Strictly Professional

By

Sherri Hayes

Strictly Professional
Sherri Hayes

Copyright 2016 by Sherri Hayes
ISBN: 978-0-9985652-4-8

Cover Photo and Design: Sara Eirew Photographer
Layout Design: Riane Holt

This book was originally published through The Writer's Coffee Shop in December 2010 as Hidden Threat. The book has been extensively edited for re-release in 2016.

Other Books by Sherri Hayes

Finding Anna series
Slave
Need
Truth
Trust

Daniels Brothers series
Behind Closed Doors
Red Zone
Crossing the Line
What Might Have Been

Serpent's Kiss series
Welcome to Serpent's Kiss
Burning for Her Kiss
One Forbidden Night

Single Titles
Strictly Professional
A Christmas Proposal

Summary – Strictly Professional

A phone call from her father sends Cali back home to Chicago to look after the family business. Being CEO of Stanton Enterprises is never something she wanted to do, but when her father tells her she's the only one he can trust to run the company in his absence she can't say no.

Within hours of stepping into her father's office she comes face-to-face with her father's head of security, Matthew Andersen. The attraction is instantaneous and undeniable. Unfortunately, Cali can't act on it. She's his boss for the next three months and it wouldn't be appropriate to cross that line.

Little does she know, fate is determined to throw them together at every turn. Someone is after her father's company and now he's set his sights on her. Can Matthew and Cali figure out who's behind the threats before it's too late and still keep things strictly professional?

Dedication

To my readers.
Thank you for coming along with me on this journey...wherever it takes us.

Acknowledgements

Publishing a book is always a long process that involves a lot of people. I want to thank my two editors, Wyndy and Andrea for helping to make my words the best they can be. To my street team who helped me proofread the story, thank you for the many hours you sacrificed for the read through. Thank you to Sara Eirew for the amazing cover photo and design. And a special thank you to Riane who not only formats my stories, but also lets me bounce ideas off of her any time I need to.

Chapter 1

Cali Stanton gave her appearance one final appraisal in the full-length mirror. It wasn't an image she was used to. Not anymore, at least.

She'd spent over an hour getting ready, making sure her hair and makeup were just right before donning one of her new power business suits. Normally she left her hair down or pulled it back into a ponytail, but today, to give herself a more professional appearance, she'd twisted her reddish-brown hair up off her neck and secured it on top of her head with a clip that scraped against her scalp as she adjusted it.

To add to her tailored appearance, she slipped her feet into a pair of three-inch black pumps. The saleswoman had assured her that they would go well with her sleek black pantsuit, and they did. The fabric of the suit hugged her curves and the heels made her legs look long and elegant.

Sighing, she ran a hand down the front of the suit. "Ready or not, here I come."

Cali grabbed her matching handbag from the bed and made her way downstairs. Her father's house was huge. It was a far cry from the small dwellings she'd inhabited for the past two years in Africa with Doctors Without Borders. The vast amount of extra space was taking a while to get used to, even though she'd grown up here.

As she descended the large central staircase, Cali could hear Jessie in the kitchen. Cali smiled as she thought of the older woman. Jessie had been her dad's housekeeper for over twenty years. She'd seen Cali through the tough years after her mother's death and stuck by her side during her not so tame teenage years. Jessie was like a mother to Cali and she was glad to have the older woman back in her life again.

Jessie glanced up when Cali entered the kitchen, and smiled. "Good morning."

Taking an exaggerated step back, Jessie gave Cali a thorough once-over before whistling her approval. "My, my. Don't you look like something this morning?"

Cali blushed. "Thank you."

She walked over to the counter and took a seat. Jessie placed Cali's breakfast in front of her and once again she felt her love for the older woman surge. She hadn't asked Jessie to make her breakfast this morning but she had anyway.

Digging in to her food, Cali asked, "You don't think it's too much, do you?"

Jessie waved her comment away. "No, no, of course not. But you *will* make a statement. Maybe you can give some of those stuffy businessmen a run for their money."

Cali laughed. "Somehow I doubt that. I'm just hoping I'm able to hold things together until Dad's well enough to come back."

Jessie's face became serious. "I don't know what I'm going to do with that man. He's not twenty anymore."

"I know," Cali said. "I don't know what possessed him."

"I'll tell you what possessed him. He's feeling his age, that's what. You came back just in time. It's a midlife crisis or something. Trying to learn to water ski at his age." Jessie shook her head in dismay.

Cali didn't know how to respond, so she said nothing. She agreed with Jessie. A midlife crisis was the most logical conclusion because it wasn't like her dad to be so adventurous.

Forty minutes later Cali stood outside Stanton Enterprises. She took a deep breath and marched through the large glass doors that led into the first floor lobby. Situated in the center of the room was a massive reception desk. A smaller security station was nestled into the far corner. Both desks had an occupant who looked up at her entrance.

Since it was already after nine in the morning, most of her father's employees were already at their desks working. That left the large lobby area feeling even bigger and impersonal.

Her shoes clicked on the tile floor as she walked toward the receptionist. The woman stood. "Good morning."

"Good morning." Cali plastered a smile on her face. "Could you let Lisa Morgan know that Cali Stanton is here?"

Shock crossed the woman's face a moment before she went into action and reached for the phone. "Oh. Oh, yes. Of course."

While the receptionist called Lisa, her father's assistant, Cali took another look around the lobby area. The office hadn't changed much over the years. In fact, the only thing she noticed beyond a fresh coat of paint on the walls was the addition of several security cameras. Cali wondered if that had anything to do with what her father had shared with her last night over the phone. Not that he'd told her much, only that something was going on and that his heads of security, Matthew and Jason, would fill her in.

The elevator doors opened and she pushed thoughts of whatever mystery situation awaited her out of her mind. Her father's assistant glided elegantly into the lobby. Lisa made walking in four-inch heels look easy. Her legs looked a mile long and her long brown hair curled against her shoulders, bouncing with every step she took.

Lisa skipped the formalities and hugged Cali. "It's good to see you again."

Cali returned the embrace. Over the years, she'd gotten to know Lisa well. "Same here."

Taking a step back, Lisa grinned and motioned toward the elevators. "Shall we?"

They made their way up to the top floor where her father's office was located. Lisa gave her a brief tour and then left her alone in her dad's office. She sat down behind the imposing desk—the desk that would be hers for the next three months—and tried to take it all in.

One week ago, she'd been standing over a tiny cot examining a young boy with deep cuts covering his entire body. He'd been unconscious when a group of villagers had brought him into the makeshift hospital the night before. No one knew what had happened, so Cali and one of the nurses cleaned the boy's wounds and made sure he was comfortable. They were watching him closely for any sign of infection.

She'd felt someone approach her from behind and figured it was Rachael Michaels, one of her fellow doctors, so Cali hadn't turned around to look.

"How's he doing?" Rachael asked.

"No fever, which is good, but he's not out of the woods yet."

She came up beside her and placed a hand on Cali's shoulder. "I'll finish up here. You have a call."

Cali knew only one person would make an unscheduled call to her in the middle of Africa—her father.

She stood and handed the wet towel she'd been using to wash the young boy's wounds to her colleague. The sun beat down on her as she exited the small hut where the boy was being treated and trudged through the heat over to the small rundown metal shack that housed the only working phone. Chad, one of the locals, handed her the phone as soon as she entered.

"Thanks," Cali said as she placed the grungy handset that looked as if it had been around for at least thirty years to her ear. "Hello?"

"Cali? Cali, honey, is that you?"

"Yes, Dad, it's me. Is everything all right?"

"No, sweetheart, it's not. I need you to come home."

Cali collapsed into the beat-up wooden chair Chad had recently vacated. "Come home? Dad, what's going on? What's wrong?"

He released a sigh followed by a low moan.

She'd been a doctor long enough to know that he was in some level of pain. "Dad?"

"I kind of went and did something stupid."

She tensed. "What did you do?"

He hesitated. "I went waterskiing with Henry."

"You what?" Cali's voice reverberated through the small metal building.

"I know, I know. Stupid, right? Not something a man my age should be doing. I've already heard it all from Jessie."

Cali tried to tamp down the fear running through her body. "What happened? Were you hurt?"

"Well . . ."

"Dad?"

Her father released another sigh followed by a more pronounced moan. She closed her eyes and gritted her teeth as she awaited his response.

"I broke my hip and a couple of ribs. The doctors say I'm going to be out of commission for about three months."

"Oh, Dad." Cali's voice was laced with disapproval.

He pretended not to hear her. "So that's why I need you to come home. I need you to run the business while I'm away. Look after things."

"Dad . . ."

"Now listen to me, Cali. I know you've told me that you don't want to take over for me when I retire. And although I'm not happy about that, I will respect your wishes. However, at the moment there are some things going on and I would feel much better with someone I trust watching over my interests."

"What about Peter? I thought you were grooming him to take over?" She was grasping at straws and she knew it, but the last thing she wanted to do was travel halfway around the world to run her dad's company. Even if it would only be for three months.

"Peter is very good at what he does, and maybe someday I'll feel confident turning the business over to him, but he's not ready. He's not family." Her father paused. "You're the only family I've got, Cali. I need you for this. Only you."

The guilt trip was working. "I don't know . . ."

Alvin Stanton turned on the charm. "Please? Your old man needs you."

Cali giggled.

Her father knew he'd won.

"How soon can you get here?" he asked.

She thought about it for a moment, going over the logistics in her head. "I can get a ride into town tomorrow and catch the bus from there. It will take me most of the day to reach the airport so . . . I should be able to make it back to Chicago by Thursday or Friday."

"Call me when you have your flight information. I'll make sure someone picks you up from the airport."

"Okay, Dad." She arose from her seat, her mind going to all the things she needed to get in order before she left the next day.

"Cali?"

"Yes?"

"I love you, sweetie."

Her lips curled up into a soft smile. "I love you, too, Dad."

The phone on the desk buzzed, startling her. She placed a calming hand on her chest and pushed the intercom button like Lisa showed her. "Yes?"

"Matthew Andersen is here to see you." Lisa's voice came through clear and confident.

"Who?" Cali asked.

"Mr. Andersen. Head of security."

Well . . . nothing like jumping in with both feet.

"Send him in."

Cali stood and straightened her suit jacket. She could do this.

The door opened and a man not much older than her entered. He strolled confidently across the room and offered her his hand. The most intriguing blue eyes she'd ever seen stared back at her.

She cleared her throat as her gaze drifted over his dark hair and broad shoulders. "You must be Mr. Andersen."

For a moment, she didn't think he was going to answer. "And you must be Ms. Stanton."

They stood there for a moment, and the air around them felt heavy and charged. She felt warmth rushing to her cheeks and looked away.

Swiping her hand back, she attempted to collect herself and hurried back behind the desk. It didn't matter that she could still feel the burn of his palm against her skin. Or that the way he seemed to own that suit he was wearing reminded her how long it had been since she'd had a man in her bed. She had a job to do and it didn't include fooling around with one of her father's employees.

Cali cleared her throat. "Um . . . why don't you take a seat, Mr. Andersen?"

He lowered his tall frame into the offered chair.

She retook her own seat and placed both her hands in her lap.

They sat in silence for several moments. He seemed to be assessing her. For what, she had no idea, but Cali wasn't sure she liked it.

"My father said there were some things you needed to discuss with me." She attempted to sound as businesslike as possible.

"Yes." He paused. "What did Alvin tell you?"

Cali tried not to let his brisk tone bother her. "Not much. Just that he needed someone he could trust running his company right now." She gathered up her courage and leveled a look at him Cali saved for her most difficult patients. "What's going on?"

***

Matthew Andersen had seen pictures of Alvin's daughter before. Pictures of her when she was little and even one from when she'd graduated from medical school. None of those had prepared him for the woman sitting in front of him.

When security had called to let him know the boss' daughter was here, he'd been dreading the encounter. Alvin had called him to say that he wanted his daughter, Cali, to be brought up to speed on the current situation. She had no idea what was going on—what she was walking into—and Matthew didn't have time to hold her hand. But that's what he was going to have to do because it was part of the job.

Of course, his brother Jason had blown off the meeting in typical fashion. Jason didn't like what he referred to as the 'suit and tie' part of the job. He was much better with the hands-on aspects where Matthew thrived on the technical and theoretical side of things. Jason preferred to be out in the action, while Matthew liked to work alone.

As Matthew sat across from Cali Stanton he recalled exactly what his brother had said when he'd gone to get him. "The last thing I want to do this morning is entertain a pampered princess."

Looking at her sitting across from him at her father's desk, Matthew wondered if his brother would have the same opinion upon meeting her. Cali did have that air about her that said she came from money, but there was also something else. An edge that he couldn't quite explain. He'd done his research on her and knew she was twenty-eight and had been working as a doctor with Doctors Without Borders for the last two years. And while he knew working outside the US had its challenges, he couldn't imagine what she would have seen for him to be getting such a vibe from her. But Matthew had learned long ago to trust his instincts and something told him that she wasn't a pampered princess as his brother had suggested.

The black pantsuit she wore wasn't any different than what most of the other women in the office wore, but it had him struggling not to squirm in his seat. Her jacket hugged her waist and had a V-neck that plunged low enough to give a hint of the skin beneath. The reddish hair he remembered from the pictures was pulled away from her face and into some fancy hairdo that left a few stray curls caressing her face. He wanted to twirl the hair around his finger and see if it was as soft as it looked.

Then there were her eyes. They were brown with a hint of copper. He could easily get lost in them.

That thought brought him up short. This was his boss' daughter. His boss for the foreseeable future. He had no business thinking about how soft her hair was or how easy it would be to slip her jacket off her shoulders and . . .

Matthew shifted his focus to the window behind her in an attempt to clear his thoughts. He had a job to do and, damn it, he was going to do it.

For roughly the next hour, Matthew explained the situation to her. She took it better than he thought she would. After all, it wasn't every day you found out people were threatening violence to you and your company.

Cali listened closely to what he had to say, stopping every now and then to ask for clarification. While he could see concern in her eyes, he didn't see panic. That impressed him. Although Matthew understood why Alvin had wanted his daughter to run things in his absence, he was aggravated with the old man as well. Being thrown into a situation like this was no place for a woman like Cali Stanton. Once word got out that she was running the company, Matthew had little doubt that the threats her father had been receiving would transfer to her.

As Matthew left Alvin's office, the danger threatening his new boss bothered him more and more. It wasn't often something rattled him, but by the time he returned to his office, his frustration boiled over. He slammed his door shut, marched over to his desk, and fell into his chair.

Two knocks sounded on his door. Matthew ignored them. He didn't want to deal with anyone right now.

Unfortunately, his brother wasn't known for leaving well enough alone. Jason opened the door and gently closed it behind him. Matthew leaned his head back and closed his eyes, willing his brother to go away.

He should have known better.

"Meeting with the princess didn't go well, I take it?"

Matthew ran a hand over his head and met his brother's gaze. "Don't call her that."

His brother raised both eyebrows but didn't comment on Matthew's outburst.

Matthew reached for his keyboard and logged in to his e-mail, doing his best to ignore Jason's scrutiny. "The meeting went as well as could be expected. She didn't have the slightest clue about what's been going on. I still can't believe her father didn't warn her."

"Well, at least now she knows."

"Yeah." Matthew glanced down at a Post-It note on his desk. "How are things looking for Friday?"

His brother hesitated. "Good. Everyone's keeping their ears to the ground. I'll be notified if they hear something."

Matthew nodded, pushed away from the desk, and stood. "I'll stop by your office later. I need to get the security clearance finished for Ms. Stanton."

Without waiting for Jason to grill him about his unusual behavior, Matthew side-stepped his brother and strolled out the door.

Chapter 2

The rest of Cali's day was uneventful. She knew that had a lot to do with her father's assistant. Lisa was amazing. She had an answer for every question that had arisen and there had been a lot of them. It seemed every time Cali turned around there was something else she needed help with. Lisa had probably spent more time that day in her father's office than she'd spent at her own desk. Cali would have to remember to talk to her dad about giving Lisa a raise. Whatever she was making, Cali was sure it wasn't enough.

During her teenage years, Cali had spent a lot of time helping her dad at the office. She knew the basics of the business and how it worked. Since Stanton Enterprises dealt in medical equipment, her medical knowledge had come in handy. It was the business side of things that had her somewhat lost.

Peter Carson, Stanton Enterprises' CFO, stopped by to see her after lunch. "I hope I didn't disturb you."

Cali set aside the paperwork she'd been working on and gave him her full attention. Peter had been working for her father for the past ten years—since he'd graduated college—and he'd worked his way up the ranks. "Not at all. Come on in."

He strolled into the office with confidence and took a seat. "Are you getting settled in?"

She looked at the stack of paperwork and thought about the

dozens of e-mails waiting for her. "Getting there."

Peter chuckled. "Well, if you need anything, let me know. I'm more than happy to help."

"I appreciate that."

"Quite a change of pace from Africa, I'd imagine. How are you adjusting to being back in Chicago?" he asked.

"To be honest, I haven't had the chance to enjoy much of it yet. Between moving back into my father's house, following up with my dad and his condition, and preparing for today, I haven't had time for anything else."

He nodded in understanding. "How is your father? I haven't spoken to him in a few days."

"Stubborn."

They both laughed.

"No, really. He's doing well." She paused. "At least, that's what they tell me."

"His doctor's still saying he's going to be out for the whole three months?" Peter asked.

She sighed and leaned back in her chair. "That's what he said. I'm really hoping it's sooner than that, but I'm not getting my hopes up."

The two of them talked for several more minutes and Peter made arrangements to stop by later in the week to go over some of the financial statements with her. She wasn't looking forward to that. While she used math as a doctor, Cali wasn't an accountant. The thought of all those figures and graphs made her head spin. She was grateful for Peter's help and expertise.

After Peter left, Cali hunkered down to try and clear some of the work off her desk. She'd been so focused on what she was doing that the next time she looked up at the clock it was a quarter after five. Cali knew there would be days when she'd have to stay late but it wasn't a habit she wanted to start on her first day.

She selected two of the reports she'd been working on that day and stuck them in her new briefcase. When she walked out of her office, Lisa was still sitting at her desk. She glanced up when Cali appeared.

"Leaving for the night, Ms. Stanton?" Lisa asked.

Cali halted her progress toward the elevator and grinned at her father's assistant. "Please call me Cali. After all, I couldn't have made it through today without you."

"You're doing fine, Cali."

"Thanks." Cali herself wasn't sure of Lisa's assertion, but she let it drop. "Are you heading home soon?" she asked instead. Cali experienced a pang of guilt at the thought that Lisa was probably behind on her own work after all the time she'd spent helping Cali that day.

"Yep. I just have to finish this up and then I'm heading out."

Cali frowned.

Lisa waved her concern away. "I'm fine, really. I should only be another twenty minutes or so, tops."

"You're sure? I mean, I could stay and help you if you want."

"Thank you for the offer, but I'm good. Go enjoy your evening and relax." A slow smile spread across Lisa's face. "You have a whole new day of this again tomorrow."

Cali grimaced. "Don't remind me."

Lisa chuckled. "Good night."

Hesitating for only a moment, Cali said good night to Lisa and made her way over to the elevator.

The drive home was exactly as she remembered it to be. Rush hour traffic was brutal. It had taken her almost an hour to reach her father's house.

Jessie had dinner warming in the oven and Cali helped herself to a large helping of the chicken casserole and blueberry cobbler before heading upstairs. Stripping out of her clothes, she ambled into the bathroom and began filling up the tub. What she needed was a nice long soak.

As Cali sank down into the warm water full of bubbles, she tilted her head back, closed her eyes, and released a loud sigh. It had been a long time since she'd taken a bubble bath. One didn't get many opportunities for such things in Africa.

The bubbles swirled around her as she pondered her first day as acting CEO. Of course, that led her directly to her meeting with Matthew Andersen. She was still trying to wrap her head around what he'd told her. It wouldn't have crossed her mind that Stanton Enterprises would be targeted like that. They manufactured and shipped medical equipment all over the world, including to foreign countries that couldn't afford it. Practicing medicine in a third world country for the last two years, she'd gotten to see firsthand how vital that was. The fact that her father and his company were under attack both shocked and angered her.

She'd also found out from Mr. Andersen that for the last two years—the entire time she'd been in Africa—shipments on their way to hospitals and major medical facilities had been stolen. It began shortly after the company started receiving harassing letters from a group who didn't feel enough was being done in impoverished nations of the world. What the people behind the threats and violence didn't seem to understand was that when the shipments to paying customers were sabotaged, the supplies going to charities like Doctors Without Borders decreased or disappeared altogether.

Of course that issue was a drop in the bucket compared to the next bomb he'd dropped on her. Six months ago, the threats had turned personal—against her father. They were in the same vein as those sent to the company saying that he wasn't doing enough to help and that they held him personally responsible. According to Matthew Andersen, there hadn't been any physical violence against her father as of yet, however he didn't feel it was wise to ignore the possibility either. Apparently, the letters her father had been receiving were getting more frequent as well as more aggressive.

While she mulled over her conversation with Matthew Andersen, she tried to ignore her body's reaction to him. Even now, hours after their meeting, there was still something about him that drew her in. As he'd relayed the information about the threat to her all she could concentrate on was his mouth and it had nothing to do with the words he was speaking. It was his lips. His full, very kissable lips. She had the strongest desire to know what it would feel like to have them pressed against hers.

It had taken every ounce of willpower for her to pay attention to what he was saying. The whole thing was crazy. He worked for her. Well, he worked for her father and, in turn, for her. At least, for the next three months.

Cali lowered herself farther down into the tub and let the water engulf her entire body until only her head was above the surface. Maybe she was overanalyzing the connection with him. She was a healthy female, after all, and he was a very attractive man. Yes, that was it. It had to be.

By the time she stepped out of the bathtub, Cali had nearly convinced herself that she was blowing her reaction to Matthew

Andersen out of proportion. She changed into her pajamas and crawled into bed with the book she'd started on the plane. By the time she turned off the lights and curled up in her bed, she was feeling more like herself. But as she drifted off to sleep, she found herself dreaming of crystal blue eyes.

***

Tuesday morning Matthew went through his normal routine, making sure everything was secure and that there hadn't been any incidents overnight. He did a quick sweep of the security footage and looked over the night watchman's notes. Everything appeared to be in order.

He sat down at his desk and began going over his to-do list for the day. At the very top was a note to take Cali Stanton on a walk-through of the building. He needed to verify her security code was functioning properly and that she knew how to access all the different areas. She'd been gone for two years. A lot had changed since then—especially when it came to the building's internal security.

Glancing down at his watch, he realized it was only seven thirty. Matthew doubted she was in the building yet, but he figured he didn't have anything to lose so he picked up the phone and dialed Lisa's number.

The phone rang ten times. He was about to hang up when Lisa answered. "Hello?"

"Lisa?" She sounded out of breath. "Is everything all right?"

Lisa giggled. "Yeah. Everything's fine."

Matthew was confused by her reaction. "Are you sure? Do you need me to come up there?"

"No!" She took a deep breath and released it. "Really, Matthew. I'm fine. It's another crazy morning in the office, that's all. What can I help you with? As much as I love to hear your voice first thing in the morning, you don't usually call just to chat."

Although something still felt off to him, Matthew could hear the smile in her voice. Maybe he was reading more into it than he should be. She didn't sound as if she were in any danger, at least.

He cleared his throat and got down to the reason why he'd called her in the first place. "I need Ms. Stanton for about three hours at some point today. I want to walk her through the building and make sure she's familiar with all the new security upgrades. Do you think you could clear some time in her schedule?"

Lisa was quiet for several minutes but he could hear her fingers clicking away on the keyboard. "Looks like she should have some time around ten and I can push back her afternoon appointments. Would that work?"

Matthew cross-referenced his own schedule. "That should be fine."

"Anything else?" she asked when he didn't contribute any more to the conversation.

"No. I think that's it. Thank you, Lisa. I'll see you at ten."

Before he could say anything else, the call was disconnected.

He stared at the phone for a moment. Shaking his head, he returned the receiver to his desk and turned his attention to his computer. He needed to go over the logistics for Friday's shipment. This one needed to go through without a hitch. It was their third attempt at the same delivery and the client was getting restless. If this one didn't arrive at its destination, the receiving hospital would most likely begin looking for another supplier. It was his job to make sure that didn't happen.

***

Cali felt better after a good night's sleep. Her dreams disturbed her a little, but they were pleasant enough. Too pleasant, if she was being honest with herself, but she was trying not to read any more into them than what they were.

She left early and arrived at the office with almost a half hour to spare. Taking the elevator up to the top floor, Cali waited patiently for the doors to open.

When she stepped out of the elevator, Lisa stood behind her desk with a huge smile on her face. "Good morning, Cali."

Cali took in Lisa's appearance and then that of the man standing next to her. Crossing the room, Cali approached her assistant's desk and extended her hand to the man she didn't know. "Hello. I don't think we've met. I'm Cali Stanton."

The man gave her a quick once-over before taking her hand. "Jason Andersen. Nice to meet you."

"You work in security, too, right?"

Jason smiled. "Yes."

She dropped his hand and gave a quick glance in Lisa's direction before returning her gaze to Jason. "Is everything all right? Did something happen? Is that why you're here so early in the morning?"

His grin deepened and Cali imagined this man had no issue attracting attention from the female sex. "Oh, no. I ran into Lisa on my way in this morning and offered to help her carry some files."

"That was very nice of you."

He looked almost embarrassed. "Yes. Well . . . um . . . I should be getting back downstairs. It was a pleasure meeting you, Ms. Stanton."

Cali waited until the elevator doors closed before turning back to her assistant with a knowing grin. "So . . ."

A blush colored Lisa's cheeks a split second before she turned until Cali could no longer see her face. It seemed that her assistant wasn't immune to Jason Andersen's charm either. But Cali wondered if it were more than that. Was that whisker burn on Lisa's neck?

"You have a meeting with the board at nine this morning," Lisa said, redirecting Cali's thoughts away from wondering just what her assistant and Jason Andersen had been up to before she'd walked in on them. "I put all the information you'll need to know on your desk for review. And I've cleared your schedule from ten to two. Matthew Andersen needs a few hours with you to go over building security. I also figured you'd want to get lunch at some point. Also, you have a meeting with Mr. Carson at three to go over the financials."

Her assistant was babbling, adding to Cali's suspicions. But Lisa's list of things Cali had to do that day left her with a sinking feeling in her stomach. How was she supposed to do this? On top of everything she had to deal with—Stanton Enterprises, her father— she had to find a way to deal with Matthew Andersen as well?

How she was feeling must have been plain on her face.

"You'll be fine," Lisa said.

Cali took a deep breath and smiled at her assistant. "Yeah. I'll be fine."

She turned on her heel, strolled into her office, and closed the door. Cali leaned back against the solid wooden surface and attempted to steady herself. Across the room, she could see the folders Lisa mentioned stacked in a neat pile on her desk. Cali knew she needed to go through them before her meeting, otherwise she wouldn't be able to contribute much to the conversation.

That's what she needed to do, but the only thing she could think about was seeing Matthew Andersen again. Knowing she would be in such close proximity to him for an extended period of time was tearing at her weak assurances to herself that she'd imagined her reaction to him the day before. It couldn't be that bad, right? It couldn't be. He was only a man, after all, and in her profession she had to work with men all the time, some of whom were drop dead gorgeous. In the past, she'd been able to block it from her mind, control her body's responses, and get the job done. She'd just have to do that again.

Squaring her shoulders, Cali pushed away from the door and went to her desk. She picked up the first folder and began studying the report in front of her. Matthew Andersen was just another employee and she would treat him as such.

She managed to look over all the files and feel halfway prepared for the board meeting. Over the years she'd attended many long, drawn-out meetings, and this one was less awkward than most. All the board members welcomed her with open arms. They accepted her as acting CEO in her father's stead without question and welcomed her insights into the issues that were brought up.

The meeting was a technicality. They went over previous business and asked about her time overseas. She'd known many of the board members her entire life. There were a few new faces, but even they joined in and did their best to welcome her.

While the meeting wasn't unpleasant, Cali really didn't see the point. No one brought up the hijacked shipments she'd been told about the day before. She wondered if that was because they didn't know or if they were unsure how much she knew. Either way, she was glad. Thinking about the stolen shipments led to more thoughts of the man who'd delivered the news to her and that was the last thing she needed.

Cali shook everyone's hands at the conclusion of the meeting, thanking them once again for their warm welcome. They all filed out, leaving her with no choice but to head back upstairs to her own office. It was already after ten and she was almost certain Matthew

Andersen would be there waiting.

Stepping onto the elevator, she tried to breathe normally as the doors closed and the car began to rise. A soft ding sounded as she arrived at her floor and the doors opened. Sure enough, he was there, and everything she told herself—that her reaction to him hadn't been a big deal—went out the window.

Her heart rate picked up at the sight of him. Then he met her gaze and, for a moment, she thought she saw something in his eyes. But before she could put a name to it, it was gone.

He remained seated until she was almost in front of him.

"Ms. Stanton," he said, rising to his feet.

"Good morning, Mr. Andersen." She needed to snap out of it. Whatever *it* was. "Um . . . give me a minute to . . . to put these things on my desk and then I'll be ready."

He nodded.

Cali glided past him and into her office. She needed to get control of herself.

After closing the door behind her, she swiftly deposited the folders on her desk and took several deep breaths. When she finally felt as if her heart wasn't going to beat its way out of her chest, Cali walked back out to where he was waiting.

This time she was better prepared, but her heart still reacted. She covered it up by clearing her throat and squaring her shoulders. "After you."

He hesitated, and then turned toward the elevator.

Her gaze traveled down the length of his body as she followed him across the room. She chided herself on her unprofessionalism, but that didn't keep her from roaming down to where the end of his suit jacket brushed against his backside.

Chapter 3

Matthew spent the next two and a half hours showing Cali Stanton around the building. He'd made her use her security code at the entrance to every department to make sure it not only worked, but that she knew how to use it. There had been a lot of upgrades to the system since he and Jason had taken over and he needed to ensure she was familiar with them.

The more sensitive areas required a person to place their index and middle fingers on a pad to be scanned. She seemed somewhat shocked by this, but he didn't know if that was due to the level of security or if she was surprised he'd been able to get his hands on her fingerprints.

As they moved from area to area, he pointed out security cameras and why they were placed where they were. They ended up in the first floor lobby. He took her over to the reception desk and showed her the setup of small monitors. She listened intently and he shared each level of protection with her as he watched realization sink in. He hadn't been exaggerating the serious nature of the threat. No company spent this kind of money on security unless there was a reason.

He ushered her over to the large glass doors at the front of the building and pointed out the last two cameras. Matthew had spent so much time talking, trying to be professional, that he realized he was probably coming across as rude.

Placing both hands in his pockets, he studied her face, looking for some sign of how to proceed. "Are you hungry?"

She blinked. "Excuse me?"

Matthew tried not to let her reaction deter him. They were going to have to work together, so they were going to have to figure this out. "It's lunchtime and I thought maybe if you were hungry . . ."

He was hoping she'd say something—anything, really. Hell, he would have been okay if she'd refused, said she needed to get back to her office. It was better than the silence he was met with.

Since she needed to respond, he tried again. "Would you like to go to lunch?"

She stared at him for another long minute. "You're asking me to go to lunch with you?"

He pressed his lips together trying not to grin. "Yes."

Matthew saw her swallow and wondered if she was going to refuse after all.

"Look, it's no big deal. Don't worry about it. I just thought—"

"Sure."

This time he didn't try to hide his smile.

He opened the door and motioned for her to go ahead of him. "After you."

She smiled back, clutched her day planner to her chest, and brushed past him out the door. The spark he felt at her touch had him closing his eyes and sucking in a lungful of air.

By the time they arrived at the restaurant a few blocks from the office, Matthew was wondering what the hell he was doing. He'd worked so hard to keep things professional all morning and now he was sitting across from her in a cozy little Italian place that seemed way too romantic and date-like. They'd passed several cafés on the way but he'd convinced himself they would be too crowded. He wanted a place where they could talk and he could brief her on the upcoming shipment.

That's what he'd told himself. But the truth of the matter was that he had no desire to discuss business. Matthew wanted to get inside her head, find out what made her tick. Then maybe she would stop consuming his every thought and he could concentrate on what he was supposed to be doing—his job.

He watched as she took in her surroundings. What he wouldn't have given to know what she was thinking at that moment. Was she wondering why he'd brought her to such an intimate setting?

She glanced at him and then picked up her menu. Matthew followed suit and scanned the restaurant's offerings, all the while sneaking peeks at the woman who sat across from him. On one such stolen look their gazes met and he smiled, hoping to ease the tension. It was as thick as it had been during their first meeting in her office. He knew she felt it, too.

Before he could think of something witty to say, their waiter approached, and they both turned their attention to him. "Good afternoon. My name is Seth, and I'll be your server today. Did you need a few minutes, or are you ready to order?"

"I'm ready if you are," Matthew said to Cali.

She nodded and gave Seth her order.

Once their server left them alone, Matthew decided he should get down to business. Or at least try and get the conversation started.

He took a sip of water. "Your dad said you were a doctor."

"Yes. That's right."

When she didn't continue, Matthew asked, "Have you always wanted to be a doctor?"

She reached for her drink and took her time answering. "Pretty much. My mom died of cancer when I was eleven." She paused. "Which I'm sure you already know."

He smiled.

Cali set her drink back down on the table and continued. "Anyway . . . after watching her suffer and not being able to do anything to help her, I knew I never wanted to be in that type of situation again. If someone I loved got sick, I didn't want to feel so helpless."

Matthew nodded. He was having a difficult time keeping his attention away from her lips and wondered if they were as soft as they looked.

He cleared his throat and sat up a little straighter. "It's hard losing a parent."

She raised her eyebrows in question.

"I lost my mom when I was eight. I was young, but I still remember how helpless I felt."

Cali's eyes softened. "I'm sorry."

"It's okay. It was a long time ago." There was a long pause and he knew he needed to get their conversation going again. "Alvin . . . your dad . . . said you were working with Doctors Without Borders."

Her entire face lit up. "Yes. I was working in Africa when I got the call from Dad."

It was obvious she enjoyed her work. "How long were you there?"

"Just shy of two years. I wasn't in one place the entire time, though. They move us around to wherever they need us."

Their server picked that moment to bring their food.

Once they were alone again, Cali picked up where she'd left off. She told him about the little camp she'd worked in right before she'd returned home and all her friends there. It sounded very basic and reminded him of many of the small villages he'd passed through during his time in the military.

They were almost finished with their lunches when Cali dropped the next piece of information on him. "I met Jason Andersen this morning."

Matthew paused with his fork halfway to his mouth. His mind was racing, trying to figure out when and how Jason and Cali's paths would have crossed. Sure, they worked in the same building, but Jason avoided the executive floors like the plague.

"When?" Matthew snapped.

Then he realized how that must have sounded and who he was talking to. "Sorry. I didn't mean it to come out that way. It's just . . . Jason doesn't tend to . . ." There was no easy way to say this. "He deals more with the operational end of things. I'm surprised you crossed paths with him, that's all."

She smiled and he hoped that meant his slip was forgiven.

"He was outside my office when I came in this morning," Cali said.

Matthew couldn't hide his surprise. "He was?"

Cali giggled and speared a piece of chicken. "Yes. Apparently my assistant, Lisa, needed some help carrying in a few things."

He was quiet for several minutes while he processed the information. Surely his brother wasn't . . .

But when he met Cali's gaze again he knew the truth.

Matthew shook his head, trying to fend off the irritation that was growing inside him. "How did I not see that? How did I not know?"

"Ma—Mr. Andersen, you can't be expected to know about

every relationship happening between coworkers. I'm sure they aren't the only ones."

He calmly set his fork down and leveled a stare in her direction. "First of all, yes, I should know. It's my job. Emotional ties mean possible vulnerabilities. And two . . ." He took a deep breath. "Being my brother, he should have told me."

Cali dropped her fork and it clattered onto her near empty plate. "Your brother?"

It hit him that her father must have left her completely in the dark. "Your father didn't tell you anything, did he?"

She sighed. "Apparently not."

Matthew tamped down the impulse to pummel his brother, and picked up his fork again. "Let's see if we can fix that."

She hesitated for a moment, and then nodded.

"A little over two years ago, your father received an anonymous letter. It caused him enough concern that he contacted a friend at the Chicago Police Department. That's how we came on board."

"You worked for the police department?"

Matthew shook his head. "No. We just have several friends in the department."

Before she could ask any more questions, he went on to tell her about their initial meeting with Alvin Stanton and what they'd been doing since to try and unravel the mystery. Luckily, she went with the flow of the conversation and didn't probe into his vague answer on his past. It wasn't that he was ashamed, more that given what he knew about her so far, he wasn't sure how she'd react to his past work history. The last thing they needed was another complication to deal with.

For that reason, he focused on the information she needed to know. "The next shipment goes out on Friday. Jason and I will be there personally to make sure everything goes as planned."

Cali didn't respond right away. She was staring blankly at the now empty table—their server had cleared their plates some time ago—so he waited.

"I should be there, too."

"No." His tone was firm. There was no way he was letting her anywhere near that shipment. There was a potential target on her back as it was.

"If this shipment is as important as you say it is, then an extra set of eyes could help."

"No," he said again. "It's too dangerous."

At that she sat up a little straighter and her eyes narrowed. "I've lived in Africa for the last two years, Mr. Andersen. I think I can handle a simple shipment of medical supplies."

He tossed his napkin onto the table, pushed his chair back, and stood. "It's my decision and I say it's too dangerous."

Cali looked up at him for a long moment and then got up. She clenched both her fists as if trying to control her temper as she met his gaze. "I'm *your* boss, Mr. Andersen."

Matthew didn't waver. "Not on this you're not."

He didn't give her time to argue. Turning on his heel, he marched toward the door, leaving her no choice but to follow.

The walk back to the building was tense. The crazy part about it was that instead of yelling at her, what he wanted to do was throw her up against one of the buildings and kiss her senseless. Maybe then she'd drop this ridiculous notion of being there on Friday.

They didn't speak the entire way back. He rode up in the elevator with her and exited on the thirteenth floor with every intention of going back to his office to decompress. As soon as he stepped off the elevator, however, he was waylaid by a member of his security team. He'd gotten wind of a possible threat to Friday's shipment.

Matthew immediately headed to his brother's office with Scott in tow, but Jason was nowhere to be found. This wasn't something that could be put off, though. The shipment was too important.

Sighing in frustration, Matthew crossed the hall to one of the conference rooms and ushered Scott inside. For the next twenty minutes, Scott answered Matthew's questions. To be honest, the man didn't have much information. They needed a solid lead to follow and thus far, all they'd gotten were bits of phone calls, letters, and a lot of headaches.

After getting all he could out of Scott, Matthew had sent him back down to the security desk and headed to his own office. He fell into his chair and reclined his head back against the soft leather. So much was going on right now and all he could think about was his lunch with Cali Stanton. He'd screwed up, let her get under his skin. He was a professional, damn it. Not some punk kid who couldn't control his emotions. Just thinking about her suggestion of joining them to see the shipment off had his blood boiling again. He needed to stop thinking about it. He needed to stop thinking about her.

Leaning forward, he let his head fall into his hands as he pondered the other, equally disturbing revelation from his lunch. His brother was fooling around with Lisa Morgan, Alvin's—Cali's assistant. A wave of agitation flowed through him. How could his brother keep something like that to himself? Emotional attachments meant vulnerabilities and that was something they didn't need right now.

Running both hands over the top of his head, he released something akin to a growl from his throat. He was going to have to talk to Jason about it.

Matthew lifted his head and glanced over at the clock. It was already after six. Had he really been sitting there that long?

Obviously.

He shut down his computer and turned off his light. What he needed was a good workout—something to take his mind off what had happened that day.

As he stepped onto the elevator and pushed the button that would take him down to the parking garage, he wondered how his life had gotten so complicated in such a short period of time.

***

Cali strolled out of her room the next morning and was immediately hit with the delicious aromas coming from the kitchen. She took a big whiff and practically skipped down the stairs. It was amazing what a good night's sleep could do to one's mood.

After her lunch yesterday with Matthew Andersen, she'd returned to her office. Peter was already there waiting for her.

"I hope you don't mind," Lisa said. "Mr. Carson was a little early, so I went ahead and showed him into the conference room."

"It's fine." Cali shrugged. "It's not like I can avoid it forever, right?"

Lisa chuckled. "Do you need me to get you anything?"

"Just let Peter know I'll be there in five minutes."

She'd spent those five minutes attempting to get her head on straight. As much as she hated to admit it, Matthew Andersen had rattled her. She used the breathing techniques she'd learned. In

Africa, you never knew what kind of stressful situations you'd encounter and staying calm was the number one priority. Situations could escalate fast, especially if you didn't project complete confidence in what you were doing.

The breathing exercises had helped and she was able to meet with Peter, go over the financial documents, and not feel as if she were completely useless to the conversation. Most of it was way over her head with all the graphs and spreadsheets, but at least Cali hadn't been completely lost.

When she strolled into the kitchen, she put yesterday out of her mind. Jessie stood at the counter with a stack of pancakes and sausage. Cali took a seat at the island and Jessie set the plate in front of her.

"Special occasion?" Cali asked as she picked up her fork.

"Nope." Jessie smiled. "Just felt like pancakes and sausage this morning, so eat up."

Cali reached for the syrup. "Thanks."

Jessie fixed a plate for herself and sat down. "How's everything going?"

"Not bad," Cali answered between bites of the sweet, buttery pancake.

"I'm glad."

Neither said anything for several minutes as they ate. Eventually, though, Cali had to break the silence. It felt as if Jessie was keeping something from her. "Did Dad say anything to you about some trouble with the company?"

She finished chewing her food . . . slowly.

"Jessie?"

The older woman sighed. "He didn't say anything specific, no, but he'd been putting in some late nights. And two of his security guys came over to the house to check out the home security system. They weren't happy with it or something, so they ended up installing that fancy alarm system." She pointed to a keypad right off the kitchen.

Cali was almost positive the two men had been Matthew and Jason Andersen. After spending half the day with Matthew, she got the impression there were some things he preferred to oversee personally. She had no doubt that he would consider the security of his boss' house to be one of those things.

"Well, it looks . . . secure," Cali mumbled, going back to her food.

Jessie grunted. "Complicated is what it is."

Cali didn't comment. What could she say? It didn't sound as if her father had shared what was going on with Jessie and the last thing she wanted the older woman to do was worry.

Plastering a smile on her face, Cali asked Jessie if there were any new stores in the area she should check out. Jessie enjoyed shopping and used to take Cali when she was younger after Cali's mother died. It was then and over quiet meals when her father was working late that she and Jessie had bonded. If she'd missed anything about Chicago, it was this—her family. And while Jessie might not be related by blood, she was still family.

Chapter 4

Matthew turned the wheel of his car a little too fast as he pulled into his assigned parking spot. He hated being late. It was one of his biggest pet peeves. But for whatever reason, his alarm clock hadn't gone off. Now he was more than an hour late.

Turning off the engine, he snatched his jacket off the front seat, and exited the vehicle. He double-checked his tie in the window's reflection before engaging the alarm on his car. While he waited for the elevator doors to open, he looked down at his watch. Eight forty. His entire morning routine was ruined. He'd be playing catch-up all day.

The ride up to the thirteenth floor Matthew mulled over his schedule for the day. He still had to go over the security footage from the night before—late or not. What could he move around or reschedule in order to carve out the time he would need for that?

He was about to duck into his office when his brother spotted him. "There you are. Where have you been, man? I was starting to worry."

Matthew rolled his eyes and let himself into his office. "I overslept."

A sly grin crossed Jason's face. Of course, his brother would think the reason for Matthew being late had something to do with sex, or a woman, or both.

"You got a minute?" Matthew asked. His brother may have sex on the brain, but they had work to do.

"Yeah, sure."

Matthew sat behind his desk while Jason took the seat directly across from him. The smile on his brother's face hadn't diminished, but Matthew chose to ignore it and got down to business. "Scott intercepted the end of a phone call yesterday. He didn't hear much, but it was enough for him to think the shipment on Friday has been compromised."

"The call came from inside the building?" Jason asked.

"Yes." They'd always figured the information was coming from someone inside the company. It was too accurate not to be.

His brother sat there for several minutes with the tips of his fingers steepled in front of his lips. "Scott didn't recognize the voice?"

"No. It was a man and a woman. That's all he could say for sure."

He'd considered pulling phone records, but Matthew knew it wouldn't be that easy. There were too many phones that could be used by anyone in the building. Plus, the call happened during business hours. There was no telling how many calls went out and came into the building during that time frame. It would be like trying to find a needle in a haystack. Besides, if their previous interaction with this mole was any indication, Matthew doubted he or she had used their own phone to make the call.

"We need to move up the shipment," Jason said. "Give . . . whoever this is . . . less time to react."

"I agree."

They spent the next hour hashing out the details. It wasn't as simple as bumping up the time. None of the shipments had been stolen at the docks. All the thefts had taken place while the orders were en route to their destinations. Knowing that had potentially been compromised again, all of it had to be reworked. However, no matter how or what they rearranged, the start and end points remained the same. It created vulnerability.

Matthew ran a hand over the back of his head. "It would be nice if we could move the shipment the day before to another warehouse and then ship it out from there."

His brother shook his head. "It won't be ready in time. We're going to be asking a lot of the warehouse as it is. Those guys are going to have to get here at three in the morning."

As much as Matthew hated to admit it, Jason was right.

"I think I need to go with this one," Jason said.

They'd talked about providing the trucks with armed security before, but Alvin hadn't been a fan of that idea. "I agree. We need that shipment to make it to Ohio this time."

"It's settled, then. I'll start moving things around . . . clear my schedule. And I'll let the warehouse manager know what's going on." Jason placed his hands flat on the arms of his chair and stood. "You can brief Cali on what's going on."

Matthew gritted his teeth at the casual way his brother said her name. It also reminded him that he needed to talk to Jason about Lisa.

Before he could open his mouth, however, there was a knock on the door. "Come in."

Mariana, Matthew and Jason's assistant, strolled in. "Sorry to bother you, Matthew, but Brad called asking if you wanted to take a look at last night's security tapes before he archives them."

Jason glanced at his brother and then to Mariana. "I'll let you get back to work. And remember what I said. You just have to kick them out when you know you have to get up for work in the morning."

His brother jogged out of the room, chuckling.

Matthew pretended his brother hadn't commented and responded to Mariana. "Call Brad back and let him know I'm on my way."

She nodded and closed the door behind her as she left.

His gaze fell on his still dark computer screen and he realized he hadn't even booted it up yet. While he needed to check his e-mail, the security tapes had to come first.

Leaving everything as it was, he grabbed the radio he kept in his office and headed down to see Brad. Once that was off his list he'd be able to focus on everything else. Including figuring out just how much he was going to tell his new boss.

***

It was almost five o'clock and Cali wasn't close to being done with all the work she had to get through. The pile of paperwork seemed to be growing instead of shrinking. Maybe that was because, with every meeting she attended, she had another two or three items added to her to-do list. How did her father keep up with it all?

Alvin Stanton was a big believer in communication. Because of that, he met with all his department heads and managers once a week to touch base and address any problems they were having. Earlier, she'd spent more than an hour meeting with marketing and another two hours with human resources. It was a great idea from a morale standpoint, but it was time consuming.

The second meeting ended right in time for lunch. Cali had been starving, but there was no time for her to go out and get something. She had too much to do.

Luckily, Lisa was used to her father's crazy schedule. She'd taken it upon herself to order food from a local deli and have it delivered. Cali had devoured it while hunched over yet another folder full of figures.

The afternoon was more of the same—paperwork, paperwork, and more paperwork. What happened to the notion of becoming a paperless society? Her only break from the monotony was a call she'd received from one of their biggest clients. It was somewhat disturbing that reassuring the president of a hospital board that they would get the equipment they'd ordered was one of the highlights of her day.

Her computer beeped, alerting her of a new e-mail. She was happy to redirect her attention away from the report she'd been working on and clicked on the message.

Nothing happened.

Thinking maybe something was wrong with her mouse, she double-checked to make sure everything was hooked up correctly then opened another file to make sure. Everything appeared to be working properly.

She tried again, but still nothing happened.

Cali hated to bother her assistant, but she couldn't see a way around it.

"Lisa?" she asked through the intercom on her desk.

"Yes, Cali?"

"I'm sorry to bother you, but I'm having trouble opening an e-mail and I'm not sure why."

Lisa didn't hesitate. "Who's it from?"

That was a good question. Cali moved the mouse to reveal the name. Matthew Andersen. Out of all people, why did it have to be from him?

"Cali?"

"Sorry." She'd gone almost the entire day without thinking about him. "It's from Matthew Andersen."

"Ah," Lisa said as if Cali had provided some vital piece of information. "You have to enter your password. It's a private message."

"A private message?" Cali asked. Her mind immediately went somewhere it shouldn't.

"Yes. It's a message 'for your eyes only.' Sometimes they send new security procedures that way so they can keep track of who has received them and who hasn't."

It was a good thing Lisa didn't know what Cali was thinking. "Oh."

A long moment passed before her assistant seemed to realize that Cali still had no idea what she was supposed to do next. "If you click on the little lock icon in the right-hand corner, a box will pop up for you to enter the password."

"But what's the password?" Cali asked.

Lisa laughed. "I can't help you there. Matthew was very insistent that no one share their password with anyone else. Not even their assistants. Besides, even if I knew your dad's, yours is probably different."

"Makes sense."

"If you're not sure what your password is, you'll probably have to check with Matthew."

Based on what Lisa had said, Cali figured that would be the case. "Okay, thanks."

"Anytime."

Cali clicked the intercom off and sighed. Talking to Matthew Andersen was the last thing she wanted to do, but if he'd sent her something important then she needed to know what it was. Before she could chicken out, she picked up the phone on her desk and dialed his extension.

The line forwarded to his assistant, Mariana. "Matthew Andersen's office."

"This is Cali Stanton. Is Mr. Andersen available?"

"I'm sorry, but he appears to be on another line. May I take a message or is there something I could help you with?"

"I received a message from him, but I'm having difficulty opening it. My assistant, Lisa, said I need some sort of password."

"Oh. Yes. You'll definitely have to talk to Matthew about that," she said.

"Okay, well, thank you."

"Did you want to leave a message for him?" Mariana asked.

Cali thought about it for a moment. "No. That's all right."

After hanging up with Mariana, Cali considered her options. Sure, she could put it off until morning, but what if it was important and needed her attention right away?

She powered down her computer and stuffed several of the folders into her briefcase for some 'light reading' after dinner. Matthew Andersen's office was on her way out, Cali reasoned. She'd stop by and see if she could catch him before she headed out. If he was there, then she'd suck it up and deal with him like the professional she was. If not, then it clearly wasn't meant to be.

Lisa smiled at her as Cali left her office and headed toward the elevator. "Good night."

"Don't stay too late."

"Just finishing up," Lisa responded.

Cali nodded and waved goodbye to her assistant as she walked into the elevator.

When she arrived at the thirteenth floor, she noticed it was eerily quiet. For some reason she'd imagined that the security floor would be buzzing at all hours of the day, but apparently not. She took her time walking down the hall, not at all eager to reach her destination. All too soon, however, she came to a closed door with a brass nameplate with Matthew Andersen on it. Steeling herself, she raised her arm and knocked.

"Come in," a clipped voice said from the other side of the door.

She swallowed, turned the knob, and entered.

Matthew Andersen sat behind his desk, his gaze firmly on the computer monitor in front of him. He didn't spare her a glance as she gently closed the door behind her and moved toward him.

It wasn't until she was standing directly in front of his desk that he looked up. He blinked several times as if he couldn't quite believe what he was seeing. It made her wonder who exactly he'd been expecting.

When he didn't say anything, she knew she was going to have to break the ice. "I'm sorry if I'm interrupting you."

He looked down and then back up again, placing his palms flat against his desk. "No, no. Not at all. What can I do for you, Ms. Stanton?"

"You sent me an e-mail today."

"Yes, I did." He sounded confused.

Her lips suddenly felt very dry and she darted her tongue out to moisten them. Why was this so difficult with him? "What you sent me is password protected."

His eyes darted to her lips and then away again.

Then she wondered if she'd only imagined it when he sat up in his chair and calmly placed his fingers on his keyboard. "Let's see what I can do."

Curious as to what he was doing, Cali went around his desk and moved to stand behind him so she could see. He typed in several groups of numbers and letters—a password of some sort, she imagined. Cali leaned closer to get a better look.

Matthew cleared his throat and pointed at the screen. "This is the backdoor system."

Another minute passed with him entering in even more numbers. Then he smiled.

"Here we go," Matthew said as he turned to face her.

The words died on his lips. His face was only inches from hers and she could feel his warm breath tickling her skin. She didn't know what she should do. Cali knew what she wanted to do. She wanted to turn toward those lips that had made a starring appearance in her dreams for the last two nights.

Her body responded without her permission and she tilted her face, bringing it closer to his. Their gazes met and held, the energy building in the atmosphere around them, urging her closer.

His computer beeped, breaking the spell. They both jumped back and she saw Matthew shake his head as if to clear it. She knew the feeling. Cali felt as if she'd been on some sort of high and had a bucket of cold water thrown in her face.

He hit two more buttons and then turned to retrieve something from the printer. Matthew handed it over to her with businesslike efficiency. "Do whatever you need to do to memorize that tonight and then destroy it. Password protection means nothing if someone is able to get their hands on it."

"Yes. Of course." She needed to get out of there. Now. She rushed to the door, paper in hand. "Thank you, Mr. Andersen. Good night."

As soon as she was out the door and it was secured behind her, Cali let out a deep breath. What was she doing? What was he doing? What were *they* doing?

She reached up to touch her lips. It had been a while since she'd been kissed. And something told her that kissing Matthew Andersen would be quite an experience. It was unfortunate that he was her employee.

Knowing it wouldn't do her any good to dwell on it, Cali tucked the paper into her pocket and headed home.

Jessie was gone by the time Cali made it back to her father's house. She let herself in, set the alarm, and strolled into the living room to throw her briefcase onto the couch. What she needed was food. Food and something to take her mind off the handsome head of security.

She walked into the kitchen to see what Jessie had left for her. Once she had her plate of food, Cali plopped down on the couch beside her briefcase and pulled out the first file while shoving a forkful of pasta in her mouth. She scanned over the information and realized it was a client complaint. Great. Just what she needed tonight.

Thirty minutes later, Cali had finished reviewing the complaint and used her father's laptop to type her response. The complaint hadn't been as bad as she'd feared. There had been some shipping problems—no big surprise there given the current situation. The client had mainly wanted some reassurances from the person in charge that something was being done to resolve the problems they were experiencing.

Cali returned the folder to her briefcase and went to retrieve the next one when the phone rang. Reaching behind her, she picked it up. "Hello?"

"How's my girl doing?" Her father's deep voice vibrated through the phone.

"Hi, Dad." She curled her feet under her, leaned back against the sofa, and settled in to talk to her father. "I'm good. Knee-deep in paperwork at the moment, but good."

He chuckled and she followed suit. It felt good to laugh a little after the day she'd had.

"The paperwork never ends. Get used to it." He paused for a moment and Cali could feel the tone of the conversation changing. "Matthew and Jason fill you in?"

She swallowed. Her thoughts immediately shifted to Matthew Andersen and their almost kiss before she refocused on the issue her father was talking about. "Yeah."

"Good," her father huffed out.

"Why didn't you tell me?"

"Nonsense. There was no need to worry you."

A spark of irritation flared. "No need to worry me? Dad, you're getting threats."

Her father sighed. "Cali, honey, I love you, but . . ."

"But?" she prompted when he didn't continue.

"Matthew and Jason are very good at what they do. That's why I hired them."

She wasn't sure how to respond to that.

Before she could, her father shifted the conversation to Jessie. "I hope you're keeping Jessie on her toes. You know how she likes to stay busy."

Cali decided not to push. It probably wouldn't have done any good anyway. Her father had run his own company for the last twenty years. If he didn't want to talk about something, then he wouldn't talk about it. "As much as I can. I've eaten more since I got back than I think I did the entire time I was gone."

They talked for almost an hour before saying good night. It was still early—only eight thirty—which was good. She still had several more files to get through before she could call it a night.

Figuring she might be up late, Cali took her empty plate into the kitchen and put on some coffee. As much as she'd love to sit around and daydream about a set of piercing blue eyes, she had work to do.

Chapter 5

As Matthew drove into work on Thursday morning it dawned on him that he'd yet to confront his brother about Lisa. It wasn't something he was looking forward to, but it needed to be done. While Jason was his older brother, it often didn't feel that way. Not anymore. Not since they'd both became adults.

Growing up, Jason was fiercely protective of his younger brother. He was strong, confident, and popular. All the things that worked to his advantage in school. But Jason was also impulsive. Sometimes that was a good thing. He was good at making split-second decisions in tight situations. It didn't, however, mean he tended to think about the long-term implications of those decisions.

Matthew had been up late the night before, but getting up and moving early hadn't been a problem. Lying in bed the night before, his mind wouldn't shut off. He kept running through the events of the previous day. Arrangements had been made to drop off the surveillance tape to a friend of his at the police department. When he'd reviewed yesterday's footage he'd noticed someone hiding in the shadows of the parking garage. It could be nothing, but he wanted to know who it was nonetheless. His gut told him it was important, so he had to try . . . even if it was a long shot that they'd be able to figure it out given what they had to work with.

But what had kept him up last night more than anything—more

than his brother's escapades or the mystery person hanging out in the shadows of the parking garage—was the memory of what had almost happened with his new boss. Even now, he could remember how it had felt to be so close to her and that frightened him. He'd almost thrown every ounce of professionalism out the window and kissed her. What was wrong with him?

Yes, he was attracted to her. What red-blooded male wouldn't be? She was a beautiful and intelligent woman.

If that was all there was—physical attraction—it would be easy enough to deal with. The problem was that Matthew feared it was much more than that. They'd spent close to four hours together on Tuesday and he found himself remembering the way she smiled at something he'd said as they'd sat across from each other at lunch or how she'd tucked a stray hair behind her ear while typing in her security code during their tour of the building.

Even losing his temper when she'd suggested being there on Friday was out of character for him and screamed this wasn't your run-of-the-mill physical attraction. Matthew never lost his temper. At least, he never used to lose his temper. Not before her. Since meeting Cali Stanton, however, he'd lost it twice.

He shook his head and stepped onto the elevator. When he reached his floor, he wasn't surprised to see it was deserted. None of the staff would be in at this ungodly hour.

His office door stood like a sentry guarding his personal space that would shield him from whatever the day would bring. It was too bad that sentry hadn't been able to protect him last night when Cali Stanton had waltzed into his office. Matthew wasn't sure if anything could have. She seemed determined to haunt him. Every time he closed his eyes, she was there. He couldn't shake her or his desire to know what it would feel like to kiss her.

At the same time, he knew acting on such an impulse was wrong.

Matthew marched into his office determined to get some work accomplished. He booted up his computer and did a quick scan of his e-mail before heading downstairs to view the previous night's security tapes.

"Good morning, Brad."

Brad looked up from the security monitors. "Morning, Mr. Andersen."

"Quiet night?" Matthew asked.

"Just the way I like it." Brad stood and walked over to the coffee machine along the back wall.

"You and me both," Matthew said as he took Brad's seat.

It was a routine they'd repeated every day for the past two years. Every day, that is, except for one.

Matthew pushed the thought aside, knowing that if he let it fester it would only lead to more thoughts of what had led to him oversleeping in the first place—his boss.

A little over an hour later, Matthew pushed away from the desk and gave Brad back his chair. If anything had occurred in the last twenty-four hours, it hadn't been picked up by any of the security cameras.

He patted Brad on the shoulder and left the man to his work.

When he returned to the thirteenth floor, his first stop was at his brother's office. Unfortunately, it was empty.

"I think he's still down in the warehouse," Mariana said, coming up beside him.

"Thanks."

Since his brother wasn't available at the moment, Matthew went to his office and retrieved the flash drive containing the security footage from the day before. He slipped his jacket on and powered down his computer. No reason why he couldn't run the drive over to his buddy while Jason was off taking care of the arrangements for Friday's shipment.

It was almost noon by the time Matthew arrived at the police station. The front desk clerk gave him a familiar smile as he went in search of Detective Martinez. It didn't take him long to spot his bald head hunched over a desk in the far corner of the room.

"Need some help?"

Martinez snapped his head up at the sound of Matthew's voice. When he saw his friend, he smiled. "Nah. I think I can handle it. Besides, you need to leave the real work for the *real* detectives."

Matthew laughed.

Martinez stood and offered his hand in greeting. "How you doing, man?"

"Good," Matthew said, shaking his friend's hand. "I brought you something."

Nodding, Martinez motioned for Matthew to follow him.

The two men ducked into a tiny conference room. It was set up with a computer and large screen monitor. Not wanting to waste any time, Matthew handed him the flash drive. Martinez inserted it into the computer and, after a few key strokes, the screen came alive.

Martinez looked up at Matthew from where he sat perched on the edge of the table. The image looked even worse on the bigger screen. "Well, man, whoever your mystery man or woman is, I'd say they know where those cameras of yours are. It's too much of a coincidence that they picked that exact spot."

"I agree." They watched for a few more minutes, but whoever it was never moved out into the light. "Do you think your guy can do anything to clean it up?"

A slow smile crossed Martinez's face as he hopped off the table. "Don't know, but my *guy* can give it a try."

He disconnected the flash drive from the computer and slipped it into an envelope. "Come on. Let's go get some grub. I'm starving. And we can drop this off to Nikki on our way out."

Matthew paused.

Martinez winked and then strolled out of the room, his shoulders vibrating with his suppressed laughter.

***

Cali had sat behind her desk that same morning drinking her coffee. It was a beautiful day. The sky was blue and clear, and the sun brought with it the promise of warmth. It couldn't have been more perfect. Too bad she wasn't in the mood to enjoy it.

She'd been up late combing through all the folders she'd brought home with her. At some point, she must have fallen asleep on the couch. The sound of Jessie arriving had been what had awakened her. It was slightly embarrassing to be found lying there still in her work clothes from the previous day. Jessie had been great about it, of course. She'd helped Cali pick up the scattered papers and then shooed her upstairs to shower and change.

The one advantage to passing out exhausted the night before was that she hadn't dreamed. It was great. Sort of. But since she hadn't spent the night dreaming about a certain blue-eyed employee her mind seemed to think it needed to catch up.

It started when she'd stepped into her shower. The steam had

50

warmed her skin, reminding her of the day before and the feel of Matthew's breath on her face. No matter how hard she tried, the memory wouldn't leave her. She'd finished her shower and dressed only to be met with the sun streaming in through the windows—the warm sun. It even seemed as though her coffee was adding to the fluttering she felt in the pit of her stomach.

With a frustrated sigh, Cali pushed the mug away from her and ran a hand through her loose curls. This wasn't good. She needed to get Matthew Andersen out of her head if she was going to get any work done.

Unfortunately, that was easier said than done.

As the morning passed, she tried to keep herself busy as much as possible. Even so, every now and then, when she'd least expect it, she'd catch herself lost in thought about a man she shouldn't be thinking about in any way except in a professional capacity.

Cali had been so busy trying to wipe the thoughts of Matthew Andersen from her brain that it was two o'clock before she remembered the e-mail he'd sent her yesterday. Her fingers hovered over the keyboard. She knew she needed to check it. He'd sent it to her protected by a password. It could be important.

If it had been so important, though, why hadn't he simply told her what it was last night in his office?

A rush of warmth inched up her neck to heat her cheeks. What was it about the man that made her feel like she was back in high school again with her first crush?

Sighing, Cali typed in the password Matthew had provided her the night before. A box popped up on her screen wanting her to confirm that she was, in fact, Cali Stanton. She clicked 'yes' and waited. A long moment later, the e-mail appeared on her screen.

> *Friday's transport may have been compromised. As a precaution, we are moving the departure from Friday evening to Friday morning at 6am.*
>
> *Everything is in order, and I will give a full report after the delivery is underway.*
>
> *~M. Andersen*

She stared at her keyboard, unmoving. After reading through several files last night, the importance of getting this shipment safely on its way was made abundantly clear. She wanted to be there on

Friday. She needed to be there.

Matthew's reaction to her being there came back to her. He didn't want her there—didn't feel it was safe. Her father trusted him and Cali knew she should, too.

She worried her bottom lip with her teeth as she weighed her options. Sure, she could stay safe up in her ivory tower and let Matthew and Jason do their job. She could wait for Matthew to handle everything and fill her in after the fact. That was probably what her father would do.

But Cali wasn't her father. She wasn't used to sitting back and waiting for things to happen. Someone was gunning for her father and his business. She couldn't stand by and do nothing.

A buzzing noise from her phone brought her back to the present.

Cali hit the intercom button. "Yes?"

"Mr. Carson is here to see you," Lisa said. "Should I show him in?"

Peter was here to see her?

She tried to recall scheduling a meeting with him for today, but was drawing a blank. "Sure. Send him in."

Closing her e-mail, Cali took a quick assessment of her appearance, and stood as the door to her office opened. Peter Carson strolled in looking as confident as ever. He smiled in greeting. "I hope I didn't interrupt anything."

"Not at all, Peter. Come in. I was just going through some e-mails." Cali motioned for him to take a seat.

He unbuttoned his suit jacket and lowered himself into a chair. "I thought you might want to see this."

She took the folder he handed her and a sea of numbers bombarded her. "Um, what am I looking at?"

"Production stats. Even with the shipping problems we've experienced, profits are up after the adjustments your father and I made. I thought with all the negative you could use a little positive."

Cali grinned at him and glanced back down at the numbers. She still had no idea what she was looking at, but he was right about one thing. Good news was in very short supply lately and she'd take what she could get.

By the end of the day, Cali was ready to curl up in bed with a book and shut out the world. Peter's news had been a bright spot in her day. It was what she'd needed to get her mind off the next day's shipment.

Jessie had dinner warming in the oven when Cali arrived home. She swiftly scarfed down her food and trudged up the stairs to her room for some downtime. If she hadn't known any better, she would have thought she'd just finished a twenty-four-hour shift in the ER.

Given her day and the less than stellar sleeping conditions the night before, Cali turned in early. She was sleeping soundly when the doorbell rang several times, waking her up.

She glanced at her alarm clock. It was eleven thirty. Who could possibly be calling at this time of night?

Cali padded down the hall, rubbing the sleep out of her eyes. Whoever it was rang the doorbell again as she was making her way down the staircase.

"I'm coming," she mumbled.

Cautiously, Cali went to the door and looked out the peephole. A uniformed officer stood on the other side of her door.

Quickly disarming the security system, she opened the door.

He lifted his head. "Sorry to disturb you at this late hour, ma'am, but we received a call about a prowler in the area."

Cali perked up at that. "A prowler?"

He nodded. "Yes, ma'am. My partner and I are going door-to-door asking if anyone has seen anything suspicious this evening. Anyone crossing through the yard? Hiding in the bushes?"

"No, I'm sorry. I haven't."

The officer handed her a business card and took a step back. "Thank you for your time. If you think of anything, please give us a call."

"I will. Thank you, officer."

He tipped his hat to her and turned to leave.

As he disappeared from view, Cali closed the door and rearmed the security system. She leaned back against the solid wood door. A prowler? In this neighborhood?

Shaking it off, she headed back upstairs to bed. This was her father's business. He'd trusted her with running it. For her that meant making sure everything ran smoothly in his absence. Including this shipment. If Matthew Andersen didn't like it, that was too bad. He was her employee, after all. Not the other way around.

She crawled into bed and pulled the covers up to her chin. It wasn't cold, but for some reason she felt a chill rush through her.

What if something happened tomorrow and the shipment didn't get to the hospital? She didn't know the details of how the other shipments had been hijacked. Was Matthew right? Would it be safer if she stayed away?

Cali gritted her teeth and balled her fists. She'd thought she'd finally put all the indecision behind her.

She rolled over and tucked her pillow underneath her head. What she needed was sleep.

But try as she might, her mind wouldn't shut off. She tossed and turned all night.

When her alarm clock woke her at five thirty, she groaned. The urge to hit the snooze button was strong, but she resisted. She had a job to do and she was going to do it.

Kicking off the covers, Cali got out of bed and stumbled toward the bathroom. What she needed was a shower and some coffee—strong coffee. Then she'd be ready. Ready for pages upon pages of reports. Ready for orders and shipments and clients. Ready to deal with hijackers. And even ready to come face-to-face with Matthew Andersen.

Chapter 6

Matthew arrived to work as the sun was beginning to peek its head above the horizon. He would have loved to have been able to sleep in another hour, but with the delivery truck scheduled to leave at six he didn't have that option. His morning routine had once again been interrupted by thoughts of Cali Stanton. The woman was messing with his head.

As he'd stepped out of the shower and dried off, he questioned his decision to send her that e-mail notifying her of the time change. He wanted her to stay far away from this morning's activities. Matthew must have argued with himself a dozen times before hitting the send button. However, in the end, his professionalism won out. If it had been Alvin, Matthew would have sent the e-mail.

He'd half expected to have a voice mail from her when he returned from his lunch with Martinez yesterday. Not only wasn't there a message, but she hadn't responded in any way to his e-mail even though the message was marked as read. He hoped that meant she was going to follow his instructions. Alvin trusted his professional opinion, but he didn't know Cali well enough to say one way or another—and every time he got in the same room with her, Matthew's hormones went haywire.

It was chilly when he walked onto the loading dock at five thirty. He surveyed his surroundings, looking for anything that appeared to be out of place.

Jason came up beside him. "Morning."

His brother had forgone his normal work attire of a dress shirt and slacks. Instead, he wore faded jeans and a long-sleeved shirt that hung loose around his waist. Matthew knew that under his shirt Jason had his weapon, just as Matthew had his. If something happened, they weren't going down without a fight.

"Morning." His brother's voice was gruff. Jason had never been a morning person.

Matthew lifted a steaming cup of coffee to his lips as he continued to scan the area. "I talked to Martinez last night."

"Anything?" Jason asked.

"Nikki's still working on it, but she says our mystery person is a woman. I'm supposed to check back with him later today to see if he's got anything more for us."

"I'm amazed she got that much."

Matthew nodded. "So am I. If not for the movement, I probably would have missed it entirely when I reviewed the video."

The brothers slipped into silence as they watched the workers load the truck to capacity. Everything looked to be on schedule. There was no sign of a threat. That didn't mean they were going to let their guards down, though.

Several minutes went by as they waited for the workers to finish. Matthew took another sip of his coffee and glanced across the street. He'd been watching a car that had pulled up roughly ten minutes ago. No one had gotten out. They just appeared to be waiting.

He shifted his weight and Jason noticed.

It didn't take long for his brother to zero in on what had caught Matthew's attention. "How long?"

"At least ten minutes."

"No movement?"

"No." They continued to watch the vehicle, but nothing happened. "They must be planning something once you're underway."

His brother nodded. "We'll be ready."

Alec and Sam, both friends of Jason's who had been brought in to help get the delivery to its destination, approached them. Matthew gave them a sharp nod in greeting.

"All set?" Jason asked.

"Yes, sir," Sam replied.

Jason cocked his head to the side, motioning toward the vehicle they'd been watching for the last fifteen minutes. "That's good. It looks as if we might have some company."

Neither Sam nor Alec made an attempt to look across the street. Everyone involved with the transport knew an attempt at hijacking the delivery was a possibility.

"Everything on time?" Alec asked.

Jason glanced over at the truck. "Looks that way. Be ready to go in five minutes."

The two gave clipped nods and backed away, leaving Matthew and Jason alone once more.

His brother stayed in place until the driver of the truck climbed into the cab, and then he moved toward the steps that would take him to ground level. He climbed halfway down before jumping the rest of the way.

Matthew watched Jason stroll casually over to the truck. "Jason?"

Stopping in his tracks, Jason faced his brother. Their gazes held for a long moment. Then Jason turned and made his way around to the passenger side of the truck.

Matthew watched as the truck pulled away from the dock and drove out of sight. He finished off his coffee as the car across the street lurched forward, following the truck. They'd waited less than a minute.

If he'd had any doubt before, he didn't now. They all knew the likelihood was high that this shipment would be targeted. Chances were good that they'd wait for the truck to get out on the open highway and away from traffic before making their move.

He crushed his empty cup and tossed it into the garbage. As long as it was only one car, Matthew wasn't worried. Sam and Alec could handle one target. They might even be able to defuse the situation before any action was taken.

In any case, it was out of his hands. Sam, Alec, and Jason would have to deal with whatever came and Matthew had complete confidence that they could.

He walked back into the building and headed straight for the elevator that would take him up to his office. There was nothing to do now but wait.

***

Cali made it to work with ten minutes to spare. She'd spent the entire morning going back and forth with herself. One minute she was ready to rush across town and be there on the docks with Matthew and Jason. The next she was reminding herself that she was a doctor and needed to leave these things to people like Matthew who knew what they were doing.

Lisa was already behind her desk surrounded by paperwork when Cali reached the executive floor. Her assistant smiled when she saw Cali, but something seemed off. Lisa wasn't her usual upbeat self. "Everything all right?"

"Yes, yes. Everything's fine." Lisa seemed startled by Cali's question. "Um. I e-mailed today's schedule to you. It's not too bad. You might even be able to cut out early."

"That would be nice." Cali paused, giving Lisa a once-over. "Are you sure you're okay?"

"Absolutely," Lisa said with a little too much enthusiasm.

"All right, then. I guess I'll be in my office."

Lisa smiled, but again it felt fake to Cali.

A few minutes later Cali was going through her morning e-mails. When she came across a short message from Matthew letting her know the shipment had left on schedule it hit her why Lisa wasn't quite herself this morning. The delivery.

Finally, it made sense. Matthew had mentioned Jason would be escorting the delivery. It was understandable for Lisa to be worried since she and Jason were in a relationship. Especially if it was more than a casual office fling.

Cali figured she'd give her assistant as much space today as possible, so she began work on her to-do list. Lisa had been right. It was much smaller than it had been the day before. Maybe she would be able to duck out of there early.

To that end, Cali took lunch at her desk. She was finishing up when her phone rang. It was her personal line, not the main one that came through Lisa. "Hello?"

"Hi, sweetheart."

Cali smiled. "Dad. How are you feeling?"

Alvin Stanton laughed and then released an agonizing groan. "Well, if I don't laugh . . ." He paused. "How are things there? Did the shipment get off all right?"

In her quest to get through the things on her desk, she'd almost forgotten that Matthew was supposed to come by her office and brief her. Since he hadn't stopped by yet, she had to assume all was well.

"Things are good." She hoped he didn't press her for details.

"Good. Glad to hear it." He sucked in a sharp breath. "Ouch."

"Dad, are you okay?"

Her father sighed. "Yes. I'm fine. The nurse is just in here poking around."

Cali bit her tongue. She knew he was in good hands. He didn't need her hovering.

"Anyway . . . that's the reason I'm calling," he said. "They're releasing me from the hospital tomorrow morning."

"That's great." It was the best news Cali had heard since she'd been back in Chicago. "I'll have Jessie get your room ready. Do we need to get a hospital bed set up for you?"

"No, no. I'm not coming back to the house."

Shock then irritation surged through her. "What do you mean you're not coming back to the house?"

He must have sensed how upset she was. "Honey, don't get all worked up. It's just . . . well, the doctors want me to rest. And I know if I'm that close to work, then that's not going to happen. Besides, I don't want to get in your hair."

"Dad." All her frustration was concentrated in that one simple word.

"Cali, I love you. But, honey, you have a lot on your plate right now and you don't need me in the way. I trust you to run the company while I can't." Before she could say anything else, he continued. "So I'm going up to the lake house. I was hoping that since tomorrow is Saturday maybe you could come have a late lunch or early dinner with me."

While she didn't like the idea that her father would be up at the lake house by himself, she also knew it was no use arguing with him once he'd made up his mind. "I'd love to."

There was a knock on her office door.

"Hang on, Dad."

Figuring it was Lisa, Cali yelled for her to come in.

As her father began talking again, she refocused on him. "I know you're busy, and I don't mean to keep you. Does three o'clock sound good to you?"

"Yeah, Dad. That sounds . . ." The words got clogged in her throat. Her visitor wasn't Lisa. It was Matthew. "Fine."

"Oh, good. Well, I'll let you get back to work, then. I need to get a hold of Matthew anyway. See if he can send someone down to make sure the security at the lake house is in working order."

Cali bit her lower lip. "Um. You might want to wait a while."

"Wait to call Matthew? Why?"

"Because he's not in his office at the moment." She hesitated. "He's here."

"Oh, good. Well then, that just kills two birds with one stone, doesn't it? Put us on speaker," her father said.

"Sure." She wondered if her father picked up on the lack of enthusiasm in her voice.

Apparently not. As soon as she hit the speaker button, her father's voice filled the room. "Matthew! How are things?"

"Very good, sir. How are you?"

"Not bad. Not bad at all. I get to finally leave this joint tomorrow." Alvin paused. "As much as I want to ask you how things went with the shipment, I won't. I trust you and my little girl are handling it."

Matthew glanced over at her and she felt her cheeks heat. His gaze lowered to her mouth and she realized she was biting her lip again. He clenched his fists and looked away.

She'd been so transfixed with Matthew that she missed some of what her father had said. "I was wondering if you could send someone up this weekend to take a look at the security system. I hate to ask, but—"

"That's not a problem, sir. I'll take care of it personally. Will tomorrow work?" Matthew asked.

"Tomorrow would be perfect." Her father's voice echoed in the large office. "Say, why don't you ride up with Cali? No sense in wasting gas when you're both heading in the same direction, now is there?"

Cali and Matthew stared at each other across the space. She had no idea what he was thinking.

"Matthew, you can take a look at things while Cali and I do

some catching up. Then we can all sit down to an early supper before you both head back."

She felt Matthew's gaze on her but she focused on a picture on the opposite side of the room. The thought of being trapped in a car for an hour with him had her heart racing to near dangerous levels. But it wasn't as if she could tell her father that. Not without some sort of explanation.

Cali waited for Matthew to respond to her father, but he never did.

"Great," her father said after a prolonged silence. "I'll see you both around three. Oh, and Cali?"

"Yes, Dad?" She tried her best to keep the panic out of her voice.

"Love you."

"You, too."

Her father hung up and with every second that passed Cali felt the awkwardness increase.

"The delivery is on its way. We had a tail, but it was taken care of." Matthew's voice was monotone and formal. "The truck should arrive in Columbus before the end of business today. I'll inform you if that changes."

Cali attempted to regain her professional footing. She looked him square in the eye. "Thank you for the update."

He nodded and turned to go.

When Matthew reached for the doorknob, he paused. "I'll pick you up tomorrow a little before two."

He didn't wait for her to respond before opening the door and leaving her office.

Alone once more, Cali let her head fall back against her chair. What had her father just gotten her into?

She pressed her fingers against her temples and took several deep breaths. Work. That's what she needed. Something to keep her mind off Matthew Andersen.

By three o'clock, Cali had made it through the stack of folders Lisa had assembled for her and double-checked her e-mail. Any other Friday she would have been more than happy to breeze out of work two hours early, but if she went home, all she would do was fret over her upcoming trip to the lake house.

Staying at work wasn't an option—with no work to keep her

busy it would only give her more time to think—so she decided to go shopping. Cali wasn't one to hang out at the mall for hours on end, but it was better than sitting at home, watching television, and stuffing her face with a boatload of carbs.

Getting out of the house and being around people worked for a while. The shops weren't very busy and she found a new outfit for tomorrow—a pair of jeans that did amazing things for her backside and a fitted T-shirt. Nothing special. She'd been tempted to find something dressier, but this was her dad. He wouldn't care what she wore.

And that was all that mattered. Spending time with her dad. Having dinner with him at the lake house.

The fact that Matthew Andersen would be joining them held no relevance at all. He was there to do a job for her father. He was an employee. That was all.

She passed by a pizza shop and her stomach rumbled. Grinning, Cali snuck inside and grabbed a bite to eat. It had been years since she'd had real brick oven pizza. With every bite, she thought she'd died and gone to heaven.

Her belly full, Cali took her bags and headed out of the mall. She had every intention of going home when she passed by a movie theater. There were lines of people standing in front of the box office and she could smell the buttery popcorn wafting from the concession stand. In that moment, going home was the last thing she wanted to do. Plus, it had been ages since she'd seen a movie in a real theater.

Cali changed direction and marched up to the ticket counter. She scanned over the movie options and picked the first one that struck her fancy. Ticket in hand, she made her way over to the concession stand and ordered a small popcorn and a large pop.

As the previews started, Cali got this weird feeling that she was being watched. A quick look around her didn't garner anything unusual. She turned back toward the screen to watch the movie and tried to shake off her unease. It was probably just paranoia left over from her encounter with Matthew earlier that day.

Almost three hours later, she returned home and wandered up the stairs to her bedroom. The movie had been packed with action. There had been explosions and bullets flying everywhere. The hero had to protect the ambassador's daughter from a group of terrorists. It kept her on the edge of her seat the entire time.

Halfway through the movie, Paul and Joan, the two main characters, were hiding out in a hotel room after a big gunfight. Paul had been hurt—shot in the arm. Joan insisted on bandaging him up and the sexual tension that had been building since the beginning of the movie came to a head. As she finished securing the bandage, they embraced in a sensual kiss. The chemistry was unbelievable.

As she laid out her new purchases and changed for bed, Cali still felt keyed up from all the adrenaline. She closed her eyes and did her best to relax.

Finally, she managed to drift off to sleep, the bedroom scene fresh in her mind. Gradually the actors morphed from Joan and Paul to her and Matthew. Her mind and her body sank into bliss as she imagined Matthew's hands and lips doing to her what she'd seen on the screen.

She woke up on Saturday morning tangled in her sheets. As the memories came back to her in the light of day, Cali groaned. She'd had her own personal, very detailed fantasy starring Matthew Andersen.

Cali took hold of her pillow with both hands, placed it over her face, and released a frustrated scream.

Chapter 7

Matthew drove up to the Stanton house a little after one thirty on Saturday afternoon. He was early, but he'd done everything he needed to do that morning and couldn't stand sitting around his place doing nothing any longer. Normally he didn't mind the solitude. His comfort in being alone for hours on end had served him well in the military.

Today, however, even his favorite author couldn't keep his attention. The only thing he could concentrate on was his upcoming afternoon with Cali Stanton. He'd dreamed about her last night. Then again, he'd dreamed about her every night since laying eyes on her. Even still, it was different. His dreams last night had a new edge to them and he woke up primed and ready.

He'd been so frustrated from his nocturnal thoughts that he'd added an extra thirty minutes to his usual hour-long Saturday morning workout. Matthew needed to expel some of the extra energy that was coursing through his body before spending time alone with the woman who was currently occupying his fantasies.

Placing the car in park, he reached to turn off the engine, but movement caught his eye. Cali must have been watching for him because she bounded out the door toward the car with incredible speed. Or maybe it only seemed that way. Heaven knows he'd been dreading seeing her again. Not because he didn't want to see her, but because he *wanted* to see her . . . and touch her . . . and a whole host of other things that he couldn't—wouldn't—do with his boss.

Matthew couldn't take his eyes off her as she walked down the path toward him. She had on jeans and a pink top that should have been completely innocent, only it wasn't. Not on her. She had pulled her hair back into a ponytail that swayed as she walked. The urge to remove the band holding her hair in place and run his fingers though her hair had him gripping the steering wheel so tight his knuckles were turning white.

All his efforts to center himself with exercise had been in vain.

Somehow he managed to smile as she slid into the passenger seat beside him.

"Hello." She met his gaze for a split second then shifted in her seat to look out the window.

"Hi," he said. "Ready to go?"

"Yes."

He did his best to keep his focus on the road as he maneuvered them onto the highway. Aside from the way she pulled at her fingers every now and then, she stoically watched the passing scenery as they drove farther out of the city. It was the only indication she gave as to her discomfort at being alone in a car with him. Matthew couldn't say he disagreed. He was feeling pretty uncomfortable himself.

They'd been driving for almost thirty minutes before she spoke, startling him. "Do you mind if I turn on some music?"

"No. Not at all." To be honest, the silence was beginning to get to him.

Cali flipped through the stations until she found one playing eighties music. It wasn't his first choice, but it would work.

Bon Jovi's "Livin' on a Prayer" came on and he was surprised to hear Cali singing it to herself. The melodic sound of her voice pulled him out of his own thoughts. He looked over to find her mouthing every word perfectly. The desire to tease her bubbled to the surface. "I didn't picture you as a hair band fan."

She shot him a grin that made his heart stutter in his chest. "What can I say? Who doesn't love 'Livin' on a Prayer'?"

"True." Matthew laughed, and it felt good. "So is it just Bon Jovi, or are you into all the other hair bands of the eighties as well?"

Cali shifted in her seat to face him. "I would have to say that I was—and still am—quite smitten with most of them. How about you? Were you a hair band fan?"

He loved the teasing lilt of her voice. "As you said, who doesn't love 'Livin' on a Prayer'? And I'm quite a fan of The Bangles, too. You know, 'Walk Like an Egyptian.' "

She giggled. "Oh my, does that bring back memories."

Matthew smiled. "What were some of your other favorite songs from the eighties?"

They spent the rest of the drive trying to outdo each other with their knowledge of eighties bands and music. It was fun and Matthew hadn't had that type of fun in a long time.

With fifteen minutes to spare, Matthew pulled the car in front of the Stantons' lake house. It wasn't as grand as the main house in the city, but it wasn't what most would consider small by any means. The Stantons' lake house was still bigger than the house Matthew and Jason had grown up in.

Matthew turned off the engine and got out. He smiled over at Cali as she followed his lead. The second half of their trip had been full of laughter. They'd shared awkward teenage memories in between bouts of singing. All the tension from before had disappeared.

As they made their way to the house, a man about their age appeared at the back door. "Cali! It's so good to see you again."

She grinned and let the man pull her in for a hug—a rather intimate hug from Matthew's perspective. "It's great to see you again, David. Is my dad keeping you busy?"

The man, David, chuckled. "Doesn't he always?"

Not liking the way the man was looking and touching Cali—and at the same time knowing he shouldn't care—Matthew cut into their blissful reunion. "Do you know where Alvin is?"

Cali jumped a little at his clipped tone. It was a complete one-eighty from his carefree mood of a few minutes ago. He couldn't help it. This David person rubbed him the wrong way and Matthew didn't want to examine too closely why that was.

"Yeah. He's down the hall in the master suite," David answered Matthew's question. Then to Cali, "It looks to be a pretty sweet setup. I don't think I've ever seen so many gadgets in one room before."

Matthew gave the man a curt nod—it was the best he could

manage when what he wanted to do was punch the guy—and marched down the hall to see if he could locate Alvin. The only thing he could hope was that this David character wouldn't be joining them for dinner.

***

Cali was beyond confused.

She watched Matthew walk away from them, holding himself stiff and taking each step with deliberate purpose. It was a far cry from the smiling, laughing man she'd shared the last half hour with.

Trying to shake it off, she turned her attention back to David. "How's your dad been?"

David's father had been the groundskeeper of the Stanton lake house for many years before he finally retired and let his son take over. She and David had grown up together. Cali couldn't remember how many times his dad had lectured them about messing in his flowerbeds or trampling his garden.

"He's good. Restless," David said. "He comes out here at least once a week. Says it's to visit me, but he always finds some chore that needs doing and insists on helping me with it."

Cali laughed. "That sounds like your dad."

"Yeah. I think if not for the arthritis in his hands, he'd have kept working here until the end."

The two of them stood in the small foyer and talked until dinner was served. David excused himself, saying he had some things to finish before heading home for the day.

"Don't be a stranger," he said as he hugged her goodbye and disappeared out the door.

Cali strolled into the dining room to find her father and Matthew already seated at the table. She knew the moment Matthew was aware of her. He sat up a little straighter and the muscles in the back of his neck flexed. She ignored it as best she could and took a seat on the opposite side of the table.

The tension was palpable. Even her father noticed. He kept looking back and forth between the two of them as they ate. Conversation was stilted at best and after a while her father gave up entirely.

Carolyn, the live-in nurse her father had hired, appeared beside her to take her plate.

"Thank you."

Carolyn nodded.

One by one, she cleared the plates from the table and then left them alone once more.

Matthew cleared his throat. "If you'll excuse me, I'm going to go take a look around."

He didn't look in Cali's direction and she tried not to let it bother her.

Carolyn placed a cup of coffee in front of her along with cream and sugar. Cali gave the woman a grateful smile and lifted the delicate china to her lips to take a sip.

"Tell me, sweetheart, how are you adjusting to life back in civilization?" her father asked.

She shook her head. "I wasn't gone that long, Dad."

He chuckled.

Cali rolled her eyes. "I'm adjusting fine. Jessie's been a big help. It's great to have her around again. I didn't realize how much I missed her."

Alvin sighed. "She is something, isn't she? I know I miss her cooking after two weeks of hospital food."

It was Cali's turn to laugh. "I imagine so. Speaking of which . . . how did you manage to get released so quickly?"

He waved his hand in front of his face dismissively. "I was done with that hospital nonsense. All I did was lie around killing time and there's no reason why I can't do that here."

"Very observant of you." Cali tried to hide her smirk behind her cup.

There was a brief lull in the conversation before he turned the tables on her. "How are things at the office? Matthew said the shipment yesterday made it to the hospital. You two taking care of things? Getting along?"

She tried to keep the emotion out of her voice when she answered. "Of course. As you said, Matthew is very good at his job."

Cali smiled, but she could tell her father didn't believe her.

Luckily, he let the subject drop. "Yes. Quite."

Matthew was gone for almost an hour before he ambled into the sunroom where Cali and her father had relocated after dinner. He glanced in her direction and then turned his attention to her father. "I don't mean to cut your visit short, but we should probably start heading back."

"Oh, of course," her father said, reaching over to grasp her hand. "Thank you for coming to spend some time with your old man."

She stood and placed a kiss on his cheek. "Call me if you need anything."

"Don't worry about me. Carolyn will make sure I have everything I need. And David's here."

Cali waved to her father and then followed Matthew out.

He said nothing as they made their way back to the car. She climbed inside and settled herself into the plush leather. Something told her it was going to be a long drive back to Chicago.

***

Matthew did his best to block out the woman sitting beside him and concentrate on the road. Although he knew he was allowing his emotions to dictate his actions, he didn't care. Something in him sparked to life when he saw Cali being all chummy with the man he later found out to be the groundskeeper.

When David wrapped his arms around her and pulled her close, Matthew saw red. He knew it was irrational. Knew he had no claim on her. But logic wasn't playing a big role in his thinking at this point.

The sun began to set as they drew closer to the city. With each mile they traveled, the realization that he was jealous gripped him and wouldn't let go. He was jealous of a man Cali clearly had a history with. Someone who could openly show her affection—be her friend and more if that was what she wanted—without any barriers between them.

As much as he ached to deny it, he couldn't anymore. He wanted Cali Stanton more than he'd wanted any other woman in his life. The problem was that he couldn't have her. She was his boss. And even more than that, he'd heard her tell her father that she had plans to return to Africa as soon as her father was back on his feet. A relationship with her was out of the question.

He was going to have to find a way to stay away from her. Somehow. Avoiding all contact would be impossible given their situation, but he would have to minimize it as much as possible.

Because the more time he spent with her, the stronger his feelings for her grew.

After dropping her off and making sure she was safely inside the house, he took the long way home and drove by his brother's apartment. He didn't really expect Jason to be home, but he wanted to see it with his own eyes.

Sure enough, his brother's place was dark. To be certain, Matthew called his landline. The sound of it ringing could be heard out in the hall, but no one was inside to answer.

Shaking his head, Matthew made his way back to his vehicle. His brother was coming over tomorrow and they were going to have to have a talk.

By the time Sunday morning arrived, Matthew wasn't in the best of moods. He'd slept like shit and nothing, not even running ten miles, had managed to clear his head. It did, however, remind him that he needed to call Martinez and see if they'd been able to glean any new information from the security footage. Cali Stanton was messing with his head.

He debated calling Martinez on his day off, but decided to wait until Monday. Even if they'd found something there wasn't much he could do until then anyway.

After taking a shower, he turned on some relaxing music and sat down with the book he'd started reading the other night. His brother would be there around one. They were going to grill some burgers and watch the game—hang out. Until then, Matthew needed to try and get his head on straight and forget about his new boss.

Jason arrived ten minutes late, as usual, with a grocery sack full of food. He carried it into the kitchen and began laying the items out on the counter.

"Did you buy out the whole store?" Matthew asked.

His brother laughed. "Of course not, little brother. I only got the essentials."

Apparently the essentials included three different kinds of potato chips, potato salad, coleslaw, macaroni salad, cookies, and a cheesecake. It was a feast of carbohydrates. Good thing Matthew ran those ten miles this morning.

Jason didn't seem worried about the carbs or anything else as he finished unloading the goodies he'd bought. When he had everything on the counter, he plucked one of the cookies out of the box and took a huge bite.

Matthew shook his head and chuckled. Jason would be, well . . . Jason.

Having got a plate out of the cabinet, Matthew started making the hamburger patties while his brother put the potato salad, macaroni salad, and coleslaw in the refrigerator. Then he ducked outside to heat up the grill.

Sunday afternoons were a tradition for Matthew and Jason. They lived mostly separate lives the rest of the week, but Sundays were special. When their dad was alive, they'd both go over to his place, stuff themselves with food, and yell at the television. After their dad passed away, they'd moved the gathering to Matthew's place. It hadn't crossed either one of their minds to stop doing it.

Jason strolled back into the kitchen as Matthew was washing his hands. After taking his time drying his hands, he turned to face his brother.

It took a minute or two for Jason to realize Matthew was staring. "What?"

"You're seeing Lisa Morgan." Direct was always best with Jason.

His brother reached for a beer and popped the cap off before answering. "Yeah, I am."

"And you didn't mention it to me because?" Matthew tried to keep the irritation out of his voice, but he didn't think he succeeded.

Jason slammed the bottle down on the counter. It was a wonder it didn't break. "Because I knew how you'd react, that's why."

Matthew shot his brother a look that said he was waiting on a better explanation than that.

Instead of answering, Jason grabbed the plate of burgers and stalked out to the patio.

Sighing, Matthew shook his head and followed his brother. Like it or not, they needed to talk about this.

His brother stood in front of the hot grill, studiously ignoring him. Jason's attitude was seriously pissing him off. "If you needed to get some action, then you should have gone to a club or something. But when it comes to work, you need to keep it in your pants. I don't have to tell you how dangerous it is. You've seen what can happen. We have enough problems as it is without yet another complication. Whatever it is you've got going on with her, it needs to stop. Now."

Jason closed the lid to the grill with a bang and whirled around to face his brother. "Not going to happen, Matty."

"Excuse me?" Matthew's temper was in danger of boiling over. He took a deep breath to steady himself.

"I said it's not going to happen. I will see whoever I like, whenever I like." Jason advanced, getting in his brother's face as he continued. "And neither you nor some half-wit who thinks it's fun to mess with people is going to have any say in my life."

His brother didn't wait for Matthew to respond before turning on his heel and storming back into the house.

Matthew spent the next few minutes replaying what had happened. His brother had always been a bit of a ladies' man. None of his relationships ever lasted more than a few weeks. While he'd expected to encounter some resistance, Jason's blowup had been a lot more than he'd bargained for.

Figuring Jason needed some time to cool off, Matthew stayed outside until the meat was finished cooking. He brought the burgers inside and set off to find his brother.

Jason was on the couch, his gaze firmly fixed on the television. He was still angry.

"How long have you been seeing her?" Matthew asked as he took a seat a few feet away from his brother.

"About three months."

Matthew sighed and leaned forward, resting his elbows on his knees. "I'm sorry I jumped to the wrong conclusion."

His brother didn't respond other than to relax the set of his shoulders.

"There's still a danger, though. You know that."

Jason leaned back and met his brother's gaze for the first time. "I know. That's why we've kept it quiet."

"Cali Stanton figured it out in her first week here."

His brother grimaced. "That was . . . unfortunate."

"Is that what you call getting caught fooling around in the office with the boss' assistant? *Unfortunate*?"

"Nothing happened and you know it." There was a hard edge to Jason's voice.

"Do I? I'm beginning to wonder. The Jason I know changes women like they're a pair of shoes."

Jason narrowed his eyes.

Matthew continued before his brother lost his temper again. "Obviously this one is different. But, Jason, this *is* dangerous. What happens if whoever our mole is finds out, huh? What if you have to choose between her and the job? I want you to be happy. I do . . . but is this really something you should be doing right now? With everything we have to deal with?"

He watched the emotions play out on his brother's face before Jason shook his head. "I don't know, man. I don't know. But I won't give her up."

A long moment passed as Matthew considered what his brother had said.

Without any concrete answers, Matthew stood. "Are you hungry? The burgers are getting cold."

One side of Jason's mouth lifted into a half smile. "Good. I'm starving."

Chapter 8

Cali had spent her Sunday relaxing. She'd even dug out her old bathing suit and taken a dip in her dad's pool. It had been years since she'd had the opportunity to swim, but she loved it.

But as she'd been floating on her back, enjoying the sun beating down on her, a noise had startled her out of her peaceful meditation. When she'd righted herself, she scanned the area for something out of place. Her gaze fell on a big orange cat. The feline had a string in its mouth that led back to a small shed in the backyard. Apparently, the gardener had forgotten to close it after leaving for the weekend because the door was wide open.

She had breathed a sigh of relief that it had only been a cat, but even still, Cali couldn't shake the feeling that she was missing something.

The feeling was still with her when she went into the office on Monday. Cali had always been a fighter, but it was hard to fight something you couldn't see. She was starting to think all this talk of threats and hijacking was making her paranoid.

Lisa was already at her desk when Cali exited the elevator.

"Good morning, Cali." The genuine smile on her assistant's face helped to brighten Cali's morning. Jason had made it back safely. If he hadn't, Lisa wouldn't be so perky.

Cali returned Lisa's greeting. "Did you have a good weekend?"

"Yes, thank you." A blush tinted her assistant's cheeks, giving Cali the impression that it had been a very good weekend indeed. "How about you?"

"It was good." She shifted her weight and edged closer to her office. The last thing she wanted to do was talk about her weekend. "Do you have my schedule for today?"

"Already on your desk."

Cali grinned. "Thanks."

She gave Lisa a little wave and then disappeared into her office. Once she was safely inside, Cali strolled over to her desk and scanned through the list Lisa had put together. She only had two meetings lined up for the day and Lisa had compiled all the paperwork Cali would need for each of them. The woman was amazing. Cali had no idea how she would have managed to get through this without her.

As she was flipping through the stack of paperwork, about halfway down there were five menus. Cali chuckled. Lisa obviously expected Cali to be eating in her office today. After a brief look over her workload, Cali figured she was probably right.

She took a few minutes to go over the menus and jot down what she wanted for lunch before reviewing the rest of her schedule. As Cali worked her way down the list, she was thinking today wouldn't be so bad until her finger landed on the information regarding her second meeting of the day. All the air left her lungs as the words 'Security Briefing' stared back at her in bold black ink.

No, no, no. Not today. She couldn't see him today. Not after the way they left things on Saturday.

A weight settled into the pit of her stomach as she remembered the long drive back home. How he'd put the car in park—not bothering to shut it off—unlocked the door, and sat there without a word waiting for her to get out. He was as still and stiff as a robot. She had no idea what had changed, but Cali got the impression that he was upset with her for some reason.

In all honesty, she wasn't sure she'd wanted to know. So instead of confronting him, she'd rushed into the house and clicked the bolt shut behind her. Seconds later, she'd heard him leave.

Thinking about it now, days later, had her blood pounding through her veins. She had no idea how she was going to be able to sit through a meeting with him. What would he say? How would he act? Would he be the man who had driven her up to see her father or the one who drove her home?

Her eight thirty meeting with Nathan Reese, one of the board members, kept her from obsessing over her impending meeting with Matthew. Even though theirs was a business meeting, she liked Nathan. She remembered him from her teenage years when she used to come to the office with her father. In some ways, they had a lot in common. Nathan had taken over his father's seat on the board ten years ago. At the time, he'd had no interest in such a thing but after his father had suffered a stroke, Nathan didn't have much choice. He was the youngest of all the board members at forty-eight.

She said goodbye to Nathan around ten and set about to get through some of the paperwork on her desk. Cali was so lost in her work that she almost forgot about lunch until Lisa popped her head into Cali's office a little before noon.

"I can't believe it's lunchtime already."

Lisa grinned. "Enjoying your work that much, huh?"

"Not quite." Cali smiled and handed her the order she'd written down earlier. "Why don't you join me?"

"Are you sure?" Lisa asked, uncertain.

"Beats eating alone."

Lisa grinned and nodded. "I'll go put the order in."

Twenty minutes later Cali and Lisa sat in a cozy sitting area inside Cali's office, eating their sandwiches. Although they'd worked together for a week now, they hadn't spent any time together outside the boss/employee structure. It made casual conversation awkward at first.

"How do you like being home?" Lisa asked, and then rushed to correct herself. "I mean, I'm sure you would like it better if your dad hadn't gotten hurt and you had to come deal with the business and—"

Cali chuckled. "It's okay. I knew what you meant. The circumstances might not be ideal, but I did miss Chicago. And I missed home. Jessie is an amazing cook and she makes sure I'm well fed."

"I've eaten some of Jessie's desserts Alvin has brought in. They're out of this world."

They fell into silence again and Cali knew she was going to have to be the one to break through the wall of professionalism.

"One of the things I miss most about Chicago, though, are the bathrooms."

Lisa wrinkled her brow. "The bathrooms?"

"Yep. You'd be amazed at the accommodations some of the villages had for us. The worst was when we had to go into this tent and there were two holes dug into the ground. They both had these pieces of wood with holes in them. That was our toilet. For two months."

"You're kidding me?" Lisa's eyes were wide.

"Nope." Cali took a drink of her water. "I'm most definitely not kidding."

"What did you do for showers?"

"Oh, we had showers. Sort of. They were outside and someone had to pump the water while you stood under the spray."

Lisa shook her head. "I don't know if I could do that. I need my privacy and hot water."

Cali tilted her bottle of water toward Lisa in salute. "Modern conveniences."

"Modern conveniences," Lisa agreed, mimicking Cali. "Let's hope I never have to live without them."

The two laughed.

Once they'd both gotten control over themselves, Cali picked up her sandwich again. "I've wanted to ask you something, but I don't want to intrude."

Lisa swallowed. "Let me guess. It's about me and Jason, right?"

Cali smiled sheepishly. "Have you guys been together for a while?"

Having finished her sandwich, Lisa gathered her trash, dumped it into the trashcan beside Cali's desk, and then returned to her seat. "Three months. So, no, not too long."

"Well, you look happy," Cali said. The last thing she wanted was to make Lisa feel uncomfortable.

Lisa's smile lit up her entire face. "I am."

Her assistant got a dreamy look on her face that made Cali envious. Her experience with men was limited. She hadn't done much in the way of dating since her rebellious teenage years and she didn't think those males really qualified as men. Once she'd decided she wanted to become a doctor she'd pretty much sworn off the opposite sex and focused on her studies.

"What about you?" Lisa asked, drawing her attention.

"What about me?"

Lisa rolled her eyes. "Men, of course. Is there anyone special in your life? Anyone you're reconnecting with now that you're back in the States?"

Cali shook her head. "No. I don't really date much."

"Why not?" The other woman seemed genuinely perplexed.

"When I was in college I didn't want the distraction. After that, well, I dated some but nothing serious." To be perfectly honest, none of the men she'd dated as an adult had done much for her. She'd been attracted to them physically, but after one or two dates the newness faded and she lost interest. No man had ever kept her up at night or filled her head with fantasies of what it would be like to spend the night in his arms. Not until she'd met Matthew Andersen.

She was still lost in her daydream when Lisa's voice broke through her thoughts. "That settles it, then. You have to come out with us."

Cali blinked.

"I mean, if you want to," Lisa added. "We'd love for you to come. It's just a small group of us, but there is this club we go to. The dancing is great and the guys . . ."

Cali chuckled. "I thought you were taken."

"Doesn't mean a girl can't look, now does it?" Her grin was wicked.

"Definitely not." It had been a while since Cali felt so carefree.

"So you'll come?" Lisa asked.

"Sure." How could Cali say no?

"Great!" Lisa said, standing and straightening her skirt. Their lunch hour was up. "I'll let Becky and Jen know you'll be joining us for our next girls' night. Does this Friday work for you?"

Cali stood and gathered up the remnants of her meal. The break had been nice, but she had a million things waiting for her on her desk. "Friday sounds great."

Lisa nodded and headed back out to her desk, leaving Cali alone. She strolled back over to the stack of paperwork she'd been working on before. As she picked up the first folder, Cali's gaze drifted to her calendar and the notation of her afternoon meeting. She swallowed and averted her gaze.

***

Matthew went about his day pretending he didn't know he had a security briefing scheduled with Cali Stanton that afternoon. He'd woken up that morning the same way he had since he'd met her—with a painful hard-on that screamed for relief. It was getting ridiculous. Like it or not, he was going to have to do something about it soon.

In an effort to distract himself, Matthew dialed Martinez. He needed to know if they'd found out any more information about the woman on the security footage. They needed something that would lead them to the mole and Matthew was hoping this woman was it.

This whole thing—whatever it was—with his new boss was making him sloppy, which only proved to drive home how much getting involved with her would be a bad idea. He had to think about her as his boss and keep her in that nice neat box. They had a working relationship and that was all they were ever going to have.

His brother often frequented clubs to find willing women to warm his bed, but that had never been Matthew's style. It wasn't appealing now, but he wasn't sure he had much of a choice. He felt on edge.

The thought of trolling a club for a hookup to release his urges felt like the act of a desperate man and it irritated him that he'd even been thinking of doing such a thing.

He let his head fall back against his chair and closed his eyes as the department's hold music played on the line. Whenever he needed to pass the time as a sniper in the Army he'd run through mathematical equations in his head. It had been years since he'd had to resort to that, but he found himself doing it now. Arranging numbers in his head calmed him and he felt the tension in his shoulders beginning to ebb.

The music coming through the phone changed. This new song was soft and melodic. It sounded like something you would dance to while holding your lover close, breathing in the scent of her auburn hair.

Matthew opened his eyes. He ran his hands over the top of his head and leaned forward to rest his elbows on the edge of his desk. Why couldn't he go one day without thinking about her? Why couldn't he go one morning without waking up in a heated state ready and willing to take her?

He sat up and slammed his hand down on the desk.

"You okay?"

In his frustration, Matthew hadn't realized the music had stopped and his friend had answered.

"Yeah." Matthew blew out a frustrated breath. "Yeah, I'm good. Please tell me you've got some good news for me."

"I do have some news, but I don't think you're going to like it much."

That seemed to be the story of his life lately. "What did you find?"

"Like I told you before, Nikki's good. She managed to clean up the file quite a bit. I think you should take a look at the footage again and see if you can recognize anything."

Matthew waited. Martinez liked to draw things out. He was such a drama queen.

"She worked her magic, but she couldn't get a face." He paused. "She's not happy about that."

"So what are you saying?" Matthew asked, getting impatient.

Martinez hesitated. "Someone tampered with the tape. Man, you not only have a mole within the company but one on your security team as well. That is unless your security has holes in it, and knowing you I highly doubt that."

Matthew slumped in his chair. Could this get any worse?

"Thanks, Martinez. I appreciate it. I'll stop by today or tomorrow to pick up the file."

"Anytime. Sorry it couldn't have been better news."

"Better to know, right?" Matthew said as he typed out a quick e-mail to his brother letting him know they needed to talk.

"Drop me a line if you need anything else."

"Thanks."

Matthew hung up the phone and contemplated the new information. One of his team was in on it. That would explain why they'd had so much trouble making any headway ferreting out the mole. It also explained how, even after they'd changed the delivery schedule the week before, the information had been leaked.

But who?

He didn't have an answer to that.

When three o'clock rolled around, there was a knock on his

door. He'd spent the last ten minutes staring at his phone trying to come up with an excuse to cancel his meeting with Cali Stanton, but he couldn't think of one. Not a creditable one, anyway.

The person at his door knocked again, louder. Matthew knew it could only be one person.

"Come on in, Jason."

A moment later, his brother opened the door and swept into the room. He walked up to stand directly in front of Matthew's desk with his hands on his hips.

"What?" Matthew demanded.

Jason raised both eyebrows. "You're supposed to be upstairs right now in a meeting. Why are you still sitting here in your office?"

Matthew had no answer for his brother since he'd been contemplating that exact question before his brother had shown up.

"What's going on?" Jason asked. "You haven't been yourself in days. Now you're missing meetings? This isn't like you."

Matthew didn't need his brother to tell him what he already knew. "I've had a lot on my mind lately, that's all."

The look on Jason's face told Matthew his brother didn't believe a word of it.

Deciding a change of subject was in order, he grabbed onto the first thing he could think of. "I spoke with Martinez. His expert says the footage has been tampered with."

He knew the moment Jason realized what that had to mean. "Who?"

Matthew tapped his fingers on his desk and glanced at his computer screen. "I don't know, but we need to figure it out. Until we do, we have to assume it could be anyone."

His brother nodded. "What do you need me to do?"

Although Matthew knew his brother was referring to whoever their mystery woman was, he had a more pressing need that Jason could help him with. "Do you think you could cover the meeting for me today? I'd like to pick up that file from Martinez this afternoon and take another look at it for myself."

Shock crossed Jason's face. "Yeah. Sure. Of course. I'll take care of it."

"Thanks. I owe you one."

Jason shot him a curious look, but let it go. "I'll call you later."

Matthew waited until his brother left the room before taking one last look at his computer screen. The flashing message reminding him of his meeting taunted him. He'd pawned off his meeting to Jason like a coward, but he couldn't face her today. Matthew needed his space . . . some separation. A little time to get his head back on straight. Then all would be normal again.

He powered down his computer and grabbed his jacket and his keys before making a beeline for the door. Maybe he could convince Martinez to grab a drink with him. It was a long shot, his friend didn't go out much now that he and his wife had a baby, but for some reason the idea of Matthew picking up a woman in a bar while hanging out with his buddy didn't sound as bad as going clubbing with his brother.

Chapter 9

Thursday morning Cali did her best to make sure she didn't look as if she'd just rolled out of bed before racing downstairs to the kitchen. Jessie was there at the stove. When she heard Cali enter, she stopped what she was doing and glanced up. A look of surprise crossed her face. Cali didn't usually come downstairs for breakfast for another thirty minutes.

Ignoring the older woman's curious expression, Cali pulled out a stool at the large island and sat down. She felt as if she were running an hour late instead of a half hour early. If she didn't slow down she was going to be worthless by the time she reached the office.

Cali took a deep breath in and let it out, trying to steady herself.

"Could I just get some toast this morning?" She smiled at Jessie. The woman looked as though she was about ready to ask Cali to explain herself, and she really didn't want to go there.

She was acting like a crazy person, but it wasn't really her fault. Ever since her meeting with Jason on Monday afternoon she'd felt off balance. She'd been preparing herself all day to see Matthew again. Then when he didn't show up, she'd been filled with a mixture of disappointment and relief along with the tiniest bit of anger. She was trying not to analyze it too closely.

On top of that, Lisa had insisted the two of them go shopping after work tonight for a new outfit. She was adamant a new outfit was required for their girls' night out tomorrow. That was the whole reason for her rushing around this morning. She needed to get to the office early and finish the stack of files on her desk, but she kept hitting the snooze button instead of getting out of bed like she should have. Now she was running behind.

And why had she continued to hit the snooze button over and over again? Because she hadn't wanted to let go of the dream she'd found herself in—one where she had her arms wrapped around the man who never seemed to leave her thoughts. In her dreams, he'd had his mouth and hands on her in so many delicious ways. She hadn't wanted it to end.

Cali sighed. The same man who'd been ignoring her all week.

She knew it had to be intentional. Not only had Matthew not shown up for their meeting on Monday but on Tuesday Mariana, Matthew and Jason's assistant, had hand-delivered some confidential documents to her. There had been a note from Matthew requesting that Cali e-mail him to confirm she'd received them. She couldn't understand why he hadn't brought them to her himself if they'd been so important, but she'd convinced herself that he must have been busy.

What had changed her mind, however, was when she'd called down to his office on Wednesday afternoon trying to find out about the next shipment. She had it marked on her calendar, but with all the issues recently Cali wanted to make sure it was still happening. Mariana had answered the phone and placed her on hold. Cali figured after a few moments she'd be transferred to Matthew but that didn't happen. Instead, Mariana had returned to the line and told her that Mr. Andersen was in the middle of something and could not be disturbed. He was requesting that she e-mail him whatever she needed to talk to him about instead.

While each of those things separately didn't mean much, put together in such a short period of time told her that Matthew Andersen was avoiding her.

"Milk or orange juice?" Jessie asked, causing Cali to blink several times.

"Orange juice, please."

Jessie placed two pieces of bread in the toaster and poured Cali her juice.

Cali took several slow sips as she waited for her toast. Jessie stayed silent until she set the toast down in front of Cali. "Are you okay this morning?"

"Of course. Why?" Cali tried to instill a level of confidence in her tone she didn't feel.

The older woman leaned back against the counter and crossed her arms. "I've known you most of your life, Cali . . . ever since you were running around here begging me to make you cookies."

Cali swallowed down a bite of toast. It felt overly dry even though she'd slathered on a healthy portion of butter and jelly.

"I know you've been gone for two years. Maybe it's that, but you look . . . frazzled."

"Frazzled?"

Cali choked out a laugh and Jessie waved a dismissive hand in front of her face. "Maybe that's not the right word. It's just that you seem to be on edge lately. Like your senses are on high alert or something."

Again, her observations had Cali squirming in her seat. It was something Jessie had been able to do for as long as Cali had known her.

"I know I'm just the help," Jessie said, softer this time, "but I do worry."

Placing her toast onto her plate, Cali met the older woman's gaze. "Jessie, you're not *just* the help. You've been there for me more times than I can count and I love you for it. But really, I'm fine. Work is just stressful. Guess I'm not as used to it as Dad."

She grinned and hoped the woman was reassured enough to drop the subject. Jessie was right, of course. Cali's nerves were on high alert, but it had nothing to do with the job. Not directly, anyway.

After several long moments, Jessie pushed herself away from the counter. "That reminds me . . ."

Cali picked her toast back up as Jessie crossed to the other side of the room, sorted through a stack of letters, and removed one. "Here it is."

She walked back over to where Cali was sitting at the counter and handed her the letter. It was a standard white envelope, but it was stamped 'confidential' on the front.

"This came yesterday. At first I thought it was for your father, but then I saw it had your name on it and thought maybe it had to do with your Doctors Without Borders stuff."

It didn't look like something from the nonprofit group she'd been working for, but she didn't have time to worry about it for the moment. She took the envelope and tucked it inside her briefcase. "Thanks, Jessie."

Cali finished her toast and juice and stood. She blew Jessie a kiss, grabbed her briefcase, and headed out the door to work.

Twenty minutes later, Cali parked her car in her designated parking space. One of the advantages of being the boss was that she didn't have to go driving around trying to find somewhere to park. The other advantage was that her spot was only thirty feet from the elevators.

She exited her vehicle and set the alarm before walking over to the elevator. As she rounded the corner, Cali saw the doors beginning to close and picked up her pace. She slammed her hand against the button, praying the doors would reopen and she didn't have to wait.

Cali breathed a sigh of relief when the doors reopened. She scrambled inside.

When she realized there was someone else in the elevator already, she turned to apologize. The words died in her throat, however, when she found herself staring into the crystal blue eyes she'd been dreaming about the night before. It felt as if she had suddenly swallowed a mouthful of cotton balls.

She pressed herself against the opposite wall of the elevator, trying to gain both a little distance and to keep herself upright. Cali couldn't speak. And as she stared into those mesmerizing blue eyes they grew hard—cold, until finally he broke their connection and looked away.

The elevator began its ascent and the farther up they went the more rigid Matthew's posture became. He stared at the metal doors as if somehow he could will them to open.

Matthew didn't say anything until the doors opened to his floor. The pause was slight, but she noticed it. Of course that might have been because she was hyperaware of him.

"Good morning," he whispered.

Then he walked away, leaving her standing there more confused than ever.

The elevator doors closed once more and Cali took several deep breaths. He hadn't spoken directly to her for almost a week and he'd acted as if telling her 'good morning' had taken an excruciating amount of effort on his part. But his eyes . . . the way he'd looked at her for that moment before he'd closed himself off . . .

She made her way to her office as soon as she reached her floor. Lisa would be in soon, but Cali needed some time to herself before she had to face anyone else. Matthew Andersen was driving her insane.

***

Matthew sat behind his desk in a daze. There was an e-mail open on his computer but he couldn't say what it was for or even who it was from. His head was too wrapped up in *her*. No matter how hard he tried, he couldn't get the way she'd looked this morning out of his mind.

She was out of breath when she'd rushed into the elevator. He knew she didn't notice him at first. It should have given him time to school his features, but seeing her had been a shock. He hadn't had time to prepare himself. When her gaze met his he'd been drawn into their depths just as he had the first time he'd met her. He'd hoped distance would help, but it hadn't. If anything it had made things worse. His dreams hadn't dissipated, nor had his longing to know what she tasted like.

Then this morning . . .

He groaned as the memory hit him again with as much force as it had when she'd been standing beside him.

This morning Cali hadn't been wearing her normal pantsuit. Today she wore a skirt and blouse with a jacket that hugged every last curve she had. Her legs had called to him the moment he'd laid eyes on her and he wanted to press her against the wall, push her skirt up around her hips, and take her. To hell with her being his boss.

It had been that thought that had pulled him out of his fantasy. So instead of giving in to his urges, he'd fixed her with a hard stare. He had no idea what she was doing to him. It wasn't appropriate to be thinking that way about his boss, and yet he couldn't stop. Keeping his distance wasn't working. He didn't know what else to

87

do.

A knock sounded at his door and his brother entered before Matthew could tell Jason to come in. Of course, Matthew had been expecting him. They were going to go over the security footage together that Matthew had picked up from Martinez. After viewing the footage more times than he could count, Matthew knew he needed some fresh eyes.

"Hey," Jason said as he pulled one of the chairs closer to Matthew's desk.

"Hey."

Yesterday during one of the hundreds of times Matthew had viewed the footage, he'd gotten a vague feeling that something about the woman was familiar but he couldn't put his finger on it. He was hoping Jason could. While Jason might not be as detail-oriented as he was, sometimes his brother's view of things was exactly what was needed.

His brother gave him a long look. He knew Jason was wondering what was going on with him. Matthew had lost his temper more than once this week. That wasn't like him.

But instead of probing into what was going on with Matthew, Jason turned to face the monitor. "Let's get this over with."

Relieved, Matthew brought up the footage and directed his attention to the screen and their mystery woman. It was the same thing he'd seen before, but he tried to pay attention to anything that could give them a clue as to who this was.

He had no idea how many times they watched and re-watched the footage but an hour later, they still had no idea who she was. All they had was a body type and some of her mannerisms. It wasn't a lot but, considering that before they'd had next to nothing, Matthew would take it.

They did know that it was a Stanton Enterprises employee. That narrowed down the list, but not by much. Also, since the file had been tampered with, there was a good chance this person was someone with access to the building's security.

As Jason left his office to check on the next shipment schedule, the thought occurred to Matthew that he should go over this new information with Cali. It's what he would've done had Alvin still been in charge. But he wasn't, and Matthew couldn't bring himself to face her again. The last thing his mind or body needed right now was another run-in with Cali Stanton.

***

Cali sat at her desk for what seemed like hours unable to focus on much of anything. She'd already downed several cups of coffee hoping that might help, but all it did was make her jittery so she'd finally dumped the rest of what was in her mug down the drain. Cali had a million things to do and instead of doing them she was remembering her encounter with Matthew Andersen this morning in vivid detail. What was it about that man that had her unable to concentrate on anything but him?

At nine thirty she needed to step away from everything for a few minutes, so she decided to call her dad. Hopefully talking to him would get her mind off things.

"This is a pleasant surprise," her dad said as he answered the phone.

"Thought I'd take a break and see how you're doing today."

"My nurse says I'm progressing nicely, whatever that means." She could almost see him pout as he said it.

She smiled. "That's good. Make sure you do everything she tells you to so you can get better faster."

"I should have known you would side with her."

Cali laughed. She really had missed her dad.

"How are things going in Chicago? Anything I need to know about?"

Her thoughts went to Matthew and whatever was going on between them. "No. Everything is good here. I'm working my way through a pile of paperwork. Not all that exciting."

He snorted. "Sounds about right. The paperwork never ends."

There was a knock on her door and Cali turned to see Lisa poking her head in.

Her father must have heard it or her hesitation. "Do you need to go?"

"Sorry."

"Don't worry about it, sweetheart."

"Love you, Dad."

"Love you, too, Cali. I'll see you soon."

By four thirty, Cali had only made it through about half the stack of paperwork, but she'd had enough of numbers and reports for one day. It would still be there tomorrow.

She took a few minutes to organize what was left. It would make things a little easier the next day.

As she sifted through some of the folders near the bottom of the pile, she found a letter with her name on it. Cali picked it up and noticed that it was still sealed and had no postmark. She flipped it over and opened it.

Inside was a sheet of paper. She took it out and read the single sentence typed on the white page.

Africa misses you.

Cali flipped the sheet over, but there wasn't anything else.

She even held it up to the light thinking maybe there'd be a watermark or some other writing not immediately visible. Again, she came up empty.

Strange.

What was 'Africa misses you' supposed to mean?

Trying to figure out the cryptic message made her remember the letter Jessie had given her earlier that morning. She'd completely forgotten about it.

Tossing the paper in her hand on the desk, she dug into her briefcase and extracted the mysterious piece of mail marked *Confidential.* It was thick—much thicker than the one she'd just opened. No wonder Jessie had assumed it was from her old employer.

Curious, Cali tore open the envelope and removed the stack of folded papers. There had to be at least ten sheets in total.

Cali unfolded them and jerked back slightly when she realized that she was looking at pictures of herself. There was a picture of her kneeling beside a little boy who'd broken his arm. She remembered him. He'd been one of her patients almost a year ago. He and his father had been hunting outside their village and he'd tripped while running. The boy had fallen trying to keep up with his father.

But where had the picture come from? She didn't remember anyone being there taking photographs.

She flipped to the next one. It was also from her time in Africa, but it was with a different patient.

As she worked her way through the photos, Cali noticed they were all of her in Africa. Each one with a different patient she'd treated.

More than a little disturbed, she picked the envelope up again looked for any indication as to who had sent it. All she could tell was that it had been mailed locally. That didn't mean anything, though. Doctors and nurses came and went frequently. It could have easily been a friend who'd sent the pictures, but why no note, no explanation? And why no return address?

Before Cali could dwell on it too much Lisa knocked on her door. "About ready to go?"

She took one more look at the papers she held in her hand and threw them down on her desk. "Yeah. Let's go."

The paperwork, the envelopes, and even Matthew Andersen would all be there tomorrow.

Chapter 10

She walked into his office looking stunning as ever. Her hair hung down around her shoulders in loose curls.

Matthew stood as she approached and moved out from behind his desk. He closed the distance between them—their eyes locked onto one another as they let their attraction take hold. Then he wrapped his arms around her waist and covered her mouth with his.

He crushed her against his chest, holding her as close as humanly possible. Her lips were so full and soft under his, just begging to be sucked and licked and nibbled on.

She brought her hands up to cup the back of his head, moaning into his mouth and begging him for more. He needed more of her.

He used his tongue to trace the outline of her lips, teasing her . . . silently requesting entrance.

Cali opened and he dipped his tongue inside her mouth for the first time. She tasted wonderful—exactly how he knew she would.

Her tongue twisted with his, urging him on and fanning the flames he already felt would consume him at any second. Cali's responsiveness thrilled him.

He reached between them to release the button on her jacket. Once it was free, he broke their kiss and looked down. There was nothing between him and her skin except a black lace bra.

Matthew slid his fingers inside her jacket and up her sides until they were on either side of her breasts. He shifted the position of his hands so his thumbs could graze her nipples. At the sensation, Cali's breath caught in her throat and she arched into his hands. Her hips pressed into him and he knew she could feel how hard he was for her.

Bending down, he pushed the thin lace of her bra out of the way and took one of her breasts into his mouth. She gasped and ground her hips against him as his lips circled around her nipple and he sucked.

A low groan rumbled in his chest. He wanted her. He wanted her here. Now.

He released his hold on her breast and flipped their positions so she was leaning back against his desk. Cali didn't resist. Her brown eyes were dark with her arousal. She wanted him as much as he wanted her.

He helped her up onto the edge of his desk then ran his hands up her legs until he found the silky piece of material separating him from what he was seeking. He hooked his thumbs on the sides of her panties and worked them down her long legs. With the barrier removed, he made quick work of removing his pants and positioned himself between her legs.

Pressing into her heat, Matthew couldn't remember a time when he'd ever felt better. He bent to kiss her as he began a slow and steady rhythm. She circled her arms around his neck and met every one of his thrusts with one of her own. Her breathing became more labored and the little sounds she was making were driving him crazy.

He was close. It wouldn't take much more to send him over the edge. All he needed was . . .

His phone beeped but he ignored it. No way was he letting go of the woman in his arms to take a phone call. Not when he finally had her.

But whoever it was wouldn't give up. He reached over to hit the button that would accept the call, but the thing kept right on beeping.

Matthew's eyes flew open. It took only a second for him to realize that he wasn't in his office. He was in his bedroom. And the beeping that he thought to be his phone was his alarm clock.

He turned off his alarm and flopped back against his pillows. What the hell was wrong with him? He hadn't reacted like that to a dream—or a girl, for that matter—since high school.

Kicking the sheet off him, he hopped out of bed. It looked as if the extra workouts he'd been doing weren't working. He was going to have to get relief in some other way and soon. This was getting out of hand.

After the way Matthew's morning had started, he wasn't surprised when the day dragged on without seeming to end. His head wasn't in work. It was still stuck in his bed fantasizing about a woman he couldn't have . . . which was what led to his decision to stop by Jason's office.

He'd been putting it off for hours, but as four o'clock rolled around Matthew was running out of time. If he was going to do this then he needed to do it. Before he could chicken out, he knocked on his brother's door.

Jason mumbled something on the other side, which Matthew took as an invitation to come in. He made his way inside to find his brother on the phone. He took a seat and waited for Jason to finish.

When he ended his call, Jason sat back in his chair looking as if he were king of the mountain. He didn't say anything, just waited for Matthew to spit out whatever it was he was there to say. It wasn't often he ventured into Jason's office. Usually it was the other way around.

Matthew cleared his throat. "I was wondering if you'd like to go out tonight. Hit a club or something."

His brother raised an eyebrow, and then lowered his gaze to the arm of the chair Matthew was sitting in. Unconsciously, he'd begun tapping out a steady rhythm with the tips of his fingers.

Matthew closed his hands into a fist and sat up straight.

Jason smirked and then blinked as if what Matthew said finally registered. "You want to go to a club?"

Matthew swallowed. In for a penny, in for a pound, right? "Yeah."

His brother looked unsure and for a moment Matthew wondered if Jason would pass.

"All right. How about I swing by and pick you up around seven?"

Matthew ran his hands down his legs in a nervous gesture and then stood when he realized what he'd been doing. Jason already suspected something. He didn't need to give his brother any more ammunition.

"Sounds good. I'll see you then," Matthew said, and then rushed out the door.

By the time he was back in his own office, Matthew was second-guessing himself. Then he recalled the way he woke up that morning and knew he didn't really have a choice in the matter. He was a grown man and he had needs. Since he couldn't have the woman his body was craving, he was going to have to find someone else who could fulfil those desires. It didn't have to be any more than two people taking what they needed and going their separate ways.

Matthew ran a hand over his head as he stared blankly at the wall in front of him. He only hoped it worked because if not he had no idea how much longer he was going to be able to resist Cali Stanton.

***

Cali had managed to forget about the two letters she'd received when she was out shopping with Lisa the night before. Having a little girl time was just what Cali had needed and she was looking forward to more of it tonight when she'd get to meet Jen and Becky. In fact, the letters had completely left her mind until she'd walked into her office on Friday morning and found them waiting for her on her desk, exactly where she'd left them.

They lay there almost mocking her as she tried to work through what was on her desk. She had no idea where they'd come from and no amount of racking her brain brought her any closer to a solution.

"Enough," she muttered and hid them at the bottom of her briefcase as if that would somehow make them go away.

All through the board meeting, she was preoccupied.

Peter noticed. He lingered after the meeting was over to talk to her. "Are you feeling all right, Cali?"

She grinned up at him. "Yeah, I'm fine. Just didn't get much sleep last night."

He frowned. "Did you want to reschedule?"

It took her a minute to figure out what he was referring to, but then she remembered. Because of the trouble the company had experienced over the last two years, her father had been meeting once a week with Peter to go over the financials. That was now her job and she'd completely forgotten that they were supposed to meet immediately following the board meeting.

Cali did her best to project a level of confidence she didn't feel. "Not at all. I'm fine. Really."

He studied her for several moments and then nodded. "Okay then, did you want to do it here or in your office?"

At the mention of her office, Cali thought of the letters tucked away in her briefcase. "Why don't we just do it here?"

He pulled out the chair next to her and sat back down. "Ready?"

She took a deep breath. "As I'll ever be."

Eight and a half hours later Cali ran down the stairs to answer the door with one earring in and the other stubbornly refusing to cooperate. She pulled the door open with a flourish as she attempted once again to get her earring to go into the tiny hole in her lobe.

Lisa stood on the other side of the threshold with an amused look on her face. "Hi."

Taking a step back, Cali motioned Lisa inside. "Come in. I just need to grab my shoes."

Cali jogged over to the bottom of the staircase where she'd ditched her heels earlier. As she knelt down to get her shoes, she felt the post of her earring slide into place. "Finally."

Lisa giggled. "Having problems?"

"Nothing a little determination can't fix," Cali said as she slipped into her shoes.

They headed to a casual barbecue restaurant called Hoggies. Jen and Becky were already there waiting for them.

"Jen, Becky, this is Cali Stanton. Cali, Jen and Becky," Lisa said, introducing them.

"Welcome, Cali," Becky said. "Lisa tells us you're a doctor."

"I am." The server came to get their orders, interrupting their conversation. Once he left, Cali turned the tables on them. "How about you? What do you ladies do?"

"I'm a project manager," Jen said.

Becky leaned back as their server returned with their drinks. They were sticking to pop until they got to the club. "I'm an interior designer."

"It's great Lisa convinced you to come tonight," Jen added. "We've all known each other for so long it's good to have some new blood."

Jen winked and everyone laughed.

"But enough about us," Becky said. "Tell us about you. What was it like living in Africa?"

"Did you see any lions?" Jen asked.

"What about the food? I've heard they eat their meat raw." Becky shuddered.

They were spouting off questions so fast Cali was having trouble keeping up. "Um. Well . . . Africa is beautiful. Hot, but you can see for miles. As for the lions, yes, I saw lions, but they usually stay away from the villages."

"What about the food?" Becky asked.

Cali shrugged. "It would depend, but there's a lot of rice, meat, and locally grown vegetables."

Before they could pepper her with more questions, Cali asked a question of her own. "So how long have you all known each other?"

"We went to college together," Lisa said.

The four sat and talked as they filled themselves with barbecue. Cali learned more about Jen and Becky. Jen had moved away after college but when her sister had some complications with her pregnancy, she'd moved back to help. Becky, on the other hand, had fallen in love with Chicago when she'd moved there from southern Illinois to go to college and never left. It was easy to see how close these women were and Cali was grateful that they welcomed her into their group so easily.

For dessert, they'd ordered a brownie that was as big as her hand and piled high with vanilla ice cream. It was the perfect dessert to share and they each dug into it with a casual comfort that Cali couldn't believe existed after one shared meal.

Jen took a bite of the warm brownie and swallowed. "You haven't told us how you and Jason are doing."

Cali glanced over at Lisa and then back to Jen and Becky. Apparently Lisa and Jason's relationship was old news to them.

Lisa blushed as she took a bite of dessert. "We're good."

"Come on," Becky chided. "You've got to give us more than that. We're living vicariously through you at the moment since our love lives are pretty much nonexistent."

"He came to see me after his trip to Ohio last weekend . . . didn't even stop home first."

Jen sighed. "I need a man like that."

"Did he rip your clothes off and make love to you against the door?" They all turned to stare at Becky. "What? You know you were all thinking it, too."

Jen laughed.

"Not quite." Lisa rolled her eyes. "And I'm not giving you perverts a play-by-play."

Becky wasn't deterred. "Did you make it to the bed?"

The blush was back. Lisa lowered her gaze to their dessert and kept it there. "Yes. Barely."

Both Jen and Becky roared with laughter. Cali tried to rein hers in, but it was contagious. She hadn't laughed that hard in a long time.

They finished their dessert, paid the check, and then ducked into the ladies' room to freshen up their makeup.

"Have you ever been to Faux before, Cali?" Jen asked.

"No."

"You're in for a treat, then," Becky said. "The dance floor is always full and the bartender's not bad to look at either."

They walked out the door and piled into Lisa's SUV.

She pulled out into traffic and took a right toward downtown. "The place should be hopping by the time we get there."

"I haven't danced in years," Cali admitted.

Lisa turned onto the highway. "Not much opportunity for dancing in Africa, I bet."

"No." Cali chuckled. "But I did get to dance in a couple of tribal dances. That was fun."

Becky shook her head. "I don't think I could do it. I mean no takeout. No shopping."

"How did you survive?" Jen asked in mock horror.

Becky stuck her tongue out at her friend and they all broke into another round of giggles.

It took around twenty minutes to reach the club, which was in a trendy neighborhood full of bars and restaurants. There were people milling about on the sidewalks as they found a place to park. It was only when they got closer that Cali realized most of them were waiting to get into the club.

"Come on," Lisa said. "I know the bouncer."

They crossed the street and followed Lisa as she made her way up to the front of the line.

When the bouncer saw them, he grinned. "Out for some fun

tonight, ladies?"

"You know it."

He unhooked the rope and motioned for them to go ahead. "Be safe tonight, ladies."

Jen led the way inside. "I need a drink. A real one this time."

"Me, too," Becky said as she followed Jen through the crowd over to the bar.

Cali took in her surroundings. It was loud, but that was to be expected. The room was dim, but there were enough lights to see most of what was going on. She could imagine, though, that if a couple wanted to find a dark corner somewhere it wouldn't be difficult.

"What do you think?" Lisa asked, stepping to the side to let a couple pass.

"Do you come here often?"

Lisa shook her head. "Not anymore. I used to. Before I met Jason."

Cali grinned at her friend and they moved farther into the fray toward the dance floor.

***

The place was packed. Matthew shifted his weight for what felt like the hundredth time trying to keep from bumping into someone. Maybe this wasn't such a good idea.

Jason tilted his head toward the bar before disappearing into the crowd. It was obvious that his brother expected him to follow.

Sighing, Matthew weaved his way through the throng of people until he found Jason leaning against the bar already with a beer in his hand. Matthew moved to stand beside Jason and motioned to get the bartender's attention. "Couldn't have ordered me one while you were at it?"

His brother brought the bottle up to his mouth and took an exaggerated sip as he turned to lean back against the bar so he could face the dance floor. "Nah. I wouldn't want to spoil the experience for ya."

Matthew shook his head, gave the bartender his order, and sat down on one of the stools.

The bartender appeared less than a minute later with his drink and Matthew placed his money on the bar along with a tip. He took a long pull on his beer and surveyed the room. So many of the women he saw were much too young. He was a thirty-one-year-old man and while some men his age would be fine with sleeping with a girl a year or two out of high school, he was not.

Jason stood patiently beside Matthew as he scanned the room. It took more than ten minutes before he spotted someone who had potential. The woman had long brown hair and looked to be in her mid to late twenties. She was attractive and looked as if she was up for a good time.

He watched her for several minutes as she danced with a small group. Although she was friendly with them, she didn't appear to be attached to anyone as she moved freely from one to another.

Finishing off his drink, he set the empty bottle on the bar behind him and stood. He took a deep breath, bracing himself for what he was about to do.

Matthew walked toward where she was still dancing in the center of the room. Bodies pushed into him as he drew closer to her, but he ignored them and focused on his goal.

The song changed moments before he reached her. It was slow and sultry. Perfect.

He tapped her on the shoulder and she turned around to face him. She looked him up and down once before meeting his gaze.

"Would you like to dance?" he asked.

Without a word, she stepped toward him and wrapped her arms around his neck.

Matthew placed his hands on her waist and pulled her into his arms. She felt good, but something wasn't quite right. The woman in his arms was soft and warm and sexy, but she wasn't the right woman—the woman his body had been craving.

She rubbed up against him and he couldn't prevent his body from reacting. It had been too long since he'd been with a woman.

He tried to concentrate on the feel of her against him . . . tried to let his body guide him in the sultry dance they were engage in. The woman he was dancing with was making her intentions clear with every move, every caress.

It wasn't working.

Matthew looked up and, right when he did, he found himself staring into the eyes of the woman who had starred in his dreams last night. He stiffened. What was she doing here?

His dance partner noticed the change in his mood and glanced over her shoulder to see what he was looking at. She turned back to him and reached up to whisper in his ear. "I'm willing to share."

Matthew only half registered what she said. He couldn't take his gaze off Cali.

Then the woman who held his complete attention from several feet away turned on her heel and disappeared into the crowd. It was as if a cold bucket of water had been doused on him. Any desire he had to sleep with the woman grinding her body against his vanished.

Chapter 11

Cali felt sick.

Before she realized what was happening, her feet were moving. She pushed her way through people until she reached the far corner of the bar. There was an empty seat so she sat down. The bartender appeared in front of her and she ordered a drink, although she wasn't sure what. It didn't matter. She just needed something . . . anything after seeing that woman with her body wrapped around Matthew like that.

She didn't know what to do. It felt as if she'd had the breath knocked out of her.

The bartender returned and placed a drink in front of her—a shot of something. She stared at it, lost in a feeling of emptiness, not making a move to pick it up.

"Are you all right?" Jen asked as her new friends surrounded her.

Cali nodded. It was the best she could do.

Lisa placed her hand on Cali's shoulder and turned her around to face them.

Cali didn't resist. She didn't have the energy.

Lisa reached up to wipe the moisture from Cali's cheeks. She hadn't even realized she was crying.

A frown pulled at Lisa's lips and she embraced Cali. "Do you want to go home?"

It took several moments before Cali could work through all the emotions that were clogging her throat to answer. "Yes."

The women didn't waste any time ushering Cali toward the door and out of the club. Without a word, they all climbed into Lisa's vehicle. Cali looked out the window as they pulled away from the curb. She wondered if he would be taking that woman home with him. And in the next thought she asked herself why she should care. She didn't have any claim on him.

The next morning Cali rolled over and opened her eyes. When she realized she wasn't in her own bed she experienced a moment of panic. Then she remembered that Lisa had refused to let her be alone and had ended up letting Cali crash in her spare bedroom.

A soft groan escaped Cali's lips as she recalled the events of the night before. She felt tears sting her eyes and willed them away. Why was she feeling like this? It wasn't rational. It wasn't logical. She'd known him all of two weeks.

But that wasn't what it had felt like last night.

Seeing that woman with her hands on him . . . with his hands on her . . .

Whether or not it made sense, she'd been jealous. The question now was what she was going to do about it.

A soft knock sounded on her door and Lisa peeked in. "Oh good, you're awake."

There was no use pretending. She might as well face the music. "Morning."

Lisa took a step into the room. "I made breakfast, and I laid some clothes out for you in the bathroom. I figured you might like to take a shower."

Cali ran a hand through her hair. She hoped it didn't look half as bad as it felt. "Thanks."

Giving her a brief smile, Lisa turned on her heel and left Cali alone once again. She tossed the blankets aside and went in search of the bathroom.

Not only had Lisa laid out some clothes, but she'd also provided a hairbrush and toothbrush, both of which were still in their packages, a washcloth and some toothpaste.

After stripping out of her clothes, Cali leaned behind the curtain to turn on the shower. When she was confident the water temperature was right, she held the vinyl aside and stepped into the spray. It felt good to wash away the dirt and grime of the previous night, but it did nothing to change what was going on inside.

Freshly showered and dressed in some of Lisa's clothes, Cali headed out to the main living area where she knew she'd find Lisa.

When Lisa saw her, she motioned for Cali to take a seat at the table. They both filled their plates with eggs, bacon, hash browns, and toast. Everything was delicious and before she knew it, the food on her plate was gone.

Lisa took her plate to the sink and returned with a pot of coffee. She topped off their mugs before sitting back down.

Cali knew what was coming.

"Do you want to talk about it?" Lisa asked.

Picking up her coffee, Cali took a sip, stalling.

"It might help," Lisa offered.

Cali glanced over at her friend. "I know. I just . . . I don't know what to say."

Lisa held her mug in both hands as she addressed Cali. "Is there something going on between you and Matthew?"

"No. Maybe. I don't know." Cali sighed and ran a hand through her still damp hair.

Her friend looked confused. "What do you mean 'maybe'? You don't know?"

Cali pulled at the legs of the loose-fitting pants she wore. She didn't want to talk to anyone about what may or may not be going on with Matthew until she figured it out for herself. The last thing she wanted to do, though, was make Lisa feel bad. "Thank you for the offer, but there really isn't anything going on between us."

Lisa opened her mouth and Cali quickly cut her off.

"We work together. That's all."

"I understand if you don't want to talk about it," Lisa said. "But I'm here if you change your mind. Based on what I saw last night I think you're deluding yourself if you say nothing's going on between the two of you. Something *is* going on. Even if you both don't know it yet."

"Impossible," Cali mumbled.

"Why?"

Cali sighed and shook her head. "We work together. And . . . well . . . we shouldn't . . . we can't . . . it's just impossible even if he did feel something for me."

Sitting up, Lisa reached out to touch Cali's arm. "Why is it impossible? If you two feel something, then why shouldn't you explore it?"

"I'm his boss."

"For the next two and a half months," Lisa pointed out.

Cali sat up in her chair, pulling away from her friend. "It doesn't matter anyway. You saw him last night. It's not like that."

Lisa opened her mouth again and once more Cali cut her off.

"I should get home," Cali said, standing. She headed back into the spare bedroom where she'd left her purse and clothes from the night before.

Lisa grabbed her keys and met Cali at the door.

The drive back to her house was somewhat awkward. She knew Lisa was dying to say something, but luckily whatever was going through her friend's mind she kept it to herself.

Lisa pulled into Cali's driveway. "Thank you for last night. And for the clothes."

"You're welcome."

Cali reached for the door.

"Call me if you need to talk. I'll listen. No judgment."

Nodding, Cali exited the vehicle and went inside.

After changing into her own clothes, she sat on the end of her bed as the weight of everything that had happened in the last twenty-four hours overwhelmed her. Before she knew it, she was on the verge of tears.

Seeing Matthew last night with another woman had caused an ache that radiated through her entire body. Whether it made sense or not, she was attracted to him and seeing him with someone else hurt.

There were times—moments—when she'd thought that Matthew was attracted to her as well. Maybe she'd read the signs all wrong.

Cali wiped the tears from her cheeks. What did she actually know about him anyway besides what her dad had told her? Not much. Although her dad's confidence in Matthew's ability to do his job well was a high endorsement, it didn't tell her much about the man himself.

Did he have a girlfriend? Was that his girlfriend? She hadn't thought about that possibility before. For all she knew that woman he'd been dancing with was the love of his life.

The possibility hurt more than she wanted to admit.

But what if he she wasn't his girlfriend? What if he wasn't seeing anyone? Could they? Should they?

If so, would he want a fling or . . .

Cali couldn't let herself finish that thought. She didn't even know where she would be after her father returned to work. Africa was always an option, but so was staying here in Chicago. She had to admit that being home, being close to her father had made her realize how much she'd missed out on by living halfway around the world. Even if whatever was going on between her and Matthew amounted to nothing more than physical attraction, Cali had something to stay for.

The phone beside her bed rang and she stood to answer it. "Hello?"

"What's my girl up to today?" Hearing her father's voice made Cali smile.

"Not much. I just planned to hang out around the house."

"Think you might want to come up to the lake house and keep your old man company for a few hours?"

"Sure, Dad. I can be up in a couple hours." She paused, not wanting her dad to hear the swell of emotion she was feeling. "I can't wait to see you."

***

The sound of someone banging on his front door woke Matthew up—not that he'd been sleeping all that well, but he'd been hoping for another hour at least. Last night had been . . .

Matthew sighed. He really didn't want to think about it.

Whoever was pounding on his door this early in the morning wasn't giving up, so he forced himself to get out of bed and find out what the emergency was. When he reached the front door barefoot and with only a pair of jeans on, he opened it and found his brother standing on the other side holding two cups of coffee in a flimsy cardboard container.

Matthew ran a hand over his face. "What time is it?"

"About eight," Jason said then pushed past Matthew into his apartment.

106

Shutting the door, Matthew followed his brother into the kitchen. Jason pulled a chair up to the counter, handed Matthew one of the coffees, and sat down.

"So what's with the early morning wake-up call?" Matthew asked with a hint of agitation after taking a sip of his coffee.

Jason studied him for a long moment but didn't say anything.

"What?"

His brother set his coffee down on the counter and advanced on Matthew.

Matthew's muscles automatically tensed ready to react if needed.

Jason came to a stop directly in front of him. "I want you to tell me what's going on with you."

Before he could open his mouth to respond, Jason went on. "And don't tell me it's nothing. You haven't been acting like yourself for the last two weeks. You're blowing off meetings, losing your temper more often than I've seen you do since we were kids. And then last night . . ."

His brother whirled around and started pacing. He stopped halfway across the room and looked Matthew in the eyes. "I'm not going to beat around the bush here. Are you involved with Cali Stanton?"

"Why are you asking me that?" The little bit of coffee Matthew drank churned in his stomach.

Jason snorted. "Why? You're seriously asking me why?" His brother mumbled something under his breath. "Matthew, you are one of the least impulsive people I know. I've never known you to go to a club with the intention of hooking up. After watching you last night, I know that was your intention."

Matthew didn't know what to say, so he remained silent.

"Then . . ." Jason laughed but there was no humor in it. "Then when you had a girl who was all over you and clearly willing, I get a look at your face and you look like you're trying to figure out the world's toughest math problem.

"The next thing I know Cali shows up and you can't get away from your dance partner fast enough." Jason walked toward Matthew, slower this time. "I know you better than anyone, little brother. Something is going on between you and Cali Stanton. The look on your face, and hers, gave you both away."

Matthew's head was spinning. His brother had it half right. The woman he'd been dancing with the night before had been willing—more than willing. He could still remember her grinding against him. Matthew's body had been completely on board with what she was offering. His mind had not.

And that was all before he'd caught sight of Cali. Everything else around him had faded into the background as she came into view and he locked eyes with her. He'd felt his heart rate pick up and it had nothing to do with the woman he was dancing with.

After Cali had disappeared in the crowded club all thoughts of finding release in someone else had vanished. All he wanted to do was get out of there.

"Matthew," Jason said in a huff.

"No," Matthew said. "There's nothing going on between me and Cali Stanton. She's my boss and I'm her employee. There's nothing else."

His brother looked at him as if he'd grown two heads.

Not giving his brother a chance to start up again, Matthew marched out of the kitchen and headed up the stairs. Jason, of course, followed.

Matthew walked into the room he had set up as a home gym and grabbed a set of free weights. Jason stood right inside the door as Matthew did a full set of bicep curls. He set the weights down and the next thing he knew his brother was standing in front of him, blocking his path.

"Move, Jason." Matthew's voice held a warning.

"Not going to happen, little brother. You're going to tell me what's going on with you."

Matthew clenched his fists at his side and contemplated driving one into his brother's face.

Then, as if a switch had been flipped, the anger he felt dissipated and he was left feeling completely deflated.

He backed away and walked over to the window. "I don't know."

Jason didn't respond right away and when he did it was in a much calmer tone. "What do you mean you don't know?"

Matthew shook his head. "There's this . . . connection with her or something."

"You're attracted to her. That's understandable, I guess. She's an attractive woman. Not my type, but . . ."

Matthew turned around. The look on his face must have made his brother think twice about whatever he was going to say.

Jason sighed. "Why don't you just ask her out?"

"No. I can't do that. She's my boss—Alvin's daughter. It wouldn't be right. We have to work together." Why couldn't his brother understand that?

"So what are you going to do?" Jason asked.

"I have no idea. I've tried staying away from her, but that didn't work." Matthew shook his head. "It would have become a professional problem anyway. Part of my job includes interacting with her. I don't think I could have avoided her for more than another week at most."

His brother hesitated, which wasn't like him. "Look, I'm not going to tell you what to do here, but you do need to do something. Because what you're doing now—the avoiding and . . . well, whatever you want to call last night—it isn't working."

"I'm going to spend tomorrow at Lisa's. If you need me, call." Jason moved toward the door. "But you need to figure this out."

Matthew stood at the window for several more minutes. He listened to his brother make his way down the stairs and out of his apartment.

Matthew walked over to his weights again and picked up where he'd left off. With the burn in his muscles came the realization that Jason was right—about one thing anyway. Matthew needed to figure out what he was going to do. Avoiding Cali was obviously not the answer. Neither was finding another woman to ease his sexual frustration. Even if Cali hadn't shown up last night, Matthew wasn't sure if he would have gone through with it.

But if avoiding Cali wasn't the answer, then what was? The last time he was alone with her all he could do was think of what it would be like to be with her. He closed his eyes and groaned as an image of his dream flashed through his mind. When he opened them again, he stared back at his reflection in the mirrors he'd installed last year to help him with his form. He was drenched. Sweat dripped down his face and chest, and there was a bulge pressing against his jeans that had nothing to do with the curls he'd been doing.

Setting the weights down once again, he made his way into the bathroom. He peeled off his sweat-soaked jeans and stepped under the hot spray.

Cali Stanton was his boss—his boss' daughter. The thing was his body didn't seem to have gotten the memo that she was off limits.

A sarcastic chuckle escaped his lips. Matthew couldn't believe he was standing in his shower trying to talk himself out of crossing a line when he had no idea how Cali even felt about him. Even if he was willing to break his own professional code of conduct, she might not feel any attraction to him at all. He couldn't believe how self-centered his thoughts were. It only proved how unfocused he'd become in the last couple of weeks.

He closed his eyes and let the water stream down his neck and back as he remembered the look in her eyes when she'd visited him in his office. Her face had been inches from his and the spark between them was hard to deny. A part of him wanted to believe she was dealing with the same struggle as he was.

Matthew rolled his shoulders in an effort to dispel the thoughts going through his head. It would be so easy to toss aside what was right and be with her the way he desired. So easy to forget about her being Alvin's daughter . . . a man he respected.

At this point, however, he knew himself well enough to know that if the opportunity presented itself, he would take it, no matter what the consequences. He wanted Cali Stanton and only Cali Stanton.

Chapter 12

Cali ended up spending the entire weekend with her father. It was the perfect distraction. They talked about her time overseas and he told her more about the incident that had landed him in the hospital with a broken hip. She still couldn't believe he'd thought going water skiing was a good idea. Her dad wasn't even a very good swimmer. He usually avoided boats and water.

She'd even gone twenty-four hours without thinking about Matthew Andersen. In and of itself, that was quite an accomplishment and something she'd desperately needed.

It was a long commute from the lake house to work on Monday morning, but she hadn't been able to pull herself away from her father. His joy at getting to spend the weekend together—just the two of them—had further helped her take her mind off the emotional mess she'd been when he'd called her on Saturday morning. She knew once she was alone again with nothing else to distract her she'd probably break down, but there wasn't much she could do about that. Cali had been through worse. She'd get through this, too.

When she arrived at the office a little after eight, Lisa was already behind her desk.

"Good morning, Cali." Lisa smiled at her but it didn't quite reach her eyes.

"Good morning."

Cali walked over to her office door, opened it, and then turned to face Lisa. She opened her mouth, but didn't get the words out before Lisa said, "Everything should be on your desk. If you need anything else, just buzz me."

"Thanks." Cali shook her head and strolled into her office. Maybe she was only imagining things. Lisa was probably worried about her after the way Cali had acted on Saturday morning.

As she rounded her desk, it hit her that it was Monday and that meant a security briefing. Cali double-checked the schedule Lisa had left on her desk and there it was in big bold letters. Would Matthew be the one who showed up this time or would he send Jason again? The crazy thing was Cali didn't know which she would prefer.

She took a series of deep breaths, but after a few minutes, she realized it wasn't working. All the progress she'd made over the last two days to forget about what happened at the club came flooding back to her. It was almost as if it was taunting her for keeping it under wraps for so long. Tears stung her eyes as she recalled seeing Matthew on the dance floor. How in the world was she going to face him if he came waltzing through her door?

It took her a while to get control of herself, but eventually she did. Cali turned on some music and began going through reports and checking e-mail. Every now and then her mind would drift, but for the most part she was able to focus on whatever she was working on. All she had to do was forget that in a few short hours she might come face-to-face with him again.

When lunch rolled around, Cali ate alone. Lisa had offered to sit with her, but Cali was afraid that would only lead to another breakdown.

At two fifty, Lisa knocked on Cali's door and asked if she needed anything before her meeting. She knew her friend was only trying to help, but there was nothing Lisa could do.

"No. But thank you."

Lisa shot her another smile tinged with sadness and closed the door again behind her.

Ten minutes later the intercom on her phone buzzed. "Yes?"

Lisa's voice came through loud and clear. "Matthew Andersen is here to see you."

Cali swallowed and she felt her palms growing damp. "Send him in."

She braced herself as best she could, but it was nowhere near enough. The moment she saw him her heart began pounding in her chest and she felt a little dizzy. Maybe she was coming down with something.

He met her gaze and her breath caught in her throat at the intensity she saw behind his blue eyes. It was almost as if he were daring her to look away.

"Would you like to do this here or at the conference table?"

Cali was so focused on his eyes that she almost missed what he said. She blinked and averted her gaze as she considered his question. The desk would provide a barrier between them, something she was desperately in need of at the moment. Cali turned back to him ready to answer when she noticed he'd brought a folder with him. If he had something to show her then being at the conference table would allow them more room to view whatever it was.

As much as she wanted to insist on staying in her office with the protection of her desk between them, Cali knew she had to put the needs of the company first. "I think the conference table might be better."

He nodded in agreement and followed her through an adjoining door that led to a small conference room.

Cali pulled out a chair and sat down.

Matthew lowered himself into the seat beside her.

For a long moment, he didn't say anything. Then he cleared his throat and opened the folder he'd brought.

He removed several pictures from the file and laid them out in front of her. "Jason went over the footage of our mystery woman again this weekend and he noticed this."

Matthew pointed to the woman's hand.

At first she didn't see anything. "Is that . . . is that a ring?"

"Yes." He handed her another photo. This one was of the same hand, only it was blown up so you could see more detail. "It's grainy, but I think it's enough. If we can find out who owns that ring and works for Stanton Enterprises, we'll have the lead we've been looking for."

Cali took a good look at the ring in question. "I don't think I've seen a ring like that before, have you?"

"I don't know," he said, sitting back in his chair a little. "It looks familiar to me, but I can't say I'm in the habit of noticing women's jewelry."

She was glad to get a little breathing room. His presence affected her too much.

Her relief lasted for about as long as a heartbeat because as soon as he smiled at her—a real smile this time—she felt as if he'd knocked the air out of her all over again.

Matthew reacted to her apparent distress in a matter of seconds. He reached out, placing a hand on her shoulder. A shot of electricity charged through her at his touch and she flinched. He swiftly retracted his hand. Matthew watched her closely as she did her best to relax her muscles and return her breathing to normal.

"I'm fine." She smiled, hoping it looked reassuring.

He didn't look convinced.

"So what now?" she asked, needing to get the conversation back on track. "I mean, what do we do next?"

Matthew didn't take his gaze off her, but at least he'd put some space between them. "Jason and I are doing some surveillance ourselves and my contact at the police department got me the name of a jeweler in town that might be able to give us some information about the ring itself. I'm going to swing by there this evening."

Cali nodded as she continued to eye the close-up of the ring. "I want to come with you."

"What do you mean you want to come with me? Come with me where?" His sharp tone had her lifting her head to look at him.

She sat up straight and stared him in the eye. "To see the jeweler."

Before she even got the sentence out, he was shaking his head.

Cali continued talking, ignoring his protest. "The person with this ring could be the link to whoever is terrorizing my father's company. I want to be there."

That watchfulness was back. He pressed his lips together and she wondered for a second if he was going to give himself an aneurism. Right when she thought he was going to tell her no, he gathered up the photos, stuffed them back into the folder, and stood. "I'll meet you outside your office at five and we can go."

She pushed away from the table and stood. "I'll be ready."

He took another long look at her and then turned on his heel and left.

As soon as Cali was alone, she sank back down into her chair.

What in the world had she just done?

***

Matthew stepped onto the executive floor for the second time that day. He'd spent the last forty-five minutes irritated with himself for not coming up with a valid reason to say no to Cali, while at the same time being grateful for the opportunity to spend some additional time with her. Something was seriously wrong with him. He shouldn't want to spend time with her.

She was standing beside Lisa's desk. When he approached, she looked up long enough that he knew she was aware of his presence and then went back to talking to her assistant. He wondered if she'd say anything about him being five minutes late.

To be polite, he waited a respectful distance for her to finish her conversation. He knew he would need to keep his distance from her tonight for both their sakes.

"Hello again, Matthew. Cali says you two will be spending the evening together." Lisa had a knowing smirk on her face and Matthew wondered just how much his brother had told her.

Cali picked up her briefcase and scowled at her assistant. "That isn't exactly what I said."

Lisa grinned.

Ignoring her assistant, Cali turned to face him. "Are you ready?"

He took a step back and motioned that he would follow her.

They made it all the way to the elevator before they heard Lisa call out, "Have fun. Don't do anything I wouldn't do."

Her laugh resonated in the small confines of the elevator and seemed to linger long after the metal doors had closed.

It only took fifteen minutes to get to the jewelry store. Neither of them had spoken during the drive. He couldn't help but wonder what she was thinking. Her earlier reaction to his touch continued to replay in his mind. If she had a problem being near him then why insist on coming with him tonight?

He was still trying to figure it out when they walked into the small store that boasted having the finest selection of new and antique jewelry in town. A bell sounded announcing their arrival and an older man appeared from behind a curtain. When he saw Matthew and Cali his eyes lit up. "Ah, hello. And how can I help you this evening? A look at some engagement rings, perhaps?"

Cali sucked in a breath beside him. Her reaction registered, but he was caught up in his own reaction to the man's suggestion. Of course the man thought they were a couple. Matthew doubted many couples came into a jewelry store who were not romantically involved. He needed to say something, but he was suddenly tongue-tied. Because as much as it didn't make sense, for all his good intentions and planning, he wanted it to be true.

It was movement from Cali that made Matthew realize he needed to respond to the man. "Uh, no. We're looking for Mr. Baker."

The man's eyebrows rose in question. "I'm Mr. Baker. How can I help you?"

Matthew put on his most professional smile and extended his hand. "My name is Matthew Andersen and this is Cali Stanton. Detective Martinez thought maybe you could be of some assistance to us."

At hearing Martinez's name, the man visibly relaxed. "Yes, yes. He did call and say a friend of his was coming in with some questions." Mr. Baker lifted a section of the counter. "Let's go back to my office and take a look at what you've got, shall we?"

Matthew hung back, allowing Cali to go first. As much as the professional in him knew he needed to stay focused on their mission, the man in him wanted to know what Cali's reaction to Mr. Baker's suggestion meant. Was someone thinking they were a couple appalling to her? And if it was, then why did he care?

He shook off his musings and followed Mr. Baker and Cali behind the counter and down a short hallway into an office. They each took a seat around an old wooden desk that had seen better days. Mr. Baker clasped his hands in front of him on the desk. "What can I do for you?"

Matthew removed the picture of the ring from the folder and handed it to the jeweler.

"A beautiful ring."

"Yes," Matthew agreed. "Can you tell us anything about it?"

"Hmm. Let me see." Mr. Baker swiveled around and began looking through a row of binders he had along the back wall of his office.

For the next hour and a half, they sat there as the jeweler

thumbed through catalog after catalog trying to find the exact ring they were looking for. Their time finally paid off when he found not only the ring but the manufacturer. "I've got it!"

"You found it?" Cali asked.

Mr. Baker nodded and handed Cali the catalog.

Matthew leaned in to glance at it over her shoulder. It was their ring, right down to the small diamond on the side.

Cali stiffened and Matthew moved away.

She handed the binder back to Mr. Baker. "I can't believe we found it."

The jeweler held up a single finger. "I've got one better."

Before Matthew realized what was happening, Mr. Baker had left the room.

He glanced over at Cali, but she looked as confused as he was.

About five minutes later, Mr. Baker returned, this time with a ring in his hand. "Here. This is your ring."

Matthew took the ring and examined it next to the picture. That was their ring all right. "How many of these do you think have been sold?"

"Well . . ."

To Matthew's surprise, Cali leaned in, placed her hand lightly on Mr. Baker's arm, and in the sweetest voice he'd ever heard asked the jeweler if there was any way they could get a list of people who'd purchased the ring.

He held his breath as Mr. Baker considered her request.

"Please? We really need to find out who this ring belongs to. It would really help us."

The man crumbled under her charm. "Give me a few minutes and I'll see what I can do."

She flashed the jeweler a brilliant smile and Matthew's heart skipped a beat. "Thank you."

It took them another thirty minutes, but Matthew wasn't complaining. They walked out of there with a list of everyone who'd ever purchased that ring in the last five years. As much as he hated to admit it, if Cali hadn't come with him then the night probably would have been a total bust.

Once they were in the car, Matthew glanced over the list. There were three full pages. He would have plenty of reading to do tonight, which was a good thing . . . a very good thing.

Within moments of them climbing back into his car the tension between them returned. Matthew wanted to change it, but he wasn't sure how. Cali had him all tied up in knots. He knew what he wanted to do, but he also knew that wasn't an option.

He started the car and pulled out into traffic. Out of the corner of his eye, he could see Cali tangling her fingers together. Was she as nervous as he was?

The urge to reach out and caress her was strong. He wondered if her hands were as soft as they looked. That led to thoughts of what her hands would feel like on other parts of his body and he felt his body temperature begin to rise.

Cali shifted in her seat and his gaze moved to her mouth. She was biting her lower lip again—another nervous habit of hers.

He quickly looked back toward the road, trying to keep his thoughts from going where he knew they would if given the opportunity.

She took a deep breath. "Do you think that will help?"

"I don't know. It will take some time to go through, but maybe we'll get lucky." He had to be honest with her. The list could end up being a dead end.

They fell back into an awkward silence.

Matthew cleared his throat. "Are you hungry? It's after seven. We could stop and get something before I drop you off at your car."

He saw her gaze dart in his direction before she looked back out the window. "No. I'll just get something at home."

Five minutes later they pulled into the parking garage located under the Stanton Enterprises building. There were a few cars still around, but most of the employees had already gone home for the night—the people still around worked security or IT, both of which operated 24-7.

Out of habit, Matthew parked in his usual spot. It was late, but since he was already there he figured it wouldn't hurt to head up to his office for an hour or so and review the new information they'd obtained. There was a deli within walking distance of the first floor lobby where he could pick up something quick for dinner.

He turned off the engine and they both exited the vehicle.

"Thank you for coming with me. I don't know if I would have been able to do what you did." Matthew smirked, trying to lighten the mood. "At least, not with the same results."

Cali blushed and Matthew almost lost it. He wanted to touch her, to crush her body against his and kiss her within an inch of her life.

Instead, he backed toward the elevators. "I'll see you tomorrow."

She grinned and began walking to her car.

He hesitated, then shook his head and continued toward the elevator.

As he waited for the elevator to reach him, he heard an engine rev. A small smile pulled at his lips as he thought of Cali heading home.

The elevator dinged right as a squeal of tires caught his attention. He whirled around in time to see a dark blue sedan he didn't recognize speed up the exit ramp.

His heart pounded in his chest as he took off at a full-out run.

Cali.

When he turned the corner, his heart nearly stopped. Cali was on the ground next to her car. She was unconscious and there was a small trickle of blood coming from her forehead. He didn't see anything else, but he knew from experience that sometimes the most dangerous injuries were the ones you couldn't see.

Kneeling down beside her, he wrenched his cell phone from his belt and dialed 911.

He rattled off the information to the dispatcher and hung on the line until he heard the sirens in the distance. After disconnecting the call, Matthew brought his face close to hers and brushed his lips along her cheek. "You'll be okay, Cali. You'll be okay."

The next thing Matthew knew he was being shoved out of the way by the paramedics.

Chapter 13

Less than a minute after the paramedics took over, the first police officer arrived on the scene. The officer insisted on talking to Matthew even though he didn't want to leave Cali's side. He was asked one question after another. What color was the car? Did he see the driver? Did he get the license plate? It seemed as if the questions weren't ever going to end.

It didn't help that the officer appeared to doubt Matthew's version of events. That is until he explained that he was head of security for Stanton Enterprises and that the company had been receiving treats, all of which were on record with the police department. After that, he seemed to take Matthew's account more seriously.

When the officer headed back to his cruiser to look up the little bit of information Matthew could provide, Matthew saw Martinez pull up. "Hey."

"Hey," Matthew said with a lot less enthusiasm. While he was happy to see his friend, his focus was on Cali and only Cali—she was still unconscious.

The paramedics lifted her onto a gurney and up into the back of the ambulance. Matthew knew that as soon as they had her hooked up to an IV they would be off to the hospital and he was going with her.

"How is she?" he asked one of the paramedics.

"Nothing obvious outside of the bump on the head, but they'll need to run some tests once we get her to the hospital."

Matthew nodded and stayed close, waiting.

Martinez jogged up beside him and glanced into the ambulance at Cali's still form. "She'll be okay."

He wanted to believe that, but . . .

"I don't know. They need to run some tests. Make sure she doesn't have any internal injuries."

His friend remained silent. Martinez must have realized that he needed a moment to pull himself together. Every cell in his body was screaming at him to forget about everything else except making sure Cali was okay, but he knew he couldn't do that. "You've got to help me figure out who did this. I didn't . . . I didn't have time to look around. Can you . . ."

Martinez laid a reassuring hand on Matthew's shoulder. "I'll do it personally, man. Don't you worry."

Matthew nodded. He made an effort to smile, but he wasn't quite sure he pulled it off.

There was some movement inside the ambulance and Matthew knew they were getting ready to leave. He didn't hesitate before he climbed into the back of the ambulance, closed the doors behind him, and took a seat.

The paramedic who had been tending to Cali looked up at the sound. "Sir, you can't—"

"I'm not leaving her. So either we're going to sit here arguing about it, wasting time, or we're going to get going and get her the help she needs."

The man looked at him for a long moment and then gave the signal to the driver to go.

They were only five minutes away from the hospital but it felt like much longer than that. Matthew held Cali's hand the entire time, clinging to that small connection he had to her.

When the vehicle jerked to a stop, the doors flew open and four people in scrubs and jackets swarmed the back of the ambulance. They maneuvered the gurney down onto solid ground within seconds, leaving him at a loss as to what to do. One of the doctors was asking the paramedic questions about Cali's blood pressure, heart rate, and a host of other things Matthew didn't understand.

Then they were pushing Cali inside and down a long hallway. Matthew followed until a firm hand landed against his chest. "Sir, you need to wait here."

The woman didn't give him time to protest. She disappeared behind a set of double doors along with Cali and he was left wondering if she was going to be okay.

Matthew had no idea how much time passed before a volunteer appeared beside him and asked if he'd fill out some paperwork. He nodded and took the clipboard without really looking at it. He was going to have to call Alvin to tell him that his daughter had been hit by a car. He hadn't thought his night could get any worse, but he was wrong.

As quickly as he could, Matthew filled out the form the volunteer had given him and returned it to her.

"Thanks," she said, smiling up at him.

"I need to make a call, but I'll be right outside if . . ."

"I'll make a note in case the doctor comes looking for you."

Matthew nodded and walked outside. He pulled out his cell phone and dialed Alvin's number.

"Well, this is a surprise. I didn't expect to hear from you tonight." Alvin's cheerful voice echoed through the phone.

When Matthew didn't respond right away, Alvin's tone changed to one of concern. "What is it? Did something happen with another shipment?"

"No. Nothing like that." Matthew paused. "It's Cali. She's . . . she was hit by a car tonight."

It took some doing, but Matthew convinced Alvin not to come. The man was recovering from his own injuries and at this point there was nothing he could do.

Once Cali was assigned to a room, Matthew breathed a little bit easier. She had regained consciousness and there was no evidence of internal injury. He'd called Alvin with the good news and he could sense the man's relief through the phone. "I can't lose her, too."

Matthew knew Alvin was referring to Cali's mother.

"I'll watch over her. I promise."

Alvin didn't question him. "Take care of my little girl."

When he finished his call with Alvin, Matthew dialed Jason's cell. Matthew figured his brother would be with Lisa, but he was in the parking garage with Martinez. They were going over the scene.

A part of him wanted to be there with them, but he couldn't bring himself to leave Cali.

"We'll keep you in the loop, little brother. Don't you worry."

"Thanks," Matthew said. "I should probably get back upstairs. I don't want to leave her alone for too long."

His brother didn't press him as to why he was so insistent to get to the bedside of a woman he wasn't in a relationship with, which surprised him. Matthew wasn't going to look a gift horse in the mouth, though.

He walked into Cali's room a few minutes later to find her awake. His heart picked up its pace as a warmth spread through his chest. She was going to be okay.

Cali smiled up at him and then he watched as it faded into a more serious expression.

Matthew took a seat beside her bed. "How are you feeling?"

She rolled her eyes. "Like a car hit me."

He chuckled. "I called your dad and let him know what happened and that the doctors said you'd be all right."

"Good. I don't want him to worry."

"He's your father. It's in his nature to worry."

She didn't say anything.

"I also talked to Jason while I was downstairs. He's overseeing the investigation from the company's end and will make sure things are running smoothly until we get back."

Cali furrowed her brow, but didn't comment.

He didn't want to crowd her, so he remained quiet.

After a few minutes, she shifted and one of her pillows slipped down. He rushed to readjust it behind her. As he did so, his fingers brushed against her arm and she jumped.

"Sorry," he said, retracting his hand.

"It's okay," she mumbled as she leaned back against the pillows.

Matthew felt at odds with what to do, so he walked over to the window and pulled the curtains shut. It was almost midnight and Cali would need to get some sleep. So would he, but he wasn't worried about himself at the moment. He'd slept in much worse locations over the years than an uncomfortable hospital chair. She was what was important.

***

Cali knew she'd overacted, but there was a war raging inside her. Part of her longed for him to touch her—really touch her—while another part was terrified of getting hurt. Matthew Andersen already meant more to her than he should, which meant he also had the power to rip her heart out if he wanted.

She took in the stiff set of his shoulders as he stood with his back to her and wondered what was going through his mind. "Matthew?"

He returned to her bedside. "What do you need?"

The walls around her heart cracked a little more at his concern. "Nothing. I just . . . thank you. For helping me with the pillow. I shouldn't have reacted like that. You just startled me earlier, that's all."

What he did next had the butterflies in her stomach fluttering around at top speed. Matthew covered her hand with his and began rubbing his thumb across her knuckles. She was sure it was meant to be comforting, but his touch was sending tingling sensations up the entire length of her arm. He met her gaze and smiled down at her with those mesmerizing blue eyes of his, making her forget about everything in that moment except him.

They stayed locked in their own world until a nurse bustled in to take her vitals.

Matthew dropped her hand and backed away.

Cali felt the loss immediately.

"How are you feeling, Ms. Stanton?" the nurse asked, completely oblivious to what she'd interrupted.

"Fine," Cali answered. Matthew was watching her from where he was leaning against the opposite wall, but he was careful to stay out of the nurse's way.

"Any pain?"

"Nothing of consequence," Cali said.

The nurse raised her eyebrows as she checked Cali's vitals and entered them into the system. Once she was done, she placed a hand on Cali's arm and squeezed. "Let me know if your pain increases and I'll get you something. Otherwise, your vitals look good. The doctor wants to keep you overnight for observation. As long as you have a good night, you should be able to go home in the morning."

Cali hated being on the other side of things. She hadn't even been able to have a decent conversation with the doctor whose care she was under since she'd seen him all of five minutes after she'd regained consciousness and her brain had still been foggy. Now that she was thinking more clearly, she had lots of questions for him. She knew she didn't have any internal injuries otherwise she would be in surgery and she didn't think she had a concussion but gauging that for oneself was never wise.

"Are you okay?" Matthew asked upon seeing her agitation. "Did you need me to get the nurse back in here?"

"No. I'm fine. I just wish I had been able to talk to the doctor."

He sat down next to the bed and gave her a halfhearted smile. "I've heard doctors make the worst patients."

She couldn't help but grin back.

"Did you want to get some rest?" he asked.

Cali sighed. "How about some TV?"

Matthew grabbed the remote control from the table beside the bed and handed it to her.

They ended up watching reruns of *I Love Lucy*. It felt good to laugh, but she had to be careful. Even though she didn't appear to have any broken bones, she did have a fair amount of bruises.

About an hour into their *I Love Lucy* marathon, Cali's stomach started growling.

"I guess that's my cue to go find us something to eat." He stood and walked to the door. "I'll be right back."

Cali waited until the sound of his retreating footsteps disappeared before reaching for the phone beside her bed. She dialed her father's number and waited for him to pick up.

"Cali?"

"Hi, Dad."

"Honey, are you okay?" he asked.

"Yeah. I'm fine. They say I should get to come home tomorrow."

Her father was quiet for too long.

"What's wrong?"

"I should be there," he said.

"Dad, I'm fine. Really. Besides, you have your own accident to recover from." The last thing she wanted was for this to derail his recovery.

"An accident? Cali, do you really think this was an accident?"

She hesitated. "I don't know. I didn't see the car coming until it was too late to get out of the way."

Her father made a grunting noise into the phone at the same time Matthew strolled back into the room with a large paper sack. "What does Matthew say?"

Cali bit her bottom lip as the man in question set the bag down on a rolling tray table and began laying out the food he'd bought. "I don't know. We haven't really discussed it yet."

Her father didn't like that answer.

"What do you mean you haven't discussed it yet? Where is he? Have the police been by to take your statement? Is there a forensic team on the scene?" With every question, her father's voice got louder.

"Dad, don't get so worked up. It's not good for you."

"You're my daughter. Of course I'm going to get worked up."

She sighed. "Matthew's here, we just haven't talked about it yet with everything else going on. As for the police . . . no, they haven't been here to take my statement. And I have no idea about the forensic team."

Her father didn't respond right away. "Matthew's there?"

"Yes."

"Let me talk to him."

"Okay." Cali handed the phone to Matthew. "He wants to talk to you."

Matthew held the phone up to his ear. "Alvin—"

It was clear her father cut him off, probably peppering Matthew with the same questions he'd asked her.

"Jason and a friend of mine from the Chicago PD are in the parking garage looking for clues and Jason is going to go through the security feed as well. Yes, sir. Don't worry. I'll not let her out of my sight."

Cali swallowed upon hearing Matthew's words. Was he serious?

He met her gaze when he handed her back the phone.

"Dad?"

"Matthew seems to be on top of things for now," her father said, sounding much calmer than he had moments before. "Are you sure you're okay?"

"I have some bruises, but nothing serious. I'll be fine."

"You'll call me if you need anything?"

"Of course," she assured him.

"I love you, sweetheart."

"I love you, too, Dad. Get some rest."

Matthew took the phone from her and pushed the tray with her food in front of her before hanging the phone up. He sat down and balanced a large container of fries on his lap while taking a bite out of his burger.

Cali unwrapped her cheeseburger and her mouth started to water. She hadn't realized how hungry she was. "Thank you for dinner."

"You're welcome."

They finished their meals and then Matthew gathered up their trash and dumped it in the waste bin.

Cali yawned.

"You should get some rest."

"What about you?" she asked as he made his way back over to his chair.

Matthew leaned back, stretched out his legs, and folded his arms over his chest. "What about me?"

She realized he meant to stay. "Aren't you going home?"

"Nope," he said, closing his eyes.

A little voice inside her whispered that she should tell him that wasn't necessary, that he should go home and sleep in his own bed. That would be the right thing to do—the rational thing. The problem was she wasn't feeling all that rational right now. She felt safe with him there.

After another long look at him stretched out in the uncomfortable chair, Cali rolled over so she could watch him for a while. A few minutes went by before his breathing evened out and he fell asleep.

Little by little, sleep called to her as she felt her lids growing heavy. She snuggled into her pillow and closed her eyes, remembering what it felt like to have him touch her and imagining how good it would be for him to hold her in his arms.

Chapter 14

Every time one of the hospital staff came in to check Cali's vitals, it woke Matthew up. Cali would turn to look at him as if she were confirming he was still there then would turn away. Once he was sure she was all right, he would close his eyes again to give her some privacy for whatever poking and prodding needed to be done.

The night went on like that until sunlight began peeking through the lone window in her room. Matthew splashed some water on his face and worked out the kinks in his neck. It had been a while since he'd slept in such an uncomfortable place.

"Hi."

He grinned. "Morning."

Cali ran a hand over her hair as if trying to tame it. "What time is it?"

Matthew checked his watch. "About seven thirty."

She reached for the remote control for her bed and adjusted it so she was sitting up. "What are the chances of me getting some coffee, do you think?"

"Let me see what I can do." He ducked out of the room and headed down to the nurses' desk to ask where he could get some coffee.

As luck would have it, the nurse on duty appeared to have a sweet spot for him and swiped him two cups from the nurses' lounge. "You're a lifesaver."

The nurse blushed. "No trouble, really."

He flashed her a smile before returning to Cali's room.

When he handed over the cup of coffee, she held it under her nose and inhaled. "It's sad how addicted to this stuff I am."

Matthew took a sip of his coffee and sat down. It wasn't great, but again, not the worst he'd ever had. "You had a rough night."

"So did you," she pointed out.

He shrugged.

Luckily he was saved from any further discussion when the doctor came bustling through the door.

"How are you feeling this morning, Ms. Stanton?" he asked without sparing her much more than a glance.

"No worse than I did last night."

He looked at her then and began a cursory exam. "It looks like you had a good night and your vitals are stable. I'll get the discharge paperwork started."

It took another thirty minutes for the nurse to arrive with the discharge papers and a list of instructions. Once that was taken care of, the nurse offered to help Cali get dressed. Matthew excused himself to give her some privacy and to call his brother for an update.

Jason answered on the fourth ring. "Ugh! What time is it?"

"Almost nine o'clock. Why aren't you at work?"

"Because I didn't get home until after four this morning."

"Did you find anything?" Matthew asked.

His brother groaned. "Look, can we table this conversation until I'm awake and had a few cups of coffee?"

Matthew let out a frustrated sigh. "Sure."

"Good. Oh, and I dropped off your car last night. It's in the hospital parking garage. Level three." He paused. "You're welcome."

Getting home hadn't even crossed Matthew's mind with everything else going on. "Thank you."

"Yeah, yeah. Now, go take care of Cali and let me worry about everything else for now."

Before he could say anything else, Jason had hung up.

Running a rough hand over the top of his head, Matthew went to check on Cali. She was sitting on the edge of the bed waiting for him.

"I thought you got lost?" she said. "I was about to call a cab."

He grinned. "Not a chance. Are you ready to go?"

"Yep. I was just waiting on you."

Cali pushed the nurse's button and a few minutes later an aide showed up with a wheelchair. "If you want to head on down and bring your car around, I can wheel her to the front entrance."

Matthew hated to leave her unprotected, but he didn't see where he had much choice. "Don't let her out of your sight."

The woman blinked then nodded. "No, sir. I won't."

It didn't take him long to find his car, or to make his way out of the parking garage and over to the front entrance, but Cali and the aide were already waiting for him. The aide helped Cali into the car and waved goodbye.

He pulled away from the curb and out into traffic. "Do you want to stop for breakfast, or would you rather go home?"

Cali thought about it for a moment. "Home, please. I'm sure Jessie is worried sick."

Matthew nodded.

It took them almost a half hour to get to their destination with the early morning traffic. He pulled into the driveway, but before he could even turn off the engine, Jessie ran out the door toward his car. She wrenched open the passenger side door and enveloped Cali in a bear hug.

After a long moment, Jessie took a step back but she didn't let go of Cali. "Are you all right, dear? Your dad called and told me what happened."

Jessie, however, didn't wait for a response before ushering Cali toward the house. "Come. Let's get you settled and I'll make you some breakfast. You must be starving. No one can eat what they call food in those hospitals."

Matthew trailed behind the two women into the house. Cali looked a little overwhelmed, but in a good way.

He was following along when Jessie stopped, her eyes wide as she stared at Cali. "We need to get you into bed. I can bring you breakfast. How does that sound? Anything you want. You just name it."

"Jessie, I'm fine. Really. I can eat in the kitchen." Jessie opened her mouth to protest but Cali cut her off. "But maybe at the table today instead of the island."

The older woman brushed a hand down the side of Cali's face in a comforting maternal gesture. "Sure. What would you like?"

Love radiated from Cali's features and Matthew felt an ache down deep in his chest.

"Pancakes?" Cali asked.

"Of course. I'll have them ready in a jiffy."

Jessie disappeared into the pantry. When she reappeared with her arms full of supplies, her gaze fell on Matthew. "Will you be staying, too, Mr. Andersen?"

He cleared his throat. "Yes. Please. If you don't mind?"

At that, Jessie turned her back on him and got to work.

Cali lowered herself into a chair at the kitchen table and he saw her wince. No matter how tough she acted, Cali was sore. He was filled with the desire to take care of her.

He pulled out the chair beside her and took a seat. The last thing he wanted to do was leave her today, but he didn't have a choice. "I need to go into the office and get an update on what's going on."

"I understand. Jessie and I will be fine." She placed her hands in her lap and began twisting her fingers together like she'd done the night before when she'd been nervous.

"How long is Jessie here today?"

She glanced up at him and then over to Jessie. "Oh. Um . . . she's usually here in the mornings. She leaves around noon, I think."

Jessie strolled up to the table and placed a plate of warm pancakes in front of them both. She smiled and headed back into the kitchen.

Matthew checked his watch. It was already after ten. There was no way he'd make it to the office, his apartment, and back here in under two hours.

"Jessie?"

She spun around at the sound of her name. "Hmm?"

"Do you think you could stick around a little longer today? I don't want Cali alone in the house and I have a few things I have to take care of."

He noticed Cali had stopped mid bite.

"Of course," Jessie agreed.

Matthew turned his attention back to Cali and his pancakes. She smiled, lowered her gaze, and began eating again. For a moment, he wondered if she was going to try and argue about Jessie staying, but she didn't.

Less than ten minutes later he had cleaned his plate and was pushing away from the table. "I'll be back in a few hours. Call if you need anything. And, Jessie, if you could please find a room for me to use?"

Jessie nodded.

"You don't have to babysit me, you know."

He met her gaze and felt that surge of protectiveness again. "I promised your father I would take care of you and I will."

Matthew stood and walked toward the door. He reached for the doorknob and turned to Jessie. "I'll be back soon."

His first stop was to his apartment. He needed a shower, a clean suit, and enough clothes to last him for a few days. Matthew had no idea how long he'd be staying at the Stanton home, but he knew he'd be there at least until Cali was well enough to return to work. When he'd spoken to Alvin, Matthew had been completely truthful—he didn't intend to be far from Cali until he was positive she was no longer in danger.

Once he felt like a human being again, Matthew drove the short distance to the office. As he pulled into his parking space, he could still see the crime scene tape marking off the area and surrounding Cali's car. He wondered if his brother and Martinez had found anything. Jason hadn't exactly been forthcoming on the phone earlier, but then again his brother had never been a morning person even after his years in the military.

A sense of déjà vu hit Matthew as he walked across to the elevator. A shiver ran up his spine. He never wanted to relive last night again.

His brother was waiting for him when he arrived on the thirteenth floor. Neither spoke as they made their way to Matthew's office and closed the door.

"How is she?" Jason asked once they were alone.

Matthew went straight to his desk and booted up his computer. "She's all right. Bruises mostly."

Jason took a seat across from Matthew as he pulled up the camera feed with the correct time stamp. He watched the numbers on the bottom of the screen move but all he was seeing was static.

Matthew closed the file and reopened it, but it was the same.

"It's no use. Martinez and I were awake half the night going through the security footage. All the ones that matter weren't working." Jason's voice had a sarcastic edge to it.

"What do you mean 'not working'? How? We check them every day." Then it hit him. "The mole."

The need to be where Cali was became top priority. He had to keep her safe.

He turned off his computer, stood, and dashed toward the door.

His brother grabbed his arm as he passed, stopping him. "Matthew, there's more you need to hear."

As much as he wanted to get to Cali, he knew he needed to hear whatever it was Jason had to say. His brother's expression told him that much. "Tell me."

Jason released his hold on Matthew's arm and reached into his pocket. He pulled out several folded sheets of paper and handed them to his brother. "Martinez has the originals, but he let me make copies. I knew you'd want to see them."

Matthew flipped through the pages and nearly fainted. They were pictures of Cali—pictures of her here in Chicago—in outfits he'd seen her wear. These photos were recent.

In the last one, she was wearing the same outfit she'd had on last Thursday. He knew that because he had spent a lot of time taking it off her in his dreams that night.

"Someone needs to go through every single tape from this building over the last twenty-four hours. We need to know who went in and out and when," Matthew said as he tucked the pictures into his suit jacket.

"I'll get on it today." Jason clasped his hand on Matthew's arm again, this time in a show of solidarity. "We'll get them."

Matthew gave his brother a hard nod before making a beeline for the elevator. He had to get back to Cali. Now.

In his rush, Matthew almost forgot that he had to stop by the pharmacy and pick up the pain medication her doctor had prescribed. She had enough to get her through the day, but she would need more come tomorrow. As tempting as it was to put it off, it was easier to get it done while he was out and knew someone was with her.

He arrived at the pharmacy, handed the woman behind the counter the script the nurse had given him earlier that morning, and took a seat in the small waiting area. After pulling out his phone, he dialed the Stantons' home number.

Jessie answered on the third ring.

"Everything good there?"

"She's upstairs resting."

Not exactly what he'd asked, but he'd take it. "I had to stop and pick up some prescriptions the doctor gave her. I should be there soon."

"Don't worry about it. I'll be here."

He hung up with Jessie and scrolled through his e-mails on his phone. Most of it was normal stuff. He'd take care of it once he got settled in.

Fifteen minutes later, he was on his way. The wait had been one of the most nerve-racking of his life, which was saying something.

Matthew felt a surge of relief when he pulled up to the Stanton estate. He parked around back, grabbed his things out of the trunk, and made his way into the house.

"You're back," Jessie said almost as soon as he walked through the door.

"How is she?"

The older woman smiled. "Same as the last time you asked."

Matthew grunted, but didn't comment.

She lowered her gaze to the bag he carried. "Come."

Jessie led him up the main staircase and down a long hall.

"This is Cali's room," she said, pointing to a room on the left.

Cracking open the door, he peeked inside. Cali was lying on her bed, facing the door. Her hair was fanned out on the pillow and her cheeks were flushed. It was hard to pull himself away. He wanted to take in every detail and memorize it.

"She was tired," Jessie said, interrupting his thoughts. "Almost as soon as you left she came upstairs to lie down."

He hiked his bag higher on his shoulder. "She needs her rest." Then he turned to Jessie. "Were you able to get a room ready for me?"

Jessie nodded and headed farther down the hall.

She stopped at a room that was only two doors away from where Cali slept. "I thought you'd want to be close to her. This used to be Cali's playroom years ago."

The room was a bit smaller than the one Cali slept in, but it still held a large, comfortable-looking bed with plenty of room left over.

"This will work. Thank you."

He walked into the room and tossed his bag on the mattress.

"Did you need anything before I go?" Jessie asked.

Matthew strolled over to the window and looked out at the grounds below. The backyard was exactly how he remembered it from the last time he was here to install Alvin's new security system. There were places to hide if one was careful, but they'd still have to get past the alarm system.

He stuffed his hands in his pockets and turned to face Jessie. "No. I think that's everything. Thank you again for staying."

"I would do anything for her. She's like a daughter to me."

Matthew nodded. "Let me walk you out."

He waited at the door until Jessie was in her car and backing out of the driveway before he headed back upstairs. On his way to his room, Matthew stopped again at Cali's door to watch her sleep. She was still on her side but now her arm was stretched out in front of her as if she were reaching for something.

Before he realized what he was doing, he was striding toward her. He knelt down until his face was level with hers. She was so beautiful.

He took her hand in his and rubbed small comforting circles on her palm with his thumb. A soft sigh escaped her lips.

It would have been easy to stay there for hours watching her sleep, but he would only be torturing himself. Placing her hand back on the bed, he backed away and continued on to his room. He needed to unpack and then he had work to do.

Chapter 15

Cali felt as if she'd been sleeping forever. When she looked over at the clock, she realized it was almost five. Maybe not forever, but she'd been sleeping for almost six hours.

After using the bathroom, she made her way downstairs in search of some dinner. The main floor was quiet except for the sound of typing. She walked into the kitchen to find Matthew sitting at the island, working on his laptop.

"Hey."

He swiveled around to face her. "You're awake."

She ignored his comment and went to the refrigerator to see if Jessie had left her anything.

Matthew hopped off the stool. "Are you hungry?"

Cali rolled her eyes. "Nope. I'm just scouring the fridge to see if mold is growing."

He laughed. Not a polite type of chuckle, but a deep belly laugh.

When he got control of himself again, Matthew grabbed hold of the door and pulled it wide open. "Why don't you go sit down and I'll make you something?"

She narrowed her eyes at him, but he only stared back at her with a hint of amusement.

Figuring it was easier to give in for now, she walked over to the counter and gingerly sat down. "You don't have to stay here, you know. I don't need a babysitter."

Matthew glanced over his shoulder with an impassive look, but otherwise she might well have been talking to herself.

He took something out of the refrigerator—leftovers, most likely—and proceeded to warm them up.

Cali pressed her lips together and waited until he carried over two plates full of some sort of chicken casserole. She let him sit down next to her before she started in again. "I'm perfectly safe, you know. The house has an alarm system. No one is going to break in without me knowing about it. You can go home. I'll be fine."

For a long moment he didn't say anything. Then he rested his elbows on the counter, folded his hands under his chin, and met her gaze. "Someone wants to hurt you. I don't know who, but I will find out."

The look in his eyes was intense.

He lowered his hands and redirected his attention to his food. This time when he spoke, his tone was softer, almost pleading. "Let me make sure you stay safe."

A lump formed in her throat. "Okay."

Neither moved right away. They both seemed to be stuck in some sort of spell.

Matthew eventually cleared his throat and picked up his fork. "I talked to Jason today when I went into the office. He and Martinez found something by your car."

She stiffened. What now?

He slid off the stool and walked over to where he'd hung his jacket. When he returned, he handed her several sheets of paper.

Cali unfolded them.

"Have you seen these before?" he asked.

She shook her head.

"Are you sure?"

"Yes. I'm sure."

Matthew released a heavy breath. "Have you gotten anything else like this? Pictures or letters? Anything?"

Cali couldn't believe what she was seeing. Who was doing this and why?

"Cali?"

Hearing him call her by name again sent a little thrill through her.

"Sorry." She shook her head to clear it. "No. It's not. I . . . I got something the other day. Two things, actually."

She started to get up, but he placed a gentle hand on her arm. "Just tell me where."

Cali pointed toward the kitchen table. "In my briefcase. They're near the bottom."

Matthew strolled over to the table and rooted around in her briefcase until he found the two envelopes. He brought them over to where she was sitting and held them up. "These them?"

She nodded.

He opened the first. It was the one with the single sheet of paper that said 'Africa Misses You' on it.

Seeing it again made her shiver. "That was the first."

Matthew laid that one down on the counter and opened the second.

"Africa?" he asked, looking over the pictures.

"Yes."

The look on his face was guarded. "Why didn't you tell me? Why didn't you come to me?"

"I . . ." She had no idea how to explain it. "When I got the first letter with the message I didn't know what to think. It didn't sound hostile to me. I thought maybe it was a doctor friend of mine joking around or something."

He sat motionless as he waited for her to continue.

"As for the pictures . . . they were weird, yes, but again, they could have been from a friend so I didn't think much of it."

Matthew opened his mouth, and then hesitated. "Cali, you can come to me with anything. I hope you know that."

He'd called her Cali again, not Ms. Stanton. Did he even realize he was doing it?

"I know. I'm sorry. I should have come to you. It was stupid. If I'd said something maybe last night wouldn't have happened."

"Maybe. But we're going to be more careful from now on." His eyes softened. "I meant what I said. I will keep you safe."

The way he said it made it sound like a vow.

Cali ducked her head and went back to eating.

The rest of their meal was pleasant enough until she started to get up.

"I'll get it," he said, taking her plate from her and loading it in the dishwasher.

"I'm not helpless, you know. I did spend two years in the backcountry of Africa. I'm capable of putting my plate in the dishwasher."

Matthew was on the other side of the island with his hip resting against the counter. He was watching her and it took everything in her not to squirm.

When the doorbell rang and Matthew went to see who it was, she took a few minutes to get her bearings again. Her body was still tingling when she heard voices in the foyer. She followed the sound.

"We drove separately. I didn't even know she was coming. I swear." Jason had his hands held up in surrender.

"It's true," Lisa said. "I have some papers for Cali to sign."

Matthew had looked as if he was ready for a fight when Cali had first walked around the corner, but at Lisa's admission he relaxed.

"She's—"

Lisa brushed past Matthew when she saw Cali standing there.

"I'm so glad you're okay." Lisa wrapped Cali in a tight embrace, causing her to wince. "Sorry."

Matthew appeared by her side almost as if by magic.

Lisa took a step back and eyed her boss. "We were all worried about you."

"We?" Matthew asked.

Jason came up to stand beside Lisa. "You knew there was no way to keep this kind of information contained. Between the police, her missing an entire day of work, and all the security activity, it didn't take long for people to start asking questions."

Matthew released something that sounded like a mix between a grunt and moan. Cali could tell he wasn't happy with the news, but there wasn't much that could be done. Working at a company was a lot like living in a small town. Like it or not, gossip traveled—especially juicy gossip.

After a few uncomfortable moments, Matthew looked at his brother and tilted his head. "We can talk in Alvin's study. Excuse us, ladies."

Jason followed Matthew and they both disappeared into her father's study.

Cali turned to Lisa. "You said you had something for me to sign?"

"Let's go sit down. You probably shouldn't be up moving around too much anyway."

What was it with people trying to coddle her?

Once they were seated on the couch in her father's formal living room, Lisa removed two contracts from her purse and handed them to Cali. She read them over and then signed her name.

"Now that that's done," Lisa said, tucking the contracts back in her bag, "let's get to the important stuff."

"Like?"

Her friend scooted closer. "You know, I think he likes you, too. And not just in a boss-employee type way."

She wasn't sure how she should respond to that.

Luckily, Cali was saved from having to answer as the man in question strolled into the room.

***

Matthew had led Jason into Alvin's study so they could have some privacy. If his brother had made the trip out here then he had to have something important to say.

What he hadn't expected was that the first thing out of Jason's mouth had nothing to do with work. "You've moved in?"

Matthew narrowed his eyes. He'd assumed his brother had come to talk about work.

Jason ignored him. "Does this mean you've decided to do something?"

Instead of answering, Matthew folded his arms across his chest and leaned back against the desk.

"Have you kissed her yet?"

How could Jason be asking questions like this after what had happened? "Cali is still my boss. Nothing has changed. It's my job to protect her and that's exactly what I'm doing."

Jason shook his head and handed Matthew a piece of paper. "Keep telling yourself that if it helps you sleep better at night."

Matthew unfolded it and skimmed through the names, ignoring his brother's comment.

"That's a list of everyone who was in the building an hour before the incident. Martinez and I reviewed the tapes ourselves today." Jason paused. "I hope I never have to do that again."

140

Several security personnel were listed, as well as IT people, a few assistants, two people from upper level management, the CFO, and the COO. The list was longer than Matthew thought it would be. "Can I keep this?"

"Knock yourself out. I've got a copy back at the office. I was planning to start going through it one by one tomorrow."

Matthew nodded and laid the paper down on the desk beside his laptop.

Jason moved toward the door. "You gonna be in tomorrow?"

"I don't know. Cali hasn't said if she's going in or not."

His brother smirked. "Call me in the morning if you don't make it in. We can talk strategy."

Jason opened the study door and walked out into the foyer. Matthew could hear his footfalls on the tile floor.

He waited until he heard the front door open and close before pushing away from the desk and strolling out into the foyer himself. Cali's voice coming from the living room drew him closer.

When he walked into the room, Lisa noticed him first. She shot Cali a smile and then stood. "I should probably get going. Call me if you need anything, all right?"

It took Cali a few extra seconds to get up from the couch to follow Lisa out. Seeing her struggle, he'd been tempted to offer assistance but he'd stopped himself. They didn't have that kind of relationship. They didn't have any kind of relationship.

Lisa stopped abruptly when she reached the door.

"One more thing," she said as she spun around to face them. "I need to know if you're still going to the gala this Friday night or if you need me to call and cancel."

Cali blinked. "What gala?"

"Oh," Lisa said almost too innocently. "Your father didn't tell you?"

"No, he didn't. What gala?" Cali sounded a little irritated. He couldn't tell if it was over the gala itself or the way Lisa was dragging things out.

"The yearly fundraiser for Chicago Memorial. Your father goes every year and I assumed you were going in his place. It's on your calendar."

He watched Cali's face as she processed the information. A variety of emotions played out on it before she seemed to sigh in defeat. "Don't cancel. I'll go. Chicago Memorial was one of my father's first clients. It wouldn't look right if I didn't."

Lisa grinned and reached for the doorknob.

Matthew had been watching the exchange silently up to this point, but he couldn't stay quiet any longer. "Who was accompanying Alvin to the gala?"

"No one. He was going solo."

He didn't even think about it. "Can you arrange for another place next to Cali? She won't be going alone."

"Sure. Whose name shall I have them put on the invitation?"

"Mine." Matthew said the word with a finality that echoed deep in his core. It was a feeling he didn't want to examine too closely.

A ringing sound awoke Matthew from a sound sleep the next morning. He'd been dreaming about Cali again, but then again when didn't he dream about her? Any time he let his guard down she was there in his thoughts.

Matthew rolled over and reached for his cell phone. He turned off the alarm with one hand and threw the sheet off him with the other. Sitting up, he turned and placed his feet on the floor as he rubbed the sleep from his eyes.

It had been a late night. After Lisa left, Cali had asked if he'd like to watch a movie. He should have turned her down—gone back into the study and started going over the list Jason had brought him—but instead he'd found himself agreeing. They'd found an old action movie in her father's collection and it turned out to be one of the most relaxing evenings he'd had in a while.

Shaking off the memories of the previous evening, Matthew went to the bathroom to grab a towel and then headed for the Stantons' home gym. It was an impressive setup. The room itself was half the size of his apartment and it had everything his exercise room had multiplied by ten.

He climbed onto one of the treadmills and programmed it for a one-minute warmup into a hard five mile run. The belt beneath him started moving. He adjusted his pace as it gradually sped up until he fell into the familiar rhythm of a brisk run.

Energy was flowing through his muscles, he could feel it, but this morning something was different. It took him a minute or two to figure out what it was. He wasn't as tense this morning as he normally was—or at least he wasn't as tense as he had been these last few weeks since Cali had appeared in his life.

Maybe staying away from her hadn't been the best idea. Maybe it had been a horrible idea. Having her close seemed to provide him with a level of peace. Even the night before in her hospital room had been different. It hadn't felt as if he were teetering on the edge of a cliff about ready to fall without any net below to catch him.

The treadmill beeped and then slowed to a walking pace. He'd completed his five miles and he hadn't thought of anything other than Cali.

Once his heartbeat slowed down to a normal pace, Matthew hopped off the treadmill and ambled over to where he'd left his towel. He wiped off the worst of the sweat that was pouring off him and checked his watch. Fifteen minutes before he had to shower and get to work. He glanced over at the free weights, but the urge to check on Cali was strong—so strong that he didn't bother trying to fight it. He wrapped the towel around the back of his neck and jogged up the stairs that would take him to her room.

Outside her door he began to have second thoughts. He argued with himself over whether or not it would be creepy to open the door and check on her. In the end, however, he'd convinced himself that in order to make sure she was okay he actually had to see her.

He opened the door slowly, trying to be quiet in case she was still sleeping. When he saw she was awake but still in bed, Matthew glanced down, filled with a sudden bout of shyness. "Sorry. I didn't know if you were awake."

Cali tried to sit up. Again, he noticed she was struggling. He wanted to help her.

"It's okay," she said. "I was just getting up."

Matthew nodded, trying not to notice how her shirt molded against her chest. "I was going to take a shower but if you'd like to take one first I can wait."

She smiled and he felt his chest clench. "I've got my own bathroom, but thank you."

"Of course." Matthew averted his gaze. He didn't want her to catch him staring. She was his boss and he had to remember that. "I'll just meet you downstairs, then."

He backed out of the room before he did something really stupid like forget that he was her employee and that he was in her house to protect her, not jump her bones.

Frustrated with himself, Matthew marched into the room he was using and dug out a clean pair of boxers. He darted across the hall to the bathroom he'd been using, shut the door, and locked it. Matthew wasn't sure if he was locking it for his protection or hers but he felt that at the moment he needed some sort of barrier between them. Otherwise . . . well, he didn't want to think about it.

By the time he finished his shower he almost felt like himself again. Matthew walked back to his room to get dressed, only pausing once to see if he could hear her moving around in her room down the hall. He couldn't, of course, but the little pang of disappointment still lingered.

Matthew was almost positive Cali wouldn't be going into the office today, but he dressed in his normal dress shirt and pants. He even threw on a tie. He needed to remember who they were and he was hoping his attire would help him stay professional. Last night they'd crossed a line of sorts. Bosses and employees didn't hang out and watch movies together. That was what friends and lovers did. They weren't either and he needed to remember that.

Taking a cleansing breath, he headed down the stairs to see the woman who seemed to hold all his fantasies in the palm of her hand. The one woman who was off limits.

Chapter 16

Cali walked into the kitchen to find Matthew was already there making breakfast. He had his back to her and she stood there taking him in. The sleeves of his dress shirt were rolled up to his elbows and his muscles flexed as he reached into a cabinet above him. She swallowed, trying to block out the memory of him earlier when he'd stopped by her room to check on her. He hadn't been wearing a shirt then and just thinking about it was making her want things she shouldn't.

She cleared her throat. "Where's Jessie?"

Matthew glanced over his shoulder and grinned. "I gave her the morning off."

"I see," she said moving farther into the kitchen. Her body still ached, but she was feeling better than she'd been the day before. That was something, at least.

"I thought since she had to stay the day before that she deserved some time off. Besides, I'm not completely helpless. I can handle breakfast." He winked at her and went back to what he was doing.

Cali eased herself up onto one of the stools at the island. Sitting at the kitchen table would have been more comfortable, but she didn't want to feel as if she were miles away from him.

"How do you like your eggs?" he asked.

"Scrambled is fine." She wasn't picky, but she figured that was the easiest option.

He nodded and reached for another skillet.

When he handed her a plate full of eggs, bacon, and hash browns, she had to admit she was impressed. "Thanks."

Again he smiled at her and it did crazy things to her insides.

Matthew sat down beside her and began eating.

Cali was a little more hesitant. "I want to go into work today."

He stopped, looked over at her, and then went back to eating. "Are you sure?"

"Positive."

"Only if you promise me one thing."

She raised her eyebrows and waited, curious as to what he was going to say.

"Promise me if it becomes too much, or if you start hurting, that you will let me know and I'll bring you home."

Cali released a shaky breath. All things considered, that was a reasonable request. "I promise."

She finished eating and he cleaned up. Cali didn't fight him because quite frankly, she was already questioning her decision to go into work. Every time she moved it hurt.

As if he could sense her pain, Matthew handed Cali her pain pills.

"Thanks."

He gave her a tense smile and turned. "I'm going to go get my things. Do you need anything from upstairs before we go?"

She shook her head even though he wasn't looking at her. "No. I think everything I need is down here."

Matthew nodded and disappeared up the stairs.

He drove her to work and rode in the elevator with her. She felt as if she had a shadow. He even walked with her over to Lisa's desk and gave strict instructions that Cali was not to be left alone for any reason and that her office door was to remain open at all times. She was a little unnerved by all the restrictions. With Matthew's new guidelines, Cali would have no privacy.

Once he finished spouting off his list of instructions to Lisa, he followed Cali into her office. Matthew closed the door behind them, effectively disregarding his own orders. She gave him a questioning look but he only shrugged and sent her a smile that had those butterflies in her stomach going again. "The rule doesn't apply to me."

Cali couldn't help but smile back. "I see."

They stared into each other's eyes and the tension that always seemed to be hovering in the background when Matthew was around rose to the surface. She felt her heartbeat pick up and wondered if he was experiencing the same thing she was.

Matthew closed his eyes, breaking the spell.

When he looked at her again, all the electricity she'd felt before from him was gone. He was all business again. "I need to head down to my office for a while. I want to go over a few things and see where we are on the investigation."

"You don't have to babysit me. Really, I'll be fine," Cali insisted. "I mean, who's going to bother me in my office with Lisa right outside?"

It was meant to be a rhetorical question. Matthew, however, didn't think so. He closed the distance between them, his eyes blazing. "Someone tried to kill you two nights ago. At the very least, someone is stalking you. I'm not taking any chances with your safety."

By the time he'd finished speaking, he was right in front of her—so close their noses were mere inches apart. She could feel his breath on her face. They hadn't been this close since that time in his office—the time she could have sworn he'd almost kissed her.

Cali knew the moment he realized their position. The color of his eyes changed slightly and his breathing grew shallow. Neither moved.

She stole a glance at his lips—they were so close to hers. Cali knew right then in that moment that she wanted him to kiss her. To hell with who she was . . . who he was. The thought of his lips on hers was the only thing that mattered.

Her gaze returned to meet his and she saw the same emotions she was feeling reflected back in his eyes. He looked down at her mouth and leaned in, closing the gap between them.

A soft knock sounded on her door the second she felt his soft lips touch hers and he jerked away from her.

Lisa strolled into her office completely unaware of what she'd walked in on. "Sorry to interrupt, Cali, but Mr. Russell is on line two and he's demanding to speak to you."

Matthew took a step back and headed toward the door. He

paused and looked back in her direction but he didn't meet her gaze. "I'll be back before lunch."

It wasn't until he was gone that Cali felt as if she could breathe again. "Thank you, Lisa."

Her assistant hesitated for a moment and then left.

Cali limped over to her desk and took a seat in her chair before picking up the phone. "Good morning, Tony. What can I do for you?"

The next few hours passed by in typical fashion. Lisa checked on her a few times, but other than that, she sat in her office and tried to get as much work done as possible. That's not to say that she got a lot done exactly. She was going for more of a 'slow and steady wins the race' philosophy.

Matthew returned a little before noon as promised. There was an air of professionalism about him that had been missing the last two days and she wasn't sure she liked it. Without uttering a word, he closed her office door and made a beeline for the far corner of the room.

"What are you doing?" Cali asked, perplexed.

He spared her a quick glance then grabbed a chair and slid it against the wall. "I'm installing a camera."

She watched as he removed two small objects from his pockets and waited for him to elaborate.

He didn't.

Cali was about to ask him to explain when her office door opened again and Jason strolled in with Lisa hot on his heels carrying several bags of food.

"Cali," Jason acknowledged with a nod before closing the door behind Lisa and going to help his brother.

Lisa walked into the adjoining room and began laying out the food.

Cali stood there completely baffled. Aside from the brief recognition of Cali's presence when Jason had entered the room, she might as well have been a ghost for all the attention they paid her.

Ten minutes later, Matthew climbed down from the chair and pulled out his cell phone. He tapped on the screen and showed it to his brother. Jason grinned and so did Matthew. Whatever it was they both seemed to be pleased about it.

Matthew lifted his head and walked toward her. He held out his phone so she could see the screen.

It was them. All of them. Here in this room. Now.

She looked up at him and then over to the camera he'd just installed.

"I've set up the camera feed to come directly to my phone. No one will know it even exists except for the four of us," he said.

The entire time this thing had been going on, Cali had been sitting behind her desk. She felt the need to do . . . something . . . so she stood. Unfortunately for her she moved a little too fast and pain shot down her side, causing her to wince.

"Are you hurting, Cali?" All the professionalism had vanished from his tone and the caring Matthew was back.

"I'm fine." It was an automatic response. She wasn't fine. Not at all.

She took a deep breath and tried again. "Don't you think this is a bit much? I mean, the chances of someone—"

"I'm not taking chances. That's the point. I can't physically be with you every minute of the day. This is the next best thing." There was a hint of pleading in his voice that she'd never heard before and she didn't know what to make of it.

Cali opened her mouth to argue, but he cut her off.

"You're not going to change my mind about this." The hard note in his voice was back. His decision was final. She could see it in his eyes. Matthew wasn't going to budge on this and she didn't have the strength to argue it out with him.

"Did you need some help?" Lisa asked, appearing next to Cali. She'd been so caught up in her conversation with Matthew she hadn't noticed.

"No. Thank you."

***

Matthew hung back as Cali made her way over to the conference table. He could see she was in pain and it ate at him. Maybe he should have insisted that she stayed home this morning, although he could image the argument that would have set in motion.

He kept an eye on her through lunch. With every minute that passed her pain seemed to be getting worse. When she reached for her drink and he saw her face scrunch up and air hiss through her teeth, he'd had enough. Pushing away from the conference table, he went to her desk, got her pills and brought them to her.

She looked up and held his gaze. "Don't tell me you don't need them. It's my job to see the details and I know you're in pain."

Cali only hesitated for a moment before taking the pills.

Matthew retook his seat and went back to eating.

"We've been working on the list I brought over last night," Jason said. "We still have about thirty names to go, but we're making progress."

"So far there are two names that stand out, but it's still early," Matthew added.

Lisa paused mid bite. "That's good, right? I mean, two is better than what you started with."

Jason nodded. "Yes, but the only thing we have on those two is that they appear to have been alone at the time the car hit Cali and don't have alibis. That isn't concrete evidence."

His brother and Lisa continued to talk about what they'd found out so far, but Matthew was focused on Cali. Her eyelids were starting to droop and she was having trouble holding her head up. He knew it was time to go.

Matthew stood and Lisa and his brother followed suit. He came up beside her and knelt down next to her chair. "I'll take you home."

She nodded and he helped her to stand.

Lisa brought Cali her purse and briefcase and gave her a hug. "I'll make sure everything here is taken care of. You get some rest."

"Thank you," Cali mumbled.

Matthew wrapped an arm around her waist and helped her to the elevators. She was leaning on him heavily by the time the doors opened. Peter Carson, Stanton Enterprises' CFO stared back at them with a look of confusion on his face. Then his gaze morphed into something else entirely. Matthew couldn't tell if it was curiosity or something more along the lines of interest. Either way it had him pulling Cali closer against him.

Clearing his throat, Matthew pulled Peter's attention away from Cali. "Ms. Stanton's had enough for today. I'm going to see that she gets home safely."

"Oh." Peter blinked several times then seemed to get a hold of himself. "Cali, if you need a ride home I would be more than happy to provide one."

For some reason Peter's offer grated on Matthew's nerves.

Luckily, Cali answered Peter, saving Matthew from making a snide comment about where the CFO could shove his offer. "It's okay. Besides, you have to make sure our financials are on track since it doesn't look like we're going to be able to meet this week."

Peter nodded reluctantly. "All right, then. Well, if you need anything you be sure to call me. I did promise your father that I would look after you in his absence."

Matthew adjusted his grip and moved them past Peter into the elevator. The look on Carson's face was priceless as the doors closed to take Matthew and Cali down to the parking garage and he found himself grinning.

"Are you okay?" Cali asked once they were inside his car.

He chuckled as he maneuvered out of the garage and onto the street. "I was going to ask you the same thing."

She laid her head back on the seat. "I'm just tired."

Her voice trailed off and he glanced over to find she had closed her eyes. He left her alone for the rest of the drive, figuring she needed her rest.

He parked in the Stantons' driveway near the side door that led to the kitchen. Matthew gently woke her up enough to help her inside and up to her room. She was barely conscious as she leaned against him.

As it turned out, getting her up to her room had been the easy part. She'd worn a three-piece suit to work—one she looked stunning in, he might add. He didn't, however, think it was a good idea for her to sleep in it.

Matthew weighed his options. He could leave her be and hope she didn't ruin her designer clothes, or he could undress her enough for her to be comfortable. The question was could he undress her and keep himself in check?

He was still debating what to do when she spoke. "Help me with my jacket and shoes? Everything else I don't care about."

Her voice was barely above a whisper, but he followed her instructions. He unbuttoned her jacket and slid it down her shoulders, trying not to think about all the times he'd done the exact same thing in his dreams. After laying it as neatly as he could on the back of a nearby chair, he returned to help her with her shoes.

Cali was sitting on the edge of the bed. He knelt down in front of her and removed her shoes one at a time. His fingers lingered a little too long on her soft ankles, wanting to explore more—to see if the rest of her legs were just as soft—but he shook off his desire and stood.

Offering her his hand, he helped her under the covers. "Get some sleep. I'll be right downstairs."

A soft sigh escaped her lips as her eyes fluttered closed. She was asleep within moments.

He hovered by the door for a few minutes, watching her. Cali Stanton was beyond beautiful.

Before his body could betray him again, Matthew closed the door and headed downstairs to Alvin's study. He left the door cracked open in case Cali needed him, and then booted up his laptop. While she slept, he had work to do. He needed to get through those thirty names and narrow down his list of suspects.

Several hours later Matthew heard movement on the stairs. He closed his laptop and went to investigate. Matthew knew it was probably Cali, but he wasn't taking any chances.

He scanned the foyer and made his way down the hall where he heard something. When he glanced around the corner, he saw Cali's copper hair as she limped around the kitchen, and breathed a sigh of relief. He propped himself up against the doorframe and put his hands in his pockets. "Hungry?"

Cali jumped.

She glanced over her shoulder and met his gaze. "Yeah. A little."

He pushed off the wall and strolled over to her. "What are you in the mood for?"

"Pizza is sounding really good, but I don't think we have any." She frowned. "My dad isn't big on pizza."

Matthew raised his eyebrows. Who didn't like pizza?

Cali laughed at his expression then groaned in obvious discomfort. "Strange, I know, but it's true. He's more of a steak and potatoes type of guy."

"Can't argue with steak and potatoes." Matthew thought about it for half a second and then reached for the phone. "What do you say we have one delivered? What do you like on your pizza?"

She closed the refrigerator door. "Anything but anchovies."

Matthew grinned. "Ah, my kind of girl."

It wasn't until he was on hold with the pizza place that he realized what he'd said. Where had that come from? Cali wasn't his girl and she never would be. He needed to get those types of thoughts out of his head post haste or else he was going to find himself in a world of trouble.

Chapter 17

Cali lay in her bed that night thinking about her day. When Matthew had told her father that he wouldn't let Cali out of his sight he hadn't been exaggerating. She still wasn't sure how she felt about the camera in her office. Having Matthew around was nice—more than nice, if she was being completely honest with herself—but his presence was also very confusing. She felt drawn to him by some unknown force and unless she was misreading him, Matthew felt it, too.

Closing her eyes, she could still feel his lips as they had brushed against hers earlier that day in her office. Cali knew without a doubt that if Lisa hadn't interrupted them he would have kissed her. And she wanted that kiss. Right or wrong, she wanted it. The more time she spent with Matthew the softer that voice inside her head screaming that she couldn't be with him because she was his boss became.

Matthew, on the other hand, had spent the rest of the day acting like nothing had happened between them . . . like nothing had changed.

She rolled over onto her side and glanced at the clock beside her bed. It was almost midnight and her mind wouldn't shut off. Matthew was only two doors down from her. Was he asleep or was he thinking about their almost kiss, too? And if so, what was he thinking? She knew he wasn't completely unaffected by whatever it was between them, but she also remembered how furious he'd been when he found out about Jason and Lisa. He'd been so afraid someone would find out about their relationship, but thus far no one knew except Cali and Matthew.

Could they explore what this was between them and keep everyone else in the dark? Would Matthew want to?

Cali sighed. As much as she tried to suppress the thoughts and feelings running through her, it was impossible. The seed had been planted and it wouldn't be ignored. She wanted that kiss . . . and so much more.

It took Cali almost two more hours to fall asleep. She got up on Thursday morning, ate breakfast with Matthew, and went to work. She stayed until her body began to protest too much and Matthew insisted on taking her home.

That night he made her spaghetti and meatballs and they sat around the kitchen table, eating and talking. It all felt very domestic except for the fact that they weren't actually a couple.

On Friday, she refused to take her pain medication.

"Cali, your doctor prescribed it for a reason," Matthew said.

"I'll be fine. I'm not as stiff as I was yesterday."

He pursed his lips and she knew he wanted to argue with her.

"Come on. We need to get going or we're going to be late."

He drove her to work and left her alone for most of the day although she was positive he was keeping tabs on her through the camera he'd installed. Her suspicions were confirmed when he strolled into her office just before four o'clock declaring it was time to go home.

"It's only four," she said, looking at the clock.

He was already gathering her things. "Yes, but we have a gala to attend tonight."

"That isn't until seven."

Matthew pulled her chair back away from her desk and offered his hand to her.

She ignored it and stood on her own without his assistance. Even though it was true that her body was aching and she could no longer get comfortable, Cali didn't want to admit that to him. She wasn't helpless.

Matthew sighed. "I don't want you to be rushed getting ready.

Besides, I can tell you're exhausted."

"I'm fine . . ." The words died on her lips when she glanced over at him. It was clear she was wasting her breath. He didn't believe her posturing.

Over the last few days, she'd learned how stubborn he could be, especially when he felt he was right about something. And in this case he was right. She was exhausted. The stabbing pain of the first two days had faded into a dull ache. It was almost as if she had the flu, but only from the chest down.

Cali let him guide her out of the office and into his car. Neither said much on the drive home, but once they were inside the house he suggested that she go upstairs and lie down for a while. She could have argued with him—a part of her wanted to—but instead she nodded and dragged herself up to her room.

Alone in her bedroom she stripped down to her underwear and crawled under the covers. She could hear Matthew moving around downstairs and it was comforting to know he was there, watching over her. It wasn't something she was used to. Being on her own overseas, she'd learned that most of the time all she had to rely on was herself. That wasn't the case now and she knew that. Matthew had made that very clear. He was sticking by her no matter what. At least until whoever was driving the car that hit her was caught.

She closed her eyes and let the sounds of his movement downstairs lull her to sleep. He would protect her. Her very own knight in shining armor. Or at least a knight in a suit and tie.

***

Matthew stood at the bottom of the stairs until he was confident Cali had made it to her bedroom then he set out to get some work done. He was worried about her. She'd pushed herself today when she should have been taking it easy. They still had the gala tonight to get through. He was hoping a nap would give her the energy to make it through the event because he was almost positive she was going to refuse to take any more of her pain medication until it was over.

When he couldn't put it off any longer, Matthew tiptoed up the stairs and into her room. He paused next to her bed, watching her sleep. Cali was on her side facing the door, her mouth slightly open.

He couldn't pull his gaze away from her mouth. It had been in his thoughts a lot over the last two days. He'd almost kissed her—his boss—and he'd been berating himself about it ever since it happened. Especially since more than anything he wanted a repeat performance, this time without them getting interrupted.

Matthew shook off those very dangerous thoughts and nudged Cali's shoulder. "Cali? Cali, you need to wake up."

"Matthew?" she moaned.

The sound sent a shot straight to his groin and he jerked his hand back as if he'd been burned. It made him want to do things to her—things that he couldn't do, things that he wouldn't do.

He needed to get out of there. Now.

Matthew took a step back and in that moment Cali opened her eyes. She looked up at him with the most innocent expression. She had no idea what she was doing to him.

"What's wrong?" she asked, her voice groggy from sleep.

"Nothing," he said, trying to hide the panic he was feeling. "It's time to wake up. You need to start getting ready for the gala."

"Oh."

Matthew glanced over at the door, then back at her. "Can you be downstairs in an hour?"

She sat up, holding the sheet to her chest. Of course, his gaze went right to her breasts. He needed to get out of there.

"Sure."

Before she could say anything else, he darted out of the room.

Matthew speed-walked down the hall to the room he was using and shut the door behind him. Only then did he feel as if he could take a deep breath. He had to get control of himself. Tonight they were going out in public and he needed to be on top of his game, not acting like some horny teenager at the mercy of his hormones.

Roughly thirty minutes later Matthew was showered and dressed in the tux he'd rented for the evening. He was headed down the main spiral staircase to wait for Cali when the doorbell rang. They weren't expecting anyone, which immediately put him on guard.

As it turned out, Jason was the one standing on the other side of the door.

He looked Matthew up and down, taking in his appearance. "You clean up nice, little brother."

Matthew rolled his eyes and stepped back to let his brother

inside. "And to what do I owe this impromptu visit? Did something happen?"

Jason shut the door behind him and chuckled. "No. At least I don't think so." Then he wiggled his eyebrows suggestively. "Did it?"

His brother's meaning wasn't lost on Matthew. "No."

Jason sighed and shook his head.

"Was there something you wanted, Jason? Other than trying to meddle in my life? Cali will be down any minute and we'll need to get going." Matthew glanced at his watch and realized that he should probably check on her. "I'll be right back. I need to make sure she's okay."

His brother placed a hand on his arm. "Let me. I need to use the facilities anyway."

Before Matthew could object, Jason was already halfway up the stairs. It also hadn't escaped Matthew's attention that his brother had never gotten around to sharing the reason for his visit.

Shaking his head, Matthew made his way into the study and opened the top drawer of Alvin's desk. He opened a small wooden box and removed what appeared to be a pen—a very nice pen. Making a few adjustments to the outer casing, the pen came apart to reveal a small knife. It wasn't much but it was all he would get since weapons were prohibited at tonight's function. There was no way, however, that he was going in there empty-handed, not with someone after Cali. A well-placed knife in the jugular was quite effective in taking someone out. Messy, but effective.

Matthew heard noise on the stairs and swiftly reassembled the pen. He tucked it into the inside pocket of his jacket and exited the study.

The moment he laid eyes on Cali his breath caught in his throat. She looked magnificent in an elegant black and white ball gown that hugged her curves to perfection. His body reacted to the sight and for once, he didn't care.

She descended the stairs and made her way over to where he was waiting. He barely registered his brother's presence in the room as she came toward him. Cali stopped three feet away from him— just out of reach. That was probably best since he was having a hard time keeping his emotions in check at the moment.

Jason cleared his throat.

How long had Matthew been standing there staring at her?

He shifted his gaze to his brother who wore a knowing smile. "I've gotta go. I'm having dinner with Lisa tonight and I don't want to be late. You two kids have fun."

Jason waved goodbye and was out the door before Matthew could form a coherent thought. He needed to focus.

"Are you all right?" Cali asked.

"Of course." He took a step forward, opened the door, and motioned for her to go first. "Shall we?"

Cali nodded and walked through the door. He took a deep breath and told himself to relax. Everything was going to be fine.

They arrived at one of Chicago's best hotels a little before seven. One valet opened the passenger side door for Cali while another met Matthew on the driver's side and slid behind the wheel. Matthew walked around the front of the car and offered Cali his arm. She took it and he led her into the hotel.

The gala was taking place on the second floor and they rode up in the elevator with another couple also decked out in their finest attire. When they stepped off the elevator the high society atmosphere permeated the room. All the men were in tuxedos and all the women were in fancy ball gowns like the one Cali was wearing. As he watched them milling about, it hit Matthew that this was the life Cali had been born into. It was what she was used to. A life far removed from the one he'd led growing up.

He glanced over to find Cali looking up at him. "Are you ready?"

She smiled and nodded.

Matthew wrapped his arm around her waist and guided her through the outer area and into the ballroom. He took a quick survey of the room, noting the exits. There were several security guards stationed around the room. It was good to know that he wouldn't be acting completely alone should something happen.

His gaze returned to one of the security guards and he smiled. Charles.

At that moment the man looked in Matthew's direction and his face broke out into a matching grin.

Charles Westbrook had been a close friend of Matthew's father. Charles had taken Matthew under his wing and helped him figure out what to do with his life after college. Without Charles, Matthew had no idea where he'd be.

Cali shifted, drawing his attention.

"Everything okay?" she asked with concern.

"Yeah. Just saw an old friend, is all."

"Oh. Well . . . um . . . are you ready to do some socializing?"

He took one last look in Charles' direction, then back to Cali. "Lead the way. I'm at your full disposal tonight."

Her gaze locked with his for a moment and he saw the muscles in her neck move as she swallowed. A moment too late, he realized the double meaning of his words.

She looked away.

He was still trying to come up with something to break the tension between them when she started moving. Matthew followed close, never more than a step behind.

***

Cali talked to a few people who recognized her before she and Matthew found their table. Dinner was delicious, of course for the amount of money it cost it should have been. Five courses later and she was stuffed.

The waiters came to the tables and began gathering up the plates and Jackson Gerber, the CEO of Chicago Memorial, arose from his seat to say a few words. It was a nice speech as far as speeches went and she'd been somewhat surprised when he mentioned Stanton Enterprises specifically. When he was finished, everyone clapped as he exited the stage and a band in the corner began to play.

Several couples around them got up to dance and Cali looked on with envy as they swayed to the music. She loved to dance, but it had been a long time—three years to be exact.

"Would you like to dance?"

She looked up to find Matthew standing beside her with his hand outstretched.

Cali hesitated, unsure if it was such a good idea. Her body, however, seemed to have no such issues and she found herself placing her hand in his as she stood.

They weaved their way through several tables until they reached the dance floor. Cali's stomach was full of butterflies as Matthew placed his right hand against her lower back and pulled her close.

The band played a smooth waltz and Matthew led them around the dance floor as if he'd been doing it for years.

"I didn't know you could dance."

He smiled down at her. "I'm sure there are a lot of things you don't know about me."

"Is that so?" Some of her nerves melted away as they moved together.

Matthew's chest vibrated under her hand. "I have many, many secrets. I'd tell you, but then I'd have to kill you."

He winked and Cali laughed. She had no doubt that he told the truth. Matthew didn't let his guard down often and she was finding that she loved it.

They continued to dance to several more songs before Cali's muscles began to protest. He noticed her distress without her having to voice it and escorted her off the dance floor. Unfortunately, they didn't make it back to their table as quickly as she would have liked. Several people stopped them wanting to talk to her and ask how her father was doing. She appreciated the support, but all she wanted to do was sit down.

By the time they did make it back to their table it was already after eleven and every time she moved she could feel it.

"Are you in pain?" Matthew asked, whispering in her ear so no one around them could hear.

She pulled out her chair and sat down. "Just a little. I'll be okay, though."

He reached into his pocket and retrieved two of her pain pills. She hadn't even known he'd brought them with him.

Matthew picked up her water and handed it to her along with the pills. "Here."

Cali shook her head. "I can't."

"Why not?" he demanded as he lowered himself into the chair beside her. "You're in pain and you don't have to be."

"You've seen what happens when I take them. They knock me out. I can't be falling asleep at the gala. It wouldn't look right."

He ignored her argument, opened her hand, and placed the water in her grip. "It's after eleven, Cali. You've made your appearance. No one is going to think anything if you leave."

She looked around at the still crowded room. Dancing probably hadn't been the best idea and she was sure she would pay for it tomorrow, but she wouldn't have traded it for anything—not even her aching muscles. "All right. Just let me say goodbye to Jackson before we go."

Cali went to set her water down when his hand stopped her. "Take the pills first."

It was on the tip of her tongue to argue, but she decided against it. He was only looking after her.

She chased the pills down with a large drink of water. "Happy?"

Matthew grinned, seeming pleased with himself despite her irritation. "Extremely."

Cali narrowed her eyes at him, but he seemed not to notice.

He stood and held out his hand as he had earlier when asking her to dance. "Shall we?"

She grabbed her purse and went to find her longtime friend. Matthew's hand never left her lower back. He stood by her side as she said her goodbyes to Jackson, and then led her out of the hotel.

By the time they arrived home it was well after midnight and Cali's medicine had kicked in. She was having a hard time keeping her eyes open. Cali was vaguely aware of the car ride home and of Matthew opening her door, unbuckling her seat belt, and picking her up. She slid her arms around his neck and rested her head against his shoulder. He smelled of soap and something a little spicy. She skimmed her nose along his neck, wanting more of the tantalizing scent.

"Are we home?"

"Yes," he whispered, his mouth close to her ear. "I'm going to get you up to bed and then you can sleep."

Cali opened her eyes and tilted her head a little so she could see his face. He didn't look happy that he had to carry her. "I can walk. You can put me down."

Instead of letting go, he tightened his grip.

If he didn't want to be this close to her then there was no reason he had to be. She could walk . . . or at least crawl up the stairs. It was better than seeing that expression on his face. So she did the only thing she could—she started to squirm.

After a minute or so of struggling with her, he set her on her feet, but he didn't go far. He stayed behind her as she slowly tried to make her way up the stairs.

On the sixth step, she lost her footing and he grabbed onto her waist to keep her from falling. Her momentum caused him to lose his balance and in order to break her fall he twisted her around to face him, bracing his knee on the stairs to support her back.

She opened her eyes to find Matthew's face inches from her own. He looked afraid, something she'd never seen from him before tonight.

Without thinking, she reaching up and caressed the side of his face.

Matthew closed his eyes and leaned in to her hand.

Cali snaked her hand around to cup the back of his neck and used the leverage to pull herself closer to him. She licked her lips, anticipating the feel of his mouth on hers. He was so close.

All of a sudden Matthew's eyes flew open and his arms that were still holding her up stiffened. There was no time to take in his expression before he swung her up into his arms and carried her to her bedroom.

Her mind was reeling. Was he going to give in to this thing between them?

The moonlight illuminated his face when they entered her room and it wasn't full of passion as she'd hoped. His face was devoid of emotion. She'd seen it before, but it was still a shock . . . especially after the moment they'd shared.

Matthew placed her on the edge of her bed, took off her shoes, and pulled back the covers. "If you need anything, I'll be in my room."

Then he was gone and she was left aching in a very different way.

Chapter 18

Morning came way too early for Matthew. It'd had been a late night. Not only had they not gotten in until after midnight but sleep had been a long time coming once he'd made it to bed.

With a groan, he dug in his bag for the items he would need and headed across the hall for a shower. There was no sound coming from Cali's room, which hopefully meant she was still asleep. Matthew wasn't ready to face her yet. He needed more time to figure out how everything got so screwed up.

Most days he could shower and shave in less than fifteen minutes. Being in the military you learned to get in and get what you needed done then get out. This morning he drew it out, taking his time. He was hoping he would have had some answers by the time he was finished, but as he went back to his room to get dressed he was still as clueless as he was when he'd woken up.

Since it appeared to be raining, he doubted they would be going out today, especially after the long day Cali had yesterday. He dug out a pair of jeans from his bag and put them on then reached for his wallet to put the items he'd taken with him last night to the gala back inside. It was an old habit, but he didn't typically carry his wallet when he was on assignment and last night he had been working—even if it was a lot more pleasant than some of his past ops.

When he opened his wallet to double-check everything was in

its place, he noticed something behind his last twenty-dollar bill that hadn't been there the day before. He pushed the money aside and, sure enough, there was a single condom. It didn't take a genius to figure out who'd put it there either.

Matthew closed his wallet and stuffed it in his pocket before grabbing his cell phone and practically running down the stairs to Alvin's office. Once inside, he closed the doors with an exaggerated slowness. He was pissed. In fact, he wouldn't be surprised if there was steam coming out of his ears.

Leaning back against the door, he closed his eyes and tried to calm down. He was going to kill his brother. What the hell had Jason been thinking?

After a few minutes, Matthew felt somewhat better—as well as he was going to get given the circumstances—and dialed his brother's number.

Jason's groggy voice answered the phone on the fourth ring. "Hello?"

Hearing his brother's voice made all of Matthew's attempts at calm go out the window. "What do you think you're doing?"

"Well, good morning to you, too, little brother."

Matthew huffed. "Tell someone who wants to hear it, Jason. I asked you what you think you're doing. And don't tell me it wasn't you."

His brother laughed. "Found my little presents, did you?"

"Jason . . ." Matthew paused when he realized exactly what his brother had said. "What do you mean 'presents'?"

His brother's only response was to laugh even louder.

"Jason," Matthew said through gritted teeth.

"Sorry," Jason muttered, sounding anything but. "I'm guessing, then, that you only found the one in your wallet. Didn't open your nightstand this morning, did you?"

"No." Matthew began pacing. "Why are you doing this? Why can't you just stay out of it?"

Jason released what sounded like an exasperated sigh. "Because you can't see what's right in front of you. Matthew, you have a beautiful woman you're attracted to—who appears to be attracted to you in return—and you're doing what about it? Nothing."

"She's. My. Boss." Why couldn't he get that through his thick skull?

"Get over it."

Matthew stopped pacing. "What did you just say?"

"I said *get over it.*"

"I can't just—"

"Yes, you can. She's going to be your boss for another two months and then what? Are you seriously going to let her walk away? Matthew, I know you better than anyone. She's different and you know it." He paused. "So don't blow it."

Matthew ran a rough hand over the top of his head, but what he really wanted to do was punch something. Preferably his brother.

"Now," Jason said, interrupting Matthew's musings, "if you don't mind, I'm going to go get some lovin' of my own."

Before Matthew could come up with any type of response, his brother disconnected the call.

He stood there staring at his phone, unable to believe what had transpired. Was his brother serious?

Of course he was. Jason didn't care about breaking the rules. Case in point was the fact that he was currently lying in bed with Cali's assistant.

Shaking his head, he opened the study doors and marched into the kitchen. He needed coffee and he could hear Cali moving around upstairs. She'd be down soon and he was sure she'd be hungry.

Matthew had no idea what he was going to say to her.

He opened the refrigerator and was happy to see that Jessie had left them some fresh cut fruit. He took it out and placed it on the counter while he dug around to see what else was in there.

As he worked to serve up the fruit and muffins Jessie had provided, what had happened last night on the stairs replayed in his mind. He'd almost kissed her last night. Again.

It would be easy if he could chalk it up to the situation and them both being tired after the crazy week they'd had, but that was a lie. He wanted to kiss her then and he wanted to kiss her now. But no matter what Jason said, it wasn't possible. She was his boss and even when that would no longer be the case, she was still Alvin's daughter. He liked and respected Alvin. He couldn't cross that line.

The sound of Cali's footsteps on the stairs caused his heart rate to speed up. He just needed to stay calm—act normal—and everything would be fine.

He hoped.

***

Cali inched her way down the staircase. She could hear Matthew already in the kitchen and braced herself to see him again.

He was facing away from her when she entered, reaching into the silverware drawer. When he shut the drawer, he seemed to sense her, looked over his shoulder, and smiled. She felt her stomach do a little flip.

"Good morning."

She pushed a lock of her hair behind her ear and took her usual seat at the island. "Good morning."

Matthew brought two bowls of fruit and two muffins over before sitting down beside her. He grabbed a muffin and started eating.

Cali stole several glances at him, but he continued to stare at his food. It was like she wasn't even there.

He speared his last piece of fruit with his fork and paused before taking a bite. "Did you have anywhere you needed to go today? I know my presence is intrusive but it shouldn't stop you from your normal activities. I'll try to make myself as inconspicuous as possible."

She froze with her fork midway to her mouth. Was he really doing this? Again? Was he really going to ignore what had happened? What *kept* happening?

Dropping her fork down in her bowl with much more force than necessary, Cali stood and marched over to the sink. She couldn't believe him.

The bowl clattered against the stainless steel surface of the sink as she not so gently placed it inside. She stood with her hands gripping the sink, trying to breathe through the emotions running through her.

Cali felt Matthew come up beside her and whirled around to face him—ready to do battle.

"Cali? What's—"

"Don't you dare ask me what's wrong!"

He stood there looking lost.

She clenched her fists, trying to keep her temper in check, but she was livid. Was he really this clueless?

"You're really going to do this, aren't you?" She didn't really expect an answer. "Again."

Matthew gave no response. Other than to flex his jaw, he didn't move.

Cali combed her fingers through her hair in frustration and then let her arms fall back down to her sides. She needed to get away, so she pushed off the counter and walked away. "I give up."

She only made it two steps before Matthew grabbed her arm to stop her.

He scanned her face as if he were looking for the answers to solve the world's deepest mysteries. "Cali?"

"How many times?" she asked. "How many times and then you just close down and act like nothing happened?"

"Three," he said, his voice flat.

She stepped closer and looked into his eyes. She hadn't expected him to answer her. Or if he did, she was expecting something more along the lines of, 'I don't know what you're talking about.'

Matthew met her gaze with firm determination. "In my office."

He took a step closer. "In your office."

Cali watched the movement of his throat as he swallowed. The room seemed to be getting warmer.

Matthew took another step, closing the distance between them. "Last night."

Her heart was hammering in her ears. He was right in front of her now. Close enough that she could feel the heat radiating off him. Close enough that she could smell the cologne he was wearing.

"That's how many times I've almost kissed you," he whispered, his breath ghosting across her face, his lips mere inches from hers.

She couldn't pull her gaze away from his.

"Four." He said it so soft she could barely hear.

Cali's heart skipped a beat and it felt as if all the air had been sucked out of the room.

He tilted his head forward, bringing their lips even closer. "Tell me no, Cali. Tell me to stop."

Matthew's eyes were pleading with her—almost begging her to stop him—but she remained silent. She wanted this. More than anything she wanted this.

A deep moan tore from Matthew's chest when he realized she wasn't going to stop him. He took her face in his hands and claimed her mouth with his. Her entire body filled with heat the moment their lips touched. It wasn't a soft, sensual kiss. This was a kiss of desperation—need. And she needed it as much as he did.

Cali wrapped her arms around his neck, pulling herself closer. She'd been waiting for this too long and she wanted to feel his body pressing against hers.

He circled his arms around her waist, holding her close, as he sucked on her lips until she opened for him. They both moaned as their tongues came together for the first time and explored. She couldn't get enough.

The kiss built quickly. They'd been repressing their attraction for the last three weeks and the floodgates had been opened.

Matthew backed her up against the counter and lifted her onto the hard granite surface. Their lips parted briefly with the new position, but Cali opened her legs and pulled him back into her embrace and within seconds, they were making out like teenagers again. Cali wasn't thinking. She could only feel.

He ran his hands up her thighs as she trailed her fingers along his cheek and jaw. His skin was smooth from where he'd shaved that morning, but she could feel the strength beneath as he continued to kiss her.

His hips pressed against her center and she could feel him through his jeans. Knowing that he wanted her as much as she wanted him only fueled her passion more. Why had they waited this long to do this?

She darted her tongue along the corner of his mouth and it seemed to flick some sort of switch in him. Matthew took hold of her hips, yanked her against him with deliberate force, and ground himself against her.

While it felt good on a primal level, she was still recovering from her injuries and she couldn't help the small whimper that left her lips as pain shot down the length of her leg at the new position.

He started to pull away, but she locked her legs around his waist, refusing to let him go.

Matthew brought his hand up to caress her cheek and rested his forehead against hers. "I'm not going anywhere. I just don't want to hurt you."

They stood there looking into each other's eyes for several minutes before he reached behind him and removed her legs from around him. He helped her down from the counter and made sure her feet were firmly on the floor.

Releasing his hold on her waist, Matthew laced his fingers with hers. "You never answered me earlier."

Cali was still trying to come to terms with the fact that this was really happening. Matthew had kissed her and they were standing in the middle of her father's kitchen holding hands. He wasn't pulling away. "What did you ask me?"

One side of his mouth pulled up in a half smile. "Do you have any plans today?"

Oh, that question. She did vaguely remember him asking that.

What Cali really wanted to do with her Saturday was curl up somewhere with him and take advantage of the current openness he was offering her. His thumbs were moving softly back and forth over her knuckles, sending tingles up her arms. It was incredibly intimate.

As she looked up at him, though, she noticed his eyes were guarded. How long would this new openness last?

He was waiting for an answer.

Even though all Cali wanted to do was lock herself away for the rest of the day with Matthew, she'd promised her dad that she would visit him. He hadn't seen her since the accident and he was sick with worry. "I'm going to visit Dad at the lake house."

Matthew nodded. "When do you want to leave?"

He still hadn't released her hands and she was in no hurry to have him let go either. What if once they broke the connection everything changed? Cali didn't know if she could handle his indifference again.

"About an hour."

Matthew gave her fingers a final squeeze and then released them. She felt the chasm building between them almost immediately.

He went to the sink and began rinsing the bowls and loading them into the dishwasher. "Go get ready. I'll clean up down here."

"It's okay. I can do it." She felt bad. He'd been doing so much for her lately.

"Nonsense. I'm already dressed and ready to go. I've got this." He reached for a cloth to wipe down the counter.

She was still standing there, unsure if she should argue, when he did something that had her insides melting into a puddle of goo. He skimmed his fingers down the outside of her arm and gazed into her eyes, all pretense falling away.

"Go," he whispered with a hint of a smile.

Cali swallowed and forced her legs to move.

***

Matthew watched as Cali made her way out into the hall and up the stairs. Once she was out of sight, he slumped against the counter and hung his head in shame. What had he done? Nothing had changed. She was still his boss. He was still her employee.

But things had changed. With one kiss, everything had changed. Cali hadn't pulled away—she hadn't told him to stop even though he'd given her every opportunity to.

That was an understatement. He'd begged her to tell him no, to say he was crazy for wanting her the way he did, but she'd only gazed at him with those deep brown eyes of hers and pleaded for him to close the distance between them and kiss her.

He stared at the grout lines in the tile floor as a level of sadness overtook him. Now that he'd crossed that line, he didn't know if he could go back to the way things were before. He knew he didn't want to. Kissing her had been amazing. He wanted more. Hell, he'd been ready to take her right then and there in the kitchen.

He picked up a dish towel and finished cleaning up. How sick was he to have wanted to take her like that after what she'd been through? Remembering her whimper of pain filled him with guilt. What kind of a man was he?

Matthew threw the towel next to the sink and contemplated what he was going to do about Cali. He wanted to explore what was between them even though he had no idea how long it would last. She was heading back to Africa in two months—maybe three—and a cross-continental relationship didn't sound that appealing.

Then again, maybe he was getting ahead of himself. Cali may not want anything long-term. For all he knew she was only looking for a fling . . . a way to pass the time while she was in Chicago.

Could he do that? Did he want to do that?

His gaze landed on a picture of Cali and her father across the room. She was leaning in to her father, smiling, and he felt a response deep in his core. Smart or not, Matthew had his answer. He would take Cali however he could get her for as long as she was willing. He had no idea how he'd deal with it once she returned to Africa, but that didn't matter. What did matter was that for now she was here and she wanted to be with him.

The peace he felt at that decision was soon followed by fear. No one could know about this. Cali was still very much in danger. Whoever it was who came after her the other night was still out there and he didn't want to give them any more of an advantage than they already had.

He blew out a harsh breath and stood up straight. They were going to have to set some ground rules.

The thought made him smirk. Cali hated his rules already. Matthew could imagine her response to the limitations running through his head. He'd just have to find a way to make it up to her.

His smirk turned into a full-blown smile as he allowed himself to think of the possibility of being with Cali. She hadn't wanted him to pull away before—hadn't wanted him to stop—so he had to assume there was a high probability that they'd be sharing a bed soon. That both excited and scared him. She was still healing. They'd have to be careful.

Matthew had to stop thinking along those lines. Cali would be back downstairs any minute and they'd be going to see her father. The last thing Matthew needed was for Alvin to notice something had changed. It still felt like a betrayal of sorts. Even though he knew Cali was a grown woman and perfectly capable of making her own decisions, Alvin was his boss and would be after Cali went back to her life overseas.

Shaking his head, Matthew strolled out of the kitchen to wait for her in the foyer. Worrying about it wasn't helping anything. He'd made his decision—he'd chosen Cali. For better or worse, he was going to have a relationship with his boss . . . with his boss' daughter.

Chapter 19

Matthew waited by the door for Cali with keys in hand. When she reappeared at the top of the stairs, she looked somewhat hesitant and he wondered if she was having second thoughts. While he knew he should be glad if she decided to call a halt to this thing between them, he couldn't bring himself to feel even the slightest bit of relief, let alone joy.

He stayed close as she climbed into the passenger seat and then went to get behind the wheel. They needed to talk, but he had no idea how to approach something like this.

After they'd been on the road for ten minutes and neither of them had said anything, Matthew knew it was going to be up to him to get the ball rolling. He cleared his throat. "I think we need to set some ground rules."

She glanced over at him. "What kind of rules?"

"Your father can't know there is anything going on between us." He paused. "No one can. That means no kissing or touching of any kind if other people are around . . . even Lisa and Jason."

He heard her suck in a breath, but she didn't comment.

"We need to keep up appearances."

"I understand."

She didn't say anything more and so he let it go.

Cali was staring out at the passing scenery when her cell phone rang. "Hello? Oh hi, Dad. Yeah. I'm still coming up. We're on our way, actually. We just left. Yes, Matthew's with me." She held out the phone to Matthew. "He wants to talk to you."

Matthew took the phone. "Hello, sir."

"How's she doing?" Alvin asked, his voice laced with concern for his only daughter.

"She's fine. I'm taking good care of her, sir."

He made a noise that sounded like approval. "I'm glad you're with her. I can't imagine anything ever happening to her. She's all I've got left."

"Don't worry, sir. I promise I will do everything in my power to keep her safe."

Cali talked to her father for a few more minutes after that and then went back to looking out the window.

Forty-five minutes into the hour-long drive, she remained quiet and with every mile they drew closer to her father's house the more anxious she seemed to become. He didn't think she was thrilled with his rules but they were for her own safety and she said she'd understood. Her body language, however, was saying the exact opposite. Something was bothering her and he needed to figure out what it was.

He reached out and placed his hand over hers in a comforting gesture.

Cali whipped her head around to look at him. That was when he noticed the uncertainty in her eyes.

"What's wrong?" he asked.

She glanced down at their hands and then back up at him.

A lightbulb went off inside his head. Here he was laying down all his rules and yet he hadn't touched her since the kitchen. She had no idea that while he was trying to be all cool, calm, and collected on the outside that on the inside all he wanted to do since he saw her come downstairs was spend the rest of the weekend getting to know every inch of her. Matthew knew she needed reassurance that he still wanted this.

He saw a sign for a nature reserve and took the turnoff. The road led back to several picnic areas, most of which were deserted given the rain. He found a place to park but kept the engine running.

Cali's face was full of curiosity.

Matthew unbuckled his seat belt, turned, and did what he'd been wanting to do since seeing her come down the stairs—he kissed her.

It was a hard kiss at first, one meant to show certainty and determination. She hesitated for only a moment then pressed her lips against his with equal fervor. Soon what was meant to be a kiss of reassurance deepened. He cradled her face in between both his hands and she slid her fingers up his chest until her hands settled comfortably around his neck. Nothing had ever felt more right.

This time it was Cali who pulled back. She rested her forehead against his as he'd done to her earlier. Her gaze was unwavering.

He caressed her face and leaned back in his seat, separating them even more, but he didn't let her go completely. Matthew reached for her hand and held it securely in both of his. His gaze was once again drawn to her very kissable lips. If he wasn't careful they would end up going at it in the backseat and that wasn't what he wanted. Cali deserved better than that.

They sat there for several more minutes enjoying the moment before he couldn't ignore the voice inside him that said they needed to go. They were too vulnerable here. And besides, her father was expecting them.

Sighing, he placed a kiss on the inside of her palm and released her hand. He secured his seat belt and put the car in gear. Out of the corner of his eye, he saw her return her hands to her lap as he maneuvered the vehicle back onto the highway. She was biting her lip and looked to be deep in thought about something.

They drove another half mile and she moved her hand a fraction of an inch toward him then retracted it. He realized she wanted to touch him. Cali was usually so headstrong. It was out of character for her to be so hesitant but considering how he'd acted up until now, he wasn't surprised she was overthinking things.

He took her hand in his and placed it on his leg. They weren't in public yet, or even in front of her father. Hours of not being able to touch lay ahead of them. It would be their first challenge—their first attempt to see if they could hide their relationship from those around them. He didn't know about Cali, but Matthew really hoped he could stick to the rules and not give in to his desires. But for the next ten minutes or so, they were alone and he was planning to take advantage of what little time they had.

***

It was almost noon by the time they pulled up in front of the lake house. The light drizzle had turned into a steady downpour. Cali and Matthew flipped up the hoods on their jackets and darted inside. Someone opened the door for them, but Cali didn't think to look to see who it was until she'd removed her jacket. Standing there with her hand out waiting to take their coats was Jessie.

Shock crossed Cali's face. What was Jessie doing here?

Before she was able to ask, her father came rolling into the room in his wheelchair. "Cali!"

Excitement was written all over his face and she rushed to give him a hug. "Hi, Daddy."

Her father held onto her for an extra-long moment before glancing over her shoulder. "Matthew."

She moved to stand beside her father as Matthew stepped forward and extended his hand. "Alvin. How are you feeling?"

"Getting stronger every day. At least's that's what they tell me," her father joked.

Matthew grinned.

"Shall we take this into the other room?" Without waiting for an answer, her father turned himself around and exited, leaving them to follow.

Cali sat on the sofa near her father while Matthew took a seat on the other side of the coffee table. That was probably a good idea. Already she was itching to touch him again. If he was closer, she might not be able to resist.

Her father, of course, wanted to know how she was doing. He asked her dozens of questions about her health and if she was following her doctor's orders. She assured him she was and that she was continuing to rest whenever possible. As the afternoon went on, he seemed to relax some and believe her assertion that she really was okay.

At two o'clock Carolyn let them know that lunch was on the table. Cali wheeled her father into the dining room where everything was set up. She'd been so busy trying to convince her father that she was all right that she'd forgotten about Jessie being there when they arrived.

"Where's Jessie?" Cali asked as she placed her father's chair at the head of the table and took a seat beside him. "I saw her when we came in, but I haven't seen her since."

"Oh. She just stopped by to say hi and see how I'm doing. You know how Jessie is . . . always worrying."

While that did sound like Jessie, something seemed off in her father's answer but she couldn't pinpoint what it was.

Matthew took a seat on the other side of her father in her direct line of sight. He looked slightly uncomfortable but she couldn't figure out why. That was until she noticed him looking at her mouth every time she took a bite of her prime rib.

Perhaps it was wrong of her, but the urge to tease him was too strong to resist. She dipped her steak into the au jus sauce and placed it into her mouth with exaggerated slowness, purposely wrapping her lips around the tines of the fork and making a show of removing the meat. Every time she did it he swallowed and she could have sworn his eyes took on an almost dreamlike quality. Cali had no doubt she'd pay for it later, but she was having too much fun to stop.

A bit of sauce missed her mouth and she cleaned it up by running the tip of her tongue along the corner of her mouth. Matthew groaned, drawing her father's attention. "Everything all right?"

"Yes," Matthew choked out. "I'm fine."

As soon as her father's attention was back on his food, Matthew met her gaze across the table. His eyes were perceptively darker and he had a mischievous grin on his face. Yep. She was going to pay once they got home. She couldn't wait.

Cali knew she needed a diversion. "So, Dad, did your doctors say when they think you'll be able to return to work?"

"I suppose after this week you're ready to leave the corporate life behind." He chuckled. "Can't say as I blame you. Who would have thought that the wilds of Africa would be safer than Chicago? I bet you can't wait to get back."

Actually it wasn't that. In fact, she wasn't sure if she wanted to go back at all at this point. Her father was here and she was finding that she missed spending time with him. And then there was Matthew. Cali had no idea where this thing with him was going, but she wanted to find out and that would be hard to do if she was half a world away.

Her father had no idea the thoughts that were running through her head and continued talking. "No, the doc says it will be at least another eight more weeks before he'll give me the all clear to return to work. I'm already bored out of my mind. You might have to check me in to the mental ward before it's all said and done."

Cali smiled. "I'm sure that won't be necessary, Dad."

After that he switched gears and started talking about a television series he'd been watching to pass the time. She listened, but her attention kept drifting to Matthew. He was watching her intently and she wondered what was on his mind.

***

The rest of the afternoon seemed to drag on for what felt like forever as they visited with Cali's father. By the time they said their goodbyes and were on their way home the tension between them could be cut with a knife. It was very different from the atmosphere that had filled the car on the ride up to the lake house. All he wanted to do was get back to the house so he could touch Cali the way he wanted to.

Matthew hurried them both inside the house once they pulled up to the Stanton estate. He took several deep breaths trying to slow his heart rate as Cali removed her coat and tossed her purse onto the long table right inside the door. She appeared calm . . . much calmer than he was. Then she turned around and met his gaze.

She took a step toward him and he couldn't help but be drawn to her in return. They met halfway and embraced each other. He devoured her mouth with his own and she melted against him. He touched her everywhere he could reach, needing to make up for the hours that he had been unable to show her any type of affection.

"I want you," he murmured against her lips.

"I want you, too." She gasped as he moved his mouth down to suck on her neck.

Matthew tilted his head back to look at her. Cali's eyes were full of the same longing that reflected in his own. He didn't understand it, but he needed to be with her. The strong pull he felt to her didn't make sense. She filled him with a passion he'd never known before. He wanted her—wholly and completely.

Without words, he took her by the hands and led her up the stairs to his room, stopping every so often to kiss her . . . touch her. It was as if he had to keep reminding himself that this was really happening and that she appeared to want this as much as he did. His heart felt light and heavy all at the same time.

When they finally made it to his room, he stopped and looked at her. His gaze lowered to their still-joined hands. They looked right intertwined together.

He looked into her eyes again, making sure she hadn't changed her mind, but there was nothing there except heat and longing. Closing the distance between them, he kissed her. This time with a gentle passion that warmed him from the inside out. He was strangely nervous, but there was nothing that could make him change his mind about this. He was tired of denying them what they both wanted.

Cali sighed as he continued to kiss her. It was a blissful sound that caused the space in his jeans to get even smaller.

He reached for the hem of her shirt and slowly worked it up her torso and over her head. Once it was free, Cali reached for the bottom of his shirt and pushed it up over his head. He placed his hands on her hips and massaged her soft skin with his thumbs.

Cali pressed her palms flat on his chest, indicating she wanted him to move closer toward the bed. Who was he to say no?

Once they were standing next to his bed, they slowly removed their pants, shoes, and socks, leaving them in only their underwear. She was flushed and beautiful, her breasts hidden behind the black lace of her bra. Matthew traced the outline of her nipple through the fabric and was rewarded when she arched her back and leaned in to his touch. He was trying to be mindful of her injuries, but it was difficult when all he wanted to do was ravish her.

"Matthew."

His name came out as more of a moan. The sound sent a rush of pleasure through him. There was nothing more perfect than hearing her say his name like that and he wanted to hear it every day. It was so much better than how he'd imagined it in his dreams.

Matthew guided her down onto the bed and hovered over her, not wanting to press all of his weight against her. He bent his head and nipped at her breast through the lace until she was writhing against him. The way she responded to him was only increasing his desire for her. He wanted more.

She reached down between them, stroking his erection with her hand.

"Cali . . ." He reached down and held her wrist in a vise grip. He was going to go off like a rocket if she kept that up.

Their gazes locked, his heart pounding in his chest.

He captured her lips again with his own and let all the emotion he was feeling come through. Trailing a hand down Cali's body, he marveled at her perfection. Every curve felt as if it was made to be touched and caressed by him.

Matthew carefully removed what was left of their clothing until she lay naked beneath him. He snaked his hand between them, praying she was ready for him.

"Please." Her plea was the last straw. He couldn't wait any longer.

Lifting himself up, he reached across the bed and opened the drawer of his nightstand. Sure enough, the condoms Jason had teased him about were there. He sighed in relief as he grabbed one and swiftly rolled it on.

Cali stared up at him as he took a position between her spread legs. He crushed his mouth against hers as he pushed inside and she lifted her hips to meet him. The sensation caused them to break their kiss and a strangled cry left both their throats.

The world around them faded away. They were no longer Cali Stanton and Matthew Andersen. They were only Cali and Matthew. No company. No threats. No titles. Just the two of them coming together as one.

Their gazes met and held as they both neared their climax. He leaned in and took one of her nipples into his mouth, teasing her as he had earlier. Cali reacted as she had before, giving him yet another surge of masculine pleasure. He wanted to be the only one who ever made her respond like that.

Her breathing changed and Matthew knew she was close. "That's right, Cali. Let go for me."

A heartbeat later, a scream tore from her throat and her nails dug into his back. It was enough to send him right over the edge with her.

Neither of them moved as their breathing returned to normal. He was still inside her. A part of him feared that once he pulled out of her—put some separation between them—that she'd regret what they'd done. It was his worst fear.

When he couldn't justify it any longer, he rolled over, separating them. As swiftly as he could, Matthew removed the condom and tossed it into the trashcan beside his bed. He closed his eyes and took a deep breath before turning to face her, trying to brace himself for whatever he would see in her eyes.

Cali was smiling back at him. She didn't regret what they'd done. At least not yet.

He reached out and pulled her into his arms.

She came willingly, but as soon as she began to relax into him, Cali started to move away.

Matthew propped himself up on one arm. "Where are you going?"

Cali wouldn't meet his gaze. "We're both tired. I'll let you sleep."

"Stay," he whispered, brushing his fingers against her arm.

She looked up again, uncertainty still there in her eyes.

He placed a soft kiss on her lips. "Stay."

After a moment's hesitation, she nodded and rested her head back on his chest. Matthew reached for the sheet and brought it up to cover them. He tucked her hair back behind her ear and pressed his cheek against the top of her head as he held her.

Matthew held her as her breathing evened out and she fell asleep. So much had changed in the course of a day—their kiss in the kitchen . . . the car . . . their flirting over lunch . . . and finally making love. He wasn't going to be stupid anymore. No matter how Cali viewed their relationship, this wasn't a casual fling for him. He cared about her way more than he probably should and he had no idea what he was going to do when her time here was up and she returned to Africa.

Chapter 20

Cali woke up with the first rays of sun streaming through the curtains. She stretched, raising her arms above her head ready to push against the headboard—only it wasn't the solid wood she was expecting. Her fingers probed spindles instead. Where was she?

She opened her eyes and glanced around the room as the fog of sleep faded from her brain and the events of the day before came back to her. Matthew. She'd slept with Matthew.

A slow smile spread across her face as she relived the memory. He had the most magnificent hands. She couldn't remember ever feeling so cherished by a man.

Humming, she finished her stretch and looked to where Matthew should have been . . . only he wasn't. The spot next to her was empty. She ran her hand over the sheets to find that they were cold. He'd been gone a while.

A rush of sadness overcame her and she closed her eyes in an effort to keep it at bay. She didn't want him to walk in and find her crying.

Cali lay there for several minutes until she was sure she wasn't going to start crying then forced herself to get out of bed. She found her clothes folded neatly on the corner of the dresser along the wall. It was such a small thing but it tugged at her heart nonetheless and she felt tears threatening again.

After scooping up her clothes, she scurried out of the room and down the hall to her bedroom. She passed his bathroom along the way and it was empty. The entire second floor was completely silent.

Once she was inside her room, Cali threw herself on top of her bed and let the tears fall. He'd asked her to stay last night. Twice. Had she misunderstood? Had he changed his mind when he'd woken up to find her still there?

Knowing that he might not feel the same way about what had happened between them left her feeling sick—like someone had punched her in the gut. Cali had dealt with heartache before but this was different. She had to see Matthew every day. If he met her with that cold indifference again after their night together, she didn't know how she'd cope.

Cali had no idea how long she lay there crying, but eventually her tears dried up and she dragged herself into her shower. The water felt good and helped to clear her head. It was possible she was reading too much into his absence. Since Matthew had been staying at the house he'd woken up every morning to use her father's home gym. For all she knew he could be down there right now working up a sweat.

That brought with it a completely different feeling as she imagined what he would look like jogging on the treadmill with his shirt clinging to his chest. Cali moaned as heat built between her legs. She needed to stop thinking like that. For all she knew, what happened last night was a one-time thing.

She needed to stop this. All of it.

Cali turned off the water, reached for a towel, and dried herself off. She needed to get dressed and find some breakfast. And Matthew.

***

Matthew heard Cali long before he saw her. They'd dozed off while it was still light outside, so he'd found himself wide awake at four in the morning. As he lay there and watched her sleep, he'd been tempted to wake her up so he could see her flushed with arousal again. He couldn't think of a better way to start his day. But she was still healing and he knew she needed her sleep. He'd crept out of bed, leaving her lying there with her hair splayed out against the pillow and a contented smile on her face while he headed down to the gym.

It had been a less than satisfying workout. No matter how hard he pushed himself, it wasn't the release his body wanted. All he could think about was Cali upstairs in his bed.

He trudged up the stairs to the bathroom he'd been using across the hall and turned on the shower. The imagines of last night filled his vision as soon as he closed his eyes and let the water cascade over his head. Before he knew it, he was hard as a rock and desperately wanting to take her again.

Knowing he needed to cool his libido, Matthew adjusted the water temperature to cold. The spray hit him like tiny hailstones but it was the quickest way to get his body under control.

He felt better, if not a little chilled, when he strolled out of the bathroom and snuck back into his room to get dressed. Cali was still sleeping. The sheet had slipped lower, exposing her naked back to him. He couldn't help but pause for a moment and marvel at her beauty.

All too soon, he felt those familiar stirrings return and knew he needed to leave. Matthew gathered up the rest of his clothes and rushed out the door like the devil himself was on his heels.

He'd spent the time working in Alvin's study while Cali was still upstairs sleeping. Work was his best distraction.

The sun had been up for a while by the time he heard her come down the stairs. Every cell in his body vibrated as he anticipated seeing her again.

The sound of her footsteps stopped. "Matthew?"

"In here."

His palms started to sweat at the thought of seeing her again. He mentally kicked himself. This was Cali—the same woman he'd spent the last three weeks fantasizing about. The same woman who'd made those fantasies a reality last night.

The door opened and Cali came into view. She gave him a tentative smile. "Hi."

She looked just as nervous as he was and her eyes were bloodshot like she'd been crying.

Matthew stood and walked over to stand in front of her. He wanted to drive all doubt out of her mind as to his feelings about what happened last night. Skimming his hand along her cheek, he cupped the side of her face, and then threaded his fingers into her hair. "Good morning."

He didn't wait for her to reply before he lowered his mouth to hers. His lips lingered, gently probing until she opened for him. The moment their tongues touched, he felt her relax and lean in to him. She gripped his waist and dug her fingers into his back. It brought their night together back in full force.

Before he realized what he'd done, he had pushed her up against the wall and was holding her face between both his hands as he devoured her mouth. They were moving together, grinding against one another. She ran her hand up the front of his shirt and then back down the length of his chest.

As she inched her way closer to his obvious need for her, Matthew finally came to his senses. He pulled back enough for them both to get some much needed oxygen. Neither spoke for several minutes while they caught their breath.

"Good morning," Cali whispered, followed by a thrilling giggle that went straight to his groin.

He grinned back at her and kissed her neck. "Yes. It is."

With a sigh, Matthew reluctantly stepped back. If he didn't, they would end up going at it on her father's desk.

She leaned back against the wall as he crossed the room and logged off his computer.

"Are you hungry?" he asked when he was done.

"Starving."

Why did she make it sound like she wasn't talking about food?

He had to admit that making breakfast with Cali was some of the most fun he'd had in a while—minus last night, of course. They'd decided to make French toast. He'd dipped the bread into the egg mixture while she'd manned the stove. Every time he added another piece of bread to the griddle, he placed a lingering kiss on her lips. By the end, they were practically making out in front of the stove and almost burnt their food.

"What do you normally do?" Cali asked as she finished the last of her breakfast.

"What do I do?" He was confused by her question.

"Yes." She pushed her plate to the side and leaned forward, resting her elbows on the table. "I mean you're here and have basically put your life on hold. I was wondering what you would normally be doing today if you weren't here."

"Jason usually comes over to my place and we watch the game."

"Oh. Um. Will you . . ." She was quiet for a long moment and then seemed to perk up. "Why don't you invite your brother to come here today?"

Matthew stood and carried their plates over to the sink. He appreciated the sentiment, but it wasn't necessary. "That's okay. Jason and I will survive without yelling at the TV for one Sunday afternoon."

"No," she said, her tone firm. "I'm serious. Invite him over. And Lisa, too. She and I can have some girl time while you and Jason watch the game."

He stared at her from across the room and considered what she said. It would be nice to hang out with his brother for a few hours and he hadn't missed her mention of girl time. They'd both had such a tight schedule lately that they needed to relax a little. "All right. I'll give him a call."

After they finished cleaning up, Matthew strolled into the foyer and dialed his brother. "Two mornings in a row? Can't you find anything better to do while you're shacked up with a beautiful woman?"

Matthew rolled his eyes at his brother's antics. "I was calling to see if you and Lisa wanted to come over today. We can watch the game while Cali and Lisa hang out."

There was some noise on the other end and then his brother was back. "Sounds like a great idea."

"Great," Matthew said. "Around the usual time?"

"We'll be there." Jason sounded happier than Matthew could ever remember and he knew that was because of Lisa.

Matthew disconnected the call and tucked the phone into his pocket. Cali was in the living room, moving some papers out of her way so she could sit down on the oversized couch. Her hair fell down around her shoulders in gentle waves and he remembered running his hands through it the night before.

She must have felt his gaze on her because she looked up and smiled. He felt warmth spread through him as he grinned back at her. It wasn't sexual, although her body still called to him. No, this was something more.

When Cali noticed he was still staring at her, she stood and walked over to him. She was breathtaking. His entire body yearned for her—his heart ached for her. Everything about her seemed to have him transfixed. He couldn't have moved even if he'd wanted to.

She crossed the few remaining feet between them, her eyes sparkling with amusement, and that was when it hit him. He loved her.

Cali slipped her arms around Matthew's waist without hesitation. He wrapped his arms around her and their lips met in a slow and tender kiss. She pressed her body flush against his and he caressed her back with his hands. He tried to pour all the love he felt for her into their kiss.

***

Snaking her hands up his chest, Cali ghosted her fingers along the collar of his shirt. She could feel the muscles beneath as they moved against each other. It was as if she couldn't seem to get close enough to him.

She slipped her right hand below his neckline and played with the skin underneath while cupping the back of his neck with her other to pull him closer. He responded by shifting his weight and turning them slightly. A moment later, she felt the wall at her back as he pinned her against it. She couldn't stop the low moan that left her throat.

At the sound of her pleasure, Matthew leaned in to her more, allowing her to feel his weight against her. It also meant that she could feel his erection straining against his pants, begging for release. Her body temperature soared. She wanted him again. That they'd been together the night before made no difference.

Actually, it made a lot of difference. She knew what it was like to be with him now—knew what it felt like to have him inside her. To feel him touch her . . . kiss her . . .

She wrapped her leg around his waist, trying to get more friction. Their kisses were no longer gentle. She could feel his desire rolling off him and it only fueled hers even more. They were both wearing way too many clothes.

He ran his hand up the length of her leg to her hip, holding her firm as he flexed his hips and pressed his arousal against her. They both gasped, breaking their kiss. She looked up into his eyes and they had a glazed-over quality to them.

Matthew placed a hand against her cheek and took a deep breath. He glanced toward her father's study and she wondered if he was considering using her father's desk. With the way she wanted him at that moment, she would have agreed to just about anything as long as it meant he wouldn't stop, but he seemed to be struggling with the decision.

She was about to suggest they go upstairs when the doorbell rang. He groaned and rested his head against her shoulder. Cali heard him mumble something, but she couldn't make out what it was.

He sighed and lifted his head. There was a look of regret there in his eyes.

Matthew took her face in his hands and brushed his thumbs against her cheeks as their breathing slowed. He placed a whisper-soft kiss on her lips before taking a reluctant step back.

Cali tried to steady herself, but she still felt off-balance. "Are you okay?"

He reached up to tuck her hair behind her ear, lingering a little too long before he pulled his fingers away. "I'm fine. I just think Jason is going to take one look at you and know what we've been doing."

She touched her lips and stared up at him, wondering if she was as flushed as she felt.

The doorbell rang again—this time with a little more impatience.

Knowing she needed to do something, Cali gave Matthew a swift, hard kiss, and then backed away. "I'll be right back."

She walked up the stairs, knowing he was watching her. Cali couldn't wipe the smile off her face.

Once she was at the top of the stairs, she stood out of sight and listened while Matthew greeted Jason and Lisa. She waited until they'd all moved into the kitchen before ducking into the small bathroom near the top of the stairs to see what the damage was.

When she flipped on the light, she realized her swollen lips were the only telltale sign of what she and Matthew had been doing. Her cheeks were a little red, but that was already starting to fade.

The sound of footsteps on the stairs had her turning on the water and quickly washing her hands and splashing some water on her face. If she had to guess, it was probably Lisa coming to look for her.

"You in there, Cali?"

Drying her face with the towel, she reached for the doorknob and opened it. "Hi."

"Hi." Lisa had a strange look on her face. "Matthew said you were still up here. Everything all right?"

Cali gave her a puzzled look, not sure where she was going with her inquiry.

"I mean, you and Matthew are getting along all right?" Lisa asked.

"Yeah, sure." Cali stepped out into the hall. "Why?"

Lisa shrugged. "No reason. I just thought since you were up here and he was down there that maybe you two weren't speaking or something."

"Oh." Cali hadn't considered that her delay would leave that kind of impression. "No. Everything's fine."

Her friend nodded, but still looked unsure.

Cali decided she needed to take the focus off her and Matthew. "So . . . how are things with Jason?"

"Good." Lisa blushed as they made their way down the staircase. "Thank you for inviting us over today. I know it may not seem like a big deal to you or anything, but . . . well, it is to Jason. He really looks forward to spending Sunday afternoons with his brother now that they're both here in Chicago."

Cali grinned. "I'm glad you both could come. And I know Matthew is looking forward to it, too."

The two women headed into the kitchen. They grabbed some drinks out of the fridge and then went to find the guys. They were out on the back deck. Matthew had fired up her father's grill and Jason was standing off to the side with a look of awe on his face. He didn't even seem to notice them until Lisa slid an arm around his waist.

Jason glanced over at Cali, and then pointed to the grill. "That's some piece of equipment you've got there, Ms. Stanton."

Cali laughed. "Thank you, Jason. It's my dad's, but I'll be sure to tell him you approve."

When the grill was ready, Matthew ran inside to get the meat.

He returned with a tray full of pressed hamburgers. They all watched as he placed each patty on the hot grill and listened to it sizzle.

"So," Jason said, pulling Lisa tighter against his side, "you ladies gonna watch the game with us?"

Lisa glanced over at Cali and shrugged. "Sure. Why not?"

"Great!" Jason said with a little too much enthusiasm. Cali had to wonder what he was up to.

Chapter 21

With the hamburgers cooked and their plates piled high with too many salads, the four of them made their way into her father's theater room. It didn't have the high-backed seats some rooms of that type had, but instead it was furnished with a black leather couch, matching love seat, and four reclining chairs. It also happened to have a big screen television that would be perfect for watching the football game.

When they walked into the room, Jason marched over to the long leather couch and tugged Lisa down next to him. Even though the couch could have easily accommodated four people, Jason spread out, making it obvious he'd staked out the area for only him and Lisa.

Cali debated whether or not to sit down on the love seat or to take one of the single chairs. It would be safer to sit in one of the individual chairs, but they were across the room along the wall. Not only would it separate her from their guests, it might make it seem like she and Matthew were avoiding each other.

Before she could talk herself out of it, Cali sat down at one end of the love seat near Lisa. That seemed like a natural thing to do, right?

Matthew hesitated and she wondered what he'd do.

A couple of moments passed, and then he sat on the other end of the love seat. They weren't touching, but he was still close. Too close really. She was hoping she'd be able to keep her hands to herself.

Matthew seemed tense even after Jason turned on the television. Every time she would shift her weight or make a noise of any kind, he would flex his fingers. It was subtle, but she noticed.

Things changed a little after kickoff. Once the ball was in play Jason became more animated than Cali had ever seen him. He was clearly a hometown boy and it didn't take long to figure out that Matthew was, too. He was a bit more reserved about it, but she could still see the boyish elation on his face. She found she was more mesmerized by watching him than the game.

Then again, that realization shouldn't have surprised her. Matthew was captivating. He was brilliant and disciplined, and his sense of humor was swift when he came out from behind that mask he wore. Not only that, Matthew was sweet, warm, and loving.

Matthew was one of the most passionate people she'd ever met. He never did things halfway. It was always all or nothing with him and she found she greatly admired him for it.

Without realizing it, Cali had been edging her hand closer to Matthew's. Her fingers were so close to his where they lay on the love seat between them that she could feel the heat from his body. She wanted to touch him, but she knew she couldn't. Matthew didn't want anyone to know about them—not even Jason and Lisa. He figured if they could fool the two people who knew them best then they could fool everyone else. While she understood, that didn't make it any easier.

As Cali sat there, she realized that Matthew had become important to her . . . so important that she couldn't imagine her life without him. Something between a groan and a whimper slipped past her lips before she could stop it. Matthew heard her and looked over to make sure she was okay.

She met his gaze and saw all the emotions she was feeling reflected back in his eyes. Cali wanted to be alone with him. She wanted to be able to kiss him and feel his body against hers without having to worry who would see them.

Balling her hands into fists, she ordered herself to stop thinking about it and watch the game.

Much to her dismay, Jason and Lisa not only stayed for the first game but a second as well. By the time they said goodbye it was after seven.

She didn't regret inviting them. The day hadn't been all bad, after all. The best part had to be when she and Lisa had a question about a play. Both Matthew and Jason would rush to try and explain it to them. It was cute to see the brothers play off each other.

Hearing the click of the lock on the front door, Cali looked up to find Matthew staring at her. With every moment that passed, the tension between them mounted. They were alone. They didn't have to hold back what they wanted.

Matthew closed the distance between them and pulled her into his arms. He buried his face in the crook of her neck while running his hands up and down her back. "Remind me to never invite my brother over to watch a doubleheader again. That was torture."

Cali chuckled as she circled her arms around him. "Yes, it was."

He grabbed hold of her hips and pressed against her—the sensation causing him to moan.

"We should clean up the kitchen," she whispered, trying to keep her wits about her.

Matthew mumbled what sounded like an agreement, but he didn't let go. Instead, he placed a series of brief kisses along her neck. The last seven and a half hours had been the longest foreplay of her life. She'd thought the last three weeks had been bad, but now she knew what she was missing.

He opened his mouth and gently sucked on her flesh at the base of her neck. She tilted her head to the side, silently begging him for more. Cali never wanted to go so long without being able to touch him again.

Before she realized what he was doing, Matthew was backing them into the living room. Clothing disappeared as they touched . . . kissed . . . loved.

She felt overheated as he lay back on the couch, pulling her down on top of him.

* * *

Matthew was exactly where he wanted to be—naked with Cali straddling him. There was no doubt. He was totally and completely in love with her.

More than anything, he wanted to tell her, but he knew he couldn't do that. She was a doctor, not a businesswoman. When her time here was up, she would go back to Africa or wherever else they sent her. He wouldn't hold her back from doing what she loved. How could he? What kind of man would that make him if he tried?

A pain he'd never experienced before shot through his chest as he gazed into her eyes. She was only his for eight more weeks. *Just eight weeks.*

His body rebelled against that knowledge and he cupped the back of her head, bringing her mouth down to his. His hands roamed her body, the need to stake his claim on her unable to be stifled.

Feeling her bare skin against his was amazing. It felt even better than it had the first time, if that were possible. Maybe it was because he'd admitted to himself that he loved her, or maybe it was because he was becoming more familiar with her body. All he knew was that it was different. She was different.

Matthew had always cared about the women he'd been with on some level, but nothing like this. With Cali, he felt as if he had to be connected with her in every way possible.

He blindly reached for his pants on the floor where he'd kicked them off. When he felt the denim, he practically sighed with relief. He fished his wallet out of his pocket and dumped the contents onto the floor until he found the condom he was searching for.

As soon as he was suited up, he guided Cali down. Her warmth surrounded him and he released a cry deep in his throat. He loved this feeling.

Their joining seemed to have left Cali stunned. She stilled above him and closed her eyes. A look of pure pleasure crossed her face.

Matthew brushed his thumb over her lower lip. She opened her eyes and gazed down at him. There was so much emotion in their brown depths.

He lifted his hips, thrusting deeper . . . harder . . . faster. They stared into each other's eyes and he watched her as she climbed higher and higher toward her release. A moment before she got there, Cali's breath caught in her throat as she choked out his name.

Seeing her go over the edge was all it took. With one final thrust of his hips, Matthew let go.

Cali collapsed on top of him, her breathing shallow. He wrapped his arms around her and cradled her against him. He didn't want to let her go. Ever.

The next morning, he was woken up by a loud gasp and the sound of something hitting the floor. Matthew sat up with a start, instinctually situating his body between Cali and the unknown threat. Only it wasn't a threat—it was Jessie. She was standing in the doorway to his room with her hand over her mouth and a stack of formerly folded towels at her feet.

Matthew tugged at the sheet, making sure Cali was covered. Neither one of them had bothered getting dressed after making love downstairs on the couch the night before.

He held the older woman's shocked gaze for a long moment before sighing. Like it or not, their secret was out. "I'll meet you downstairs?"

It took Jessie a moment to respond, but eventually she nodded and rushed out of the room. She didn't even bother to pick up the towels.

Turning to face Cali, Matthew kissed her shoulder . . . then her neck . . . behind her ear . . .

Her breathing began to pick up and her eyes fluttered open. A slow smile lit her face as she stared up at him. Cali stretched, pushing her ass against him. He couldn't stifle the groan that rumbled deep in his chest.

That only made her smile wider.

She twisted and threw her arms around his neck. "Good morning."

It would be so easy to forget everything outside of her . . . them. He wanted to make love to her again before they had to spend the next nine hours keeping their hands to themselves. Having to sit down and explain to Jessie why no one could know anything was going on between him and Cali wasn't how he'd envisioned starting his morning.

Cali seemed to sense that something was off. "What's wrong?"

He nodded toward the door.

She lifted her head to look and her brow furrowed in confusion.

"Jessie," he said.

Cali's smile faded and she pressed her head against the curve of his shoulder. "What are we going to do?"

"Go down and explain. I don't see that we have any other choice." He skimmed his fingers along her spine. "Hopefully, she will understand why no one can know."

They got dressed and headed down to the kitchen. Jessie was already busy making breakfast. When they walked in, she blushed then turned back to face the stove with a knowing grin. She looked like the cat that ate the canary.

Matthew placed a hand on the small of Cali's back and they both took their regular seats at the island as Jessie set their food in front of them. He took a bite of the ham and cheese omelet, waiting to see what the older woman would do.

Jessie leaned back against the counter and folded her arms across her chest. She was staring them down, apparently willing to wait them out.

He kept his voice even as he spoke. "You can't share what you saw this morning with anyone."

The older woman's eyes widened. She looked first to Cali and then back to Matthew. "And why not?"

Jessie's tone made it clear that she didn't approve of them keeping their relationship a secret.

Luckily, it was Cali who answered her. "It's too dangerous for others to know."

By the look on her face, Jessie still didn't understand.

"Cali's life is in danger," Matthew said. "It's my job to protect her. And I will. But if anyone knows—and I mean anyone—that Cali and I are involved they could use it as leverage against her. Or me. Or even the company to try and get what they want. I can't let that happen." He paused. "I won't let that happen."

The last part was said with a fierceness that caused Jessie to jump. She looked back and forth between Matthew and Cali before settling her gaze on Cali. "Does your father know?"

Cali shook her head. "No. And we'd like to keep it that way."

Jessie frowned.

"I trust Matthew. If he says it's safer this way, then it is." Cali's eyes pleaded with Jessie. "Please?"

"Fine," Jessie said, pressing her lips together. "I won't say anything."

"Thank you." Cali grinned and went back to her breakfast.

"So does that mean we will be moving someone?" Jessie asked after several moments of silence.

Matthew and Cali looked at each other, both confused, then

back to Jessie.

She chuckled. "Well, it's obvious you two will be sharing a room. I just figured it would be easier if all your things were in one place."

"No," Matthew said without missing a beat. "I want everything from the outside to appear that we're still in separate rooms."

"Fine, fine. Have it your way." Jessie waved a dismissive hand and walked over to the sink. "I just hope you both know what you're doing."

An hour later, they arrived at the office and Matthew followed the same routine as he had the previous week. He escorted Cali to her office, greeted Lisa, and repeated his instructions that Cali's door was to remain open at all times and that she was not to be left alone with anyone. As he stood there handing out his instructions, both Cali and Lisa looked as if they wanted to roll their eyes at him. It didn't matter. He had to make sure Cali stayed safe.

His day went by faster than he thought it would. He worked in his office and kept tabs on Cali through the camera he'd installed. She rarely left her desk. From the looks of it, she had as much paperwork to do as he did. Even still, he made sure to check on her every fifteen minutes. Maybe it was overkill, but she'd become way too important to him for something to happen because he wasn't paying attention. Protecting her wasn't just his job anymore.

He'd been hoping to sneak up and have lunch with her, but a phone call from the production manager saying they needed to talk as soon as possible derailed his plans. So instead of spending an hour with the woman who constantly occupied his thoughts, he'd spent it going over shipping and route schedules for the next three weeks.

At two fifty, he was back working at his desk when his computer beeped and a window popped up reminding him of his security briefing with Ms. Stanton. He smiled, closed the reminder, and gathered his things. A lot had changed since last week's meeting when the two of them sat next to each other at her conference table and Cali had insisted on going with him to the jewelry store.

Tension built within him as he thought of Cali lying on the cold ground after that car had hit her. He knew he needed to calm himself down. No one could see the effect she was having on him . . . not even Cali.

He took several deep breaths as he walked out of his office and let Mariana know where he was going. She grinned politely back at him and nodded.

On his ride up in the elevator, Matthew cataloged the details he needed to go over with Cali. The production manager had heard that another attempt was going to be made on a shipment. It was only a rumor, but he wasn't willing to dismiss it either. They'd thwarted more than one hijacking on nothing more than a rumor before.

His thoughts drifted to Cali and how she'd looked this morning as he'd woken her—her lying in his bed, curled up next to him. It was difficult to stay focused on work with an image like that lingering in your head . . . especially when he was on his way to see her.

"Hello, Matthew," Lisa greeted him as he exited the elevator.

"Lisa." He looked over to see Cali's door was open. "Is Ms. Stanton available?"

Lisa startled at his use of *Ms. Stanton*, but he couldn't help it. That was how he'd referred to her before she'd become his . . . girlfriend? Lover? He had no idea what to call her now.

"Yes. She's expecting you," Lisa said.

Matthew grinned, hoping that it was enough to convey his thanks for not making a big deal out of him using Cali's surname.

He walked into Cali's office and closed the door behind him. She glanced up from whatever she was working on and their eyes met. It felt as if they'd been apart for far more than a mere eight hours.

Cali stepped out from behind her desk and strode toward him. She stopped with only about an inch separating them. "Are we alone?"

His answer was to crush her against his chest and cover her mouth with his. The folder he'd been holding fell to the floor.

She gripped his arms, her fingers digging into his flesh. He'd meant to keep it chaste but, heaven help him, he couldn't. Having her in his arms again was too much.

Matthew felt his body respond to her closeness and knew they had to stop. He slowed the kiss and moved his hands to the side of her face, putting some space between them.

Cali blinked up at him. "Hi."

He rested his forehead on hers and grinned. "Hi."

After picking up his folder, he let her lead him over to the sofa that was along the wall. She sat down and urged him to take the seat beside her. It wasn't exactly professional, but looking into her eyes Matthew couldn't deny her. He spread the reports across his lap as she cuddled up to him.

It might not have been the most professional way to conduct a meeting, but it was definitely the most enjoyable.

Chapter 22

When Cali and Matthew arrived home that evening, they found the table in the dining room set for two. There was a lovely flower arrangement with candles on either side waiting to be lit. The setup had romance written all over it.

Cali ran the tips of her fingers along the edge of the table. She and Matthew hadn't discussed the boundaries of their relationship. Were dates even an option?

She glanced over at him and found that he was doing a rather poor job at not laughing.

"Sorry," she said, tilting her head toward the table.

"Why are you sorry?" He had a full-blown smile on his face now.

Cali shrugged. "Jessie seems to be a little . . . excited."

Matthew placed his hands on either side of her face. "That's okay. I can't think of anything I'd rather do than spend a romantic evening with you, Ms. Stanton."

He closed the gap between them and pressed his lips to hers.

"Shall we see what she left us?" he murmured.

"Mmm."

Jessie had prepared a salad for each of them along with a note saying there was lasagna and bread warming in the oven.

"I'll bring the lasagna over to the table if you can grab the salads," he said, his eyes dancing with amusement.

Cali chuckled. "I think I can handle that."

Their meal was pleasant. They talked a little about their day, but most of it was random information. It really did feel like a date.

Cali dipped her spoon into the chocolate pudding Jessie had made them. "You mentioned before that you used to be in the military. What exactly did you do?"

She swallowed the delicious chocolate and scooped up another bite before glancing over at him. He wasn't looking at her, though. His gaze was unfocused as if he were somewhere else.

"Are you okay?" she asked, placing a hand on his arm.

That seemed to snap him out of it. He swiftly finished his pudding and stood, taking his bowl over to the sink.

Cali didn't understand his reaction. Had she said something wrong? Was his job in the military classified?

"I'm sorry. I shouldn't have asked. I understand if you're not able to tell me." More than anything she didn't want this to ruin their evening together.

"No. It's fine." He opened the dishwasher and put his bowl in the rack before walking back over to her. "Are you finished?"

She nodded and handed him her dish.

Matthew strolled back to the counter and repeated the process of rinsing her bowl and putting it into the dishwasher. He was stalling, only she didn't know why.

"I was assigned to a Special Forces unit six months in." He turned to face her for a moment before looking away again. "I think I'm going to work in the study for a while before turning in. I'll see you upstairs?"

It was phrased as a question, but he didn't wait for her to answer before exiting the room. She was left sitting there trying to figure out what had happened. Clearly, he didn't want to talk about his past, but why?

Not only that, but the mask was back. The one she hated. That mask of professionalism—indifference—or whatever you wanted to call it. She'd hoped she'd seen the last of it when they'd stopped ignoring the attraction they felt for each other. Apparently not. Her stomach clenched into knots as she thought of the look on his face.

Cali got up and made sure everything was put away before making her way upstairs. She paused to look at the man bent over the small laptop computer in her father's office. He still wore that blank look from a few minutes ago. She wished more than anything she could know what was going through his mind, but she didn't think approaching him while he was in work mode would get her what she desired.

With one last look, she headed up the stairs.

***

Matthew stayed in the study for as long as he could justify it. He knew his past would come up sooner or later. It wasn't as if he were ashamed of his time serving his country overseas. He just didn't know how Cali would react to the information. The fear of her taking it badly—banishing him from her house . . . her life—wasn't something he wanted to think about. He wasn't sure he could handle it.

Sighing, he powered down his computer and went upstairs.

Cali sat in his bed with a book in her lap. Her hair was pulled back away from her face revealing the graceful curve of her neck and shoulders. She was wearing a silky nightgown that was so thin he could see the outline of her nipples against the fabric. He felt his body temperature rise a few degrees.

He got in a few minutes of ogling before she noticed him standing there. Her eyes held questions and concern. Any hope he'd had of her letting the subject drop faded away.

Removing all but his boxers, Matthew climbed into bed beside her. He leaned back against the headboard, mimicking her position.

She marked her place in her book, laid it on the nightstand beside the bed, and then placed her hands in her lap. He knew she was waiting.

"After my mom died, Jason and I spent a lot of time with my dad." He glanced over to see her watching him intently. "Not that we hadn't before, but it was just . . . more.

"Dad had started his security firm five years earlier. Jason remembers when he was a cop, but I was too young. To me, Dad was always the man in charge, the one with a plan."

Cali had turned her body toward him. He wanted to reach out to her, but he needed to get this out. If he touched her, he never would.

"When I turned ten, he bought me my first rifle." Matthew

smiled at the memory. "We went hunting the weekend after my birthday, just the three of us." He met her gaze. "It was one of the best weekends of my young life."

She nodded, so he continued. "By my sixteenth birthday, I was helping my father with everything from paperwork to surveillance. If I wasn't at school or doing homework, I was helping Dad."

"Where was Jason?" Cali asked, interrupting him. "Was he helping your dad, too?"

Matthew shook his head. "No. At Dad's insistence, Jason went to college for four years. Then he joined the Marines. He wanted out of Chicago and felt that was the easiest way to do it, I guess."

"Is that why you joined? Because of Jason?"

"No." Matthew smiled and reached for her hand. He couldn't help it.

She took his hand and gave it a little squeeze of encouragement.

"Do you remember me telling you about the friend I saw that night at the gala?"

Cali nodded.

"He owned another security firm and used to work on the force with my father. They were best friends—Charles and my dad."

"Were?" She hadn't missed that he'd used the past tense.

"Hmm." Matthew chuckled. "You're making me get ahead of my story, Ms. Stanton."

She pushed against him, teasing. "Sorry."

He flexed his fingers that were still laced through hers. "When I graduated high school, I went off to college. As I said before, it was sort of a requirement with my dad."

Matthew could still see his father sitting at the kitchen table, pointing his fork at him. *"You do your homework. Get good grades. Get a college education. Make something of yourself."*

The memory made Matthew smile. "I graduated with a degree in business administration."

Cali raised her eyebrow in question.

"I know it's hard to believe, but yes, I have a degree in business, of all things."

She laughed.

When she noticed the wicked look he was giving her, she pressed her lips together. "Sorry. Go on."

He snorted. "After college I was at a loss. I really didn't know what I wanted to do with my life. I'd considered going to work for my dad—that was part of the reason I'd chosen my field of study."

Matthew knew they were getting to the part that could change his relationship with Cali forever, but he plunged forward. "Joining the police force was another option. I was an excellent marksman and knew with my dad's connections, I wouldn't have any trouble getting hired on.

"That was part of the problem, though. I was twenty-one and I'd never been away from home . . . never been out on my own." He glanced over at Cali again. "Charles . . . well, he helped me figure it out.

"He came in one Friday night when I was going over some receipts for my dad. We talked about my options." Matthew adjusted their hands so he could trace the lines on her palm. "The next day, I got a letter from Jason telling me about his latest mission. I'd received mail from him before, but for some reason this was different."

Cali didn't say anything. She just listened.

"So I started asking questions . . . talking to people. Jason, Charles—I even tried talking to my dad but as soon as I mentioned the military, he shut me down.

"Two months later an opportunity presented itself when I was at the range. I ran into an Army sergeant who was home on leave. He saw me shoot and asked me to have lunch with him. We ended up talking for over three hours."

Matthew glanced up at her, wanting to see what she'd have to say.

"So your dad isn't friends with Charles anymore because you talked to him about your future?"

"No." Matthew shifted. "That's not quite all of it. More that when I told Charles that I was going to join the Army, he didn't try to stop me."

"Oh."

Cali sat there for several minutes in silence. He wondered how long it would take her to figure out that he'd yet to answer her original question.

Matthew knew exactly when it hit her. Cali jerked her head up and turned her body so that she was facing him. "You said Special Forces earlier. So . . ."

"It was in a unit with five guys. Each one of us had a specialty and we worked as a team."

When he didn't continue, Cali asked, "What was your specialty?"

He held her gaze, trying to prepare himself for, at best, her disapproval and, at worst, her revulsion. "I was a sniper, Cali. It was my job to assassinate people."

Matthew watched as a torrent of emotions crossed over her face and her eyes went out of focus. There was confusion, shock, and maybe even a little fear, but there was nothing he could do. Lying to her hadn't been an option. He was proud that he'd served his country, but he had no idea what he'd do if his time in the Army cost him Cali.

***

It had never crossed Cali's mind that Matthew had been a sniper. Being in the military, she'd assumed he'd had to kill people before, but killing someone in a firefight and having to look into their eyes and shoot was something altogether different. She couldn't imagine what that would be like.

Cali looked into his eyes and saw uncertainty. She got up on her knees, straddled him, and then leaned forward until her lips were pressed against his.

Matthew didn't respond right away, but when he did her heart soared. He slid his hands up her bare thighs under her chemise. She arched her back, bringing their bodies in closer contact. He was already hard and all she wanted was to feel him inside her.

She lifted her arms as he pushed her nightgown up her torso and tossed it onto the floor beside the bed. He held onto her hips, running his thumbs back and forth over the thin lace of her panties. There was a raw emotion in his eyes that sent a thrill of anticipation through her, heightening her senses. She wanted to show him how special he was to her—how important he'd become. It caused an ache deep inside to think of him not being part of her life.

A few seconds later, what she was feeling for him settled over her like an all-encompassing calm. She loved him.

This newfound knowledge brought with it a renewed determination to show him in actions what she couldn't bring herself to say. Cali reached for the hem of his boxers and worked them down his legs then discarded her panties before repositioning herself on top of him. She cupped the back of his head and brought their mouths together in a searing kiss.

Matthew reached into the bedside drawer and took out a condom. Somehow, he managed to sheath himself without breaking their kiss.

Once he had the condom in place, she lowered herself down onto his erection. Cali tilted her head back and closed her eyes, overcome with all the emotions flooding through her at once. She loved this man—loved him as she'd never loved another.

As they moved together, she felt her connection to him growing. She felt it with every touch, every kiss.

All too soon, the desperate need for fulfillment surged through her. She could feel her release coming as she brought their lips together again. Cali thrust her tongue into his mouth, needing to taste him. Her climax raced through her body and she gasped, desperate not to lose the connection.

Matthew held on and didn't let go as she came down from her high. He placed one hand on her hip and the other behind her head as he gazed into her eyes and pumped into her. She almost felt as if she were floating . . . suspended in time.

His breath caught in his throat as he lifted his hips and let himself go.

They both sat there unable and unwilling to move, staring into each other's eyes. What was she ever going to do without him?

When Cali woke up the next morning, she was alone. She smiled and stretched as she remembered the feel of Matthew's fingers as they'd brushed across her skin. After they'd made love, he'd adjusted them so that they were both lying down but he didn't let her go. He'd held her against his chest until she'd fallen asleep.

She ran her hand over the spot in the bed where he'd slept. It was cool to the touch, but it didn't bother her as it had that first morning. Cali knew he was probably downstairs in the gym or working.

Feeling almost giddy, she threw the covers off and slipped the chemise back over her head before hurrying down the hall to her bedroom. She wouldn't have bothered putting anything on at all if not for the fact that she knew Jessie was somewhere in the house.

As the warm water of the shower cascaded over her body, Cali reflected on what she'd learned about Matthew last night. He'd expected her to react badly to what he'd said. She had to assume that was because she was a doctor and her job was to save lives—his had been to take them. Even now, she had trouble picturing him sneaking around a jungle or a desert, lying in wait to kill someone.

However, what struck her most about last night—more than his former profession—was his honesty. It had caused the last safety net over her heart to melt away. Matthew had stolen her heart in every way possible and it didn't matter to her that he'd killed who knew how many while he was in the Army. She knew him—knew him well enough to know that he'd done what he thought was right.

She finished her shower, got dressed, and joined Matthew downstairs for breakfast. He drove her to the office and made sure to keep a safe distance once they got out of the car. Her fingers were itching to touch him as they rode up in the elevator, but she somehow managed to keep her hands to herself.

Lisa was already at her desk when they reached her floor, so their goodbye had to be short and formal. It wasn't what she wanted, but Cali kept reminding herself that there would always be later tonight. She'd have to take comfort in that.

"I will come by to check on you around lunchtime," Matthew said, his tone holding none of the warmth it had earlier that morning when he'd kissed her hello after she'd walked into the kitchen.

Cali nodded. "I'll be here."

He turned on his heels and made a beeline for the elevator.

She waited until the doors closed before going into her office.

Lisa followed.

Cali sat down behind her desk and pulled out her calendar. "What's on the agenda today?"

"You have a meeting at nine o'clock. Then another one at ten." Lisa jotted something down on her pad. "I've left you about forty-five minutes for lunch . . . did you want me to order you something?"

"Yes, please." Cali could already feel the tension building in her muscles.

Lisa smirked. "Should I order enough for one or two?"

Cali knew what her friend was asking. "Might as well order enough for two. I don't know if Matthew will be joining me or not today. I don't know what his schedule is or what all he has planned. For all I know, he's going to install some other gadget to keep tabs on me."

She'd wanted to make it sound as if she was irritated with all of Matthew's hovering and, based on the look on Lisa's face, she'd succeeded.

"He's only trying to protect you," she whispered.

"I know." Cali sighed dramatically. "What else?"

Cali ended up spending her entire morning in meetings. Her first ran over by ten minutes, which made her late for her second. Then, if that wasn't bad enough, her second meeting ran even later and cut into half the time Lisa had carved out for Cali's lunch.

She was hoping that at the very least her twenty-minute lunch would include some private time with Matthew, but when Lisa strolled into her office with a frown on her face Cali knew that wasn't happening.

"Matthew called while you were in your meeting. He had to meet with Detective Martinez, so he won't be joining you for lunch." Lisa handed Cali the salad she'd ordered.

"Thanks," Cali said, giving her friend a weak smile.

"Did you want me to stay?"

"That's okay. I'm sure you have work to do."

Lisa made no move to leave. "It can wait."

Cali nodded and her friend pulled up a chair. While Lisa wasn't the company Cali really wanted, she did manage to keep her from dwelling on the fact that Matthew was somewhere across town trying to track down whoever was after her.

Chapter 23

Matthew was tired. He'd hoped to spend his lunch hour with Cali but instead he'd gotten a call from Martinez asking if he was free. Considering he might have something that could help them catch whoever was after Cali, Matthew couldn't say no. By the time he waltzed into Cali's office a little after five, he was beyond ready to go home and spend a relaxing evening, just the two of them.

Lisa breezed into the office before he'd even had a chance to say anything. She had a stack of paperwork in her arms that she handed to Cali.

"Thanks," Cali muttered as she stared down at the files.

"You're welcome," Lisa grinned with absolutely no remorse. "I'm heading out. I'll see you both tomorrow."

Cali sighed as soon as Lisa left the room. He could sense her weariness. He felt it, too. He wanted nothing more than to comfort her but it was too risky.

Matthew reached for her briefcase and handed it to her. He made sure to let his fingers brush against hers a little longer than was normal, trying to offer some comfort.

She lifted her head and met his gaze. Cali smiled up at him and he almost forgot where they were. The impulse to kiss her was strong.

He took a step back, putting some distance between them, and waited while she loaded the case with everything she needed to take with her. When she was ready, Cali strolled out of her office and Matthew followed. It was a good thing he'd kept his hands and lips to himself since Lisa was still gathering her things at her desk when they walked by.

Twice on the way down to the parking garage he had the urge to reach for her and both times he held himself back. Even though they were technically alone in the elevator, there were cameras. He couldn't take a chance.

Once they were inside his car, he could have given in and touched her. It was within the rules that they'd discussed. They were away from prying eyes. It was not knowing if he'd be able to stop at holding her hand or caressing her thigh that kept his hands on the steering wheel.

By the time they reached the house, Matthew was wound tight. He followed her inside and locked the door behind them before grabbing hold of her upper arm and yanking her flush against him.

Cali's breath came out in a rush as their bodies collided but she didn't protest. He heard her briefcase and purse hit the floor a moment before she gripped his waist. It was all the green light he needed. He twisted her hair around his hand, positioning her mouth exactly where he wanted it, and then kissed her as if his life depended on it.

His lips claimed hers, saying with his mouth what he couldn't with words. Nine hours was too long to go without feeling her against him . . . without tasting her.

Matthew knew how crazy that sounded. But knowing she was so close and he wasn't allowed to be with her the way he wanted was too much. He needed her.

She seemed to understand his need and reached up to undo his tie. He released her and shrugged off his jacket while she went to work on his tie. The rest of their clothes disappeared quickly and before long, he was buried deep inside Cali. Exactly where he wanted to be.

As their breathing returned to normal, the desire to tell her he loved her sprang to the surface again. He wanted to tell her but he knew he couldn't.

"I missed you," he whispered, brushing his lips against hers.

Cali hugged him tighter and kissed the spot on his neck near his collarbone. "I missed you, too."

Lowering her feet to the floor, they both gathered their clothes and raced upstairs to change into something more comfortable. Being with her felt natural. He didn't feel as if he had to work at it.

They ended up back on the couch after dinner. This time they had the files Cali had brought home with her in front of them. She had a meeting with the CFO tomorrow to go over the financials again and had wanted to do some prep.

She groaned. "I feel as if I'm reading a foreign language."

Matthew chuckled. "Would you like some help?"

"I couldn't ask you to do that."

He picked up one of the files. "You didn't ask. I offered."

Cali looked at him for a long moment and then leaned in to give him a chaste kiss. "Thank you."

It took some time, but eventually they got through everything. Even he had to admit that all those numbers were a lot to digest. He was glad he wasn't an accountant.

They were lying in bed that night, Cali curled up next to him, her back pressed up against his chest, when she asked, "Did something happen today?"

"What do you mean?" He grazed his palm down her arm and wrapped it around her waist.

"When you came into my office. I don't know . . . you just looked like you had something on your mind."

He hesitated. It wasn't as if he didn't want to tell her. It was more he didn't want to worry her.

His silence must have been enough of an answer. "Tell me."

Matthew sighed. "We think another shipment is going to be targeted."

"When?" she asked in a voice barely above a whisper.

"Within the next three weeks. I'm working with the production manager to see what we can do. It's a long shot, though. We'll probably have to send an escort like we did last time."

"Jason?"

He shrugged. "Maybe. But we have other options."

She lay there unmoving.

Matthew kissed the top of her shoulder. "Don't worry about it. Jason and I have it under control. That's our job."

"I know."

He cupped the side of her face and she rolled over to face him. There were no words as he leaned in and pressed his lips to hers. She reached up and pulled him down on top of her as both of them wiped all thoughts of shipments, hijackers, and everything else that had to do with the outside world from their minds.

The next day was a little better. Matthew managed to make it upstairs to have lunch with Cali, at least. Unfortunately, Lisa had some things she needed to go over with Cali, so the three of them had all eaten around the conference table and worked while they ate. While it wasn't ideal, being close to her was better than being apart.

That evening as they pulled out of the parking garage, he reached for her. When he'd returned from lunch, there had been an envelope waiting for him. Since Cali had showed him the disturbing correspondence she'd received, all of her mail had been prescreened by either Jason or Matthew. Today, Jason had flipped through her letters and found one that contained more surveillance pictures.

Matthew waited until they were finished with dinner to bring them up. He reached into his pants pocket and pulled out the envelope.

"What's this?" she asked as he handed it to her.

"That was in your mail today."

She paled as she looked at the white envelope. Like the other ones, there were no distinct markings that would make it stand out. It looked like hundreds of others pieces of mail that came through the office every day.

"It's more pictures."

Cali blinked. "Of what? When?"

This was the kicker. "They're from Saturday when we visited your father."

Her eyes went wide. "What? How?"

"I don't know." And he didn't. He'd kept an eye out for a tail the entire time and hadn't seen anyone. Either whoever it was had been able to blend in better than anyone he'd ever seen, or this person had been lying in wait for their visit.

"What do we do?" she asked, bringing his attention back to her and their current conversation.

He placed a comforting hand on her arm. "We continue to do what we've been doing. We pay attention. Be mindful of our surroundings."

She swallowed and nodded.

"We'll find whoever's behind this, Cali. I promise you we'll find them."

***

Cali sat there staring at the envelope. She hadn't even gotten up the courage to look inside. It had a Chicago postmark and no return address exactly like the other two she'd received.

She did her best not to let it bother her or ruin the rest of her evening with Matthew, but as she lay curled in his arms that night, she began thinking about the what-ifs. What if the mole got to her despite all the precautions they'd put in place? And if this person were to find out about her and Matthew's relationship, would he or she try to hurt him, too?

That thought had her tightening her hold on him. Matthew adjusted his grip on her, hugging her closer. His deep, easy breathing told her he was sound asleep—his action had been purely instinctual. Knowing that should have made her smile but there was too much weighing on her mind.

On Friday, Cali was sitting at her desk going over reports. The never-ending paperwork was depressing, but she couldn't seem to wipe the smile off her face. Things with Matthew were going good. Really good. He'd had lunch with her three times that week and she was hoping he would be free again today.

Cali was so lost in her fantasies about her head of security that she jumped when Lisa's voice came through the intercom on her phone. "Cali, there's a Rachael Michaels here to see you. She says she's a friend?"

This time the smile on Cali's face had nothing to do with Matthew. "Thanks, Lisa. I'll be right out."

When she walked out of her office, Rachael spotted her instantly and enveloped her in a hug. "It's good to see you again, Cali."

"What are you doing here?" Cali demanded as they broke apart and she took a long look at her friend. "Not that I'm not glad to see you. I just thought you were still in Africa."

Rachael laughed. "Up until two days ago, I was."

Cali shook her head in disbelief. She and Rachael had worked side by side for almost two years while she was overseas. "How long are you here?"

Her friend shrugged. "Not sure. I needed a little civilization so I decided to take a break. A month? Maybe two? I'm going to play it by ear and see what happens."

That sounded like the Rachael she knew.

"I'm glad you came to see me," Cali said. "It's good to see a friendly face."

"Well, I did have a reason for stopping by today. I was hoping I could persuade you to join me for lunch. Are you free?" Rachael asked.

"Yep. Just let me grab my purse."

Cali ran into her office to get her purse from where she kept it in her desk. When she turned around, however, she came face-to-face with Lisa who was holding a cell phone out in front of her.

"What—"

The phone on her desk rang before she could get her question out. With a sigh, Cali picked it up. She already knew who was going to be on the other end.

"Where are you going?" Matthew asked, not even giving her a chance to say hello. He didn't sound upset, only curious.

She leaned her hip against her desk and cradled the phone against her shoulder. "A friend of mine is in town and invited me to lunch."

"Who?" His tone was sharper this time.

Cali ran a frustrated hand through her hair. "We worked together."

"Where?"

"Africa." She was trying not to lose her temper.

He didn't answer right away. "I'm coming with you."

"No!"

"No?"

She shook her head. "You can't. How would I explain it to Rachael?"

"I don't care what you tell her or what she thinks. I don't know anything about this person. I won't take a chance with you like that." There was a hard edge to his voice that she didn't like.

"That's ridiculous. I've known her for two years."

"In case you've forgotten, someone took pictures of you in Africa as well. I don't trust people I don't know and I don't know her."

He wasn't going to back down. But neither was she.

"Well, I do."

They were both breathing hard and neither said anything for a while. She had no idea how long they were locked in a sort of limbo but movement behind Lisa caught her eye. Cali looked up to find Rachael hovering in the doorway.

"Sorry to interrupt," Rachael said as she strolled into the office.

"Take her to Marc's? I can follow behind and sit at another table," he said, almost pleading.

Cali knew that was the best she was going to get. If she refused, Matthew would find a way to follow her anyway or stop her from going altogether. "Sure."

He released a deep breath. "Thank you."

She hung up the phone and turned her attention to Rachael. "Ready to go? I was thinking of this little Italian place nearby."

Fifteen minutes later, Cali and Rachael entered the same Italian bistro where Cali had first gotten to know Matthew. They sat down at a table along the wall and she noticed Matthew and Jason enter the restaurant a few minutes later. Matthew looked her way for a split second before following Jason to a table on the other side of the room.

Cali did her best to ignore them as she and Rachael enjoyed their lunch.

"So what have you been doing since you've been back in Chicago?" Rachael asked as the server brought their meals.

"Working, mostly." Cali chuckled. "Who knew running a company was so much work?"

Rachael laughed right along with her. "Are you trying to tell me you've had no time for a social life?"

"I did go out with my assistant, Lisa, and some of her friends once."

"Oooh. Be still my heart. Once."

Cali picked up the wrapper from her straw and threw it across the table at Rachael.

Her friend picked it up and threw it right back at Cali. "Seriously, though, all you've been doing is working since you got back stateside?"

"That and visiting my dad."

"How's he doing?" Rachael asked.

"Better. They're saying at least another seven weeks before he can return to work."

"Bummer."

"Yeah."

They were quiet for a few minute as they ate, then Rachael looked at her across the table. She had a gleam in her eye Cali wasn't sure she liked.

"What are you doing tonight?" Rachael asked.

Matthew instantly came to the forefront of her mind, but considering she was still ticked at him . . .

"Nothing much. Why?"

"Come out with me. We can hit a club. Do some dancing. Who knows, maybe we'll even meet some hot guys." Rachael's suggestion didn't surprise her. The girl liked to party.

"I'm not—"

"Please?" Rachael batted her eyelashes dramatically, making Cali laugh.

"Okay, okay. I'm sure Lisa can make a recommendation."

Rachael grinned. "That's great. Maybe we can all go together. The more the merrier, as they say."

After Cali said goodbye to Rachael in the lobby at Stanton Enterprises, she went straight up to her office. She didn't see Matthew again until he came to her office to pick her up at the end of the day. One look at his face told her he already knew about her plans with Rachael for later that night and it didn't take a genius to figure out who'd told him.

He was quiet as they made their way home. She was expecting him to say something once they were alone, but it never happened. Things hadn't been this awkward between them since that first trip home from seeing her father.

Cali knew he was upset and on some level she understood but that didn't mean she wasn't angry in her own right. Rachael was her friend and Cali wasn't going to feel guilty about spending time with her while she was in town. Matthew was treating her like a child.

As they pulled into the driveway and he parked the car around the back of the house, she glanced over at him. He was staring straight ahead, his jaw tight.

Her relationship with him had been the first impulsive thing she'd done in years. She loved him, but she couldn't let him control her. There was nothing wrong with what she wanted and she wasn't going to let him talk her out of it.

Matthew climbed out of the car and she followed him inside. He marched through the door and directly into the study.

Cali didn't know whether or not she should follow him, but curiosity got the better of her. She found him sitting in front of his laptop typing away. He appeared to be totally focused on whatever he was doing.

His nostrils flared as she entered the room. It was the only acknowledgement he gave her.

"So this is your answer? Ignoring me?" she asked, her voice thick with sarcasm.

"No. My answer is to do my job to the best of my ability and try to keep you from getting yourself hurt."

"What's that supposed to mean?"

Matthew continued to look at the screen and not at her. "It means that since you will not *trust* me to do my job—"

"What the hell are you talking about? I *do* trust you."

Finally, he looked up from whatever he was doing and met her gaze. "No. You don't."

Cali didn't know what to say. She'd expected him to be angry, yes, but trust? How could he think she didn't trust him? She loved him.

She stood there staring at him in a state of shock for several minutes before forcing her body to move.

Chapter 24

Matthew heard her walk away, but he didn't look up. He was fuming inside. A part of him wanted to lock Cali in a room and keep her there for the foreseeable future. Reason, of course, told him he couldn't do that but reason wasn't making a lot of headway at the moment.

How could she not trust him? It was his job to protect her and yet she'd agreed to go out to a crowded public place with a woman he'd never even met. Not only that, but it was Lisa who'd had to tell him about the outing when he'd called up to check Cali's schedule.

It had his blood boiling that Cali didn't trust him. If she had, she would have called him immediately. This Rachael Michaels was due to arrive in less than an hour and he needed to find out everything he could about her in that short period of time.

Despite how furious he was at Cali, he still loved her. He wouldn't be able to live with himself if she got hurt . . . or worse.

After fifty minutes of digging, Matthew hadn't come up with much on this Rachael woman. Everything looked perfect—too perfect for his peace of mind. No criminal record. No citations. Not even a parking ticket.

Maybe he was looking for trouble where it didn't exist. Maybe he was letting his feelings for Cali cloud his judgment. He honestly didn't know and it was slowly driving him mad.

Shutting down his laptop, Matthew left the study and jogged up the stairs to his room. He dug in his bag until he found what he was looking for. Palming the device, he went to find Cali.

She was sitting on the edge of her bed, putting on her boots.

He paused at the doorway for only a moment and then crossed the room to stand in front of her.

"You need to wear this tonight," he said, holding out the device.

Cali stared up at him then at his hand. "What is it?"

"It's a GPS tracker. It will let me keep tabs on you even if you're not in my line of sight."

"Matthew—"

He could tell she was going to fight him on this. "This isn't up for negotiation, Cali."

Cali narrowed her eyes at him and he wondered if she was going to flat out refuse. Then she snatched the dime-sized tracker out of his hand. "Fine. Where should I put it?"

"Your bra would probably be best."

Cali sighed and lifted her shirt.

He worked quickly to secure the GPS to her bra right where the cup met the shoulder strap. It took every bit of professionalism he had in him not to pull her into his arms and kiss her until she changed her mind. She had no idea the potential danger she was putting herself in and she didn't seem to care.

When he was satisfied it was secure, he stepped back and she lowered her shirt.

"I'll wait upstairs until you're outside so Ms. Michaels doesn't see me here."

Cali nodded.

"You're going to Faux?"

"Yes." She sighed.

"Anywhere else?"

"No." She grabbed her purse and a jacket off the bed then turned back to face him. "Anything else you want to know?"

He knew she was upset with him, but Cali wasn't taking the threat to her safety seriously. Not tonight, anyway. For whatever reason, her desire to spend time with this friend was overriding her sense of self-preservation.

"Just try not to spill anything on your shirt tonight. It could disrupt the signal."

She rolled her eyes, brushed past him, and walked out the door. He heard her footsteps as she descended the stairs. And a few minutes later, he heard the doorbell ring. It was showtime.

***

Cali tried to shake off her interaction with Matthew as she went to answer the door. He'd been so cold and professional as he'd attached the small device to the inside of her bra. The lover she'd known the past few days was nowhere to be found—there was no affection in his touch.

Sighing, she opened the door to find Rachael all decked out in a flashy club dress.

"Ready?" Rachael asked.

"Yep." Cali draped her jacket over her arm and followed Rachael out the door.

As they drove through the streets of Chicago to the club, Cali glanced in the side mirror a few times looking for Matthew. He'd said he would be following them, but she didn't see his car. Then again, maybe with the tracker he didn't have to be all that close.

The longer she sat there in the car, the more her anger at him began to fade. Was he being overbearing? Yes. But Cali knew it was because he was trying to protect her. That didn't mean she had to like it.

Rachael found a place to park on the street a block away from Faux and they made their way to the entrance where Lisa, Jen and Becky were already waiting. Cali made the introductions and then they all made their way inside.

An hour later, Cali was sitting alone at a corner table watching her friends dance. She'd joined in for a bit, but her heart wasn't in it. All she could think about was her fight with Matthew earlier—his insisting she didn't trust him kept echoing through her mind. Did he really think that, or was it something he'd said in the heat of the moment?

Cali didn't understand. She trusted him with her life . . . her heart. But Rachael wasn't the enemy. She was a friend. One of the few true friends she'd had overseas. Why couldn't he understand that?

She was so lost in thought Cali didn't notice Lisa return to the table. "You okay?"

Taking a sip of her drink, Cali smiled. "Yeah."

Lisa frowned. It was obvious she didn't believe her.

"I'm fine. Really."

"Did something happen? With Matthew, I mean?"

Cali's eyes widened. "Wha-what do you mean?"

Her friend leaned forward so she wouldn't have to raise her voice over the music. "Well . . . when he came upstairs to pick you up this afternoon, he didn't seem to be in the best mood."

"And why do you think that is, Lisa? I know you told him. Why couldn't you have just let me handle it?" Cali felt her anger rising to the surface again.

"Look, I don't know what's going on with you two. Last week you were struggling to be civil to one another and this week, it's like you've both done a complete one-eighty."

"What does that have to do with anything?" Cali demanded.

"Maybe nothing. Maybe everything." Lisa crossed her arms across her chest and leveled a look at Cali. "What I want to know is why you didn't call and tell him right after lunch. You know you should have."

Cali opened her mouth ready to tell Lisa what she could do with her opinion when what her friend had said registered. Why hadn't she called Matthew and told him right away?

Before she had a chance to think on it too much, Rachael plopped down beside her. She reached for her drink and downed half of it. "Ah. That's better. You ready, Cali?"

"For?" Cali asked.

The next thing Cali knew she was being pulled out onto the dance floor. Rachael dragged her about ten feet from the table and came to a stop in front of a tall man with sandy blond hair and green eyes. "Cali, this is Lance. Lance. Cali."

Then Rachael whispered in her ear, "Let's see if we can lift that mood of yours and end that long dry spell, huh?"

A second later Rachael was gone, leaving Cali alone on the dance floor with Lance.

He took a step forward and place one hand on her hip. "Rachael says you're a doctor?"

"Yeah." Cali looked around to see if she could spot her friend, but there were too many people around. She couldn't even see their table from here.

His other hand found her waist and they began to sway their hips with the music.

"I don't think I've seen you here before." As he said this, he pressed their bodies closer together. It was subtle, but she was sure it wouldn't take much encouragement on her part and he'd be ready to take things to a more private place.

"I don't get out often."

"Beautiful woman like you shouldn't be hiding herself away." He skimmed his hand up her side and back down again.

The questions continued for three more songs. With each one, there was more touching and grinding. Unfortunately for him the only thing his actions had her doing was comparing his touch to Matthew's. She remembered him dancing at the club that night with that woman and wondered if it would ever be like that for them. Would they be able to go out dancing at a club once this was all over?

The thought of Matthew touching her . . . pressing against her body in a sensual way as they moved to the music . . .

Cali released a low moan just thinking about it.

Her dance partner heard her and misinterpreted her reaction. He took it for the encouragement he'd been waiting for and pulled Cali's body roughly against his. She could feel his excitement pressing against her stomach. There was no mistaking his intentions.

She tried to back away but he only held her tighter, smashing her breasts against his chest. Screw being subtle. Cali snaked her hands down his torso to the waistband of his jeans. She felt him twitch beneath her fingers and he arched to give her better access.

Never one to miss an opportunity, Cali reached between his legs and grabbed hold of him with all her strength.

He released her instantly and she eased up on the pressure a little before squeezing again. She looked him straight in the eye and said, "I think our dance is over. Don't bother me again."

Cali didn't wait for a response before she released him and walked away. Now she had to find Rachael and give her hell for tossing her to the wolves.

It took her all of five minutes to find her friend. She was at the bar downing shots with a cute redhead.

"Cali!" Her name came out slurred. How many shots had

Rachael done?

"Can we talk?" Although Cali had doubts her friend would remember any of the conversation.

"Sure," Rachael said a little too loud. She ran a teasing hand down the arm of the redhead. "Don't go anywhere. I'll be right back."

Cali took hold of Rachael's hand and led her across the room away from the bar and dance floor. "Are you all right?"

Rachael laughed. "Of course I'm all right. I'm having fun."

Looking into her friend's eyes, Cali tried to gauge how drunk Rachael was.

"Are you leaving?" Rachael asked.

"What?"

"With Lance. Are you leaving with Lance?" Rachael wiggled her eyebrows suggestively, but in her drunken state it just looked strange. "He's a cutie."

Cal sighed. "No. I'm not leaving with Lance."

"Why not?"

"Because he's not my type."

"See if I try to set you up again, Cali Stanton. Lance was a sure thing," Rachael huffed.

"I'm sure he was, but I prefer to find my own dates."

Rachael got a wicked smile on her face, grabbed hold of Cali's hand, and started backing toward the dance floor. "Well, then, let's get you out there so you can show 'em what you've got."

It was well after midnight by the time Lisa dropped Cali off at her father's house. They'd taken Rachael back to her hotel. She would probably have a hangover in the morning, but she'd survive. Rachael was a party girl so she was used to it.

Matthew's car was already in the driveway when they pulled up. It looked as if it had been there the entire night. She knew he was in the house waiting for her.

A war raged inside her as she waved goodbye to Lisa and strolled into the house. She wanted her Matthew back—the man who could set her on fire with one touch. But what about today? The independent woman within her couldn't dismiss that.

So instead of going to him like her body wanted, she climbed the stairs and went to her room. She needed a shower to wash away the smell of the club and the memory of Lance's hands.

When Cali slipped into bed that night something felt—off. She laid her head down on her pillow and closed her eyes, praying for sleep to come. But it didn't. Her mind was racing and her heart was aching.

She knew what the problem was. Matthew wasn't there beside her, his even breathing lulling her to sleep.

Cali fought it for as long as she could before glancing over at the clock. It was two thirty in the morning. She'd been awake for over twenty hours straight. She should be exhausted. Her mind, however, didn't seem to agree.

Her options were to continue to lie there for the next four hours—pretending to sleep—or she could go talk to Matthew. She didn't like either of those options. Her body needed sleep. As for talking to Matthew, Cali wasn't even sure he'd want to talk to her after their fight. That wasn't even factoring in that it was close to three in the morning. He was probably asleep.

She lay there for several more minutes arguing with herself before she forced herself out of bed and walked down the hallway to his bedroom. If he was asleep then she'd turn around and go back to her own room. She'd have to suffer through her sleepless night whether she wanted to or not.

Nudging open his door, Cali peeked inside. Her gaze immediately found his staring back at her through the darkness. They were clear as crystal. He hadn't been sleeping either.

Cali stepped into the room with a little more courage. She strolled over to the edge of his bed and sat down.

They sat in silence for several minutes. When she realized he was going to wait her out, she averted her eyes and swallowed. "I think we need to talk."

He sat up. "I agree."

She laced her fingers together in her lap and looked up at him. "Why did you say that I don't trust you?"

"Because you don't." His answer was so final.

She glanced over at him, but there was nothing there for her to go on. His expression was almost as cold as it had been before she'd left for the club.

"Why didn't you call me after lunch and tell me about Rachael inviting you to the club? Why did I have to hear it from Lisa when I called at four thirty to get your schedule for Monday?"

Cali stilled, remembering yelling at Lisa earlier. She was going to have to apologize.

Matthew shifted a little, waiting for her answer.

It was a good question. Why hadn't she called him? "I don't know."

He crossed his arms over his chest and narrowed his eyes a little.

She sighed and rubbed a hand across her forehead. "I guess it's just been a long time since I've had to justify my actions to anyone."

"So why didn't you say that?" He uncrossed his arms and relaxed his shoulders.

Cali shrugged and took a deep breath. "By the time we got home, I knew you were upset."

Matthew snorted.

She ignored it. "Like I said, I'm not used to justifying myself to anyone. And, well . . . you got my feathers ruffled, so to speak."

For the longest time he looked at her. It was as if he was taking her measure and it made her slightly uncomfortable.

After several minutes had passed and he still didn't say anything, Cali brushed her fingers along the length of his leg and met his gaze. "I do trust you."

He moved his hand down to cover hers and smirked. "I'm sorry I ruffled your feathers."

Cali smiled. "I'm sorry, too. You're right. I should have called you."

They sat there holding hands for a few moments. She felt as if a huge weight had been lifted from her shoulders. And with her anxiety gone, Cali could feel her eyelids starting to droop.

Matthew slid back down under the covers and tugged on her arm, encouraging her to crawl in next to him.

She climbed up onto the mattress and under the covers. They turned to face each other and laced their fingers together. He wrapped his other arm around her shoulder and pulled her against him.

Cali snuggled herself closer, enjoying his warmth. It felt good to be next to him again. She felt safe. Protected. Loved. There was nowhere else she'd rather be than here in his arms.

Chapter 25

Matthew sat at his desk on Wednesday morning reviewing the previous night's security footage when there was a knock on his door. "Come in."

The mail clerk ambled inside with a stack of envelopes.

"Just put them on the corner of the desk there," Matthew said, waving his hand in the location he mentioned.

The man nodded, placed the letters on the desk, and then left.

Alone again, Matthew went back to what he'd been doing. There'd been no additional sightings of their mystery woman in the garage, or elsewhere for that matter. Since they knew the footage had been altered, he wasn't really surprised. What he wanted to know was why whoever it was didn't delete the footage entirely if they were trying to cover their tracks. Had they ran out of time? He thought it would have been easier to delete than manipulate.

Then there was the footage from the night Cali had been hit. He'd reviewed it all himself—again—and some from the following morning hoping to find something of interest. Once more he'd come up empty-handed. There wasn't one person he could place at all three incidents.

Matthew ran a hand back and forth over the top of his head in frustration. The number of people in the building at the time in question wasn't huge, and the number in the building the night Cali was hit by that car was even shorter. If he also took into account those people who were in the building the next morning and could have deleted the footage, the list was much too long for his liking. IT. Security personnel. Half the executive secretaries and even a good chunk of the executives themselves. It went on and on.

All he needed was a break—one little mistake on the part of whoever was behind this and Matthew would have them.

Sighing, he leaned back in his chair, steepling his fingers in front of him. Over the last few days, he'd also done some more digging on Rachael Michaels. He'd done every type of search he could think of and still came up with nothing. There was something about her that rubbed him the wrong way, but he couldn't put his finger on it.

The stunt she pulled on Saturday didn't help that nagging feeling he had in his gut either. He and Cali had been about to leave for the lake house when Rachael showed up unannounced on their doorstep. She'd been understandably curious about his presence, so Cali made up some story about him having business to discuss with her father.

It sounded weak to him, but Rachael seemed to buy it and that's what mattered.

Much to his dismay, Rachael ended up tagging along with them. Her presence in the car meant they had to keep things professional. Once they arrived at the lake house, Rachael stuck to Cali like glue. The entire day was awkward.

It was almost seven by the time they got back to the Stanton estate. After spending the day keeping his hands to himself, he was looking forward to some alone time with Cali. That, of course, didn't happen. Rachael breezed inside the house and made herself comfortable.

Since Rachael couldn't know Matthew was staying there, he'd asked to use the bathroom and ducked upstairs to his room to retrieve the GPS he'd had Cali wear the previous night. When he came back downstairs, he caught her gaze and motioned toward the door. Luckily, she took the hint and told Rachael that she was going to walk me out.

He'd spent a good four hours sitting in his car down the street watching the little dot on the screen of his phone while he waited for Rachael to leave.

On Sunday, Jason and Lisa came over again to watch the game. Luck was on his side this time when Lisa announced that she had to leave about four o'clock. As soon as their car left the driveway, Cali and Matthew had walked hand in hand up the stairs to his room and stayed there for the rest of the night.

He'd only known Cali for a month, but already he couldn't imagine his life without her. It terrified and amazed him at the same time. Matthew had to constantly remind himself that he didn't have forever with her. Once her father was back on his feet, she'd be off to Africa again.

His phone beeped, reminding him to check on Cali. He tapped a couple of times on his phone and the camera feed from her office appeared. A slow smile spread across his face. She was sitting at her desk, talking on the phone. Her hair was piled on top of her head in a messy bun and little pieces were falling around her face. She was absolutely gorgeous.

Placing the phone on his desk, Matthew went back to the security footage. He wanted to have lunch with her today and in order to do that he needed to get this done.

Two hours later, he clicked the last screen closed. He went through last night's footage with a fine-tooth comb and didn't find any evidence of suspicious activity. That didn't mean much, though, considering whoever his mole was had already tampered with the footage twice before—that they knew of.

With that done, he reached for the mail the carrier had brought in earlier. The mailroom separated Cali's mail from his with a rubber band. He thumbed through his pile first. It was much smaller than hers and comprised mostly of companies trying to sell him things. Matthew shredded most of it.

Moving on, he began sorting through Cali's stack. There was an invitation from the Chicago Museum of Art for a fundraiser next month and a few things from some of their bigger clients. He laid them aside and moved on. It was unlikely they'd be sending her anything suspicious.

He paused when he came across a plain white envelope almost an inch thick. It had a Chicago postmark like the others she'd received and no return address. An empty feeling settled in the pit of his stomach. He didn't need to open it to know it contained more pictures of Cali.

***

By the time lunch rolled around, Cali was more than ready for a break. Her phone had been ringing off the hook this morning. Most of the calls were from board members irritated because they felt more needed to be done to protect the shipments. She'd tried to assure them that everything possible was being done, but some were more easily placated than others.

She sat at her desk with her head in her hands when someone knocked at her office door. It was open per Matthew's orders.

Cali looked up, trying to prepare herself for whoever it might be. When she saw Matthew waltzing into the room, she relaxed. "Hi."

He closed the door behind him. "Hello."

Something wasn't right.

Matthew walked to the conference table and she got up to follow him. He set the food down on the table and sat.

Cali lowered herself into the chair beside him, but didn't pick up her sandwich. "What's wrong?"

He stopped with his food halfway to his mouth. "You got more pictures today."

"Oh," she said, finally reaching for her food. "Can you tell when they were taken?"

"Yes."

When he didn't elaborate, she began to get worried. "Well, that's a good thing, right? I mean, at least it's something."

"Yeah, it's something," he muttered. Maybe she was imagining it, but she detected sarcasm.

Cali debated if she should let it go, but then she remembered the last time they'd let something fester. She placed her hand on his arm and he met her gaze. "What's wrong?"

He hesitated then set his sandwich down and placed his hands flat on the table in front of him. "The pictures were taken Friday at the club." Matthew held her gaze. "They were there, Cali. Inside. With you."

"I didn't see anyone," she whispered, trying to recall seeing anyone who looked out of place.

Matthew snorted and averted his gaze. "I seriously doubt you'd see them unless they wanted to be seen."

She still felt as if she were missing something. "Is that all?"

He looked at her then but he remained silent.

Cali picked up her discarded straw paper and twirled it absently around her finger. "I mean . . . you seem . . . distant. Was there a letter, too? Did it say something I should be concerned about?"

After what felt like forever, Matthew leaned back in his chair and crossed his arms. "No note. There were several pictures. All of them were taken inside the club. Most of them were of you . . . and a man. Dancing."

Cali knew he was talking about Lance and if the photographer had snapped the pictures at the right times, she could only imagine what had been going through Matthew's head when he'd seen them. She remembered how she'd felt seeing him at the club dancing with that woman and back then they weren't together. Not that they were together now. Not really. But he had to know she'd never . . .

When she looked into Matthew's eyes, she saw the conflict there. As she continued to stare into his eyes she realized why he looked the way he did. It wasn't that she'd danced with someone else. It was that she hadn't told him. Again. She realized that he wasn't angry—he was hurt.

She knew she had to fix this. Now. "His name was Lance. We danced. He got . . . well, he took a few liberties that I didn't appreciate, so I took care of it."

He still didn't move or break eye contact.

"It was an experience I'd rather forget, which is why I didn't say anything to you about it." She paused. "I'm sorry."

Matthew looked away then back to her. "You don't owe me anything, Cali."

"How can you say that?" It was as if he'd slapped her.

He sat up straight and shook his head. "It doesn't matter."

"Of course it does! Matthew, I . . ." She'd been about to tell him she loved him, but she let the words die in her throat. Cali had no idea how he felt about her, but did he really think it didn't matter? "I care about you. You have to know that."

This time when he looked at her the hardness was gone. "I care about you, too."

Matthew reached for her hand and laced their fingers together. He smiled and they sat there for a while enjoying the moment.

The sound of a throat clearing caused them both to look toward the door. Lisa was standing there only a few feet away with a knowing grin on her face. They had been caught.

Cali and Matthew stared at Lisa for a long minute. Neither had moved. Their hands were still linked together. She had no idea how Matthew would handle it, but she was leaving the ball in his court. They were his rules, after all.

He looked at Cali and gave her hand a squeeze before turning his attention back to Lisa. "Was there something you needed?"

Her assistant's brow furrowed. "Um . . . yes. Cali, your father is on line one asking to speak with you. If you're available."

The implication was there but Cali chose to ignore it. She stood. "Sure."

Matthew trailed behind her as she walked over to her desk. She paused before picking up the phone and turned around to find him standing only inches away. Although she knew they should still keep public displays to a minimum, Cali needed his touch. She took a step forward and within seconds his lips found hers.

Their kiss didn't last long but by the time he pulled away, Cali felt as if she were floating. She opened her eyes to find his staring back at her full of heat and her heart began to race.

Her phone beeped, reminding her she had a call waiting. She took a deep breath in an attempt to calm her erratic heart and reached for the phone.

"I'll see you at five," Matthew said as he moved toward the door.

Lisa stood several feet away and Cali had no doubt her friend would pepper her with questions the minute the opportunity presented itself. Lucky for her, she had a call waiting.

Taking another cleansing breath, Cali picked up the phone. "Hi, Dad."

"Hi, sweetheart. How's your day going?"

Her father had been calling to check on her. Apparently, one of the board members had called him and given him a heads-up about the heated discussion that had taken place the day before during the board meeting. He'd offered to talk to the board himself, but she told him she was taking care of it. What he needed right now was to rest.

Lisa must have been watching her phone because five seconds after Cali hung up with her father her assistant marched into her office, closing the door behind her. "Start talking."

"I don't know what you want me to say."

"Okay. Let's start with you telling me how long this has been going on." Cali opened her mouth to answer, but Lisa cut her off. "Was it that night after the gala? I heard you two danced together. Oh. Have you slept with him yet? Hmm. We'll have to compare notes." Lisa chuckles. "Why didn't you tell me? Does Jason know?"

Cali laughed. "If you stop with all the questions, I'll tell you."

Lisa huffed and sat down in the chair across from Cali. "Fine. Spill."

"Okay, okay." Cali held up her hands in surrender. "It happened about two weeks ago. The morning after the gala. Things had been building and, well . . . it just sort of happened."

"So you've been together for two weeks?"

"Yeah."

Lisa frowned. "Why didn't you say anything?"

She sounded hurt. "I'm sorry, but Matthew thought it best if no one knew. He figured if we could fool you and Jason then we could fool anyone since you two know us best."

Her assistant didn't look convinced. "You should have told me."

It was obvious that Lisa felt betrayed and, to be honest, Cali couldn't blame her. If Lisa had kept her relationship with Jason a secret from her now that they were friends, Cali would probably feel the same way.

"My father doesn't even know," Cali said, hoping that would help.

It seemed to. The crease in Lisa's brow eased a little.

"Wow. I can't believe we're dating brothers." Lisa giggled. Then her expression became serious again. "Does that mean you're staying?"

Cali took a minute to consider her answer. It was something she'd been thinking about a lot recently. She couldn't imagine her life without Matthew anymore, but she had no idea what he wanted. They'd never talked about the future. Plus, everything was so new.

Even with the uncertainty, Cali already knew her answer. Over the last month, Chicago had become her home. Her father was here. Her friends were here. And . . . Matthew was here.

"I'll probably stay." Then realizing how that sounded given the direction of their conversation, she added, "But not because of Matthew."

Lisa raised her eyebrows.

Cali shrugged. "I've missed my dad. And Chicago. I still don't want to run Stanton Enterprises, no matter how much fun this last month has been."

Her friend chuckled.

"I don't know. I'm sure I could get a job at one of the local hospitals. I have plenty of trauma experience so an ER is definitely an option."

It took Lisa a long moment to respond. "Does Matthew know that?"

"No. And I'd appreciate it if you didn't say anything."

Lisa sat forward and Cali already knew what she was going to say.

"I mean it. Not to Matthew and not to Jason. Matthew's got enough to worry about right now without that, too. We'll deal with it later. If there is a later."

"Cali—"

"Please, Lisa. Just let me handle this my way."

Reluctantly, Lisa nodded.

Before either of them could say more, there was a knock on the door. Lisa got up to answer it.

"Oh. I'm sorry," Rachael said. "I didn't mean to interrupt. I can come back later. There wasn't anyone out here so I thought . . . well, it doesn't matter."

Cali stood. "No, it's fine. Lisa and I were just finishing up. Come on in."

Rachael sashayed into the office and took the seat Lisa had recently vacated while Lisa slipped out of the room, leaving the door open behind her.

"I never did tell you how impressed I am with this room," Rachael said. "This is some pretty nice stuff, you know? A lot better than what passed for your office in Eldoret."

Cali laughed and sat back down behind her desk. "Yeah. My dad has good taste. Or at least his interior designer does."

Her friend smiled. "So, Cali, I was thinking. You. Me. Dinner. Tonight."

Her recent fight with Matthew came to the forefront of her mind. He'd want as much information on where they were going as possible. "Where were you thinking?"

Rachael's eyes lit up with excitement. "There's this little place I've been hearing about called Ruby's. They're supposed to have the best steak in town." She paused for a moment and lowered her voice. "I've also heard the waiters aren't bad to look at either. Who knows, maybe neither one of us will be going home alone tonight."

Cali blushed. Even if she wasn't with someone at the moment, hitting on waiters wasn't her thing. It was Rachael's, though, and she wouldn't deny her friend a good time while she was in town. "Sure. What time?"

"I'll pick you up at seven." Rachael stood, practically bouncing on the balls of her feet. "This is going to be so much fun, Cali. Just you wait."

Cali stood and walked Rachael to the door. "I'll see you at seven."

Rachael waved goodbye and headed toward the elevator.

After returning to her desk, Cali picked up the phone and dialed Matthew's number.

He answered on the first ring. "What did she want?"

"We're going to dinner tonight at Ruby's." Then for some reason Cali felt compelled to add, "She's been told the waiters are cute."

Matthew laughed. "Oh she has, has she? And what are you hoping to get out of this evening, Ms. Stanton?"

She grinned, pleased that none of the jealousy from earlier was present. "Well, Mr. Andersen, I was thinking about doing some ogling myself, but I don't think I'll find anything up to my standards."

"So you have high standards, do you, Ms. Stanton?"

"Oh, most definitely, Mr. Andersen. Most definitely."

Chapter 26

Cali's dinner with Rachael was uneventful. Matthew had attached the GPS inside her bra again as a precaution and he sat outside the restaurant in his car while she was inside. He got the impression that Cali felt it was overkill, but he wasn't willing to take any chances with her safety.

On Friday morning, Matthew opened a drawer of his desk to find a string of condoms. There was no mystery as to who had put them there or that Lisa had told Jason about Matthew and Cali's relationship.

If there had been any doubt in his mind as to who had left the condoms it was crystal clear the minute Jason strolled into Matthew's office a little before noon. "You're more than welcome to use my apartment over lunch if you and Cali need some privacy."

Matthew was only half paying attention to his brother. "Thanks, but I think we can control ourselves."

His brother grinned and waggled his eyebrows. "Wouldn't want those condoms to go to waste."

Rolling his eyes, Matthew went back to Cali's mail. "Saves me a trip to pick up more."

Jason threw back his head and laughed before sitting down across from his brother.

Matthew couldn't help but smile. He'd learned over the years that every now and then one had to relieve some tension or it would kill you.

"So, seriously, how are things with Cali?"

Glancing up at his brother, Matthew let his expression say it all.

Jason whistled. "That good, huh?"

Matthew chuckled and shoved the latest package in his brother's direction. "Here."

There were five sheets of paper—all pictures. "This is from Wednesday night, right? When she was out with her friend?"

"Yeah," Matthew said, resting his elbows on the desk. "I don't know what to make of it or even if I should make something out of it at all. The last two sets of photos have been when she was out with Rachael, but she hasn't been out in public outside of that recently so maybe that's all it is."

"You still can't find anything on the woman?" Jason asked, handing the pictures back.

"No. But maybe I'm making trouble where there isn't any. I don't know." Were his feelings for Cali clouding his judgment?

"Matthew, you have good instincts. If you feel something isn't right then I wouldn't dismiss it."

That made him feel better. "Thanks."

"Anytime," Jason said as he stood to leave.

He was halfway to the door when Matthew asked, "Did you just come in here to rib me about the condoms or was there something else? Something work related?"

Jason looked back at his brother with his hand on the doorknob. "You know me too well. And yeah, there was something else, but it's not important."

Matthew waited.

There was a long pause before Jason relented. "We lost another one today."

"And you didn't think I needed to know that another shipment was taken?"

Jason shook his head. "You've got a lot on your mind lately. I can handle it. It's my job, remember? Your job is to take care of Cali. Someone is gunning for her. She needs you. I can handle this."

"We have to figure this out, Jason." Matthew gathered up the growing pile of pictures, letters, and reports from the corner of his desk. "What are we missing?"

His brother sighed. "I don't know. But they'll trip up soon. They have to."

Matthew spent the rest of the day going through the motions, hoping that in the routine something would pop out at him.

He could tell Cali knew something was up when he went to pick her up that night, but she waited to ask him about it until they were home. "More pictures came today."

She thought about it for a moment and then asked, "From Ruby's?"

"Yeah." He let that hang in the air, not sure what to say.

"What do we do?" she whispered, wrapping her arms around his waist.

He tucked her head under his chin and held her close. "Keep doing what we're doing. Being careful. They have to make a mistake eventually."

"And if they don't?"

He didn't have an answer for her.

They spent Saturday at the lake house with her father. Matthew was extra careful on the drive up to make sure they weren't being followed, and once they arrived, he took a walk around the grounds. He found some footprints along the edge of the property, but they were far enough away from the house that he couldn't say if they were from a hiker who'd strayed off the path or someone else. If it was their mystery photographer then they had a high-powered lens they were using to get the shots Cali had been sent. It would explain why they hadn't been seen.

On Sunday, Jason and Lisa came over to watch the game and this time Cali and Matthew didn't have to hide. It was a huge weight off his shoulders not to have to pretend in front of them. Jason teased him some, but all things considered it was worth having the cat out of the bag.

That evening after their company had left Cali offered to clean up so he could go over some files on his laptop. Something was bugging him and he needed to get to the bottom of it. He spent another two hours going over the same security footage he must have viewed at least a hundred times already. It was as if his subconscious was telling him that he was missing something, but he couldn't seem to put the pieces together.

Cali walked into the study and the movement caused him to

glance up. His eyes grew wide when he got a good look at her. She was leaning back against one of the doors in a long black nightgown. The sight had him completely forgetting about work.

Matthew stood—not even bothering to shut down his computer—and stalked toward her as he took her in. The nightgown flowed gracefully down her legs, ending right above her ankles. It would be considered conservative if not for the long slit running up the side. The way she was standing made it clear that the slit went all the way up to the top of her thigh.

When he came to a stop in front of her, Matthew skimmed his palms up the sides of her bare arms and over her shoulders. "Gorgeous."

Her eyes sparkled with mischief as she leaned in and took his bottom lip into her mouth, biting it gently.

He moaned and brought his body flush with hers.

Instead of wrapping her arms around him and deepening the kiss, Cali backed away.

Matthew gave her a puzzled look.

Cali giggled and reached for his hand. She led him toward the stairs and he followed her up willingly.

They barely made it to his bedroom before he began stripping her out of her nightgown.

That night as he lay in bed playing with her fingers, Matthew pondered the connection he and Cali had. It never failed to amaze him. When he was with her, he felt a peace he'd never known before and one he knew he would never feel again.

He kissed the top of her head as she snuggled closer, closed his eyes, and drifted off to sleep.

Sometime later Matthew jerked awake. He looked frantically around the room, his panic rising, his heart pounding in his chest. Something had woken him but he couldn't spot the danger. Nothing appeared to be out of place in the room.

He lay there and listened for several minutes. When he didn't hear anything, he knew he had to get up and check or else he'd never be able to get any more rest tonight.

Easing out of bed so he didn't wake Cali, he tugged on a pair of jeans and grabbed his gun from his bag. He went room by room checking to see if there was any sign of an intruder.

Matthew was passing by the study on his way back upstairs

when he remembered he'd left his laptop running. Walking back into Alvin's home office, Matthew rounded the desk and moved the mouse to bring the screen back to life.

As he moved the cursor to begin the shutdown, he froze. Matthew remembered what had woken him so suddenly. He knew who their mystery woman in the parking garage was.

***

The alarm woke Cali up on Monday morning. She blindly turned it off and rolled over to bury her head in Matthew's empty pillow. His scent was all around her. It was mixed with her own and a hint of sex. Cali couldn't remember the last time she was this happy.

She was not a morning person—never had been. Matthew was. In fact, it wouldn't surprise her if he was already downstairs in his suit and tie.

That thought made her smile and caused a fluttering in the pit of her stomach. It was enough to get her up and moving. She couldn't wait to see him.

Cali hurried through her morning routine and rushed downstairs to join Matthew for breakfast. She was in such a rush that she almost overlooked the light being on in the study.

Peeking inside, Cali found Matthew behind her father's large desk. He appeared to be deep in thought. He gave no indication that he'd noticed her.

She crossed the room and placed a hand on his shoulder.

Matthew jumped.

"Sorry," she said, removing her hand.

He blinked up at her several times before rubbing a hand over his face. "What time is it?"

It was then she noticed that there were bags under his eyes. How long had he been up?

"It's about seven o'clock. Everything okay?"

He turned to look back at the computer screen, but didn't answer.

"Matthew?"

"I don't know," he said, shaking his head.

"Did you find something?"

He glanced up at her again, his brow furrowed in concentration. "I think so. I need to check a few things out first, though."

Matthew powered down his laptop and stood.

"Anything I should know?" she asked. Cali was somewhat concerned by his vague answer.

He finally seemed to notice her unease. Taking a step toward her, Matthew placed a soft kiss on her lips. "I don't want to jump to conclusions but I may have figured out who the mystery lady is from the garage. The one with the ring."

"What can I do?" She wanted to help if she could.

"Nothing." His eyes narrowed a little. "And if my suspicions are correct then this person is my problem anyway."

Cali frowned.

Matthew tucked a strand of hair behind her ear and trailed his fingers along her jawbone. "I'm not trying to keep this from you. I just want to make sure I'm right before I say anything. Once I'm sure, I'll tell you."

As much as she didn't like it, what he said made sense. If not for their intimate relationship, she wouldn't even know about his hunch until after he'd confirmed it. "All right."

He grinned and took a step back.

She took in his attire for the first time since walking into the room. All he had on was a pair of jeans—even his feet were bare.

"You might want to get dressed, Andersen. That is unless you were planning on working from home today." Cali lowered her voice, making it clear she was up for playing hooky if he was.

Matthew groaned, and then chuckled. He placed another kiss on her lips—one that held a whole slew of promises she knew he was more than capable of keeping—and then he was gone. By the time she opened her eyes and realized what was happening, he was halfway up the stairs.

She sighed and made her way into the kitchen to find Jessie.

"Morning," Cali said when she saw the older woman already standing in front of the stove.

Jessie smiled and there was a knowing look in her eyes. "Good morning."

Cali blushed. Although she was a grown woman, it still felt strange that the woman she saw as her surrogate mother knew she was having sex with her b—someone. Since Cali had decided to stay in Chicago, she knew that eventually she and Matthew would have to discuss what they both wanted, but for now it seemed wrong somehow to use a title like *boyfriend*. Or think it, for that matter.

The only reason she hadn't brought up the future yet was because Cali didn't want Matthew to feel obligated in any way. His job right now was to protect her. While she couldn't think of anyone else she'd rather keep her safe, she wanted him to stay with her because it was what he wanted—not because he felt he had to.

Matthew strolled into the kitchen and took a seat beside her. He looked dashing in his pinstriped suit.

"Good morning, Jessie. Smells good." When he glanced in her direction, he had a smirk on his face. "Good morning, Cali."

One look from him sent her heart thundering in her chest. She grinned back at him. "Morning."

He raised an eyebrow and she sucked in a breath, realizing that she'd been caught ogling him again. She couldn't help it.

Jessie brought over two plates full of eggs, bacon, and toast and set them in front of Cali and Matthew. The older woman was humming to herself and Cali got the distinct impression that Jessie knew exactly what Cali had been thinking. She should probably be embarrassed—and she was . . . a little, but she decided she didn't care. Matthew was her man for however long this lasted and she wasn't going to apologize for enjoying the view.

***

Matthew sat in his office, staring at the computer screen. He'd spent the first half of his morning running a new background check on her and still he had nothing. Not one thing stood out that screamed "mole."

There was always the possibility that he was wrong—that she wasn't the woman on the security footage—but he didn't think he was. He'd even watched the footage again and he was more sure now than he had been sitting in Alvin's study that morning. There was only one last thing left to do to verify his suspicions.

He saved the file, locking it with a password, and pressed the intercom button on his phone. "Mariana, could I see you in my office for a moment? Bring something to write on."

Less than a minute later, his assistant waltzed into his office and took a seat across from him. She crossed her legs and placed the pad of paper she'd brought in with her on her lap. In her right hand she held a pen, ready to take whatever dictation he was about to give her.

On her right hand was a ring—*the* ring. The one that he'd been racking his brain for the last two weeks trying to figure out to whom it belonged.

Making sure not to give anything away, he rattled off a list of reports he wanted pulled and compiled by the end of the day. Matthew also asked her to put together a list of all the drivers whose shipments had been targeted over the past six months. He needed to keep her busy for most of the day and out of his hair while he figured out what to do next.

"Anything else?" she asked, her pen hovering over the paper.

"I think that's all for now. I'll let you know if I think of anything else I'm going to need."

She nodded and left.

Matthew sat there staring at the door she'd walked out of. Something still wasn't adding up. Mariana was smart, but she wasn't that smart. She didn't have the skills to pull off something this complex. And what about the pictures of Cali in Africa? Mariana was working for him in Chicago at the time they were taken. She'd never been to Africa—he'd checked.

It was possible that she'd hired someone else to take the pictures for her, but he didn't think that was the case. This was bigger than they'd thought. Mariana was only one piece of the puzzle.

It was Monday, which meant he had a security briefing with Cali at three. He knew she'd want some answers but he needed more information before he could give them to her.

Pulling up his e-mail, Matthew shot off a quick message to Cali letting her know he wouldn't be able to join her for lunch today. Then he messaged Jason asking him if he could sit in on the security briefing in Cali's office this afternoon. Once those were off, he pulled out his cell and dialed Martinez.

His friend answered on the first ring. "Hello?"

"I've found something. Can I meet you at the police station in about a half hour? I'll bring lunch."

Martinez laughed. "You know me. I've never turned down a free meal."

Matthew grinned despite the situation. "See you in a few."

He logged off his computer, making sure nothing sensitive was where anyone—including Mariana—could access it, and then headed out the door. One way or another, he would have a plan in place by the end of the day to take down Mariana and whoever else was working with her.

Chapter 27

Matthew's lunch with Martinez only confirmed his stance that Mariana had an accomplice. Her work history was solid and there was nothing out of the ordinary in her background check. Martinez even went as far as to run her name through the criminal database, but she was clean. Not even variations on her name brought up anything.

"What's she getting out of it? That's what I want to know," Martinez said as he wiped the barbecue sauce from his hands. "I mean, she has a good, steady job. There are no discrepancies in her financials that I can see. What's the payoff for her?"

"I don't know. We have to be missing something." Matthew shook his head as he finished his food.

"Blackmail?"

"Maybe."

Martinez wadded up his trash and tossed it into the bin beside his desk. "Well, someone has to be pulling her strings."

Matthew couldn't agree more. All he had to do now was find out who.

It was almost three before he returned to Stanton Enterprises. He headed straight for Cali's office.

Lisa greeted him as soon as he stepped off the elevator. "Hello, Matthew. Go on in. Cali's expecting you."

She didn't seem the least surprised that he was fifteen minutes early for their scheduled meeting.

He strolled into the office to find Cali sitting at her desk with her head bowed. She was reading something and her hair had fallen forward so it hid part of her face. It reminded Matthew of how she'd looked the night before when she'd been riding him. His heart rate kicked up a notch and he felt his pants get a little tighter. After the last few hours, seeing her was exactly what he needed.

Matthew rounded the desk, needing to be closer to her. He dropped the papers he'd brought with him onto the corner of her desk and closed the distance between them.

Cali didn't look up from whatever she was working on until he was only a foot away. She opened her mouth to say something, but he didn't give her the chance. He took her by the shoulders, lifted her up out of her chair, and crushed his lips to hers.

When he finally let her come up for air, she blinked at him. "Wow. Not that I'm complaining, but what was that for?"

He brushed a stray hair away from her face and skimmed his index finger down her cheek to her neck . . . and lower. "Do I need a reason?"

"No." Her voice was barely above a whisper as she stared up at him with an expression that gave him a small amount of hope for the future.

A throat cleared and he took a step back. Jason was standing in the doorway with a huge smile on his face. "Am I interrupting?"

"No," Cali said. "We were just—"

Jason chuckled and walked into the room, closing the door behind him. "Oh, I know what you were *just*. I'm only wondering if you'd like some more time to *just*."

Cali's cheeks reddened and she sat back down behind her desk.

Matthew retrieved the papers he'd laid on her desk and took a seat across from her. His brother followed suit and sat down in the chair beside him. Jason's chest was vibrating with his suppressed amusement, but he kept his mouth shut.

Figuring that was the best he was going to get from his brother, Matthew got down to business. "I've figured out who our mystery woman is from the garage."

"Who?" Jason asked, all humor wiped from his expression.

"Mariana."

"Mariana? Your assistant, Mariana?" Cali asked.

Matthew nodded.

"You're sure? I mean . . ." The look on Cali's face said exactly how Matthew had felt when he'd realized that his assistant had betrayed them. Shock. Disbelief. And praying that somehow he was wrong.

But he wasn't wrong. "Yes, I'm sure. She's wearing the ring today. I saw it on her hand this morning."

Cali sat forward in her chair. "But why?"

"I have no idea. I didn't even consider her before because it didn't make any sense. Hell, it still doesn't." Matthew shook his head. "But the facts remain the same. She was the one on the security footage. Granted, all that proves is that she was somewhere she wasn't supposed to be."

"And given her position, she has access to the security feeds," Jason said, finally contributing to the conversation.

"Yes," Matthew said, gearing up for his next point. "But either she's been doing a lot of her own research into security systems, or someone else is behind this. I'm betting on the latter."

No one said anything for several minutes as they all digested the new information.

"So what happens now?" Cali asked. "Like you said, all we know is that she was someplace she wasn't supposed to be."

"Surveillance." Jason rubbed his hands together with undisguised excitement.

Matthew rolled his eyes at his brother and grinned. "I stopped to pick up some additional supplies. What we need to do this properly was going to clean us out."

A confused looked crossed Cali's face. "I don't follow. What are you two going to do and why do you need supplies?"

"We're going to tap every phone in this building she has access to—well, the most likely ones, at least. Including mine," Matthew explained.

Cali's eyes widened.

"We'll also place cameras at different angles around her desk to watch what she's doing. I'd love to be able to tap her cell as well, but we can't do that without a court order and we don't have enough to get that yet. I'm hoping it won't be necessary."

"She'll need to be followed," Jason added.

Matthew nodded. "Martinez said he'd help with that when he could, but that still only leaves the two of you since I'm not willing to leave Cali unprotected."

Cali opened her mouth to say something, but Jason cut her off. "Alec and Sam. I trust them. They've saved more than one shipment for us."

"I agree," Matthew said. "But they need to know as little as possible about what's going on."

"Agreed."

Matthew and Jason had to wait until everyone had gone home for the night before they could put their plan into action. Lisa offered to drive Cali home and wait with her until Matthew got there. He still didn't feel great about leaving her with Lisa, but he didn't have much choice. It was too much for Jason to do on his own and the fewer people who knew about the cameras and the wire taps the better.

Even with both of them working together, it took them until almost nine to get everything installed and tested. All they had to do now was watch and wait for Mariana to get caught doing something they could confront her with.

***

Cali and Lisa spent their evening enjoying some girl time. They made themselves dinner, and then popped in a movie. It was a decent movie but there was too much going on for it to hold their interest.

"How are things going with Matthew?" Lisa asked.

"Good."

"But?"

Cali shook her head. "No buts. Things are good. Getting used to each other, you know?"

"Yeah, I know. Jason is such a cover hog." Lisa laughed. "That took some getting used to. Now I just elbow him until he wakes up."

"Matthew isn't like that at all. Of course, he tends to spend most of the night lying on his back or spooning me." It felt really good to be able to talk to someone about the man she loved.

Lisa snorted. "I wish. Jason is all over the place."

They both laughed.

"Does Jason wake up at the crack of dawn, too?" Cali asked. "I know they were both in the military."

"Heavens no. Jason would sleep half the morning away if you'd let him."

They spent the rest of the night comparing notes. It was fun to learn that Jason was, in many ways, Matthew's total opposite.

The sound of the door opening brought Cali to her feet. She walked into the foyer to find Matthew removing his jacket.

"Did you get everything set up?" Cali asked.

Matthew met her gaze from across the room. "Yeah. We're ready to go. Now we wait."

"Well," Lisa said from behind her, "I need to get going. We should do this again sometime, Cali."

"Definitely," Cali said, not taking her gaze from Matthew.

"Good night." Lisa slipped on her shoes and grabbed her purse before ducking out the door.

He walked toward Cali with measured steps. "Something happen I should know about?"

"Nope." She circled her arms around his neck as soon as he was within reach. "Just girl talk."

Matthew wrapped his arms around her waist and pressed his mouth firmly against hers. They'd only been apart for a few hours. It was crazy how much she missed him.

Cali held his head in place as she leveraged herself closer, deepening the kiss.

He slid his hand down her back and dug his fingers into her hip, pulling her flush against him. She could feel his arousal against her stomach, demanding attention. It was difficult to think of anything else but having him inside her, but she forced herself to focus.

"Are you hungry?" The words were weak.

Matthew's only response was to grind his hips against her.

She rolled her eyes. "For food."

When he didn't answer her, she looked up. He was staring down at her with heat in his eyes but also something else. She realized he must be conflicted about what he wanted more. Her man was very logical, but he was still a man.

Making the decision for him, Cali took a step back and reached for his hand. He followed her willingly. She knew there weren't many places Matthew wouldn't follow her. At least for the time being.

He groaned when he realized they were headed into the kitchen and not to a bed. She smiled and pointed to one of the stools at the kitchen island. "Sit and I'll get you something to eat."

Cali went to the warming oven and removed the plate she'd made for him. When she turned around, she didn't miss that his gaze had been on her ass. She grinned and brought his plate over to him.

Matthew picked up his fork with his right hand and wrapped his left arm around Cali's waist. He tucked her against his side and held her there while he ate. Cali didn't protest. She stood patiently waiting for him to finish. He seemed to need her close and she was more than okay with that.

Once he was done eating, Matthew pushed the plate aside, stood, and led her up the stairs. He closed the door as soon as they were inside his room and molded her body to his as he walked her backward toward the bed. Neither said anything—there was no need. She could feel the desire rolling off him that matched her own.

Something would happen soon. They both knew it. Mariana was the lead Matthew had been waiting for. Although they both wanted the mystery to be solved and the threat to disappear, Cali also knew that meant things between them would be changing. With the threat eliminated, he wouldn't have an excuse to stay with her. Did that mean that their tryst would be coming to an end?

All she knew for sure was that he was hers for tonight.

They removed each other's clothes and Cali positioned herself in the middle of the bed with her head on the pillows. Matthew reached for a condom, crawled onto the mattress, and hovered over her. She reached up to cup the back of his head, bringing him in for a kiss. He lowered himself down on top of her and she welcomed his weight with open arms.

Cali tried to convey all the love she felt for him with every touch, every kiss. There was something different this time as they came together. She felt a sense of desperation that she couldn't shake as they reconnected over and over again. All she knew was that she couldn't lose him when this was all said and done. She couldn't.

Over the next few days, things went on as they normally did with the exception that Matthew kept even closer tabs on her than usual. Cali didn't know if that was because of what was going on with Mariana or if it was due to the impending changes to their relationship. To be honest, she tried not to think about it too much.

On Thursday night, however, Cali found herself lying in bed, unable to sleep. Her mind wouldn't shut off. Matthew and Jason had been watching Mariana like a hawk but so far she'd been the model employee. Cali knew it had only been three days, but she wondered why they hadn't seen anything. What was she waiting for? Shipments left Stanton Enterprises roughly every other day.

And then there was the biggest question of all—who was she working with? What was their connection?

It wasn't until the sky began to lighten with the start of a new day that something occurred to her. What if Mariana and her accomplice weren't being provided the right kind of bait? If Matthew was correct, and she had to believe he was, then the person they were looking for held a position of importance within the company. That would mean this person would have access to all routine shipping information. It was only when there were changes to normal routes or schedules that Mariana's assistance would be required.

This realization put her mind at ease and allowed her to finally close her eyes and drift off to sleep. Unfortunately, right as she was being pulled under the alarm began beeping.

Cali felt Matthew shift in bed. It was the alarm he set every morning so he could get up and do his workout before work. Usually he was able to turn it off before it woke her. It wasn't his fault that she'd been awake most of the night.

She reached out to stop him from leaving the bed.

Matthew halted, leaned over, and placed a soft kiss on her lips. "What are you doing awake, Ms. Stanton?"

Cali smiled. "Mmm. Couldn't sleep."

He moved closer and pulled her into his arms. "Are you feeling okay?"

"Yep." She pulled his mouth back down to hers, not willing to let him go yet.

Needless to say, Matthew never did make it to the gym that morning. He got plenty of exercise, though. Cali made sure of it.

Breakfast was a little awkward. Jessie kept sending her sly looks and Cali wondered whether she had a big sign on her forehead that said 'I got laid this morning.'

The thing was Jessie seemed genuinely happy for them. Cali did know Jessie had an issue keeping it a secret from Cali's father, but as far as she knew, the older woman had respected their wishes and kept things to herself.

It was on the way to the office that Cali decided to share her theory with Matthew.

"I was thinking about some things last night."

Matthew glanced over at her. "Is that why you couldn't sleep?"

She nodded. "It was bothering me that it's been three days and Mariana hasn't done anything."

"It's just going to take some time."

Cali twisted in her seat to face him. "Hear me out."

"Okay."

"You think whoever she's working with is also an employee, too, right?"

He nodded. "Yes. It makes sense. Either that or a former employee. This feels personal to me. It always has."

"I agree with you." She took a moment to organize her thoughts. "So wouldn't it make sense that this person—whoever they are— would have access to shipping schedules and all that?"

Matthew pressed his lips together. "Probably. It would depend on their position. Whoever it was would have to either be in security, production, or management."

"Which gives us a lot of options."

"So what are you thinking? That this person is just biding their time? Waiting for a specific shipment?" Matthew asked.

"I don't know about that. Maybe. But it occurred to me last night that the reason you haven't caught Mariana doing anything suspicious is because he or she hasn't had need of her help yet this week." She paused to let that sink in.

He drove into the parking garage and pulled into his spot before addressing her. "They're using her when we change the shipment routes."

"Makes sense. I mean, when things change the amount of people who know the details dwindles considerably."

"Yes. And it also means that the people who do have access can be taken off the suspect list. They wouldn't need Mariana's assistance."

Cali hadn't thought about that, but he was right.

Matthew smiled, and then sighed. "I really want to kiss you right now."

She laughed. "Sorry, Mr. Andersen. Too many people watching."

He frowned. "I know."

"Your rules, remember?"

That reminder didn't seem to help his mood in the slightest. "I know that, too."

Cali let that hang in the air for a few minutes. "What are you going to do?"

"I need to talk to Jason."

"And then?" she asked.

"Lay the trap and hope she walks into it."

Chapter 28

After seeing Cali safely to her office, Matthew found Jason and shared Cali's thoughts with him.

"Makes sense," Jason said.

"I agree. So I'm thinking we keep it simple and try to catch her in the act."

Jason leaned forward, excitement in his eyes. "What did you have in mind?"

An hour later, Matthew and Jason exited his office and headed toward the elevator, making sure to linger for an extra moment near Mariana's desk.

"You don't think it will be a problem?"

"Not at all." Jason shook his head and pulled his phone out of his pocket. "Danny said moving the delivery would only take a few adjustments."

"Wonderful." Matthew glanced down at his watch and smiled before continuing on toward the elevators. "I've got an appointment to get to, so I'll see you later?"

"Sure." Jason turned on his heel and handed a yellow envelope to Mariana. "Can you make sure these get downstairs ASAP?"

"No problem," she said, taking it from him.

The elevator doors opened as Jason disappeared into his office.

Matthew stepped inside the elevator and pressed the button for the parking garage. He'd left his laptop in the trunk of his car this morning having anticipated that he might need it when they executed their plan. Once he had his laptop, he made his way up to Cali's office on the thirtieth floor. Somehow, he didn't think she would mind the interruption.

"I had a feeling I'd be seeing you again before lunch," Lisa said when she saw him come off the elevator.

"Able to predict the future now, are you?"

She laughed. "No. You're just predictable."

"Cali inside?" he asked.

"Yep. Go on in. She doesn't have any meetings this morning."

Cali looked up when Matthew strolled into her office. "Hey."

He closed the door and crossed the room to give her a quick peck on the lips. "Hey. Mind if I use your conference room for a bit?"

"Of course not."

As he set up his laptop at the conference table, he heard her come up behind him. "Everything all right?"

"We gave Mariana the bait."

"Oh."

She moved around so she could see his laptop screen. There was Mariana. She was alone and had already opened the envelope. She was sifting through the papers, reading them. Then she picked up the phone.

"Is she doing what I think she is?"

"We're going to find out," Matthew said. He shrunk the screen and brought up the wiretap on the phone.

A second later, Mariana's voice came through. "There's been a change in Monday's delivery."

She rattled off the change in delivery information to an unknown male. His voice sounded muffled and she never used his name, but if he wasn't mistaken, the way the man spoke gave Matthew the impression he and Mariana had an intimate relationship.

Cali pulled out the chair next to him and sat down. "I can't believe it."

Matthew closed the file and raised one eyebrow.

She shrugged. "I guess a part of me was hoping we were wrong."

"So was I. Mariana has always been a good assistant. I hate that it's come to this."

"What now?" Cali asked.

"I call Martinez and get him to issue an arrest warrant."

Cali sat beside him while he made the call. They wanted to keep this as low key as possible, so Matthew made arrangements for Martinez and a uniformed officer to meet him on the thirteenth floor at five o'clock. Given it was a Friday, a lot of people tended to duck out early and he was hoping for less of an audience.

"Mind if I stick around here for an hour or so?" Matthew asked when he hung up the phone.

"Avoiding your office?"

"I made the excuse that I had a meeting to go to. It would look odd if I returned so soon."

Cali stood and gave him a kiss before going back to her desk. "Knock yourself out. All I'm doing this morning is going through these financial reports."

Matthew laughed. "Again?"

She narrowed her eyes at him. "Do you want me to kick you out?"

He shook his head and turned around, his shoulders still vibrating with amusement. "I'll just stay over here and do my own thing."

"Good answer."

Matthew ended up staying in Cali's office until after lunch. It was nice having her close, although it was a bit distracting. She was cute when she was frustrated.

Right on time, Martinez and two uniformed officers walked onto the thirteenth floor. Matthew stepped out of his office and watched as they marched straight to Mariana's desk. As they loomed over her, Mariana's eyes widened.

"Mariana Lugo, you're under arrest." He helped her to stand, pulled her hands behind her back, and placed the cuffs on her. She didn't even seem to notice Matthew standing outside his office as they read her rights to her while they escorted her to the elevator.

When the elevator doors closed, Jason joined Matthew. "I'm going to follow Martinez to the station. Meet you there?"

"Yeah. I want to update Cali and see if Lisa will drive her home again."

"I'm sure she wouldn't mind."

"All right. I'll see you there, then."

Matthew disappeared into his office to shut things down, and then made his way upstairs to Cali.

She was already waiting for him by Lisa's desk. "What happened?"

He walked over to her, careful to keep his distance since they were technically in a public space. "Martinez has taken her downtown. I'm heading down there myself. I want to be there when they question her." Matthew looked toward Lisa. "I was hoping you'd be able to take Cali home again and stay with her until I get there."

"Su—"

"That won't be necessary, Lisa. I'm going with Matthew."

"Cali, I don't think—"

"Dad gave me the responsibility of running his company while he's recovering. One of my employees is about to be questioned about her involvement with the hijacked shipments. I want to be there."

Matthew weighed the pros and cons. He didn't like the thought of her being there, but she did have a point. "Are you ready to go?"

Cali seemed relieved he wasn't going to fight her. She hoisted her purse over her shoulder and knelt down to grab her briefcase.

Jason and Martinez were waiting outside the interrogation room when Matthew and Cali arrived. If they were surprised by Cali's presence, they didn't show it.

While Jason and Martinez conducted the interview, Cali and Matthew watched from behind a two-way mirror.

They'd tried to pull the phone records from her call but it went to a burner phone. It was untraceable.

It was a very long two hours. Mariana wasn't talking—not about the shipments and not about her partner in crime. All they knew for sure was that the man she'd called was her boyfriend.

Mariana was incredibly calm during the interrogation. She didn't appear worried that she was being arrested for corporate espionage, even after she was told they had her on tape giving out confidential information.

Although it was a white-collar crime and her first offense, Matthew still thought she'd see some prison time. The evidence against her was too strong and if they could tie her to any of the shipments that were hijacked, the dollar amount would add up quickly.

They went round and round with her for another forty-five minutes before Martinez called an end to the questioning.

"Maybe a weekend in jail will loosen your tongue, huh?" Martinez stood and Jason followed, leaving Mariana in the room to wait for an officer who would take her to a cell.

Matthew and Cali stood side by side in the small, dark room as the officer came to get Mariana. She didn't fight him, just went quietly along as if he were taking her for a stroll rather than to a jail cell.

Wrapping his arm around Cali, Matthew whispered in her ear, "We'll find him."

"I know you will," she said, leaning in to him.

Matthew chuckled. "Such confidence you have in me, Ms. Stanton."

She turned and circled her arms around his neck and held his gaze. "Always, Mr. Andersen."

There was electricity in the air around them. Although their exchange was teasing, it felt like more. What did she mean when she said 'always'? He knew what he wanted it to mean.

He was about to ask her when the door opened and the moment was lost. They broke apart so that they were once again standing a respectable distance from one another.

His brother and Martinez entered the room and turned on the light. Neither one of them looked happy.

"Hopefully a weekend in the tank will shock some sense in to her. She's covering for someone. If she wises up and helps, she might get off with a slap on the wrist for this," Martinez said.

"Do you really think she'll turn her boyfriend in?" Cali asked. "She didn't seem very forthcoming in there."

"I don't know. Women are hard to predict when it comes to emotions." Martinez smiled and winked at her.

Matthew raised his eyebrows in question, but his friend ignored him.

"Interrogations always make me hungry. Who's up for some chow?" Martinez asked.

"Actually, I need to get Cali home," Matthew said. All he

wanted to do was go home and spend some time alone with her. The month they had before she went back to her life overseas seemed to be going way too fast. A month didn't seem like nearly enough time.

Martinez nodded. "Maybe next time then. Jason?"

"Sure. I can always eat."

***

Cali breathed a sigh of relief when Matthew turned Martinez's offer of dinner down. What she wanted more than anything in that moment was to go home, curl up on the couch with Matthew, eat some pizza, and watch a movie.

As if reading her mind, he stopped on the way home and picked up a large pizza and a two-liter of pop. They found a pay-per-view movie to watch on television and spent the rest of the evening cuddled up on the couch together. It was the perfect way to spend what was left of their night.

It was an action-packed movie, which was fine with her. The hero reminded her a lot of Matthew. He was smart and strong and very protective of the heroine.

The credits began scrolling across the screen and Matthew shifted their position. He took her face in both his hands and brought their mouths together in a searing kiss. She fisted the fabric of his shirt and held on while every cell in her body got lost in the feel of him.

By the time they broke apart, they were both panting.

"I will keep you safe, Cali," he vowed. "Always."

The intensity of emotion behind his declaration was as powerful, if not more so, than hers earlier that day.

Cali sat there unmoving for several moments before lifting her leg and straddling his lap. *I love you* was on the tip of her tongue but she held the words back. She slid her hands over his shoulders and down his chest. One by one, she released the buttons of his shirt.

Matthew held on to her hips as he laid them both down on the couch, her perched above him. He was looking up at her with an expression that said maybe he felt the same. Whatever it was between them was special. She didn't want to lose it.

It was different with him. With every kiss— every touch—her body craved him more.

He raised his hips, grinding his hard length against her sex, and she let everything but him fade from her mind.

They lay there after with her naked body lying on top of his. She felt content and completely relaxed. He ran his fingers down her spine while his other hand rested on her hip.

Matthew kissed the top of her head. "We should go upstairs."

"Mmm." But she didn't move.

His chest vibrated beneath her. "I guess if you're okay with Jessie finding us like this in the morning, then so am I."

"Tomorrow's Saturday. No Jessie." She could feel sleep pulling her under.

Before she knew what was happening, he had them sitting up. "Come on. As comfortable as this couch is, I don't really want to spend the entire night sleeping on it."

Cali sighed. "All right. Fine. You win."

She tried to get up, but he grabbed hold of her and gave her a hard kiss. "I'll make it up to you."

"Promises, promises," she mumbled as she stood and began gathering her clothes.

Cali was almost to the bottom of the pile when she noticed something that didn't look like a piece of clothing. She bent down, picked it up, and dropped it almost immediately once she realized what it was. Her gaze met his as her heart pounded in her chest. "Matthew, why do you have a gun?"

Without comment, he retrieved it from the pile of clothing still on the floor and checked it. "I told you I'd keep you safe, Cali, and I meant it."

She swallowed, but didn't comment.

Five days later, she was sitting in her office trying to prepare for another dreaded meeting with Peter. The quarterly financials were due to the board by the end of month. She couldn't put it off any longer.

After finding the gun mixed in with Matthew's clothes, she learned he'd started carrying it a few days ago. She still wasn't sure how she felt about it, but the next morning—and every morning since—she'd watch him make sure it was ready to go and then strap it to his ankle.

Mariana still wasn't talking. She was arraigned on Monday and the judge set bail. Both Jason and Matthew thought the amount was too low, but Martinez said that was because this was her first offense. They still didn't like it, but there wasn't much they could do.

The upside to her arrest was that Martinez had subpoenaed all her phone records and searched her apartment. They were still waiting for forensics to come back, but they were hopeful it would turn up some clue as to who her boyfriend was.

Even though Martinez was handling things on his end, Matthew wasn't willing to sit back and wait. Since they already had the wiretaps in place within Stanton Enterprises, he and Jason decided to use them. In the last three days, they'd recorded two suspicious calls—both originated from the boardroom on the executive floor.

Things were beginning to add up and Cali wasn't sure she liked it. Sure, they didn't know who had made those calls, but it did narrow down their suspect list. Only senior vice presidents, the board of directors, and Cali had access to that room. Someone very close to her father was behind this.

Lisa knocked on Cali's door, pulling her out of her thoughts and back to the present. "Don't forget your lunch meeting."

Cali was thankful for the reminder. There had been too much on her mind lately.

She was meeting Devlin and Tad, two of the board members, at an upscale restaurant in the heart of downtown. They were supposed to be discussing the rollout of a new product in the upcoming quarter.

It didn't take Cali and Lisa long to reach the restaurant and they were escorted over to Tad and Devlin's table. The men both stood and waited while they took their seats.

Lunch was all business. Most of the discussion revolved around the benefits of the new equipment, the implementation, and even the cost of the production. For the most part, she smiled and nodded. Both men were polite and professional, making sure to include her. Still, she couldn't shake the fact that either of them could be the one behind this—the hijacked shipments, the letters, the pictures . . . and even hitting her with a car.

The meeting lasted two hours. "You were such a great help, Cali. Thank you for agreeing to join us today."

She hadn't felt very helpful, but . . . "You're welcome. Glad I could be of assistance."

Cali and Lisa said goodbye to Devlin and Tad, and then headed back to the office. Her meeting with Peter was in less than an hour and Cali still wasn't done looking everything over. If she ever saw another spreadsheet again, it would be too soon. It was so bad that the night before, she'd had a nightmare involving columns of numbers that had jumped off the page and started attacking her.

"Knock, knock." Peter peeked his head into her office.

She looked up and gave him the best smile she could manage. "Come in."

"Not interrupting anything, am I?"

"Not at all. I was just finishing something up." Cali abandoned the e-mail she'd been working on and waved toward the conference room. "Let's set up in here."

Luck was on her side. Her meeting with Peter wasn't nearly as traumatizing as she'd feared it would be. He'd brought some graphs with him that showed how the money flowed from research to production to distribution. It helped. Sort of.

Logic told her that the flow of money should be simple to follow, but the graphs were all over the place. When she'd asked Peter about it, he said it was a diversification process that he and her father had come up with to make the company more stable. Not putting all your eggs in one basket type of thing. Again, it made sense . . . yet didn't at the same time.

She tried not to let it bother her that she wasn't following. Accounting wasn't her area of expertise.

When Matthew knocked on her door at five, Cali was still trying to wrap her head around all the numbers and graphs. She left the papers on her desk and walked straight into Matthew's arms.

He circled his arms around her waist, picking her feet up off the floor as he kissed her. "Ready to go?"

Cali nodded. "More than ready."

Chapter 29

Matthew's day had been filled with one headache after another. He'd contacted a temp agency to send over a replacement for Mariana. Jackie, the woman the agency sent, wasn't bad but she had zero experience with security or anything past basic phone and typing skills. But she would have to do for now since neither he nor Jason had the time to search for a more permanent replacement.

He and Jason had spent most of their day going through reports, security footage—anything they could get their hands on, really—trying to narrow down who Mariana's contact was. There were two years of information to sort through, so it was going to take some time.

They did receive some good news, though. Mariana had gotten herself a new lawyer. He wasn't someone a person living on her salary could afford. Neither could her parents. There was a good chance that her 'boyfriend' was the one footing the bill. Martinez was attempting to trace where the funds came from. It was only a matter of time before they had a name.

The drive home with Cali felt routine—normal. Home. It was her home. Her dad's home. Over the last month and a half, however, Matthew had begun to think of it as his as well. He knew it had nothing to do with the house itself. It was Cali. She was the one who made everything in his life better.

Her head rested against the seat as they drove down the street, her eyes closed. Matthew knew the stress was taking its toll. He reached over and took her hand in his.

Cali looked at him and smiled. Warmth filled his chest and he knew there wasn't anything he wouldn't do for this woman.

Inside the house, they moved together in a rhythm they'd perfected over the last month. It felt very domestic and he found that he like it.

Cali warmed up the dinner Jessie had left for them. Matthew stood behind her, placing featherlight kisses on her neck.

She leaned in to him and hummed. "You're distracting me."

"Good."

Cali wiggled her way out of his arms and began setting the table. "There'll be time for that later."

He groaned dramatically as he took the food out of the oven and over to the table.

Dinner was full of discreet touches and meaningful looks. He couldn't wait to get Cali upstairs and out of her clothes.

"I was thinking a bath sounded good," Cali said as they were loading their dishes into the dishwasher. "It's been a *really* long day."

She wrapped her arms around his waist and rubbed herself against him, causing a low moan to escape his throat.

"Want to join me?" she whispered.

Without speaking, Matthew unwound her arms from his waist and began guiding her toward the stairs. A nice long bath with the woman he loved sounded close to perfect. The small space would mean constant excuses to touch, which suited him just fine.

Matthew knew he needed to figure out a way to tell her how he felt. It had almost slipped out a few times, but something always stopped him.

They removed their clothing and stepped into the large tub. It was bigger than he was used to—easily big enough for two people. He sat down and helped her settle between his legs with her back against his chest.

The water lapped gently around them as they caressed each other. It was peaceful. A stark contrast to the day he'd spent at the office and a far cry from the years he'd spent in the military. She made him feel things he never had before—at least, not in the same way.

He tried not to think about what would happen after they found their mole. There would be no need for him to stay in the house anymore. She wouldn't need his protection.

Cupping the side of her face, Matthew tilted her head back so he could press his lips against hers. Cali twisted until her breasts were smashed against his chest and her legs were on the outside of his. Her slick heat pressed against him in the most delicious way as he continued to kiss her.

They stayed in the bath until the water began to cool. Matthew helped her out and took his time drying her off. He loved looking at her.

When they were both dry, he bent down, picked her up, and carried her to his bedroom. Their lovemaking that night was slow and sensual, full of lingering touches. It was hours before their bodies actually joined to become one and they stayed locked together for as long as possible.

Matthew and Cali lay in bed late into the night holding each other. Things were about to change, whether they were ready for them to or not.

The next day started normal enough. He drove Cali to work, walked her up to her office, and then headed down to his.

He was early, so most of his colleagues weren't there yet. It wasn't unusual. Matthew often arrived early. Luckily, so did Lisa. There was no way he would have left Cali upstairs alone. Not when they still didn't know who their mole was.

As he sat behind his desk enjoying the silence—no one demanding his attention, no crisis that had to be dealt with without delay—he got an eerie feeling that something wasn't quite right. With every tick of the clock the uneasy feeling in the pit of his stomach grew. It didn't make sense, but just in case, he did a quick walk-through of the floor and even checked the camera feed in Cali's office twice.

Matthew pushed the feeling aside and tried to get to work. It was most likely his nerves over having to say goodbye to Cali in the not-too-distant future that had him jittery. They had a connection he couldn't explain and it had been at its highest last night. He had to figure out how to tell her how he felt before it was too late.

His first priority, however, was to keep her safe, so he had to concentrate on that. Everything else came second.

Two hours later Matthew's phone rang. It was Martinez. "You free this afternoon?"

Matthew pulled up his schedule. He was supposed to do a walk-through with Jason but if Martinez had something that took priority. "Nothing I can't rearrange."

"I'm supposed to get a report back around two that will hopefully tell us who paid for Miss Lugo's hotshot lawyer. I thought you might want to be here."

"You thought right," Matthew said. "I'll see you at two."

After hanging up with Martinez, Matthew called his brother to let him know what was going on. Jason, of course, had no problem handling the walk-through on his own. Both of them wanted this thing with the mole over and done with.

At noon, Matthew went upstairs to have lunch with Cali. She put her pen down as soon as she saw him walk through the door, although she waited until he'd closed it behind him before launching herself across the room and into his arms. He held her for an extra-long time, enjoying the feel of her against him.

He kissed her and put a little distance between them. "Miss me?"

"Yes." Cali sighed as they made their way over to the table where Lisa had laid out the food. "Today has been a total nightmare."

Matthew waited for her to explain.

"It's these numbers. They don't make any sense. I mean, how am I supposed to sign off on the financial reports when I can't even figure them out?"

He knew she wasn't really expecting an answer, but he gave her one anyway. "You can't. As CEO, or acting CEO, it's your responsibility to ensure the company is as financially sound as it says it is."

"Don't remind me." She sounded miserable and all he wanted to do was make it better for her.

He placed a comforting hand on her arm. "You'll figure it out. And if you can't do it on your own then have Peter explain it to you. That's part of his job."

Cali cringed.

He didn't understand her reaction.

"Don't worry about me," she said, waving off his concern. "I'll figure it out. Somehow. How's yours going? Please tell me it's better than mine."

He told her about the meeting with Martinez. "It shouldn't take long. I'll make sure I'm back before five to take you home."

Before he headed back down to his office, he gave Cali a long kiss and let Lisa know about his afternoon plans. Jason would still be in the building if anything came up.

***

After Matthew left, Cali went back to her desk and picked up where she'd left off. She had to make sense of these numbers. Unfortunately, two hours later she was even more confused than when she'd started. They weren't adding up. What was she missing?

She understood how the money went into a main account and was then filtered through several smaller ones. Some of the smaller accounts she recognized—some she didn't. That wasn't what concerned her. No matter how she figured it, what she started out with wasn't what she ended up with.

At four o'clock, she finally gave up and called the one person she'd been avoiding all day. Peter Carson picked up on the third ring. "Cali. I wasn't expecting to hear from you today. What can I do for you?"

"I've been sitting here going over the reports you left with me and I'm having trouble getting everything to add up."

There was a long pause on the other end of the line before he answered. "I'll be more than happy to come up and go over everything with you again. I know it's a lot to take in."

"That would be great. Thank you, Peter. I appreciate it."

"Not a problem, Cali. I told you I was here to help."

She put the reports aside and checked her e-mail while she waited for Peter.

Almost a half hour later Peter ambled into her office, closing the door behind him.

Cali logged off her e-mail, ready to tackle the financial reports again. "Please leave the door open, Peter."

"I don't think so, Cali." His tone of voice made her freeze. He was staring at her with a look that was anything but friendly. That's

266

when it hit her. Peter Carson—the man her father had been grooming to take over Stanton Enterprises when he retired—was the mole.

She considered her options. As far as she knew, Matthew wasn't back yet. There was the camera he'd installed in her office, but would he be watching if he was at the police station? She didn't know the answer to that.

Her best hope was that Lisa would realize the door was shut. But why hadn't Lisa called to check on her already? Had she stepped away from her desk or something?

What if she had stepped away? If she realized the door was shut, she might come to check on Cali herself. Then what? There wasn't anything Lisa could do that Cali couldn't.

Peter stalked toward Cali. She had no idea what he'd do, but she knew she needed to stall. "Why, Peter? I mean, after everything my father did for you. Why?"

She stood, trying to put herself at less of a disadvantage, but Peter still had a good seven inches on her and at least fifty pounds.

He snorted and it was a menacing sound. "Yes, sticking me behind a desk with a measly salary for the last ten years. He really did so much for me."

"But he took you under his wing . . . showed you the ropes. How could you do this? How could you steal from him?"

Peter laughed. "Stealing was the easy part."

"What are you talking about?"

He closed the distance between them and moved to stand behind her. "Sit down, Cali." It wasn't a suggestion.

She lowered herself back into her chair.

Peter leaned down to whisper in her ear, causing a shiver to run down her spine. "I guess it wouldn't hurt to grant your last request."

Cali swallowed hard and felt him smile against her cheek. He was too close.

"You see, I have everything planned out. After a little persuading on my part, the former CFO resigned and I graciously offered to take his place. It was the perfect setup. Redirect a small amount of profits into an offshore account. With all the business Stanton Enterprises does in the course of a year, I knew that small amount would add up to a nice little bonus to supplement my income."

Peter took a step back and twirled her chair around so she was facing him with her back to the door. "Things were going well until they passed those stupid laws saying the CEOs had to take personal responsibility for the financials. Your dad decided to take an interest in what I was doing, so I had to do something to divert his attention. It wasn't hard to find a group willing to step into the role of mercenaries in exchange for goods they could sell on the black market."

"You're the one hijacking the shipments?" she asked, stunned.

"Something like that." Peter strolled over to the bank of windows and propped his leg on the sill.

Cali knew she had to keep him talking. He'd mentioned things had changed. She had to assume he was referring to Matthew and Jason. "You said something changed?"

"Yes. Your father hired the best security team he could find to come in and figure out exactly what was going on." He puffed out his chest and smiled, full of pride. "Too bad all their hard work was for nothing. I still have the money and soon the company. Problem solved."

Then his demeanor shifted and he became more serious. "I had to sweeten the pot a little for the hired guns. They wanted more than just the goods they'd stolen, and then of course, someone had to take the fall when Mr. Tall-dark-and-nosy found out the money was missing. It wasn't hard to transfer several large sums of cash into a dummy bank account with his name on it."

It took her a few moments put it all together, but then she remembered Matthew telling her about an employee they'd discovered embezzling money shortly after he and Jason had started working for her father. Matthew wouldn't be happy when he found out an innocent man had been framed.

Peter swung around to face her again and this time his hand wasn't empty. He waved a black gun carelessly in her face.

"Everything would have been fine if your father had left things alone and trusted me to take care of it!" He slammed his hand down on the desk beside her, making her jump.

"Y-you're the one who sent the notes to my father, threatening him."

The left side of Peter's mouth quirked up into a sinister smile. "You're a smart one, aren't you, Cali? No wonder Daddy wanted to put you in charge. Too bad it will cost him an heir."

Cali's heart pounded in her chest. Was this it? Her dad? Matthew? She'd never been able to tell him she loved him. Would never be able to look into those blue eyes of his again and dream that one day he could love her back.

The door to her office flew open.

"Cali, are you—"

Peter pointed his gun in Lisa's direction and she stopped talking.

"Step inside and close the door, Lisa," Peter said.

When he'd lifted his arm to point the gun at Lisa, Cali's chair had shifted a little. She could see her friend and assistant standing in the door, unable to move. There was indecision in Lisa's eyes and Cali hoped her friend wouldn't do anything stupid.

Then, before Lisa made a move one way or another, there was a muffled thump from behind her. A second later, her friend fell to the floor, unconscious.

Cali saw another figure looming in the doorway but she couldn't make out who it was until they stepped over Lisa's body.

She gasped, unable to believe her eyes.

"Sorry I'm late. Did I miss anything?"

Chapter 30

Matthew couldn't wipe the smile from his face as he pulled into the parking garage at Stanton Enterprises. The weasel had covered his tracks well, but not well enough. Peter Carson was going to pay for all the trouble he'd caused.

Martinez was getting a warrant to tap all of Peter's phone lines and put him under twenty-four-hour surveillance. Right now, the only thing they had proof of was that he was paying Mariana's lawyer, but Matthew knew they'd find a lot more than that once they had the resources they needed. Matthew and Jason could monitor his activities at work but outside would be more difficult. They didn't have the manpower to sustain something like that long term.

Since Peter wasn't hijacking the shipments himself, they would need a few weeks at least to get the evidence they needed to arrest him. Both Matthew and Martinez agreed it would only be a matter of time now that they knew who they were looking at. The important thing going forward was to make sure not to tip their hand too soon. He couldn't know they were onto him.

Cali's concern earlier about the financials not making sense kept replaying in his mind. He'd already put in a call to one of his old Army buddies who was a whiz with numbers. Matthew wouldn't put it past Peter to skim the company accounts to pad his own pocket. He probably had a nice little nest egg somewhere.

After pulling into his spot, Matthew turned off the car and jogged to the elevator. While he was waiting, he took out his cell to call his brother. He wanted Jason to meet him in Cali's office so Matthew could tell them both the good news.

It was when he looked down at his phone that Matthew realized he'd turned it off when he'd entered the police station. They'd been doing some kind of drill or something when he'd arrived and hadn't wanted any technical interference or something. He'd forgotten to turn it back on.

Matthew waited impatiently as the screen came to life. The elevator doors opened and he stepped inside. He reached to press the button for the top floor as the camera feed from Cali's office popped up on the screen. Matthew's finger paused halfway to the button.

He'd programed his phone to show him a still image of Cali's office every fifteen minutes. Matthew scrolled through the last two hours of pictures as the doors automatically closed. When he got to the next-to-last image, he could see Peter standing in her office with her office door closed.

A lead weight settled in his gut as he moved on to the most recent image which, according to the time stamp, was taken less than a minute ago. Peter was standing at the window. Cali was in her chair. By her rigid pose, Matthew could tell something wasn't right.

Instead of selecting the floor Cali's office was located on, he chose the one directly below it and hit the speed dial on his phone. He didn't wait for Martinez to finish his greeting. "He's in her office right now. Something's wrong."

His friend knew better than to argue with him. "We're on our way."

The seconds dragged as the elevator continued its upward ascent. Matthew counted each floor, willing the elevator to somehow go faster.

When the doors finally opened, he darted out of the elevator and into the stairwell. It was the best way to reach Cali's floor without being detected. He needed an opportunity to fully assess the situation before he made his presence known.

Careful not to make any noise, Matthew inched his way up the stairs to the executive level. The stairwell was empty—no one used the stairs this high up unless there was an emergency. It was also minutes before five o'clock. Before long, most of the building's occupants would be leaving for home, completely unaware of what was happening on the top floor.

Matthew freed his gun from its holster as he reached the top of the stairs and double-checked to make sure he had a bullet ready to go in the chamber. Peering through the small window in the door, he scanned the floor to see if anyone was visible. The floor was deserted and Lisa wasn't at her desk. He did note, however, that Cali's door was open.

As quietly as he could, Matthew slipped unseen onto the executive floor. He did another quick sweep for people and again came up empty although he could hear voices coming from Cali's office. She wasn't alone.

He moved closer to the open doorway, listening. Someone other than Cali and Peter was in the room. It was another female and it wasn't Lisa. Where was she?

The sound of Cali's voice rang out loud and clear through the open door and it almost caused his heart to stop beating. "What's going on? I thought you were my friend."

It was then that he recognized the other female voice. Rachael Michaels.

***

Cali stared at the woman who'd been one of the few friends she'd had during her time in Africa. Even now, she was having trouble believing that Rachael had something to do with this.

Rachael laughed at Cali's confused expression. "You know the old saying, blood is thicker than water."

"What are you talking about?" Cali glanced over at Peter, and then back to Rachael. "You're related?"

"Sometimes it's a good thing when Daddy Dearest can't keep it in his pants."

Cali's stomach churned. It was impossible to watch them both at the same time. Rachael didn't have a gun—at least not one she'd seen—but that didn't make her any less dangerous.

Rachael kicked Lisa's limp body then strolled farther into the office. It was then Cali realized that they planned to kill her. She closed her eyes long enough to say a little prayer that Matthew wouldn't be the one to find her body. Cali didn't want that to be his last memory of her.

When she opened her eyes again, Rachael was standing on her left, a gun in her right hand. She used it to tilt Cali's chin up, forcing Cali to look into her eyes. "So . . . are you going to be a good girl and cooperate or is a little persuasion in order, hmm?"

"What do you want?" Cali asked.

Rachael glanced over at Peter.

He shrugged. "I hadn't gotten that far yet. Why don't you do the honors?"

A wicked smile crossed Rachael's face. "Well, you see, we need to take care of a little business. It's nothing big, really. We just need you to sign some things. It will make everything go so much smoother."

Cali bit the inside of her cheek. There was no way in hell she was going to let them see how scared she was. "I'm not signing anything."

She cried out as a tearing pain shot up her arm and a loud popping sound echoed through the office. The room tilted as she tried to remain focused on not blacking out. Peter had dislocated her shoulder.

"You only need one arm to sign your name, Cali. And where you're going, you won't need your legs either, so what's it going to be? Do I start working off body parts here or are you going to sign the papers?"

Rachael slapped several pieces of paper in front of Cali's face, although she was having trouble focusing on them through the pain. One of them was a resignation letter stating she no longer felt able to fulfill her obligations as acting CEO and was returning to her first love—being a doctor overseas.

Cali's heart pounded in her ears. She knew what would happen if she signed that paper. Communication was sparse in Africa. Her father had been lucky she was in a place where she could be reached when he called. There'd been many times over those two years when Cali had been out of touch for more than a month. That would be more than enough time for Peter and Rachael to get rid of her and any evidence linking them to her disappearance.

"We don't have all day," Rachael said, bringing Cali back to the present situation. "You have thirty seconds to pick up that pen and start signing your name before I put a bullet in your leg."

Everything stilled.

The seconds ticked by but none of them moved.

"Five seconds, Cali."

Her mouth went dry. This was it. This was the end.

"Four."

Fear took over and her breathing came in short, rough pants.

"Three . . . two . . ."

***

Matthew knew he couldn't wait any longer. Rotating his body so that he was poised at the edge of the doorway, he shouted, "Don't move."

Rachael didn't listen and a boom filled the room as she fired her weapon.

His heart stopped for a split second before instinct took over.

Cali screamed as another shot rang out.

Rachael collapsed onto the floor, her gun falling from her hand and landing a couple of feet away.

"No!" Peter raised his gun, pointing it at his new target.

Matthew was faster. His second bullet found its home directly in the center of Peter's forehead.

Peter seemed suspended for an extended moment in time before he toppled over and landed with his top half sprawled across Cali's desk.

After making sure there were no other threats visible, Matthew knelt down to check Lisa who was lying at his feet. He found a pulse, confirming she was still alive. Hopefully, all she had was a concussion. He knew Cali wasn't so lucky.

Rushing over to Cali, the first thing he noticed was how pale she was. Her body was completely limp. The only sign of life was that he could see she was still breathing. His chest ached seeing her like this.

"Cali? I need you to open your eyes." Nothing. "Please, Cali. Look at me, baby?"

Gradually she opened her eyes. They were glassy and unfocused.

Matthew felt tears threatening, but he pushed them away. Cali needed him.

He applied pressure to the blood gushing from her leg, attempting to staunch the flow, while he dialed 911. He couldn't lose her. They hadn't had enough time together.

"911, what's your emergency?"

"I need paramedics at Stanton Enterprises. Thirtieth floor." He rattled off the address. "Three people have been shot. Two dead. One badly wounded. She's losing a lot of blood."

"Okay, sir. I'll dispatch an ambulance and an officer."

"There's also someone unconscious. Her pulse is strong, but I think she was hit over the head with something."

The dispatcher was quiet for several seconds. "All right, sir. Is there anyone else hurt?"

"No."

"Okay. Just stay on the line with me. They'll be there shortly."

"Just get them here!"

Without waiting for her response, Matthew hung up the phone. Cali was falling apart before his eyes and he wasn't going to spend what might be his last few minutes with her stuck on the phone with some dispatcher.

Time seemed to stand still until he heard the elevator ding followed by the sound of half a dozen feet running in their direction. Not even five seconds passed before Martinez poked his head through the door. He took in the scene and met Matthew's gaze.

Matthew nodded. The danger had been neutralized.

Martinez and his men did their thing while Matthew tended to Cali. Her breathing was becoming shallow and, with every rise and fall of her chest, that feeling in the pit of his stomach grew. She had lost all color in her face—even her lips were turning blue.

Where were those damn paramedics?

Martinez knelt down to check Lisa's pulse. "She's alive," he announced to no one in particular.

After firing off some instructions to one of his officers, Martinez left the room only to return a minute or so later with a towel. He retook his position next to Lisa and placed the towel over the gash on the back of her head. From the look of it, Matthew doubted she'd even known what hit her.

"I'm sorry," Matthew whispered as he held tighter to Cali's leg, willing the bleeding to stop. "I'm sorry."

It seemed to take forever for the paramedics to get there. In reality, it was probably only about five minutes. They took charge of the situation and loaded both Cali and Lisa onto stretchers.

There wasn't enough room in the elevator for Matthew to ride down with Cali, so he took the stairs. He made it to the bottom floor as they were loading her into the back of the ambulance.

Before they closed the doors on Cali, Lisa was wheeled out of the building toward another waiting ambulance. Matthew heard her ask for Jason. He was glad she was awake.

Martinez had come down with Lisa. She hadn't needed as much hands-on medical care as Cali had.

"He'll meet you at the hospital, okay?" Martinez assured her.

Matthew was only half paying attention. His focus was on Cali. They'd put a tourniquet on her leg to stop the bleeding, but he knew enough about human anatomy to know that the bullet had hit an artery. She was losing way too much blood and there was no exit wound that he could see. That most likely meant surgery to remove the bullet.

He felt lost—numb. The only woman he'd ever loved could die and there was absolutely nothing he could do to stop it.

As soon as the ambulance pulled away, Martinez yelled his name.

Matthew looked up in time to see a set of keys flying at him. He caught them easily.

"Don't break any laws getting there, okay?"

Palming Martinez's keys, Matthew nodded to his friend. "Thanks."

Matthew jogged over to Martinez's unmarked car and got in. He was only about three blocks behind the ambulance. It wouldn't take much to catch up to it.

The ambulance pulled up at the emergency room right ahead of Matthew. He found a parking spot and ran into the hospital hot on the paramedics' heels.

As they had the last time, they got to a point where a nurse stopped him from continuing on and he lost sight of Cali. Matthew tried to step around her but a security guard placed a hand on his shoulder. For a moment, he considered fighting his way through. The only thing that stopped him was knowing that if he was in jail he wouldn't know what was happening with Cali.

Matthew's face twisted in agony. He hadn't felt this empty

inside since his mom died.

He leaned back against the wall, staring at nothing, when his brother came up beside him. Jason didn't say anything and they both stood by as Lisa was brought in. She was awake and talking. It looked as if she was going to be all right.

Lisa saw Jason and called out to him.

Jason looked torn. Matthew could only imagine what he must look like if his brother was hesitating.

"Go," Matthew said.

With one last concerned look at Matthew, Jason crossed the room and reached for Lisa's hand. "I'm right here."

It wasn't long until the two of them were taken down the hall so a doctor could examine Lisa's head.

Matthew was glad his brother had finally found someone like Lisa. She was good for him.

People came and went around him but he didn't pay much attention. He wanted to be with Cali. He wanted to know she was okay.

There was no doubt in his mind that he'd screwed up. It had been his responsibility to keep her safe—he'd promised to keep her safe—and he'd failed.

Eventually his brother returned to stand beside him. Matthew didn't acknowledge him and soon he felt a hand guiding him to the waiting room. Those same hands pushed him down into a chair and placed a cup of coffee in his grasp.

He didn't drink it.

Every time there was movement at the door, Matthew looked up hoping it was the doctor with an update on Cali.

Time dragged by with no word.

Jason said something to him before getting up and leaving. Matthew had no idea what he'd said. His brain felt disconnected from his body.

At some point, his brother returned to sit beside him and they continued to wait together.

"Is anyone here for Cali Stanton?" A man in scrubs stood at the door.

Matthew shot out of his seat and crossed the room. "I am."

The doctor nodded to a group of seats in the corner and they all sat down. He took off his cap and folded his hands in his lap as he faced Matthew and Jason.

Chapter 31

Jessie walked out of the ICU, pushing Alvin in his wheelchair. Their eyes were red and their cheeks flushed. It was obvious they'd both been crying.

"How is she?" Matthew asked, desperate for news. The doctor hadn't said much other than letting him know she had made it through the surgery. He'd never been more frustrated in his life. Didn't they realize how important she was to him?

"They say she's stable," Jessie said. "But she's lost a lot of blood. They don't know . . . they don't know how long it will be until she wakes up."

Alvin sniffed and wiped at his eye. "This is my fault. I asked her to come home. I should never have—"

"It's not your fault. You didn't know."

"I should have," Alvin insisted.

"But you didn't." Jessie placed a hand on Alvin's shoulder.

Alvin looked up at Matthew. "Thank you."

"I didn't do anything." And that was the truth. If Matthew had done his job, this wouldn't have happened. Cali would be safe at home, not lying in a hospital bed attached to monitors.

"Yes, you did. You saved my little girl's life. I'll never be able to thank you enough for that."

Matthew didn't know what to say, so he remained silent.

"Come on, Alvin. I need to get you home," Jessie said.

This time when Alvin looked at Matthew it was with a scowl on his face. "Jessie and Carolyn both agree that I need to be home resting or it will delay my recovery. But I don't feel right leaving my little girl."

"I'll stay with her, sir." Matthew didn't hesitate. He wasn't going anywhere until he knew for sure she would be okay anyway.

Alvin seemed unsure, but it was Jessie who jumped in. "I think that's a good idea. Alvin can put you on the approved visitor list and that way you can keep an eye on her."

"I couldn't ask—"

"No need to ask, sir," Matthew said.

Alvin considered it for another minute before nodding his head. "All right. Just let me know if anything changes."

"You'll be my first phone call."

Matthew shared a meaningful look with Jessie before she wheeled Alvin back to the nurses' station to add Matthew's name to the list. He would owe Jessie big for this.

While he waited for Alvin and Jessie's return, Matthew shot a quick text to his brother letting him know what was going on and where he'd be. Jason had stayed with him until they'd moved Cali to ICU, then he'd gone to visit Lisa. She'd had to get nine stitches and had a pretty nasty bump on her head. They wanted to keep her overnight for observation.

By the time Matthew got back to Cali's room it was almost midnight. He sat beside her bed, holding her limp hand. It was so small in his . . . so delicate. Matthew would give anything to trade places with her if he could.

"I'm so sorry, Cali," he said, apologizing again.

She didn't stir, not that he'd expected her to. The nurse said she could wake up at any time, but it probably wouldn't be until sometime tomorrow. She'd lost a lot of blood.

At some point Matthew must have dozed off. When he opened his eyes again there was sunlight shining through the window. Someone had draped a blanket over his shoulders.

He blinked several times, trying to adjust his eyes to the brightness, then checked on Cali. She still lay unmoving, her eyes closed.

Jessie had said she'd bring Cali's father back to see her around eight. It was already seven thirty.

Taking advantage of the little bit of privacy he had left, Matthew stood and grasped hold of Cali's hand. He leaned down and placed a soft kiss to her forehead. "I love you, Cali Stanton. You make me feel things I never imagined were possible. I'm sorry I failed you and . . ." The words got caught in his throat. "And I hope you can forgive me."

He ran his fingers over the planes of her face, memorizing them. What he wouldn't give to see her smile up at him right now.

"How's she doing?"

Matthew jerked and pulled his hand back.

He turned to face Alvin and Jessie. "There hasn't been any change."

Matthew glanced back at Cali once more before walking to the door. "I'll leave you alone."

When he walked out of the hospital, Matthew turned his phone back on. There'd been several messages waiting for him—most of them left within the last half hour. He knew the best thing he could do for Cali and her father right now was to clean up the mess that was left behind.

The first message was from Brian, Stanton Enterprises' COO. He wanted to know what he was supposed to do. With Alvin, Cali, and Peter out of commission, it was up to him to run the company until Cali or her father could take over again. Matthew knew Brian and he was more than capable of stepping up, however, the police had blocked off Cali's office as a crime scene. Brian couldn't get access to anything.

The next message was from Jason letting him know Lisa was being released this morning. Matthew wondered if his brother would make it into the office today at all.

There were also a few hang-ups, but Matthew figured if it were important, they'd call back.

The last message was from Martinez letting him know he needed to come down to the station and give his statement. Martinez didn't say anything about Matthew getting his gun back, so he figured he shouldn't hold his breath. It was probably being entered into evidence. Good thing that wasn't the only firearm he owned.

Prioritizing, Matthew called his brother first. "Hey."

"Hey. I wasn't sure if you'd still be with Cali or not," Jason said.

"Her dad and Jessie are with her right now. I figured I'd see what I could do at the office." Matthew slipped behind the wheel of his car and started the engine. "I have to swing by the police station at some point today and give my statement."

"Better you than me." Jason paused. "How is she?"

"She's still unconscious but stable. They say she might wake up today." Thinking about it was getting him all choked up again.

"The doctors are saying Lisa needs to rest for at least forty-eight hours, so I'm going to take her home once all the discharge paperwork comes through."

"Give me a call once you have her settled and I'll let you know where things stand. There's no sense in you coming in if you don't have to," Matthew said.

"Don't do that."

"What?"

"This isn't all on you."

Matthew didn't say anything as he pulled out into traffic.

Jason sighed. "I'll call you once I get Lisa home. We'll get this cleaned up. *Both* of us."

Not wanting to argue with his brother, Matthew let it go. "I need to call Martinez. I'll talk to you later."

After disconnecting the call, Matthew immediately dialed Martinez. The last thing Matthew wanted to do was spend his day at the police station, but there was no avoiding it.

Martinez answered on the second ring. "I was wondering if I'd have to track you down or not."

"I was at the hospital all night with Cali."

"How is she?" Martinez asked.

"Stable. We'll know more once she wakes up."

"I'm sorry, man."

The last thing Matthew wanted was to get emotional again, so he quickly changed the subject. "I got your message. I need to head into the office and put out some fires there, but I can come down to the station in a few hours. That work?"

"Yeah, that's fine. Jason told me you have video footage from the room. I'm going to need that, too. You and I both know you wouldn't have fired unless you didn't feel you had a choice, but the powers that be need evidence to back that up."

"I understand. I'll be there before lunch."

With that call out of the way, he moved on to Brian. The man was a bit panicked, but he calmed down some when Matthew told him he'd be there within the hour. Matthew knew he'd have to talk to Martinez about getting the room released but until then they were going to have to find a way to manage.

Matthew pulled up to the Stanton estate and parked his car around back as he had for the last month and a half. It felt different this time. Each step he took toward what had become their bedroom felt heavier than the last.

He could already see evidence of Alvin's return as he walked through the foyer, up the stairs, and down the hall. Alvin was back. The danger was gone. Matthew was no longer needed. Not here.

When he entered the room he'd shared with Cali, Matthew fell back on the bed and stared up at the ceiling. It was only a day ago that he'd been lying there in bed with her, basking in her beauty and her warmth. Matthew reached for her pillow and held it to his chest. He could still smell her scent. And if he closed his eyes, he could almost imagine she was there.

The buzzing sound of his phone roused him from his memories. He fished it out of his pocket. It was a text from Jason letting him know he and Lisa were on their way home.

Tears welled up in his eyes and, for the first time, he let them fall. He'd almost lost her. He made a stupid mistake and it had almost cost him everything.

He lay there for a while before forcing himself to get up. Cali would get better. She was strong. She could do it. Matthew had no doubt about that. And he would do what he needed to do as well. He would give her back her life—the life she wanted.

***

The first thing that registered in Cali's mind was that whatever she was lying on wasn't very comfortable. That and she felt as if she'd been lying in the same position for way too long. The next was the steady beeping of a machine.

Where was she?

Cali slowly opened her eyes, only to close them again against the harsh light.

"Hey, kiddo."

She turned her head toward her dad's voice and tried to open her eyes again. "Dad?"

"It's me, sweetheart. How are you feeling?"

Cali attempted to move but her body protested with more aches and pains than she'd ever experienced.

"Don't move, dear," Jessie said from the other side of her bed. It was then she realized she was in a hospital.

"Jessie?"

The older woman smiled down at her and brushed some hair away from her face. "You gave your father quite a scare, you know?"

Cali couldn't see much in the room beyond her father, Jessie, and some of the machines surrounding her bed. She tried to see more, but it was impossible at this angle.

"Where's Matthew?" she asked.

"He was here this morning," Jessie said, patting her on the hand. "I'm sure he'll be back later."

Later? Later when? She wanted to see him. She needed to see him.

Jessie glanced over at Cali's father. Was there something they weren't telling her? Did something happen to Matthew?

"Are you in pain, sweetheart?" her father asked.

"No." At least, not any more than she had been a few minutes ago.

Jessie gave her hand a comforting squeeze and walked toward the door. "I'll go tell the nurse she's awake."

***

Matthew drove straight to the hospital the next morning. He'd had every intention of going to see Cali the night before, but Jessie had called to let him know she was doing much better and had been moved to a regular room. By the time he'd left the office it was already after ten. He didn't want to disturb her sleep after what he knew had to have been a long day. She needed her rest.

Since it was Sunday, he hoped he'd get to have a little time alone with Cali so they could talk. Luck, however, wasn't on his side. Not only were her father and Jessie there, but so were Jason,

Lisa, Jen, and Becky. It was standing room only.

Cali was awake. She didn't participate much in the conversation around her, but she listened. For the most part, she seemed glad for the company.

As noon approached, Cali's eyelids began to droop.

"I think we should go and let you get some rest," Lisa said, getting up.

Jason stood, not straying far from Lisa's side. "We'll stop by to see you tomorrow."

Jen and Becky followed their lead.

"Let us know if you need anything . . . even if it's to smuggle in some chocolate," Becky said.

Cali smiled. "Thanks, guys."

Her father and Jessie each kissed her goodbye and said they were going to grab some lunch and would be back later.

Matthew hung back. He knew everyone would expect him to leave, too . . . well, maybe everyone except for Jessie, Lisa, and Jason since they knew of his and Cali's relationship. He lowered himself into a chair beside Cali's bed. Her eyes had already closed and her breathing was slow and steady. She was asleep.

This was his first opportunity to really look her over. He knew every inch of her body intimately and it wasn't difficult to pick up the subtle changes. She was still too pale. He missed seeing her blush. And, of course, there was a sling holding her left arm tight against her body.

He skimmed his fingers down the length of her good arm, remembering how it felt to have her arms wrapped around him. He lifted her right hand, kissed the inside of her palm, and then laid it gently back on the mattress. Matthew knew he needed to go.

"Is she all right?"

He whipped his head around at the sound of Alvin's voice. "Yeah, she's the same. Still sleeping."

Alvin wheeled himself over to his daughter's bed. He placed a hand on Matthew's shoulder. "I know I said it before, but you saved her life. I owe you much more than just my thanks for that."

"You don't owe me anything. If I'd been a few minutes later . . ." Matthew didn't finish his thought.

"You weren't, though."

For several minutes neither of them spoke. The only sound in the room was the quiet beeping of the machines.

"I should probably go," Matthew said as he stood. "I'll . . . call me if you need anything."

Alvin looked confused and Matthew couldn't blame him. Before his boss asked him something he couldn't answer, Matthew left, his heart aching with every step he took away from Cali.

The new workweek brought with it a whole new set of issues. Although the mole had been found and eliminated, there was still the issue of the individuals hijacking the shipments. Martinez had narrowed it down to three possible groups operating in the Chicago area who were known for this type of thing. He had each one of them under surveillance. All they had to do was wait.

There were different versions of what happened going around the office. It was decided that it would be better to get the correct information out there—at least what they could share of it—than to let the employees speculate. Brian called a companywide meeting on Monday afternoon to do just that. Matthew had been presented as the hero, which had made him feel like a fraud.

On Tuesday, the board of directors demanded a meeting with Matthew and Jason. For two hours they sat through rapid-fire questions ranging from 'how could you miss this?' to 'when were we going to be told?' Most of the board members acted as if Matthew and Jason had known Peter was behind this all along. Or if they didn't, they should have.

Matthew also spent many hours helping Brian get things readjusted. Passwords and access had to be updated. E-mails and phones rerouted. And all without setting foot in Alvin's office since Martinez still hadn't released it.

With Matthew so busy helping Brian get up and running, Jason had to take over Matthew's usual duties. It meant they were both putting in eighteen-hour days the entire week after the shooting.

Matthew stopped by the hospital each night. It was always after midnight and Cali was always asleep. He would stand by her bed for a few minutes each night, kiss her brow, and then whisper *I love you* before going home to his lonely apartment.

Unfortunately, the second week wasn't much better. Matthew and Brian managed to untangle the financial web Peter had created with the help of Jake, Matthew's old Army buddy. He was the only reason they'd gotten to the bottom of it. In the end, they'd been able to track down all the missing money and hand over the information to the district attorney. It would take a while and no small amount of paperwork, but Matthew was fairly certain that Stanton Enterprises would be able to recover most of the money Peter had stolen.

Every day Matthew would call Jessie for an update on Cali's condition. On Wednesday, she called with good news. "They're releasing her from the hospital. Alvin and I are taking her home. Alvin's nurse has already moved her things to the main house. She can help with Cali as well, but I'm going to be staying in one of the guest rooms for a couple of weeks to help out. At least until she's able to move around more on her own."

"That's great news, Jessie." He was glad she was going home. Really he was. But it meant seeing her would be more difficult. He could drop in at the hospital any time day or night. Somehow, he didn't think Alvin would be thrilled if he showed up on his doorstep at midnight wanting to see Cali.

"How are you doing?" she asked.

"I'm fine." Matthew assured her. And physically he was fine. "I'll try and come by this weekend to see how she's doing if I can."

"Do you want me to let her know?"

"No. I-I don't know if I'll be able to or not. It's been nuts around here lately."

It turned out to be a good thing that he'd asked Jessie not to say anything about him coming to visit. He'd gotten a call late Friday from Martinez. They were pretty sure they'd found the ones behind the hijackings and his friend wanted to know if Matthew was up for a little recon.

His need to finish this compelled him to go with Martinez.

Chapter 32

"How did you find these guys?" Matthew asked as they sat in Martinez's car a block away from the warehouse they were staking out.

"I have a friend in Vice who got a tip from one of her informants."

"It's credible?"

Martinez rolled his eyes. "Would we be sitting here if it wasn't?"

Letting out a breath, Matthew tried to relax. It wasn't the stakeout that had him jittery. It had been two weeks since he'd been able to look into her eyes.

"What's with you today?" Martinez asked. "You seem on edge about something and I doubt it's this."

"No." Matthew debated whether or not to say anything to his friend, but he figured why not? If he had his way about it, the world would know about him and Cali soon enough. "Cali was released from the hospital this week."

"That's good, right?"

"Yeah. It's great. Jessie says the doctors are happy with the way everything is healing." He stared across the street at the large metal building. There hadn't been any movement yet.

Martinez was quiet for a long moment. Matthew could only

imagine what was going through his friend's mind.

"Holy shit! You and the boss' daughter?" Martinez whistled. "You got balls, man. I'll give you that."

"Yeah, well, don't get ahead of yourself. She might not be sticking around."

"What do you mean?"

Matthew took a pull from the water bottle he had wedged between his legs. "Before she moved back to Chicago to take over for her father, she was working in Africa with Doctors Without Borders. I'm pretty sure she plans to go back once this is all said and done."

"You haven't talked about it?"

"No. With everything going on and then her getting hurt, there really hasn't been a good time to bring it up."

Martinez sat there for several minutes. "If you want to be with her, man, you're gonna have to tell her that. She might feel the same way."

The afternoon turned into evening and no one had shown up at the warehouse. They already knew the loot was inside. All they needed was someone to show up so they could arrest them.

"Looks like it's going to be an all-nighter. You sure you want to stay?" Martinez asked.

"I'm not going anywhere until this is finished."

"What about your woman?"

Matthew stretched his neck. "Jessie will call me if something changes."

"That's not what I meant and you know it."

He pretended to ignore his friend's comment. "You want me to take the first shift or do you want it?"

Martinez must have realized the subject was closed for the time being. "I'll take the first shift."

Matthew nodded, leaned his head back and closed his eyes.

At twelve fifty-two on Sunday afternoon, three white males pulled up to the warehouse. One jumped out, opened the large metal garage door, and then hopped back into the car. They drove inside and, seconds later, the door closed behind them.

Matthew and Martinez exited the vehicle and crossed the street.

"Everyone in position," Martinez ordered into the radio.

They waited just out of sight along the brick wall of a

neighboring building until a response came through on the radio. "I've got eyes on them inside the warehouse, Detective."

"Any sign of weapons?"

"Negative. Doesn't mean they aren't carrying, though."

Martinez looked over at Matthew. "You're gonna have to hang back. If this gets ugly, I don't want to have to file an incident report as to why one of my suspects was killed by a civilian."

Matthew smirked. "Aye, aye . . . Detective."

His friend chuckled. Matthew had been his superior when they'd served together.

"We go on my signal," Martinez said into the radio.

He held his arm at a right angle, his hand in a fist for two seconds, and then gave the signal for his team to advance.

Matthew stayed on his six. He wouldn't shoot unless he had to, but he wasn't letting his friend go in there without him.

The Chicago PD busted down the door and rushed, shouting, into the building. Matthew was used to covert military operations. This was the exact opposite.

Two of the men dropped to the ground immediately. The third decided to try and be a hero. He ran around behind the back of some boxes.

Martinez and another officer took off after him with Matthew hot on their heels.

Four shots rang out in quick succession and the suspect fell to the ground.

Martinez kept his gun at the ready as he approached the suspect while Matthew went to check on the officer who'd been hit. So much for the suspects not being armed.

Luckily, the officer who'd been shot had been wearing a vest. He wouldn't have much more than a bruise.

The suspect would survive, too. Martinez was a good shot. He'd put two bullets in the guy's leg and one in his arm.

By three o'clock, the Chicago PD had three suspects in custody and two truckloads worth of supplies that had yet to be sold.

Martinez walked over to where Matthew was standing off to the side watching the three being loaded into patrol cars. "Thanks for your help."

"I should be thanking you. Doubt we would have caught them without your help."

"It was a team effort." Martinez smiled and slapped Matthew on the back. "Go get some rest and then go see your woman."

Matthew wasn't going to argue with him. "I'll catch you later."

"Later, man."

He slept like the dead that night. It had been years since he'd had to sleep on something other than a bed. Maybe he was getting soft, but spending the night sleeping in a car wasn't something he wanted to repeat anytime in the near future.

When he woke up on Monday morning, he had one thing on his mind. He was going to see Cali today. Nothing was going to get in his way this time.

He marched into his office determined to finish his work early and go see her, but he stopped short when Alvin was there waiting for him.

"What happened? What's wrong?" Matthew asked, fear lacing his voice.

Alvin cocked his head to the side and Matthew realized how his words must have sounded. Not exactly the greatest first impression to give your girlfriend's father. Well, not exactly the first impression since Alvin already knew Matthew, but things had changed. At least, Matthew was hoping they had.

His boss stood there watching him for several moments before he spoke. "No, she's good. Better than good, actually. Her doctors expect her to make a full recovery."

"Oh, that's good," Matthew said, moving farther into the room. It was then that he noticed Alvin's clothes. He was in a suit. "Are you back?"

"I only had two weeks left anyway." He laughed. "I had to promise all my hovering nurses, including my daughter, that I'd take it easy."

Matthew smiled. "So what brings you to my office on your first day back?"

"Cali, as a matter of fact."

At the mention of Cali, everything else that had been on Matthew's mind was forgotten. "What about her?"

"Since I'm back a little early she's decided to start packing. I told her there was no hurry or anything, but Cali's very stubborn. I'm sure you figured that out over the last few months." Alvin chuckled.

Matthew was filled with a mix of anxiety and sadness. It took him a minute to form the question he had to ask. "She's leaving, then?"

"Says she doesn't want to be in my hair or some such nonsense." Alvin waved his hand, dismissing the notion. "Anyway, I was wondering if you wouldn't mind giving her a hand with her things tomorrow since both of us are a little less mobile than usual."

Matthew's head was spinning. She was leaving? How could she leave and not tell him she was going? Did she think so little of him? Of them?

"Matthew?"

He returned his attention to Cali's father. "Sorry. You were saying?"

Alvin grinned. "I know you've been busy here, but could you possibly be out at the house around eight tomorrow morning? For some reason, she seems to be in a bit of a hurry."

Matthew's heart sank. "Sure. No problem."

"Great!" Alvin appeared completely oblivious to Matthew's distress. "I'll have Jessie save some breakfast for you."

Matthew started to protest, but his boss held up one hand to stop him. "It's the least we can do."

Not wanting to argue, he nodded and waited while Alvin rolled himself out of Matthew's office.

He had no idea how in the world he was going to go over there tomorrow morning and help the woman he loved move to the other side of the world and out of his life.

The simple answer was that he couldn't.

***

Cali had been awake long before her father came in at seven thirty to say goodbye on Tuesday morning. She couldn't sleep—not well, anyway—and she didn't need a shrink to tell her why. Matthew hadn't called or visited her after that first day. It didn't make sense. He cared . . . she knew he did.

Or at least she thought he did.

She'd picked up the phone to call him more times than she could count, but each time she stopped herself. What if it really was the end? What if he hadn't come to visit her because it was over between them? The danger was gone, after all.

And that, in a nutshell, was exactly why she couldn't sleep. When she was in the hospital, there were constant distractions. That and plenty of strong pain medication. At her dad's house, she was surrounded by memories. Everywhere she looked, Matthew was there.

On her first night back, she'd fallen asleep curled up on the bed they'd shared, hugging his pillow to her chest. She'd lain there all night watching the phone, praying he would call. Her father found her the next morning. He didn't come right out and ask, but she could see the question in his eyes.

Cali slept in her own room after that. She knew she was acting like a silly schoolgirl, but for some reason she didn't care. She missed him—she needed him—and he wasn't there. What she didn't understand was why.

That was ultimately what drove her decision to leave. She'd been home for five days and still nothing. He wasn't coming.

Cali knew she couldn't allow herself to follow through on that train of thought. It hurt too much.

She wasn't giving up, though, just postponing until she had the strength to fight for him. And fight for him she would. One way or another she was going to get the answers she needed.

Her body hurt if she moved the wrong way and walking was difficult. Jessie usually brought Cali's meals upstairs to her because the one time she'd tried to go downstairs, she'd almost fallen. For the next two weeks, Cali's arm would be strapped close to her body so her dislocated shoulder could heal. That meant she only had full use of one of her hands. It made most daily tasks challenging.

Once she was back to one hundred percent, she'd confront Matthew. He owed her that much.

But for now she was leaving. The lake house was already stocked from her father's recent stay and Carolyn, her father's nurse, had agreed to stay on and help Cali for the next month. Jessie would stay here and look after her dad. All Cali knew was that she couldn't stay here. Not without Matthew.

Cali slowly eased herself up off the bed and made her way into the bathroom to get ready. Her things were packed and her father had arranged for a driver to take her to the lake house. She wanted to be ready when they arrived.

Bathing was a challenge given she only had use of one arm, but Cali managed. She pulled a loose sweatshirt over her head and through her one good arm before limping back out into her bedroom. Her balance was off due to her injury, but what she saw when she reentered her bedroom almost caused her to lose it altogether. There, sitting on her bed, was Matthew.

The toiletry bag she'd been carrying dropped to the floor, causing him to look up. They stared at each other for several minutes before he spoke. "Hi."

"Matthew." She took a deep breath.

They fell into silence again.

"You look tired."

Cali lowered her gaze. She was filled with so many mixed emotions. Part of her wanted to yell at him—to demand to know why he hadn't called. Every other part of her, however, wanted to curl up in a ball. She didn't want to talk about her lack of sleep. This conversation wasn't supposed to happen yet. She was supposed to get well first. That was the plan.

She looked at the items she'd dropped strewn across the floor.

Matthew seemed to notice them for the first time and bent down to pick them up. "I'll get them."

"Thanks," she whispered.

He piled all the items back in the little bag and stood to face her. The tension was palpable. So many questions swam in the space between them, and yet neither seemed to be able to form words.

A knock on Cali's door caused them both to jump.

"Good morning, Matthew," Jessie said from the doorway.

Matthew took a step back and placed the toiletry bag down on the dresser. "Morning, Jessie."

Jessie grinned. "Sorry to interrupt but I wanted to see if you'd like any breakfast. I still have some pancakes downstairs."

"No. Thank you. I'm not hungry."

Nodding, Jessie left them alone once more.

The exchange had allowed Cali time to get her bearings back. She began moving toward the bed again, where she'd been headed before she'd spotted Matthew in her room.

Cali felt him come up behind her. She wanted to turn around and fall into his arms, but she held herself back. This not knowing where they stood was even worse than it had been before. Then she hadn't known what it was like to melt into him and get lost. She wanted to forget about Peter and Rachael . . . her leg . . . her shoulder. She wanted to forget about all of it. He could do that for her. Matthew could make her forget the worries and stress in her life. He was standing within her grasp, but she couldn't reach for him.

Before she made it to the bed, Matthew moved to stand between it and her. She waited for him to say something, but he didn't.

"What are you doing here?" Cali asked. "Why did you come?"

"Your dad said you were leaving." His answer was so simple, yet it didn't give her any of the answers she wanted.

"Yes."

"Why?"

Cali felt herself choking up and she mentally cursed herself. She didn't want him to see her cry over him. "I can't . . . stay here."

"Why not?" he demanded. "Your father's here. And Jessie. And what about Lisa and Jen and Becky? They seem like good friends. And—"

She saw the muscles in his throat move as he swallowed.

"And me."

At first Cali didn't think she'd heard him right then she saw the vulnerability there in his eyes.

"Matthew, I—"

"No, I just . . . I need to say this." He took a deep breath and looked her in the eye. "I love you."

Cali's eyes widened and her heart pounded in her chest.

"I love you," he said again. "And I don't want you to leave. I want you to stay. With me. I know you may not feel the same way about me, but I just—"

"I love you, too."

It took a second for the words she'd said to register, but when they did a huge smile lit up Matthew's face. He cupped her face with both hands and rested his forehead against her. "You . . ."

"I love you," Cali whispered.

Matthew closed his eyes and lowered his mouth to hers. The kiss was soft and gentle—and full of love. Cali wrapped her good arm around his waist and melted into her lover's arms the way she'd been longing to for the last three weeks.

Ultimately it was Cali's injuries that broke them apart. She couldn't stand on her leg long without pain and all too soon it demanded her attention.

"I'm sorry," Matthew said as he helped her onto the bed. He pushed her suitcase out of the way, sat down beside her, and held her close. Several minutes passed as they sat there together on the bed before he cleared his throat. "Why are you leaving?"

Cali leaned in to him. "I couldn't stay here anymore. It was too hard being here without you."

There was a long pause. "Being here? You mean in this house?"

"Yeah."

He tilted her chin up so he could see her face. "So you weren't going back to Africa?"

"No! How could you think—" What he must have thought registered in her brain. "You thought I'd just leave?"

"I didn't know," he said, his voice softer. "I hoped not, but then your father said you were leaving, and, well, I guess I panicked. I couldn't lose you."

"I was going to the lake house."

"Oh." His brow creased as if he was thinking really hard about something. "Don't go to the lake house."

"What?"

"Don't go to the lake house." He paused. "Come home with me."

"What?" Surely she hadn't heard correctly.

Matthew smiled. "Can you say something other than 'what'?"

Cali had to make sure she'd heard what she thought she had. "What do you mean when you say you want me to come home with you?"

He brushed a damp strand of hair behind her ear. "I mean I want you to move in with me. I've been miserable without you. I need to see you every day and I need you in my bed every night."

More than anything Cali wanted to say yes, but she had to ask one question first. "Why didn't you come visit me at the hospital?"

"I did." He looked confused.

"No. I know you did right after, but I was there for over a week and you never came back." She felt the tears threatening again.

He trailed his fingers down the side of her face as he spoke. "I was there. Every night I stopped by your room to make sure you were okay and to give you a kiss. Maybe I should have woken you, but I didn't. I wanted to let you rest. And I called Jessie to check on you every day." His eyes softened. "You thought I'd abandoned you?"

"You came every night?"

"It was usually after midnight, but I couldn't go to sleep without seeing you." He rubbed his thumb lightly over her bottom lip. "When Jessie told me they were sending you home I wanted to come to you, but your father was here and I didn't know what you wanted. Then yesterday I finally decided it didn't matter. I had to see you. That was when Alvin told me you were moving. I thought—"

"That I was leaving you." She reached up to caress his face.

"Yes."

"I picked up the phone at least ten times a day to call you," she confessed.

"Why didn't you?"

Cali bit down on her bottom lip. "I didn't know if you still wanted this. Us."

"I will always want you."

"Why didn't you call me?" she asked.

"I was afraid, I suppose. I promised to take care of you and look what happened. I didn't know how you felt." Matthew hesitated. "I should have called. I should have been here when you needed me."

"You should have. None of this was your fault, and I did need you."

She thought he might argue with her, but then he whispered, "I know."

Cali leaned forward and pressed her lips to his. Everything they couldn't say with words came through in that kiss. He slid his hands through the wet strands of her hair and held her close. It was one of the best feelings in the world.

A long time passed before they broke apart. When they did, she gazed up into his eyes and smiled. "Yes."

"What?" he asked, clearly confused.

She brought her hand up to stroke the side of his face. "Yes, I'll come home with you."

Before she knew what hit her, Cali was tumbling back onto the bed. Matthew's hands held her face as he gave her a hard kiss. "I love you."

Laughter bubbled from deep within her, followed swiftly by a groan of pain. "I love you, too."

"That's all I need to know," Matthew said as his mouth once again descended to claim hers.

Epilogue

Cali checked her reflection in the full-length mirror. It had been a while since she'd put on one of her designer suits. There had been big changes in Cali's life over the last two months, the biggest of which was her change in address. Matthew lived in a nice-sized townhouse in the city. It was nowhere near the size of her father's house, but there was more than enough room for the two of them.

For the most part, the adjustment had been easy. They'd already been living together before the shooting. The only difference was that her clothes now hung beside his in the closet. The main point of contention between them was her injuries. Matthew felt responsible. Cali didn't think he should.

When she'd first moved in he'd insisted on doing everything for her. All the hovering drove her nuts until she finally had to put her foot down. It had led to their second fight and, boy, was it a good one. They were both stubborn and used to getting their way. It was a good thing he didn't share walls with any of his neighbors. Cali refused to let him take the blame for something that was clearly not his fault.

In fact, no one thought Matthew was at fault for what had happened. Not her, not her father, not even the press.

The press. A month went by with little more than a small blurb about what had happened. Then the lawyer who'd been representing

Mariana dropped her case. With Peter gone the money had dried up. No one was really surprised the lawyer walked away.

No one, that is, except Mariana. When she realized she could be facing major jail time she began talking to anyone who would listen—including a sympathetic reporter. Overnight, Stanton Enterprises, Mariana, and everyone else involved in the case became front-page news. Matthew became the hero while Peter and Rachael were painted as the heartless villains.

Detective Martinez had done some more digging and found that what Rachael had told Cali minutes before she'd shot her was true. Rachael and Peter were siblings—half siblings. Peter's father had an affair with a coworker twenty-six years ago resulting in the birth of a baby girl: Rachael.

The reporter used this information to create more sympathy for Mariana. She was the poor, unsuspecting, lovesick victim.

It floored Cali how much the woman had changed. She remembered how defiant Mariana was in the interrogation room. That woman had disappeared. Mariana was now the epitome of remorse. She played the 'love is blind' angle whenever she was given the chance and the public was eating it up.

Cali didn't buy it and she was hoping the judge didn't either.

Satisfied with her appearance, she headed downstairs.

When she reached the last step, Cali paused for a second to admire the man standing in the kitchen. His back was to her and he looked edible as he stood over the stove in his dress shirt and slacks. Six months ago, she'd been in Africa oblivious to his existence. Now he was the center of her world.

Matthew glanced over his shoulder and smiled at her.

Without a word, Cali walked over and wrapped her arms around his waist. "Good morning, Mr. Andersen."

"Mmm."

"You ready for today?" she asked.

Matthew placed a lingering kiss on her lips before answering. "Yes. I want to get this over with."

Cali grinned. "Tired of the reporters trying to knock down your door for an interview?"

He snorted. "Most definitely. The sooner things get back to normal the better."

***

Matthew grabbed some plates out of the cabinet while Cali went to get the orange juice from the refrigerator. He was more than ready for this thing to be over and done with. The same day the first article about Mariana hit the newsstand, Matthew began receiving phone calls. Every media outlet within a fifty-mile radius wanted to talk to him.

It was the last thing Matthew wanted. He and Cali had survived. Peter and Rachael were dead. And Mariana was safely behind bars. As far as Matthew was concerned, the case was closed. Considering the number of reporters camped in front of their townhouse, the media didn't agree.

He'd also received half a dozen job offers over the past two months. Matthew turned them all down. He had no interest in working anywhere else. He liked his job and he was looking forward to things quieting down now that the threat was gone.

There was also the bonus of dating the boss' daughter. He was still trying to wrap his mind around that. At odd times, it would strike him that Cali was Alvin's daughter—most of the time Matthew only thought of Cali as being his.

"Don't forget about dinner at my dad's tonight," Cali said as she sat across from him, eating her breakfast.

"I'll be there. Don't worry." After the court hearing today, Matthew needed to stop in at the office for a few hours. He wasn't going to miss dinner, though. Alvin used the excuse that they all needed to decompress after the hearing, but Matthew suspected there was something else going on. Since he didn't know what it was, he'd kept his suspicions to himself.

They finished breakfast and cleaned up before putting on their coats. Cali placed her arms on his shoulders and smiled up at him. "I'll see you at the courthouse."

He took his time kissing her goodbye. With the reporters outside it was better to do these types of things inside. "I'll be right behind you."

Because he had to go into work, they took separate cars. As promised, Matthew followed behind Cali as she drove into the city to the courthouse.

The hearing was short. Mariana's court-appointed lawyer

couldn't sell the sympathy plea to the judge and a trial date was scheduled.

Mariana leaned in and whispered something to her lawyer.

As people began filing out of the courtroom, Mariana's lawyer approached the prosecutor. Matthew and Cali were close enough to overhear that Mariana wanted a plea agreement.

Matthew wasn't sure how he felt about that. Cali had almost died. Even if Mariana didn't have anything to do with that directly, she'd still helped to perpetuate the scam that had ultimately put Cali in danger. She deserved to suffer.

"She's going to get off with a slap on the wrist," Matthew muttered, disgusted.

Cali put her arm around him as they strolled down the long hallway toward the elevator. Even though her leg was almost healed, stairs were a bit of a challenge for her.

"He used her." Matthew opened his mouth to disagree, but she cut him off. "Yes, she went along with it. And yes, she made some really bad choices. But she isn't the one who hurt me."

Matthew frowned.

She hugged his waist a little tighter. "She'll get what she deserves."

He pulled her closer when they stepped inside the elevator and rested his cheek against the top of her head. "I hope you're right."

"I am." She sounded so sure.

***

The mob of reporters seemed to have grown during the time they were inside the courthouse. Cali and Matthew did their best to ignore them and their questions as they rushed to their cars.

Matthew opened the door for her and then leaned in to kiss her goodbye. Before they separated, Cali heard the flash of a camera. It wasn't the first time they'd been caught in an intimate moment and she knew it wouldn't be their last. She was the daughter of a prominent member of Chicago society. Growing up she'd been used to her picture showing up on the society pages alongside her father all the time. She was used to it. Matthew was not.

Cali saw him narrow his eyes at the man holding the camera.

"I'll see you tonight, all right?" she asked, trying to pull his attention away from the reporter. "I love you."

It worked. Matthew relaxed his shoulders and gave her another kiss, this time on the cheek. "I love you, too."

While Matthew headed to Stanton Enterprises, Cali drove to Chicago Memorial. It had meant calling in a few favors but she'd been able to secure a job in the ER. Cali missed being a doctor. She was looking forward to the challenges she would find in the ER of one of Chicago's busiest hospitals.

It took her a few hours to finish filling out all the necessary paperwork for her new job, but it felt like a step in the right direction. At four o'clock, she said goodbye to a few of her new colleagues, walked out to the parking lot, and slid behind the wheel of her car.

The drive to her dad's house took a little longer than expected. It was already after four when she left the hospital and she'd forgotten to account for traffic.

Cali pulled into her father's driveway and turned off the engine. When she made it up the walkway her dad was already there standing with the door open. "Hi, Dad."

Her father pulled her into a bone-crushing embrace. He'd been extremely protective since her brush with death.

Jessie ambled into the foyer. "I'm so glad you could come tonight. We've missed you."

Cali caught a whiff of the delicious smells coming from the kitchen and her stomach was already rumbling. "Whatever you're making smells delicious."

"Well, come on in," Jessie said, motioning Cali inside. "Let's get this coat off you and I'll find something for you to snack on while we wait."

Luckily they didn't have to wait long for Matthew, Jason, and Lisa to arrive. Cali's friend and former assistant had completely recovered from her injuries. The doctors did have to shave a section of Lisa's hair in order to stitch her up, so she was sporting a much shorter haircut these days trying to cover up the damage.

Jessie ushered everyone into the dining room where she had laid everything out. It was an impressive spread.

Dinner was great—not only the food, but the company as well. Everyone was smiling and laughing. Cali had missed this.

For dessert, Jessie brought out a chocolate pie. She gave each one of them a slice and everyone dug in. Everyone, that is, except for her father and Jessie.

It took a few minutes for Cali to notice. "Dad? Is everything okay?"

Her father grinned, but something was off. He looked nervous. "Yes, sweetheart. Everything's fine. Great, actually."

Cali tilted her head to the side trying to figure out what she was missing. If things were great, then why was her father sweating?

"I have—" Her father looked up at Jessie who was standing by his side. "*We* have something we'd like to tell you all." Taking a deep breath, her father faced the group. "Jessie and I are getting married."

Cali's fork fell out of her grasp and clattered onto her plate. It was the only sound in the room.

She knew everyone was probably staring at her, but Cali didn't care. Her attention was focused on her father and Jessie. "You're getting married?"

Then she realized how that must have sounded. "I mean . . . what . . . when . . . I don't—"

Matthew placed his hand on her knee. "This explains why Jessie was at the lake house."

Jessie smiled. "I was wondering if you'd figure that out. I'd wanted to leave when you two called, but Alvin said no."

"How long?" Cali asked.

Her father and Jessie glanced at each other and then back to her. "About fifteen years."

Cali's eyes went wide and her mouth fell open. "You've been having an affair for fifteen years?"

"We just—"

"We didn't think it was the right time," her father said. "First there were your rocky teen years. Then you were away at college and medical school. Once you were finished with that we considered saying something to you, but then you announced you were going overseas."

"So what changed?" Lisa asked, breaking into the conversation for the first time.

"Cali and Matthew," Jessie said. "We'd been worried not only about Cali's reaction but also how the outside world would see it if the millionaire married the housekeeper."

Her father took Jessie's hand and kissed her palm. "But after seeing what happened to Cali—after seeing what she and Matthew went through—we decided it didn't matter. We love each other and want to be together."

Cali brushed the moisture from her cheeks.

"Are you okay with this, sweetheart?" her father asked in a soft voice.

Pushing herself away from the table, Cali walked the short distance to where her father sat at the head. She bent to give him a hug. "I'm more than okay with it, Dad. As long as you're happy, that's all that matters to me."

Later that night as Matthew escorted Cali out to her car, he lifted her left hand to his mouth and kissed her ring finger. "You do know I plan on making it official one of these days, don't you?"

She laid her head on his shoulder and closed her eyes. "And you better not take too long about it either."

To find out more about A Christmas Proposal (A Hidden Threat Novella) and other upcoming books by Sherri Hayes, subscribe her newsletter at http://eepurl.com/J4vDb.

Preview – Welcome to Serpents Kiss

Katrina Mayer glanced at the clock. She had a few more minutes before she needed to head upstairs. It was enough time for her to glance over the newest membership application she'd received.

The applicant's name was Drew Parker. He was a firefighter and listed himself as submissive. Everything about him seemed fairly straightforward. He was twenty-eight. Single. And looking for a kinky relationship with a female dominant.

As she scanned the rest of his details, two Femdoms came to mind—Madi and Beth. Madi was a regular. The club was open every Friday and Saturday night, and Madi rarely missed the opportunity to have some fun. Every now and then, she'd play with one of the male subs, but it was rare. More often than not, Madi could be found on the dance floor.

Beth was another story. To be honest, Katrina was worried about her. Beth used to come to the club all the time with her longtime sub, Ben. Two months ago, Beth discovered that Ben had a secret life she'd known nothing about. It had left her shattered and heartbroken. She hadn't been to the club since it happened. For the time being, Beth had no desire to get back on the horse. Katrina was hoping that would change with time.

It wasn't her job to be a matchmaker, however. She'd created

Serpent's Kiss as a place where kinky people could hang out and play when the mood struck them.

Speaking of moods, Katrina was in the mood to have some fun. She pushed back from her desk and walked out into the hall. After locking the door to her office, she headed down to the main room of the club, where Ali and Brandon were getting things ready for later that night.

Brandon, her main bartender, caught her eye. She tilted her head toward the stairs, and he nodded.

Katrina rarely played while the club was open unless it was to do a demonstration. Things were too hectic, and all too often, she was needed to help with one issue or another. Plus, it was always good to mingle with the club members and make sure they were content.

It was for that reason that she tended to play before the club opened its doors to the evening crowd. Brandon and whichever submissive had signed up for the evening service arrived three hours before the club opened to prep and clean. It was the perfect opportunity for her to sneak upstairs to have a little fun while still being safe. She always kept the door open to whatever room she used, and Brandon was aware that the upstairs was off-limits during those times unless he heard someone yell red.

Ascending the stairs, she entered the first room on her right. All the rooms on the second floor had been turned into playrooms. Each was well equipped with a variety of toys that could be adapted to specific needs for whatever situation arose. She'd tried to make the rooms as versatile as possible.

Ryan was kneeling on the floor waiting. As per her instructions and their arrangement, he was waiting for her naked. His cock hadn't been erect when she'd walked into the room, but as she stood there looking at him, she saw it stiffening.

Katrina had prepared the space earlier that day with all the items she would need for the scene. They were all placed within easy reach at the back of the room. Now, all she had to do was get her submissive in place.

"Stand," she ordered.

Ryan rocked back on his heels and nimbly pushed himself up off the floor and to his feet.

She picked up a spreader bar and nudged his feet apart. With the spreader bar in place, she removed two leather cuffs from the table. One by one, she encircled his wrists and then lifted his arms above his head to attach the cuffs to the chains in the ceiling. Once she was sure they were secure, Katrina stepped back to appreciate her subject.

Ryan was thirty-five and a lawyer. You'd never know he spent most of his time behind a desk. He worked out every morning and ate healthier than she cared to think about. She had a weakness for cake. It didn't look as if he even thought about processed sugar, much less ate it.

Nonetheless, Ryan was one of her favorite submissives to play with. Katrina didn't have a submissive of her own. She had no desire for one, either. At the age of forty-three, she'd found herself widowed. And while she'd loved her husband, he had been vanilla as vanilla could be. Even role-playing in the bedroom held no interest for him.

Her husband's death had been a shock. It had also made her realize how short life was. No one knew how long they had on this earth. That was why, six months after her husband's death, Katrina made the decision to open up a fetish club. Five years later, the club was exactly what she hoped it would be. Every Friday and Saturday night, Serpent's Kiss was packed with members who paid a monthly fee for privacy and convenience.

Katrina's heels clicked on the wooden floor of the dungeon as she slowly circled Ryan. She ran a hand down his chest and could feel the anticipation rolling off him. There was something about seeing a man bound and ready for whatever she wanted to do to him that gave her immense pleasure.

She didn't take her eyes off his face as she moved her hand down over his abs, heading for the straining erection between his legs.

He lowered his head and closed his eyes. . . waiting.

When she brushed her hand against his cock, he tensed. "Have something you wish to say?"

He shook his head.

Taking hold of his balls with her right hand, Katrina squeezed. "Are you sure?"

"Yes, Ma'am. I'm sure." His eyes remained closed, but his breathing had picked up. He knew pain was coming, and what she'd just done to his balls was only the tip of the iceberg.

She released her hold on him. "Very well. Let's get things started, shall we?"

A long table along the wall held a plethora of items she'd selected for their scene. Some she would use. Some she wouldn't. She liked having options.

Running her fingers over the small metal clothespins, she grinned and placed several in her hand before returning to stand in front of Ryan. He hadn't moved—not that he could go very far.

With her free hand, she took hold of one of his nipples and worked it between her thumb and index finger until it was ready to accept the clip she had poised in her left hand. Giving his nipple a hard pinch, she replaced her fingers with the silver clip.

To his credit, he didn't react beyond a small intake of breath. Ryan liked pain. That was good, since she liked to inflict it. Katrina considered herself a sadist. She liked to mix pain with pleasure.

Without pause, she moved to his other nipple and placed another clip on the hardened flesh. He was ready this time and didn't react in any way.

That won't do, Katrina mused. Returning the remaining clothespins to the table, she grasped each clip by the extended ears and pulled sharply.

Ryan hadn't been expecting that, and his reaction was exactly what she'd been hoping for. She saw his jaw flex and then clench.

Releasing him, she gathered up the clothespins again and began placing them where she wanted them. By the time she was finished, he had forty of the miniature clips in various places on his body including his sides, arms, inner thighs, cock and balls. She'd made sure to space them far enough apart for what she had planned.

"How are you doing?" she asked, caressing the side of his face. He trusted her with his submission. She didn't take that lightly.

Ryan opened his eyes and met her gaze. "Good, Ma'am."

"Are you ready to continue?"

"Yes, Ma'am."

While Katrina didn't mind people in the club referring to her as "Mistress," she required submissives scening with her to call her "Ma'am." She wasn't anyone's Mistress. She was the club Mistress, yes, but that was different. The club belonged to her. Ryan and the other male submissives she played with did not.

She nodded and donned a pair of latex gloves. Once they were in place, she lubed her fingers and picked up one of her favorite anal toys. It had three silicone beads that gradually increased in size on one end. The beads were perfect for stimulating the prostate. Where the beads ended, the toy curved around to provide additional stimulation to the perineum. Considering the fun she intended to have with the clothespins, the added pleasure to Ryan's prostate and perineum would have him on the edge in no time.

Without warning, Katrina inserted a single gloved finger into Ryan's ass. She made sure he was relaxed before adding another finger, and then another. Once she was confident he was significantly prepped, she removed her fingers, added some lube to the toy, and pressed it in place. His cheeks flexed around the intrusion, but otherwise he remained still.

That was, until she turned on the vibrations. A ripple went through his body, and he clenched his fists.

She watched his cock grow even harder as the toy continued to work its magic. Smirking, she removed her gloves and then went to the far wall to remove her single-tail whip. When she began researching BDSM, she had known immediately that she was a top. Submission held no appeal for her. Domination, however, was a different story. The first time she laid eyes on the whip she held between her fingers, it had felt as if it belonged in her grasp. She made the decision that day to learn all she could about how to wield a whip properly, and her determination had paid off.

Unfurling the whip, she let the tail dangle against her leg before giving Ryan's backside a quick crack. It wasn't meant to hurt so much as get his attention.

Get his attention it did. Ryan snapped his head up. He'd been so caught up in all the sensations that he hadn't been paying attention to her. Well, that would change.

She stepped closer to him, running the tips of her fingers over the clothespins. "Which one should I remove first, do you think? Hmm?"

His eyes widened as what she was about to do sank in. She'd used the clothespins on him before, as well as the whip, but she'd never combined the two. Over the last few months, she'd been working diligently on her aim. It had been good for the last two years, but she'd wanted it to be excellent. After hours of practicing, she was ready. Ryan just happened to be the lucky one to benefit from all her training.

Without another word, she took several steps back, putting room between her and Ryan. A flick of her wrist later, the whip made contact with one of the clips attached to the inside of his thigh. He jerked when the clothespin detached and landed onto the floor.

She didn't give him time to recover. One by one, Katrina removed each metal clothespin with the tail of her whip, leaving the ones clinging to his cock and balls for last. By that point, he was sweating. Ryan's eyes were closed once again, and his entire body was vibrating with unreleased energy. He looked as if he were about ready to explode.

Tossing her whip to the side, she came to stand in front of him. "Open your eyes. Look at me."

Slowly he opened his lids to stare down at her. His pupils were dark—almost black in the soft light of the dungeon. "You're okay to continue?"

"Yes. . . Ma'am." The words were broken and barely above a whisper. She knew Ryan, though. He would safeword if he needed to.

She lowered her mouth over one of his nipples, grazing it with her teeth. This time, he tilted his head back. He would have been looking at the eyebolts in the ceiling if not for the fact that his eyes were closed. Ryan embraced everything she gave him. It was one of the reasons she enjoyed playing with him.

Keeping her lips on his skin, she reached between them and ripped off the three clips she'd attached to the underside of his cock in quick succession. Before he had time to recover, she wrapped her hand around his length and began scraping her nails along his erection with each pass of her palm. Katrina increased the suction of her mouth, biting down every now and then. He was trembling and completely at her mercy. She loved it.

There were still two clothespins attached to his testicles. She switched her mouth to his other nipple, treating it to the same sucking and biting as she had the first. He was close. Very close. It wouldn't take much to send him over the edge.

With her free hand, she began playing with his balls, toying with the clips. His cock was pulsing in her hand. Their play agreement didn't include her having control over his orgasms. He could come whenever he wished. Ryan, however, tended to like to draw it out for as long as he could. He was a masochist that way—another reason he made a good play partner.

She kept up her actions until she knew he was right there, teetering on the edge. Without warning, she bit down hard, sinking her teeth into his chest at the same time that she yanked the two clothespins from his balls.

Ryan arched his back, letting out a strangled cry as he let go. His climax covered her hand, and a few drops landed on the leather corset she was wearing.

With the hand that wasn't covered in spunk, Katrina leaned down and freed him from the spreader bar. Then she stood and walked around to his backside to remove the butt plug from his ass. Once that was extracted and set aside, she reached up and unhooked his cuffs from the chains that held him upright. He sagged a little, but otherwise held himself up. She led him over to the couch along the far wall and draped a blanket over his shoulders.

She sat down beside him, checking to make sure he was coming back down from his high. He seemed fine, so she went to clean herself up.

"I made a mess, didn't I?" he asked.

"Just a little." It wasn't the first time a man had come on her, and she was positive it wouldn't be the last. Sure, she could have stepped out of the way, but where was the fun in that?

When she returned to the couch, she brought a bottle of water and some chocolate with her. He might not be her submissive, but as his play partner it was her job to take care of him after.

He took the offering and downed a good portion of the water in one gulp. "Thanks."

"How are you feeling?" she asked.

Ryan snorted. "Like all my bones have turned to Jell-O."

She gave him a knowing grin. "Relax up here for a bit. I'm going to go downstairs and check on Brandon and Ali's progress. If you need anything before I get back, just holler."

When she moved to stand, he placed a hand on her arm, stopping her. Katrina met his gaze.

"Don't you want me to take care of you?"

While she never allowed her play partners to penetrate her, she did occasionally have them preform oral favors. Ryan was a huge fan of cunnilingus, and he had a very talented tongue. As tempted as she was to take him up on his offer, she had a few things she needed to do before the club opened at seven o'clock. Katrina knew if she gave in and let him pleasure her, one orgasm by Ryan's talented mouth wouldn't be enough.

"Not today. I have some work to do." She placed his hand back in his lap and headed toward the door. "Take your time."

Once she was outside the room, Katrina made a beeline for the stairs. As she descended, Brandon waved her over. "Mr. Monroe called while you were upstairs. I told him you were busy and would have to call him back."

Peter Monroe was the private investigator she used for the club. All members had to pass a background check as well as a medical exam. You could say it was overkill, but most of her members appreciated the care she took with both their privacy and their safety. Even so, the one mistake she'd made in that department plagued her regularly. She'd vowed never to let someone slip through the cracks again. "Thanks. Everything all right down here?"

"We're good. Ali is almost finished cleaning the main floor. Should I send her upstairs or wait a while?" Brandon asked.

"Have her wait fifteen minutes and then come on up. We should be finished by then."

"Will do."

As she started back toward the stairs, Brandon's voice stopped her. "By the way, you missed a spot." He had a smirk on his face, and he was looking in the direction of her leg.

Sure enough, on the inside of her thigh was a small amount of Ryan's cum. She grabbed a paper towel from the bar, dipped it in some water Brandon had sitting close by, and removed the evidence of her afternoon adventures. "Happy?"

Brandon chuckled. "I think the better question would be, are you happy? You've obviously just had more fun than I have."

She gave him a wink. "True. Speaking of which. . . I need to get back upstairs."

He nodded. "Tell Ryan to stop by when he's done. I wanted to ask him something."

"Sure."

About the Author

Sherri spent most of her childhood detesting English class. It was one of her least favorite subjects because she never seemed to fit into the standard mold. She wasn't good at spelling, or following grammar rules, and outlines made her head spin. For that reason, Sherri never imagined becoming an author.

At the age of thirty, all of that changed. After getting frustrated with the direction a television show was taking two of its characters, Sherri decided to try her hand at writing an alternate ending, and give the characters their happily ever after. By the time the story finished, it was one of the top ten read stories on the site, and her readers were encouraging her to write more.

Since then Sherri has published several novels, many of which have hit the top 100 in their category on Amazon. Writing has become a creative outlet that allows her to explore a wide range of emotions, while having fun taking her characters through all the twists and turns she can create. You can find a current list of all of Sherri's books and sign up for her monthly newsletter at www.sherrihayesauthor.com.